Mad Dog House

Mad Dog House

A Novel

MARK RUBINSTEIN

Thunder Lake Press
Wilton, Connecticut

Thunder Lake Press
196 Danbury Road
Wilton, CT 06897
www.thunderlakepress.com

Publisher's Note: This is a work of fiction. Names, characters, places, and incidents are a product of the author's imagination. Locales and public names are sometimes used for atmospheric purposes. Any resemblance to actual people, living or dead, or to businesses, companies, events, institutions, or locales is completely coincidental.

Ordering Information

Quantity sales. Special discounts are available on quantity purchases by corporations, associations, and others. For details, contact the "Special Sales Department" at the address above.

Orders by US trade bookstores and wholesalers. Please contact BCH: (800) 431-1579 or visit www.bookch.com for details.

Printed in the United States of America

Cataloging-in-Publication Data
　　Rubinstein, Mark, 1942-
　　　Mad dog house : a novel / Mark Rubinstein. -- 1st ed.
　　　p. cm.
　　　ISBN 978-0-9856268-4-6

　　　1. Psychological fiction. 2. Suspense fiction.
　　　I. Title.

　　PS3618.U3M33　　2012
　　813'.6　　QBI12-600148

First Edition

17　16　15　14　13　　　10　9　8　7　6　5　4　3　2　1

To Linda

The past is never dead. It's not even past.

WILLIAM FAULKNER, *REQUIEM FOR A NUN*

What you need to know about the past is that no matter what has happened, it has all worked together to bring you to this very moment.

ANONYMOUS

Chapter 1

When he was twelve years old Mad Dog ripped off Cootie Weiss's ear.

On the day it happened, Cootie—sitting at the desk behind him, as usual—drove his middle finger out from his thumb.

SNAP!

Pain seared through Mad Dog's ear like a voltage-filled wire. A high-pitched ringing began in his head. Heat throbbed through his face.

The teacher, Miss Moreno, was still writing on the blackboard. Mad Dog's face felt like it was on fire.

The finger snapped out again.

CRACK!

Turning, Mad Dog glared at Cootie. The older boy smirked.

The abuse had been going on for weeks. There was no civilized solution—not with Cootie Weiss. He'd been left back twice and was a head taller than anyone else. Everyone knew he was whacked out. Rumor was he sold drugs and was somehow connected. Cootie was a tough Brooklyn street kid, a real hard-ass. Nobody messed with him.

Miss Moreno was very attractive. And Cootie had been masturbating—every day, right there, behind Mad Dog. Their attached desks rocked back and forth as Cootie, hand in his pocket, rubbed away. There was muffled breathing and then the rocking accelerated until Cootie climaxed.

It went on for weeks, in front of the other kids. Mad Dog was forced into accepting Cootie doing his thing. Finally, he turned and whispered, "Hey Cootie, why don't you whack off at home?"

After that, Cootie repeatedly finger-snapped Mad Dog's ear. By the end of each day, the ear felt like a hot ember. Mad Dog held his temper—stayed calm and cool, thinking Cootie would tire of his little game.

But it went on until the day Cootie took the humiliation to another level.

After the fourth ear snap of the day, Mad Dog felt something on his right ear. It was wet, warm, and without thinking, he touched his ear shell. He pulled his hand away and peered at it. Sitting on his fingertip was a slimy wad of snot.

It was typical Cootie Weiss; he reveled in his nickname and even demanded to be called "Cootie." He often dug deep in his nose and smeared the pickings on the girls' coats. He was a filthy guy who loved sharing his bodily functions.

Mad Dog earned his moniker because when he lost his temper, he fought like an animal. He'd learned to brawl at home. His father, a violent man, had been shipped to Attica when Mad Dog was just a kid—an armed robbery during which he'd killed two men. His mother's boyfriend, Horst, drifted in and out of their lives. An abusive man, Horst punched and kicked Mad Dog mercilessly. Though he always got beaten, the kid usually landed some good shots. And there was the boxing club where he mauled kids far older than he was. So early on, Mad Dog learned to fight.

But challenging Cootie? A tough guy? One who was so crazy he insisted on being called Cootie? It was suicide. But Mad Dog had reached his limit.

He turned back, looked Cootie in the eye, and said, "Meet me behind Leo's."

Cootie smiled. For him, this would be a clinic in street fighting:

Punch-Out 101.

No one had ever—in the history of the earth—called out Cootie Weiss. It was off-the-wall-out-of-this-world. Word of the brawl-to-be spread through the school like a sea swell. For Mad Dog to punk out was guaranteed humiliation, complete disgrace.

"You're nuts," whispered Danny Burns, after class ended.

"I can't take it anymore."

"Look," Danny said, "this isn't Herbie's Boxing Club. There're no rules. This Cootie's a serious psycho. Just ask Moreno to change your seat."

It was pure Danny Burns. There were certain things Mad Dog loved about Irish Danny Burns. He was smart, had common sense, and always thought things through. But Mad Dog shook his head.

"He'll kill you," said Danny.

"Danny, you're my best friend, and I usually listen to you, but I gotta do it."

"I heard he carries a knife. Jesus, you'll end up like your father."

Mad Dog's father was belly-shanked in the shower at Attica—where he died with his guts and shit pouring down the drain. A bunch of cons watched his life ebb away, laughing as he bled out and died. It was a neighborhood myth that got chewed and spit out, again and again.

"Like father, like son," Mad Dog retorted. "I'm not scared . . ." He looked up at the hallway clock. Nearly two. By 3:10 he'd be facing off against Cootie Weiss.

"Look, kemosabe, said Danny, "you're my blood brother. I'm gonna get Kenny McGuirk and some Bay Boys."

"I don't need Kenny McGuirk or the Bay Boys."

"You'll need backup. 'Cause Cootie's gonna have the Coyle Street Krauts there."

"Doesn't matter, Danny. I gotta do what I gotta do."

"I'm getting Kenny and some Bay Boys," said Danny.

The Sheepshead Bay Boys were a high school gang—tough, Irish,

Jewish, and Italian kids—a pack of beer-drinking dead-enders.

Kenny "Snake Eyes" McGuirk, fifteen, knew everyone in Sheepshead Bay, Brooklyn—the local bookies, gamblers, and toughs. Kenny ran numbers for some mob guy in Mill Basin. He had sway. He'd bring some muscle.

Mad Dog watched Danny hustle down the corridor and then disappear in a swarm of seventh and eighth graders. He glanced up at the wall clock again: two o'clock. A little more than an hour before the shit would hit the fan.

Mad Dog knew that as quick as his hands were, they'd have to be panther fast if he didn't want to end up like his father.

Either Mad Dog or Cootie would go down.

■

The empty lot behind Leo's luncheonette sprouted tufts of grass from the sandy soil. Cigarette butts and glass fragments glittered in the September sunlight. A breeze blew in from Sheepshead Bay, smelling of brine and motor oil.

Mad Dog's legs felt like cement; his heart throbbed in his throat. The pungent smell of marijuana hung in the air. A horde of kids was there. Danny Burns stood off to one side with Mad Dog's gang, the 19th Street guys, including Kenny McGuirk and ten Bay Boys, tough-looking high school thugs. Entering the debris-strewn expanse. Mad Dog knew the mob was itching for blood.

"Kill the kraut bastard, Mad Dog!" Snake Eyes yelled.

Cootie Weiss stood there, waiting. A group of Coyle Street Krauts gathered on the other side of the lot.

Sucking on a cigarette, Cootie squinted as Mad Dog approached.

Facing Cootie, Mad Dog's bowels loosened and he thought they might empty.

"Well . . . ?" sneered Cootie. "What's it gonna be?"

"You gotta stop botherin' me, Cootie . . ."

Mad Dog heard a fear-filled warbling in his own voice. But then, fear could be a good thing, he thought. Like just before a boxing match at Herbie's gym. Butterflies. That weak, sick feeling—but then would come a pumped rush of blood, the thump of fists, frenzied speed and motion.

"Whaddaya, some kinda faggot?" Cootie growled. He flipped his cigarette away, the same finger-snapping motion he'd used on Mad Dog's ear.

Be cool, stay calm . . . don't let him think you're scared . . .

Jolts of nervous energy shot through Mad Dog. He felt his bowels close off. He'd neither shit nor blow lunch. He watched as Cootie's hands curled into huge fists. Without thinking, Mad Dog tossed his jacket to the ground. He held Cootie's stare.

"Kick his ass, Cootie!" shouted a Coyle Street guy.

"Kill him, Mad Dog!" screamed Danny Burns.

"Last chance to back out, faggot," Cootie said.

Back out? Too late for that.

Mad Dog crouched and circled slowly. Suddenly, Cootie swung— a wild roundhouse.

Slipping it easily, Mad Dog shot a fist into his belly. Cootie doubled over with a throaty gasp. Mad Dog threw a hard right to his jaw. Cootie's mouth—open as the blow landed—snapped shut with the impact. A tooth flew into the air; blood sprayed from his mouth.

Mad Dog's fists began a flurry of lightening-fast thumps to Cootie's face, a rapid-fire series of chopping blows.

Cootie staggered, wobbled and lurched to the side.

"Attaway, Mad Dog!" Danny shouted.

A raucous cheer went up from the 19th Street kids.

Cootie blinked, regained his balance and advanced.

Mad Dog slammed a fist into Cootie's nose—a quick, cracking blow. Blood jetted upward in a red spray. Cootie's head snapped back; he went down.

"Stomp his fuckin' head," Snake Eyes shouted. "Kill him."

"Don't let up," Danny shouted.

Mad Dog waited for Cootie to get up.

■

Danny Burns felt his own blood lust rise from deep within himself. "Kill him! Kill him!" he roared as Mad Dog landed blow after blow.

Click. A steely snapping. Cootie's switchblade swung out and locked into position.

Danny's heart tumbled. His breath left him and he began wheezing. His asthma was kicking in—big time. Fuck it; can't worry about it. He'd jump Cootie from behind and grab his neck. Mad Dog could work him over and gut-punch him till he fell.

Danny lunged for Cootie, but two Bay Boys clutched him, thrust him down and held him. He writhed and thrashed like a snake, but they pinned him.

"Lemme go!" Danny shrieked.

He could smell the Bay Boys' breath, rancid from beer and pot.

"The knife!" Danny screamed.

"The Dog knows how to fight," a Bay Boy yelled.

Still down, Danny watched Mad Dog back away from Cootie.

"Run. Run!" Danny screamed.

Cootie advanced clumsily, weak and wobbly. The knife blade— lethal looking, long, glinting—protruded from his fist.

Suddenly Mad Dog turned, darted to a Dumpster behind Leo's, and grabbed a metal trash-can lid. Holding the handle, he whirled.

Cootie advanced and then lunged.

Mad Dog parried the knife with the lid.

Another thrust. The makeshift shield deflected the blade.

Cootie made an arcing swipe with the knife. Mad Dog spun. The lid smashed Cootie's face, and a jagged metal edge slashed his ear. A blood runnel ran down his face.

A knee thumped into Cootie's groin. The knife dropped as Cootie crumpled to the ground.

Mad Dog's punches rained down, heavy thudding blows. He

straddled Cootie and grabbed his throat. One hand went to the side of Cootie's face.

Suddenly, the Dog stood, chest heaving.

Cootie lay still, tongue protruding—senseless—blood seeping into the sand.

Silence. A damp breeze blew in from the bay; it smelled of brine and clams.

Danny blinked; sand and soil clogged his nose. He coughed and sputtered. The Coyle Street Krauts were gone.

Danny got to his feet.

Kenny McGuirk cried, "Holy shit. Look at *that.*"

Danny felt fire in his lungs.

Then he saw it. Right there in Mad Dog's hand, something pinkish with frothy pulp and blood dribbling onto his friend's wrist. Mad Dog held it up for all to see.

There it was in the late afternoon sun.

Cootie's torn and bloodied ear was in his hand.

It was Mad Dog's day.

Chapter 2

Roddy Dolan flings his leather jacket over the razor wire atop the chain-link fence. With a sudden thrust he scrambles up the links, swings over the top, and then drops down on the other side. The night air is bitterly cold—ice crystals form in his nostrils. In the pale wash of light, vapor plumes stream from his nose and mouth.

It's dark except for a street lamp down the block. It's a silent winter night. The warehouse is a squat, two-story brick structure with a corrugated tin roof. The loading platform is stacked with crates. He treads lightly, flashlight in hand.

There's a sound—something coming very fast—and he whirls and snaps the flashlight on. There's a gleam in the light shaft: red eyes, curved fangs, and the dog leaps on him. Roddy goes down. The dog—a huge beast with hot breath—lunges for his throat. Roddy's arm goes up; the creature's teeth sink into it and tear flesh. Roddy punches at it and its jaws clamp onto Roddy's throat.

Roddy clutches the jaws, rips them open, and wrenches away. He pummels the dog with his fists, kicks at it, and bolts upright in bed. The pillow is soaked.

His body quivering, Roddy sits at the edge of the bed and waits for his heart to slow its stampede. Roddy casts off sleep's shroud and resurrects himself to a state of awareness.

Tracy lies on her side, her back to him. He doesn't want to wake her, but part of him hopes she'll say something and bring him back to their lives, together—away from the dream.

The bedside digital clock reads 5:10 A.M. on this late August morning. He has a full caseload of surgeries today. He's due in the OR at seven.

"Is it the dream again?" Tracy murmurs.

"Uh huh . . ."

She turns and reaches for him.

He snuggles against her and inhales deeply. She smells sweet, of sleep and bed linen. Her honey blonde hair is spread on the pillow. He's always astonished by Tracy's scent, which flooded him the moment they first met.

"Maybe you should talk with your psychiatrist friend, Dick Simons."

"Oh, Trace . . . I don't know . . ."

"Honey, I read about some new medication for nightmares."

Roddy knows whenever the dream wakes him, he feels depleted for the day. And he's got a long one; after today's surgeries, there are office consultations into the evening.

Roddy's certain Tracy's drifted off. He's always marveled at her ability to sleep. In the fifteen years they've been together, she's never had a bad night's sleep.

Roddy pads his way to the bathroom. He regards himself in the medicine cabinet mirror. At forty-five, he's still brawny, although he can't boast the well-cut six-pack he once had. The weight training has helped, so too have the walks with Tracy through the nearby golf course, though they're not members. They aren't country club types. But still, he looks far younger than his forty-five years. The good life hasn't turned him into some flab-assed Westchester suburbanite.

The dream. How many years has it plagued him? Maybe Tracy's right; he might just talk with Dick Simons.

Roddy shaves; the razor glides over the contours of his face—it's the minor surgery with which he begins each day. And he always thinks about things while shaving. He recalls when he and Tracy met.

He was a surgical resident at New York Hospital in Manhattan—the center of the medical universe. Browsing in the library, he knelt at the lower shelves perusing a dizzying display of journals. He barely noticed a ladder on wheels parked to his right.

Suddenly, a blurred presence dropped from the ladder and she was beside him. Roddy recalls that strange and exhilarating moment: they stood there, breathless at the sudden intrusion, each on the other. They were so close he could smell her shampoo.

"I'm so sorry," she gasped breathlessly.

"No. It's me . . ."

"It's you?" she asked with a smile. "Sorry . . . it's *me*."

She had gleaming green eyes. Her porcelain skin, Celtic features, and blonde hair were arresting. Her neck was long, pale, and inviting. Something elemental rushed through him. Amidst the musty smell of texts, her scent was intoxicating. Her skin *looked* delicious. He grew weak in the knees and knew in that second he could look at her forever.

A week later, lying naked with each other on the bed in his apartment, she laughed and said, "You know, Roddy, the moment I saw you I felt something . . ."

"What was that?"

"It was more than just attraction. I felt something go through me . . . something deep."

"Like a rush?"

"Yes. A *rush*."

"We were fated to be together from that moment," Roddy whispered, luxuriating in postcoital contentment.

"Yes. And do you know what else I knew then?"

"Don't tell me. I'll tell you," he said. "You knew we'd get married."

"Yes, I did," she said with a laugh.

After they married, they lived in Manhattan. But when Tracy was pregnant with their first—Thomas—they house-hunted, finally buying an English Tudor in Bronxville, just north of New York City.

The house had fairway views of the Siwanoy Country Club.

He got a staff appointment at Lawrence Hospital. He did mostly GI surgeries—stomach ulcers, gall bladder removals, pancreatic and large bowel surgery—along with appendectomies. He opened an office near the hospital, partnering with Ivan Snyder. There were no snags, no complications. The house was minutes away from Sarah Lawrence College where Tracy worked as a librarian. It was the life they'd dreamed of.

Roddy luxuriates beneath the steamy hot shower, contemplating the day's surgeries, wondering if any unforeseeable complications will pop up. But these—and a thousand others—are the unpredictable elements in every life. Roddy knows the hours in the OR—by now, thousands—are a gauge of the repairs he's done. They're the essence of good deeds.

Then, office consultations into the evening. Brenda, the receptionist, told him, "Your last one's at six. He wants your last appointment. His name's Egan, Kenneth Egan."

"He wanted the *last* appointment?"

"He was emphatic about it."

Back to the bedroom, he sees Tracy's side of the bed is empty. Usually she stays in bed. He always sits beside her and strokes that amazing, silken blonde hair. Caressing her is a luxury he anticipates, truly adores. He always plants a kiss on her neck, tasting the luscious tang of her skin.

He usually whispers, "I love you . . ." and she mumbles something—soft, unintelligible. Roddy's always amazed by the milky whiteness of Tracy's skin, as though it's never seen the light of day. Then he works his way to her mouth, those soft, pliant lips. And each morning he wants to rouse her from sleep and make love.

But not this morning. Not after the fucking dream. He dresses and heads for the stairs.

Tommy emerges from his room. He's incredibly tall for twelve with blond hair and those amazing green eyes of Tracy's. *A really good-looking kid*, Roddy thinks.

"Hi there," Roddy says, trying to quell the thrumming sensation in his chest.

Tommy mumbles something, casts a sour look at Roddy, and disappears into the hallway bathroom.

Tommy—or, Thomas, as Tracy calls him—is by far the smartest kid in his class. Teachers have said that even without trying, he far surpasses the other students.

"But he doesn't even *try*," said Mr. Williams, his seventh grade teacher.

"Roddy, he respects you," Tracy said last evening. "Can't you turn him around?"

"Tracy, he resents anything I say."

"Maybe you can push him."

"If I push, he'll push back."

Lately, Tommy's bloated with adolescent angst that makes him disdain all things, especially his parents.

In short, Roddy thinks Tommy's a pain in the ass, a typical teenager.

Sandy comes out of her room. She's ten years old, with golden curls ringing her pretty face. Seeing Roddy, she smiles. "Daddy, will you help me with my science project tonight?"

"Of course, sweetie. What is it?"

"I have to make a chart that shows how a heart works."

"That'll be fun. I'll bring something home from the office . . . it shows the human heart. Okay?"

"Tonight?" she asks, her blue-green eyes wide with anticipation.

"Yup, tonight," Roddy says, feeling the warmth of love so deeply it could devour him. Sandy wants to be a doctor. And Roddy's certain she'll succeed. She brings home straight As, is quite a soccer player, is popular, and loves science.

From her looks—even at ten—Roddy knows she'll be as beautiful as her mother. And there's none of that teen torment that's so *de rigueur* these days. At least, not yet.

■

In the kitchen with its granite-top counters, nickel-plated appliances, including a six-burner Garland range, Roddy watches Tracy prepare breakfast.

"The one good thing about that dream is it gets you to make breakfast," he says, slipping his arms around her. He nuzzles her neck. The kitchen is filled with the aroma of eggs and toast.

Tracy leans against him. "Roddy, I think you need to talk with Dick..."

"I will... I promise," he says, and begins making the coffee.

Roddy uses a rich blend of Sumatran and Colombian beans in the Krups coffeemaker. Tracy turned him on to mixing coffee beans soon after they'd begun living together. She'd taken a course at Peter Kump's New York Cooking School, back then, and works culinary miracles. She turned him on to freshly prepared foods, too, not the bachelor shit he'd been consuming for years.

At the breakfast table, Roddy gazes out the window. He loves watching the garden as the morning air brightens. It's like seeing it for the first time each morning—again. It confirms that everything he and Tracy have is real and good; it's not ephemeral and meaningless, like so many things in this life.

"Do you want me to turn on the radio?" Tracy asks.

"Why bother?" he asks, thinking of the crises that fill the broadcasts. "It's a disaster out there, and we can't do anything about it."

"Roddy, *you* do something every day. You *help* people..."

Yes, Roddy knows he rights wrongs, reverses the ills afflicting the human body. And he's got a full schedule today, followed by office consultations, and the last one, that guy Egan. Then home and helping Sandy.

Roddy thinks of their Bronxville house. He loves the Tudor-style architecture with its wood timbering, stone-faced fireplace, screened-in porch, and spacious sunroom. He admires the hand-hewn chestnut ceiling beams and the Old English casement windows. "It has all the craftsmanship that's missing in things today," he said to Tracy when they first toured the place.

And he thinks about his life with Tracy. She's the smartest, most commonsense person he's ever known. Roddy knows he'd never have dreamed he'd be living with this gorgeous, loving, intelligent, and sexy being—a woman with whom he shares a chemistry that's combustible, organic. They just can't keep their hands off each other, even all these years later.

"You know Trace . . . sometimes I can't believe we have so much . . ."

"We should be thankful for everything," she says, sliding eggs onto a plate.

At that moment, he knows that regardless of humanity's troubles, life in Roddy Dolan's corner of the planet is good. For him, it's heaven on earth. There's nothing else he wants.

And for all he has in this crazy and unpredictable life, Roddy Dolan is more than thankful.

Chapter 3

One night when he was seventeen, Mad Dog, Frankie Messina, and Kenny "Snake Eyes" McGuirk were at the Acropolis Diner—"the Greek's" as they called it—on Nostrand Avenue. They sat at a Formica-topped table, amidst the fake chrome, plaster columns, and bogus leather booths.

"I'm not interested in this job," Kenny said, tamping his Lucky Strike in an ashtray.

"Whaddaya mean?" Frankie said. "It's a sure thing."

"Sounds risky."

"Hey, Snake Eyes, you're a gambler. You take risks every day."

"Frankie, gambling's the art of *controlling* risk."

"Whaddaya talkin' about?"

"I always know the hand I'm dealt. That way I figure the other guy's hand. This job? I don't know the guy's hand."

Frankie's low-lying hairline sank as he scowled. "Look, Kenny, this guy's been workin' there four years. The place closes at eight and he's gonna leave the alarm off. Nine-thirty, he comes back and turns it on. We'll have an hour and a half."

"I wanna meet this guy."

"Why?"

"To dope him out. I got one rap already," Kenny said. "One more and I go away."

The waitress approached, Silex coffeepot in hand. "Will there be anything else?"

"No, sweetheart. Just you," Frankie said, ogling her breasts.

She sighed, looking bored and tired.

Mad Dog always felt embarrassed when Frankie—who fancied himself a Romeo—oozed his bewitching bullshit. Kenny looked uncomfortable. With a purple scar on his forehead, a broken nose, and weak chin, Kenny McGuirk never found a comfort zone with the girls. His true love was gambling, especially poker, and his main squeeze was the smiling queen of a royal flush.

Plopping the coffeepot on the table, the waitress ripped the tab from her pad and set it down. "Have a good night," she said, and then sauntered off.

"You too, sweetheart," Frankie called. "I'm telling you, it's guaranteed," he whispered to Kenny.

"Nothin's guaranteed," Kenny said. "And what about the kid here?" He tilted his head at Mad Dog. "One more rap, he does time."

"What're you, Kenny? His fuckin' father? Besides, for him it's juvie."

"Frankie, I gotta talk to your guy."

"You sound like that red-headed chicken shit, Danny Burns," Frankie said.

"Watch it, Frankie," Mad Dog warned.

"Yeah, yeah," Frankie said. "Don't get your Mickey Finn Irish up. Your best friend's gonna be a fuckin' accountant with his numbers."

Frankie's eyes followed the waitress down the aisle.

"Look at *me*, schmuck, not her," Kenny said. "You get me face time with your friend. Otherwise, forget it. *Capice?*"

"Yeah, yeah. I *capice*. I'm tellin' ya, my guy says the fence value in that storeroom is fifty, sixty Gs. Whaddaya gonna do with that kinda cash, huh?"

"*If* I go for the job . . . and that's a big *if*," Kenny said, "then I won't work the Parisi card game anymore. I'll start my own."

"Yeah," Frankie said with a snicker. "Kenny never saw a bet he didn't like."

"Only when I know the odds," Kenny said.

"And you, Dog?" Frankie asked. "What'll you do with that kinda money?"

"Get outta my house. Get away from that low-life bastard."

"That kraut, Horst?" Frankie asked.

Mad Dog nodded.

"You could box. Herbie Jew-Boy says you're the best light-heavyweight he's ever trained."

"Yeah, and have scrambled eggs for brains."

"With those hands you're the toughest white guy I know," Frankie said.

"There's always someone tougher," Mad Dog said. "And I don't want another rap."

Frankie kissed his Saint Anthony medallion. I'll see if my guy'll meet Kenny. Then maybe we're in business."

■

Kenny jimmied the store's back door with a crowbar. No alarm.

He and Mad Dog clambered down the steps. Another door—fastened by a hasp and padlock. Wood splintered and metal creaked, as Kenny pried it open. Their flashlight beams fell on stacked cartons: Sony, Sharp, televisions, stereos—months of inventory.

"We're gonna need a bigger van," Kenny whispered.

They began hauling. Up the stairs out the back door. Box after box. Frankie waited at the van's rear and loaded it up. Kenny scrambled back down to lug another load. Mad Dog and Frankie packed the van.

A whoop shrieked through the alley. Mad Dog's insides turned to ice. Then a cherry light whirled on the brick walls.

A silent alarm. Frankie's guy fucked up.

The walls were a mad rush of gyrating lights. "Stay where you are!" came a command down the alley. "Hands in the air where we can see 'em!"

"Don't move," yelled one officer. "Not a muscle."

They were patted down, head to toe. Mad Dog's hands were thrust behind his back, cuffs snapped on.

He felt his flesh chill as radio static and whirling lights filled the air.

■

The Honorable Alfred Waterman—bushy-haired, bespectacled—looked austere in his black robe. The legal aid lawyer told Mad Dog and Frankie, "Don't bullshit this guy. You already copped a plea and he'll hear you out for a presentencing statement."

They stood with their court-appointed lawyers.

"Young man," Wasserman said, addressing Mad Dog first, "you're only seventeen and this is your second offense. Grand larceny carries a severe penalty."

Mad Dog nodded respectfully.

"And there were only two of you?"

"Yes, Your Honor."

"You took a lot of merchandise in a very short time."

"I'm sorry, Your Honor," he said, wondering what happened to Snake Eyes.

"You're on a bad road, son; it leads to prison." The judge peered at him. "What do you have to say for yourself?"

Thoughts streaked through his head. *No bullshit.*

"I'm sorry, Your Honor. I didn't think of the consequences . . ."

"We live in a world of consequences," the judge said. "Yours is a unique situation, young man. This is the first time I've ever been contacted by a youthful defendant's teachers. They said you're a brilliant kid . . . you have enormous potential."

Wasserman seemed to be taking some kind of mental inventory. I'll tell you what I'm going to do," he said. "I'll give you a choice . . ."

Mad Dog's heart jumped in his chest.

"The first is two years in prison. It means one year at a state reformatory. And when you turn eighteen, you'll be transferred to a penal institution.

"Your second is this: you join the army, for a three-year enlistment. You'll get a chance to fulfill your potential. Now . . . which will it be?"

A year's vacation in juvie followed by lockdown with the crazies? Or the army? Who knows? Could be a chance for something . . . who knows?

"The army, Your Honor . . ."

"And, young man, if you're thrown out or discharged other than honorably, you'll do those two years in a state penitentiary. Is that clear?"

"Yes, Your Honor."

"Maybe you'll become something other than a street thug."

Chapter 4

The office of Dolan & Snyder Surgical Associates is virtually empty. The consultations have gone well—a woman with an abdominal hernia, a teenager with a brewing appendicitis Roddy will take out first thing in the morning—but no emergencies. Only one more consultation, and then it's home for dinner and Sandy's project. Roddy telephones Tracy to tell her he'll be home by 6:30.

"See you then," she says, but Roddy detects tension in her voice.

"What, honey?"

"What, what?"

"What's going on?"

"I'll tell you when you get home."

"Give me a hint."

"It's Thomas . . ."

That familiar apprehension crawls through him.

"I got a call this afternoon . . ."

"From Dean Brookings again?"

"We'll talk about it when you get home, okay?"

More adolescent bullshit . . . and the kid's only twelve; it's just beginning . . .

"All right. Love you . . ."

"And I love you."

Roddy thinks he hears Tracy sigh.

Then there's a click.

A moment later the intercom trills. "Roddy, your last consultation's here—Mr. Egan," Brenda says.

"I'll be right out. Oh, and Brenda . . . go home. I'll close up."

Roddy's scalp tingles as a cold feeling spikes its way up his neck. He's still thinking of Tommy . . . *Jesus, when he was twelve, the world was different. But doesn't every parent feel that way?*

■

Egan is fairly tall, maybe six two. Looks to be in his mid- or late forties and well muscled. He could've been an athlete in his younger days. He has dark, glinting eyes set in a narrow face with prominent cheekbones; a long, sharply pointed nose; a strong chin; dark hair—thinning slightly in front, brushed back neatly. Uses a little gel. Egan has a well-barbered look, an expensive haircut—probably seventy-five dollars at a high-end shop, no doubt in Manhattan. He has manicured, buffed fingernails, and there's a subtle hint of cologne—expensive stuff.

Egan strides in the consultation room. Roddy has the uncanny feeling Egan's sizing him up, that his eyes are roaming all over him.

There's an uneasy silence. Roddy can't tell exactly why, but he feels a twinge of discomfort, as though he's told a bad joke at a hospital board meeting where the snooty Westchester crowd gathers to discuss their latest pet project.

"You don't remember me, do you?" Egan asks, a hint of a smile on his thin lips.

"Should I?" Roddy says as a raw feeling invades him.

Remember you? From when . . . where've I seen this guy? Can't be from medical school, or college . . .

Roddy hates this feeling. It envelops him whenever he doesn't recognize someone, whether in the hospital, at a party, or in a restaurant. He'll recall a name if there's a reason to do so. But in his day-to-day routines, Roddy runs into scores of people—on the wards, in a clinic, at meetings—and there's nothing more than a quick once-over. Hardly a memorable event.

"No recollection, huh?" Egan says.

Roddy gropes for something familiar—in Egan's voice, posture, his face, anything—but there's not a glimmer of recognition. Yet, there's a disquieting cognizance about the guy, a faint flicker of acquaintance. *Egan . . . Egan . . .* Roddy flips through his mental file cabinet, his cerebral cache of people and places from over the years.

Medical training has given Roddy the ability to observe physical characteristics, especially in the office or hospital where a diagnosis can hinge on something as subtle as a patient's posture. Picking up a faint deviation from the norm can be the difference between life and death.

Roddy thinks the guy's sort of rugged looking—street-wise, even tough in the sense you can tell he's been around; he isn't some panty-waist who's had an easy life.

"I'm sorry, Mr. Egan . . . I just can't place you," Roddy says, beckoning to a chair facing his desk. But the guy stands there. It's clear to Roddy this isn't going to be a routine surgical consultation.

Egan wears a dark gray suit—midwidth lapels, jacket vented on both sides. Probably Armani. A powder-blue shirt is open at the collar. French cuffs on the sleeves. Probably custom made. Wing-tipped shoes—high-end, maybe Fendi—finish off the ensemble. The guy looks like he just stepped out of the pages of the *Times Men's Fashion* magazine.

"No idea who I am, huh?" says Egan.

Is this guy toying with me?

"Kenneth Egan . . . Egan . . . ," Roddy murmurs. "I'm sorry, it doesn't ring a bell."

Edging around the desk, Roddy moves closer and notices spider veins on the tip of Egan's nose and barely visible crow's-feet at the corners of his eyes. Any sign of plastic surgery? Not really. Roddy's become an expert at picking up those tip-offs of a surgeon's knife. In women it's the too-refined nose and the windblown look of facial skin stretched like a drum top. With men, it can be a tougher call.

Roddy gets a better whiff of Egan's cologne, subtle but detectable. Roddy feels his brow furl.

Do I remember him? It's gotta be from a long time ago. From before medical school . . . even before college . . . Egan . . . Egan . . . Egan . . .

"It's been years, and plenty's changed," Egan says.

It puzzles Roddy. How could a guy from his own past be so unrecognizable, so absent from his mental file cabinet?

"We all change with time, don't we, Mad Dog . . . ?"

Fucking *Mad Dog*? Did the guy actually utter that shit-ridden moniker? One he hasn't heard for decades. It's the sewage of a best-forgotten past.

Roddy wonders if this is some weird telescoping of time. Or maybe he's been dropped into an episode of *The Twilight Zone*. Mad Dog? He's never even told Tracy his old street name, though she knows plenty about his past. It was all centuries ago, on some distant planet. In another life.

His eyes roam over the guy, but it's a total zero. As though his brain has emptied. Is he—Roddy Dolan—going senile, turning into some doddering, underwear-staining imbecile?

Mad Dog? Mad Dog? Sheepshead Bay . . . Brooklyn . . . Coyle Street? Na . . . doesn't look German . . . he's Irish, for sure . . . 19th Street? The 8th Street Pool Hall? Leo's?

Roddy's brain virtually whirrs as names, images, sounds, even smells shuttle with mercurial speed through his brain. A flush seeps through Roddy. Jesus, it feels like his face is on fire.

Egan laughs. It's a jarring eruption that jogs something deep in Roddy's mind, a tiny seed of distress lurking just below the surface. At that moment—with Egan's laughter still in his ears—Roddy wonders if he doesn't want to remember this Egan guy, wants instead to erase the memories and forget whatever this lost connection might be.

"Hey, Mad Dog. It's *me* . . . Kenny. *Kenny McGuirk.* Snake Eyes! From the good old days in Brooklyn."

Chapter 5

"**K**enny McGuirk?" Roddy hears himself say.

McGuirk nods. A knowing smile forms on his thin lips.

It feels as though life telescopes in an instant.

Kenny McGuirk? It's impossible.

Roddy's thoughts tumble. The guy doesn't even *look* like Kenny McGuirk—not a scintilla of resemblance. *And Sheepshead Bay?* Before this moment in his office near Lawrence Hospital in Bronxville, Roddy's old neighborhood was a faded memory, estranged from everything in his life. It was a distant echo, a whisper, maybe even a shadow of a former life. But it lives and breathes right here and now.

"Kenny, is it really *you?*" he asks, aware that he's blinking, shaking his head.

"It's me, Roddy. In the flesh. Isn't it amazing what a little plastic surgery'll do? Remember that broken nose? Gone."

"And the scar?" Roddy asks, eyeing Kenny's forehead.

"Gone, too. It was always an ugly distraction. And the chin . . . I had some silicone put in there. Now I'm another George Clooney," he says with laugh.

"Kenny. I'd never have guessed. Jesus, *Kenny McGuirk.* I can't *believe* it."

"It's *Egan* now. Changed it to my mother's maiden name."

"Ken Egan . . . the former Kenny McGuirk," Roddy exclaims,

shaking his head. *It's a Yogi Berra déjà vu all over again moment*, thinks Roddy, and he's not quite sure he likes this sudden intrusion of Brooklyn into his life.

Is this for real? Or is it a dream . . . the past revisited?

"Jesus, Kenny, the last time I saw you was just before the cops got there," Roddy hears a warbling voice say.

And it all comes back to him: Frankie's idling van, the shrieking sirens, flashing lights, handcuffs, and the stench of urine in the Sixtieth Precinct's holding cell. The judge, the sentencing, the army. It's out of time—away from *this* time in Roddy's life—it seems like some weird ghosting of the past.

"I haven't forgotten that night, Roddy," Kenny says, looking somber.

The room is so quiet Roddy hears his own heartbeat.

"Jesus, Kenny, I can't believe it. That was twenty-eight years ago. Where were you when the cops got there?"

"I lucked out, Roddy. I was downstairs when I heard the siren. So I squeezed behind some boxes. They never saw me. Later that night, I snuck out. I knew you and Frankie were nabbed, but what could I do? I never got a chance to thank you for not ratting me out."

"Nobody ever ratted, Kenny."

"I know, but I always felt bad about it. Frankie's friend screwed up."

"Not your fault, Kenny."

"I never liked that you took a rap. I shoulda doped that guy out more carefully."

"You did your best. And getting away? It's what I'd have done."

"But I always felt shitty about it. It was . . ."

"Forget it, Kenny. You know I went into the army because of that."

"Yeah . . . I heard."

"It changed my life."

Roddy stands stock-still, looking at the new Kenny. *Kenny Egan,*

aka Snake Eyes, a connected guy heavy into everything—mostly illegal and vaguely mysterious to Roddy back then. He plops into the
chair behind his desk, feeling his heart thud a staccato rhythm in
his throat.

Kenny sits in the chair facing the desk. "So what's happening,
Mad Dog?" he asks, as though they just ran into each other at the
Greek's or Leo's.

Mad Dog? That absurd moniker is a universe away from who he
now is.

"What's happening, Ken? I'm just fucking amazed," Roddy says,
leaning back in his chair. "And it's not Mad Dog anymore."

"I know. And it's not Snake Eyes, either."

Roddy's being tugged back to the past and hears in his own
words . . . *I'm just fucking amazed* . . . it's the patois of the streets, the
harsh, clipped, Brooklyn lingo leaching away the last twenty-eight
years—going to college, medical school, the internship, his surgical
residency and career. It's the past leaking through his life, lapping
away its current construction, maybe dissolving the reconfigured
Roddy Dolan.

Roddy tries to get his head around it all because it's absofucking-
lutely amazing. Yes, Kenny McGuirk Egan sits in Roddy's Bronxville
office with its teakwood furniture; the bookshelves groan under surgery journals and medical texts, Sandy's papier-mâché school project
sits on a credenza, and Roddy's beloved Matisse reproductions hang
on the walls near the diplomas from college and medical school.
And there are the gold-stamped certificates from medical societies
and The American Board of Surgery; there's the Kentia palm Brenda
bought him for the waiting room; and there was Brenda herself, his
overly friendly receptionist who's been with him for ten years, now
gone home.

He's sitting behind his Scandinavian-style desk—the one Tracy
picked out for him at Bloomingdale's in White Plains—and resting
on the desk is a framed color photo of Tracy and the kids, the center

of his life, the one he's living in the here and now.

And on the other side of that desk is the new, improved Kenny McGuirk—the former Kenny *Snake Eyes,* now Kenny Egan— from the hardscrabble alleys of Brooklyn. In that instant, Roddy's reminded of the turf wars, the Sheepshead Bay Boys and the Coyle Street Krauts, the pool halls and bars, Herbie Goldstein's gym and the Golden Gloves—another era in his life. It's Rip Van Winkle–ish, like some strange dream from which he awakened, only he hasn't been sleeping. He's been living *this* life, not the one from back then— a life no longer lived.

But it's all telescoped—in the form of Kenny Egan, lounging in the patient's chair.

"Look at you . . . a doctor," Ken says.

And there it is, Roddy thinks. It's so incongruous: Kenny marvels that he's a doctor. Jesus. It's who he is; it's what he's become, what he's been for years now—in this life. Yet, to Kenny, it seems amazingly far-fetched.

Oh, the distance we travel in this life.

"So how'd you get to be a doctor?"

"I got my GED in the army. Went airborne," Roddy says.

"I heard . . . the Eighty-second . . . Fort Bragg, North Carolina."

"Right. Then I became a Ranger."

"Green Berets? Learned all that commando stuff, right?"

"Yup. Had to learn field surgery along with everything else. I loved it, so when I got out, I went to Brooklyn College. Then, medical school at the state university."

"You were always the smartest guy around, Roddy, and the toughest, too. Everyone thought you'd be a boxer, especially after the Golden Gloves."

And why is Kenny here? Roddy finds himself wondering. *To talk about the bad old days? I don't really have time for this. Besides, Tracy's waiting at home . . . and there's Sandy's project, and then there's this thing with Tommy . . .*

But Roddy realizes Kenny's different from anything he'd have expected. It's like a secret door opened, and the past—a vaporous cloud—wafted into his life.

Suddenly Roddy blurts, "You know Ken, you don't even *look* like the same guy."

"You look very much the same to me, Roddy."

"Kenny, you look . . . how shall I say it? Refined. The way you dress, even how you talk. You've *changed,* Kenny."

"I sure have. And *you?* You look a lot younger than me," Ken says. "Nobody'd believe I'm only three years older than you."

"Well, Ken, when we were kids, three years was a lifetime."

"I can't get over you, Roddy. You're a different *person.* It's like Mad Dog went away . . . that guy died."

Kenny's words remind Roddy of the dream—the warehouse, the dog with his foaming fangs and hot breath.

"What ever happened to Snake Eyes?"

"He died, too."

They laugh softly; it's a shared moment of reminiscence.

But Roddy wonders again what brings Kenny here in the middle of their lives. It's not thirty years ago, and there's no card game or rendezvous at the pool hall.

But instead of asking that, Roddy asks, "So, Kenny, what about you? You married?"

"Na, Roddy. I always liked the ladies too much to marry one."

"What happened after I left for the army?"

"I went where the action was . . . Vegas."

"You always were a gambler, Kenny . . ."

"I went to school, became a croupier. Then I landed a job at Caesars Palace, dealing blackjack. The money was great and the tips were fantastic. So, Roddy, I was earning more money than I knew what to do with. And what do I do? I gambled it away."

"You were a big-time risk taker, Kenny."

"Those days are over."

"You sure, Kenny?" Roddy asks, recalling that Kenny took to gambling like flies take to garbage.

"Ken *Egan* hasn't gambled for *decades*. People change, Roddy. Look at *you*."

Yes, people can change, Roddy thinks. *Look at yourself, Mad Dog.*

"So what then?"

"I learned that *gambler* is just another way of saying *loser*. So, I joined Gamblers Anonymous. Turned my life around. Haven't placed a bet in over twenty years."

Roddy nods, waiting.

"I got a job in a Vegas restaurant. Worked my way up. Realized I had a great head for the restaurant business. I learned how to make a place tick like a Swiss clock."

Roddy can virtually *feel* Kenny's pride—an obvious sense of pleasure in having mastered the restaurant business.

"It became my calling," Ken says.

"Sort of like surgery became mine . . ."

"Exactly. You know, Roddy, we have something in common. For you, it was the army. For me . . . Vegas. It's like that botched caper turned our lives around."

"Yup, that night was a turning point," Roddy says.

Bad leading to good . . . a new life.

"Roddy, the restaurant trade saved my life."

"Like the army saved mine," Roddy says, feeling a strange kinship with Kenny. "So what happened, then?" he asks.

"I got to be assistant manager of Neros, at Caesars Palace. Then, I managed *the* Prime Steakhouse at Bellagio, a glitzy chophouse for the high rollers. The money was top-notch. A manager can make a fortune if he does right by the patrons."

"You still there?"

"No, I left a few months ago."

"How come?"

"I want something of my own. Here in New York. Manhattan, a

place called McLaughlin's, on Broadway and West 46th."

"In the theater district," Roddy says, thinking of Old New York—how the West Side got seedy—and then the city went through heavy-duty gentrification with Giuliani and now, under Bloomberg. He and Tracy make a pilgrimage maybe twice a year to see a show or dine in a restaurant.

"Right," Kenny says. "I'm gonna buy McLaughlin's. And, Roddy, I'd like to offer you the chance to be a silent partner."

Chapter 6

The consultation room spins.

Is this for real? Am I hallucinating?

After nearly three decades, a guy from his now-distant and best-forgotten past shows up—unannounced, like an errant joker in a deck of cards—and makes a business proposition.

"What?" he hears himself say.

"A silent partner . . . a backer in a top-notch chophouse."

"Kenny . . . I don't . . . I don't think I can . . ."

"Roddy, it's a turnkey operation. The owner died and the son's looking for a buyer. And I know I'm that guy . . ."

"Kenny, I don't have time to . . ."

"It's half a notch below the famous ones, you know, places like Peter Luger, or Smith & Wollensky," Kenny says. "It's got steady patronage with a heavy bar crowd, and believe me, Roddy, that's where the profits are—in the booze."

Kenny's eyes seem to dance, as though an electric charge pulses through them.

"I've looked at their demographics," Kenny says. "Young people flock there in droves. And the older crowd, too. And believe me, Roddy, steak's back. Along with the old-time drinks—martinis, Manhattans, highballs from the fifties."

Roddy feels a ticklish sense of discomfort. He swivels his chair and finds himself wanting to end this little talk. It's almost seven o'clock and Tracy's probably wondering what's keeping him. There's dinner and the kids, but Roddy's thoughts scramble, as though a bulldozer plows through his brain.

Ken looks earnestly at him; Roddy feels heat creep into his face.

"Kenny, what makes you think I'd be interested in that kind of thing?"

Jesus, he sounds smugly superior. That kind of thing . . . shit, it's condescending, even pompous.

Don't start getting snobbish, Roddy Dolan . . . you came from the streets, too.

"It's an investment, Roddy. I don't want to sound presumptuous, but don't you invest? For your family? For the future?"

"Of course . . . but a restaurant . . . ?"

"It's not about *being* in business, Roddy. We're talking about *investing* in a business. Being a backer."

"Kenny, any investing I do is done through my broker."

"You invest in stocks and bonds, don't you?"

"So?" Roddy's legs tense up; his toes clench.

"Roddy . . . stocks, bonds, mutual funds . . . you're investing in *businesses.*"

"That's different, Kenny."

Jesus, why does he feel defensive, as though he needs to explain anything?

"Investing's *investing,* Roddy. It's putting money behind a business—whether it's in IBM or Microsoft or McLaughlin's Steakhouse."

Kenny's mentioning the corporate behemoths is fucking laughable—a steakhouse in the same league as the blue chip powerhouses? But Roddy realizes he knows surgeons who've invested big bucks in a beach club out on Long Island—the Hamptons—as silent partners. "Silence is golden," joked Harold Stanton, a vascular surgeon who sank $300,000 into it. "I have nothing to do with the operation—I just reap profits. And if there's a loss," Stanton said, "I write it off. Roddy, you can buy in, too."

"No thanks, Harold. Tracy and I talked it over. It's not for us."

There's Lou Steiner and his crew, high-flying neurosurgeons who sank a ton of dough into a restaurant on the Upper East Side, Positano. "We hooked up with this guy who was a maitre d' at some big-name place in Soho. It's a gold mine. We may put some more money into an offshoot on the West Side. You interested, Roddy?"

"No, Lou. I'm doing just fine."

And another surgeon—an orthopedist—pumped money into a Toyota dealership in White Plains. He's a silent partner. It's done all the time.

But this? A restaurant? For me?

"Look, Kenny . . . I can't be involved. I've got a whole different—"

"What's the matter, Roddy? Don't you think I can make it work?" Kenny's eyebrows arch. Roddy is suddenly reminded of how as kids, Kenny—being older—had plenty of sway with him and Danny; Kenny could cajole them into almost anything.

"I'm sure you can make it work, Kenny. It's not for me."

"But Roddy . . . *I'll* run the place. As a *silent* partner you'd profit from an investment."

"Look, Ken, I . . ."

"Roddy, you don't manage Microsoft, do you?"

"Of course not."

"But you own a piece of it, right?"

"But . . ."

"It'd be the same with McLaughlin's."

"McLaughlin's is no Microsoft, Ken."

"It's the same principle, Roddy."

"I—I don't think so, Kenny . . ."

Ken peers into Roddy's eyes. "You don't trust me, do you?"

"My God, Kenny. You don't pull your punches, do you?"

"This is no time for bullshit, Roddy. We're grown men now, not kids."

"Look, Ken . . . it's what . . . twenty-eight years later and you show up and ask me for fucking money? You pop up out of nowhere and you want me to go into business with you? C'mon, gimme a fucking break, Kenny."

"Roddy. I understand your feelings, but . . ."

"Lemme be frank with you, Kenny . . ."

"Please, Roddy. This is no time for bullshit."

"Okay, Ken. Here it is. I crawled out of that shithole—Sheepshead Bay. I avoided doing jail time; I became a paratrooper, a Ranger, and a paramedic. I saw guys jump out of planes and their chutes didn't open and they hit the ground from 1,500 feet. We scraped 'em up like paste. I tramped through swamps with snakes and leeches and saw things you wouldn't know in your most shit-awful dreams. I got a GED, went to college and medical school, became a surgeon, and I married the most incredible woman in the world. I've saved, pinched, scraped, and made financial decisions with my wife . . ."

Kenny nods his head; he's listening.

"And Kenny, the last time we were in business together—granted, it wasn't your fault—I ended up being arraigned on felony charges."

"Roddy, that was a thousand years ago. People change. *I've* changed!"

"Okay, Ken . . . all bullshit aside, just like you want it. The bottom line is simple: I'm not sure I can trust you."

Kenny swallows hard.

"I'm riding bareback here, Kenny . . . no condom. It's the *naked* truth."

"I understand, Roddy."

Roddy's heart lurches in his chest.

"Lemme answer you this way," Kenny says, "My gambling—the life I led back then—is over. That was then; this is now. I'm a businessman now, not the nineteen-year-old punk kid you knew back then. In fact . . . let me tell you exactly why I've come to you. Of all the guys I've *ever* known, Roddy, you've got the most integrity."

Kenny leans forward in the chair.

"Because I knew the DA was squeezing you. He couldn't believe only two guys loaded up all that stuff." Kenny's eyes bore into Roddy's. "You're smart and successful. But above all, you can be trusted."

Kenny pauses and then says, "As important as your not giving me up was—to my way of thinking—I remember how things were between you and Danny Burns: how much trust you had in each other back then."

Kenny looks deeply into Roddy's eyes.

"*That's* the Roddy Dolan I knew . . . a stand-up guy. And that's the kind of partner I'd want in *any* business." Kenny shrugs his shoulder. "As for the past," he says, "I'm not ashamed of who or what I *was*. And now, I *am* who I am. I know you understand, because we both came from the streets."

Ken looks down at his hands and then peers up and says, "Wasn't there a time, Roddy, when you were Mad Dog Dolan, the toughest kid on the streets, the guy headed for a Golden Gloves crown? You were a slow starter, but when a guy hit you, you got your Irish up; you were a killer in the ring."

A tide of memories washes over Roddy. He sometimes thinks about these things: Herbie Goldstein's gym, how he learned to control his aggression, execute a strategy, and be a tactician, not a street brawler and less a Mad Dog.

"Are you that same guy—Mad Dog Dolan?"

"Of course not."

"So, why think *I* haven't changed? Why wouldn't you trust me enough to make an investment in a successful Manhattan restaurant?"

It occurs to Roddy that the most clear-thinking guy he knows, Dick Simons, his shrink friend, is part-owner of a Blimpie right here in Westchester County. Like plenty of physicians he knows. These guys—work-a-day docs who see patients every day, cut bellies open, and listen to hearts and minds—sink money into these ventures.

They aren't life-changing bucks—a few thousand—maybe fifty, sixty grand.

Roddy reminds himself he's not worried about money. It's about change, a sweeping transformation in the way you see the world. Kenny McGuirk-Egan's just barreled into Roddy's life, and without trying, he's raised basic questions: *Where have you been and where are you now? And, where are you going?*

And Roddy realizes if you're lucky—as he knows he was—you get a chance to make life-altering changes. Kenny Egan—with his new name and refashioned face—is dead right: Roddy Dolan isn't the same guy he was thirty years ago. And Kenny's changed much more than his features; it's been a metamorphosis—as it was for Roddy.

Roddy waits; the room is so silent he hears the ticking of his wristwatch.

"Roddy, I assume you have a financial advisor . . ."

"Sure."

"Why don't we sit down together and see if this might be something for you?"

"You know who my money guy is?"

"How would I know?"

"My accountant, Danny Burns."

"*Irish Danny Burns?* From the neighborhood?"

"Yup."

"Danny Burns?" Kenny laughs. "He was a whiz with numbers."

"Uh huh . . ."

"And you've stayed in touch all these years?"

"He's still my best friend."

"Of course. You two were blood brothers. Right?"

"Absolutely."

"Danny Boy, you, and me. It'll be a reunion. Right outta the past."

Chapter 7

Thinking about the phone call from Robert Mitchell's mother sends a shiver through Tracy. At twelve, Thomas and Robert are doing shots of vodka. And there are other troubles.

There was the call yesterday from Dean Brookings. "Mrs. Dolan," he said, "Thomas has been having a problem with another boy . . ."

Tracy's body felt coiled, tense.

"There's been name calling in gym class. It nearly came to blows."

"Did Thomas start it?"

"We don't know. You know how these things can escalate. But Thomas has been surly lately, and he's dozing off in class. We're wondering if things are okay at home."

Now, Tracy's fingertips tingle; her lips are dry. *Thomas . . . fighting? Acting surly. Nodding off in school? Doing shots of vodka? Are drugs involved, too?* Tracy feels sickness brewing in the pit of her stomach.

Roddy will be home soon. It'll be horrible when she tells him today's new development on top of what Brookings said. No doubt, Roddy'll expect the worst: that Thomas will turn out the way he was at this age—a street kid, a dead-ender, as he puts it. Roddy's tried for years to erase his past, but he can't. Actually, who can? The past is part of who you are. Tracy knows Roddy worries about Thomas. It's like a low-level toothache. Whenever any minor thing rears its head, a dark, somber look clouds Roddy's face. And with Thomas, snags and hitches—some not so small—have begun. He has an uncanny knack for getting into scrapes. Both she and Roddy recognize that.

And Roddy wants nothing more than to be the best husband and father he can be, as though by giving everything to his kids he refashions his own horrible childhood.

Once, some years back, when they were having drinks in some trendy Manhattan restaurant, Roddy said, "The only salvation from having no parents is *being* a great parent."

"So, have you been saved?"

"Yes. By having you in my life . . . and the kids," he said.

"But you just said that salvation comes from being a great parent."

"Yes."

"From anything else?"

"Being a good husband."

"How about from being a fine surgeon?"

"I guess so."

"Roddy, my love," she said, slipping her hand into his, "your salvation came a long time ago. You're a *great* father and a *wonderful* husband. And you're a boon to your patients. And Roddy . . . I love you so much."

It was the only time she recalls him tearing up. "You and the kids are everything," he whispered. "Trace, you gave me a new life . . ."

"Roddy, your life now isn't a do-over. Only kids have do-overs. You've done so much with what was handed you. I love you more than anything. And the kids love and respect you. God, you should hear Sandy brag about you. And Thomas . . . he won't say it, but he admires you more than you'll ever know."

Thinking about it, Tracy realizes Roddy orbits his entire life around the family. He rushes home from the hospital, helps Sandy with her homework, drops everything to drive her to a friend's house, and basically spoils her to death. He'd be the same way with Thomas, if the boy would let him.

If Thomas is really getting into trouble, it would be like a fist in

Roddy's chest.

■

Roddy enters the kitchen through the door from the garage. Tracy looks pale, washed out. And her lower lip trembles. "Roddy, there's trouble with Thomas," she says.

"Another call from Brookings?"

"No. I got a call today, from Robert Mitchell's mother . . ."

"Sure, I know Bobby," he says, feeling the blood leave his face. "What's up?"

"Well, after Thomas left Anne's house this afternoon, she smelled alcohol on Robert's breath. It turns out the kids were doing shots of vodka."

Roddy suddenly feels clammy, weak.

"Maybe that's why he's dozing off in class . . ."

"Roddy, I checked the cabinet. The vodka bottle's almost empty."

Roddy's stomach eddies.

"Roddy . . . that's not all . . ."

"What else?"

"Robert told her the kids were at the golf club parking lot. Thomas hot-wired an unlocked car. He wanted to drive it into town but the other kids said no."

Nausea kicks in, big time.

"How the hell did he learn to do that?"

"On the Internet . . ."

Roddy's breath leaves him. "It's hard to believe," he says. "The smartest kid in the class. Last year he was a superachiever and now he's acting like a street hood."

"Roddy, you've *got* to talk to him."

■

Roddy wonders what he can say without resorting to trite bromides, all the stale father-son clichés? He stands outside Tommy's bedroom door with no memory of having climbed the stairs. Did he float up the staircase and waft along the carpeted hallway to Tommy's door? Is this some kid-driven-I'm-losing-it kind of trance?

"You never stop worrying about them," he said to Tracy. "Whether it's braces, their friends, school, or what happens when they're teenagers."

"Oh, Roddy. We've always had issues with Thomas," Tracy said.

"Shit, I hate that word. *Issues*. They used to be called *problems*."

Roddy knocks gently on Tommy's door.

There's no response.

He knocks again, a bit harder.

Still nothing. He puts his ear to the door: silence from within. Is the kid dozing? Sleeping off the booze?

It occurs to Roddy that Tommy can't hear the knock because an iPod is probably spewing music into his ears. Lady Gaga or Eminem or some other hormone-driven, erotic-bordering-on-violence shit. *It's part of the dumbed-down, hyper-sexed, digital culture we live in,* Roddy thinks, nearly laughing to himself.

He wonders if he's becoming Grandpa Cranky-Pants, suspenders and a belt holding his pants up, just below his nipples.

Have I become so last century—pining for the good old days? Do I sound like every other old fart?

He knocks again, forcefully—the door actually bends in on its hinges.

"Yeah . . . ," comes from inside.

Roddy enters. Tommy's on the bed, propped against the headboard, listening to his iPod. The plastic buds are buried in his ears.

"Tommy . . . I'd like to talk with you . . ."

Music leaks out around the earpieces.

The kid glances indifferently at Roddy, removes the plugs, and looks away.

A pregnant pause. Is the kid being hostile? Not really. Bored? Shit, he can't read the kid worth a damn. He used to be an open book—not now.

"Mom told me about what's going on at Bobby Mitchell's house . . ."

"Yeah . . . ?"

Tommy's blond hair has that retro look. Back in Brooklyn it would've been called *Leave It to Beaver* faggoty. It's neo-something-or-other, some generational horseshit. Like how their jeans have their crotches hanging down between their knees. But Roddy knows he'll avoid the timeworn tunes of parenthood—ones he never heard as a kid.

Tommy's got his mother's features, thank God. Blue-green eyes along with pale, Celtic skin. Someday he'll be a lady-killer. Roddy sees hints of Tracy right there. *And it's a good thing, too*, Roddy thinks, because Tracy's family's a bunch of hard-striving, middle-of-the-road types—solid citizens from northern Jersey who worked their asses off to make ends meet, trying to get somewhere in the world. And Roddy's background? A genetic shit pit of criminality—highjacking, armed robbery and murder on his father's side—alcoholism and petty thievery on his mother's. Prison, unemployment, welfare, drugs, booze, food stamps—all the degenerate DNA of his bombed-out Brooklyn childhood. A shit-ridden strand of genetic material to bestow on your kids.

"Listen, Tommy . . ."

"Don't call me 'Tommy.'"

"Why?"

"It's diminutive. Meaning small. In grammar, it denotes triviality. As a verb, one might use the word *diminish*. To make or cause to seem smaller, less important."

"Okay . . ."

Jesus, the kid's so fucking smart when he wants to be.

"How'd you learn this stuff . . . *diminutive* . . . *triviality*? I never see you crack a book."

The kid shrugs. It's clear he's indifferent.

"And Mom always calls me 'Thomas' . . . which I can't stand," he adds, fiddling with his iPod.

"Why?"

"It sounds so religious. Just call me 'Tom.'"

"Okay, Tom. I can understand that."

"Whatever . . ."

How Roddy hates that word . . . *whatever*. It's really so . . . *fuck you*.

Roddy notices the kid's hands: they're immense pale paws. Could be the hands of a boxer, heavy-boned with round, prominent knuckles. And his feet—wrapped in $175 Nike Hypermax basketball shoes—are enormous. Soon he'll erupt in a growth spurt. The hormones'll surge to his prepubescent cortex. Holy shit. His brain'll be hot-wired for sex, aggression, and rebellion. The worst is yet to come. It'll be like one of those Hieronymus Bosch paintings he saw in Tracy's art book. Another thing to worry about—an inevitable tableau of trouble—another source of dread in this life.

"Tom, we have to talk," he says, sitting at the edge of the bed.

"Talk."

"We know you're bored with school."

"A waste of time."

"Is there anything about it that interests you?"

"*Not.*"

Another shitty youth-bomb: contemptuous, total dismissal. Another *fuck you*.

"Would you rather go somewhere else . . . not public school?"

"What? A school for *troubled* kids?"

"No, for *gifted* kids."

"You mean geeks."

Despite his feelings, Roddy laughs; he wonders how the kid got to be so cynical.

"There are different kinds of gifts, Tom. There are kids who are mathematically gifted and others who can perform—sing, dance, or act."

"Yeah. Geeks and fags. Actually, Dad, I'm not sure I want to go to high school."

"Tom, that's not an option."

"Why?"

"Without a high school diploma, the world's a closed door."

But he suddenly realizes the kid's heard this pitch—this anemic parental mantra. It's as stale as four-day-old donuts sitting in the Dunkin' Donuts box.

"If I could, I'd do what you did . . . join the army."

The kid's yanking his chain. Serving up bullshit on a platter. *Twelve years old and talking about joining the fucking army? Jesus, I was seventeen, nearly eighteen when I went in and did my time.* Roddy knows he's being sucked down this deflection—away from the booze and the hot-wired car. The kid's commandeering the conversation.

Conversation. Another word that's beaten to death these days, Roddy thinks. Everybody's having a fucking *conversation.* No discussions, no talks, no head-to-head, straight-up, one-on-one-heart-to-heart-sit-downs. Just *conversations.*

"Tom," he says, his throat tightening, "I know about the drinking . . ."

"It's nothing."

"No, Tom! It's *something.*"

Tom still looks down.

"And I heard about the car."

There's no response.

"Tom?"

The kid looks at him, expectation leaching through every pore on his good-looking, twelve-year-old face.

"I'm not gonna give you bullshit about right and wrong . . ."

The kid nods. Maybe he's making headway.

"You know there *are* consequences, don't you?"

The kid nods again.

"Just so you know, Tom, there are consequences to every decision in life."

The kid stares straight ahead.

"Anytime you're gonna do something—*anything*—like hot-wire a car, or get stoned . . . there's something you *must* do."

"What's that?"

"You've got to listen to yourself."

"To *myself?*" He finally looks into Roddy's eyes.

"Yes, listen to yourself, Tom. There's a little voice inside your head. It tells you what's right or wrong. Without anyone lecturing you—me, Mom, *anyone*. You've gotta listen to that voice because it'll tell you the truth."

Their eyes lock. Roddy feels a connection. It's real, so deep and filled with meaning, Roddy feels his heart ache with love and worry and warmth. Maybe he's penetrated the kid's crust.

"Do you understand?"

The kid nods and his eyes look moist.

"So what happens now?" the kid asks, again looking down.

Roddy waits, says nothing.

"What're the *consequences?*"

"Mom and I'll discuss that."

Roddy knows anything else will sound preachy; it'll just be some overwrought, trite bullshit from the overused parental playbook; it'll bore the kid to death. So he leans closer and says, "Tom . . . you, Mom, and Sandy are *everything* to me."

The kid glances at him and looks down. Roddy asks himself if he's embarrassing the boy by saying it, true as it is. Because the three of them—Tracy, Sandy, and Tom—*are* everything to him, the entire world. They're all Roddy's ever wanted, and they're everything he lives for in this life.

Roddy feels a pinching sensation behind his eyes as they grow wet.

"It's nothing without all of you," Roddy whispers.

"Whatever . . ."

Chapter 8

D anny's office is bathed in sunlight. Danny looks at Roddy sitting across the conference table. Dan knows Roddy could've been a top-notch boxer if he'd stuck with it beyond age seventeen. But of course, there was the burglary and the army, then college and medicine. Roddy still looks physically impressive; he's tall and brawny with a full head of light brown hair, an almost heroic jaw line, straight nose, and clear blue eyes that can pierce you like a knife. Even now he still looks like a tough customer.

Back when they were just little shits—maybe ten years old—a few years before the Cootie Weiss fight, he and Roddy would sit on the rocks overlooking the Atlantic Ocean at Manhattan Beach. They'd hurl stones at the gray Norway rats sniffing for fish morsels left by the hovering army of seagulls. Sometimes they'd toss Doritos to the fuckers and watch them fight over the scraps. Looking west they could see the 260-foot-tall steel frame of the parachute jump at Steeplechase Park, in Coney Island.

One particular day while sitting there, they decided to take a special vow. They'd just seen a rerun of *Broken Arrow* with Jeff Chandler and James Stewart, and they decided to reenact the scene where the Apache warrior Cochise and the cavalry officer Jeffords cut their wrists together, mingling their blood.

"We'll be blood brothers," Roddy said.

"Brothers always," Danny said.

"This means we'll always be there for each other."

"That's right, kemosabe. Always . . ."

They called each other kemosabe—meaning faithful scout, loyal friend—which they got from watching *Lone Ranger* reruns with Clayton Moore and Jay Silverheels, a true-blooded Canadian Mohawk Indian who played Tonto, the loyal sidekick.

Danny whipped out his pocketknife and carefully slit his wrist. Then, sitting amidst the wind and sea spray, Roddy sliced his own, but the cut was too deep. Blood spurted in a crimson fountain.

Horrified, Danny ripped off his T-shirt and wrapped Roddy's wrist.

Dashing to Oriental Boulevard, they flagged down a car. While Danny pressed on Roddy's wrist, the driver rushed to Coney Island Hospital. Dan felt the hot seep of blood oozing everywhere and was sure Roddy would die.

Danny thought he'd crap his pants. There'd be blood and shit everywhere. And he thought he'd have an asthmatic attack—that he'd start gasping for air because it was so scary. But he held on and beat back the fear.

And Roddy? Calm as Cochise, he called out directions to the driver.

Turned out, he'd slit an artery.

Afterward, Roddy spent weeks at Danny's house. Ma brought him to the clinic for follow-up treatment. Roddy's mother—always drunk—never even knew it happened.

It's been thirty-six years since the blood brothers fiasco, with plenty of scrapes since then, too. But it turned out well; actually, considering their earlier days, it's been fabulous.

Danny can't recall when he and Roddy met; it's lost in the fog of memory. It was before his own father died when Danny was six. A furnace repairman, the old man had a heart attack while fixing a furnace—checked out in a heap of soot. His clock just stopped.

So, he and Roddy were two fatherless boys, always there for each other. If there's one guy he can count on in a crunch—no matter what—it's Roddy Dolan.

They never lost touch, even when Roddy was in the army. That's just the way it's been all this time—the best of friends. Bonded. Connected.

They're on the telephone a few times a week. Their wives adore each other. His wife, Angela, thinks Roddy's the kindest man she's ever met. She should have known him back in Brooklyn. But that was a million years ago.

As Roddy's accountant, Danny knows his income, expenses, investment portfolio, and retirement accounts. He's advised Roddy and Tracy about all things financial and knows everything—to the last dollar.

And right now, they could be sitting at the Greek's on Nostrand Avenue. *It's amazing how memory never really dies*, Danny thinks. Memories dim, for sure, but with the slightest prod, they rush back, flood the brain with light. It's like hearing an old song; the lyrics come right back.

"Kenny's proposal's interesting," Danny says. "I've met with him four times; we went over everything very, very carefully."

Dan knows he's always cautious. It's been his guiding principle. Angela says he's always been circumspect in business, maybe to a fault.

"Danny, it's good to be conservative with clients' money," Angela said. "But sometimes you can miss an opportunity."

"Honey, the clients value my vigilance," he said. "I'm the gate-keeper, the watchdog. And I've gotten some clients out of big trouble."

Dan's always known that Roddy's satisfied with what he has. Being a surgeon married to Tracy, he wants nothing more out of life.

"That's bullshit," Roddy says when some guy drives by in a Mercedes. "It's a sign of inadequacy."

"The guy driving the car doesn't think so," Danny would say.

"He's compensating for a short dick."

"You don't want a yacht or membership in the Siwanoy Country Club?"

"That's bullshit."

"No swimming pool in the backyard?"

"Do I look like a fish?"

Danny knows Roddy's not the acquisitive type. What money can buy isn't important to him. For Roddy, getting involved in Kenny's restaurant means reconnecting with the past, and he knows Roddy isn't favorably inclined to the proposition.

■

Roddy wonders why Danny never spent more on office furniture. The couch and chairs are Office Depot discount—bargain basement crap. The place is bottom-line simple: a conference table, Dan's desk, some chairs, an intricate computer setup, and potted houseplants everywhere—pothos, ferns, baby's tears—Dan must spend hours each week watering them all.

"Why don't you spend a little money on office furniture?" he once asked Danny.

"It's window dressing. The only thing that impresses my clients is how much money they don't owe the government."

"Just kidding, Danny Boy."

"Just like you, Roddy. I spend where it counts—on Angela, the kids, and the house," he said, referring to their center-hall colonial in Tuckahoe. "The office? It's my model of fiscal prudence."

At age forty-five Danny's kept his hair—a full mop of reddish curls framing his pale, still-freckled face. Roddy always knows when Danny's upset or angry; his face gets blotchy—red whorls form on his cheeks. It's that Celtic skin—and his allergies—the blood rush shows on his face.

Danny's looks—especially those green irises with dark rims—always drove the girls crazy in high school. They'd go dewy-eyed and croon "Danny Boy" passing him in the hallways. It was swoon time.

Mary O'Sullivan would ask Roddy, "Can I hang out with you guys?" She thought she could get close to Danny by buddying up with his best friend. And Cathy Andrews would ask, "Would you and Danny like to come to my party next Saturday night?" But the only woman who lit his fire was Angela. Her traditional Italian family wasn't crazy about her hooking up with a barrel-chested Irishman. But before long, he and Angela got married.

Danny's grown a bit thick around the middle, but he has powerful-looking arms and muscle-massed forearms covered with red-orange hair. Inherited his physique from his father—a bull of a man. Poor guy died about the same time Roddy's father checked out at Attica.

"You met with Kenny four times . . .?"

"Yup."

"Hey, kemosabe, I didn't think you'd be *that* interested."

"Roddy, Kenny's proposal isn't some dumb-ass scheme."

"Coming from you, that carries weight."

Dan leans back in his chair and steeples his fingers. "You know, Roddy, I have plenty of doctor and lawyer clients who're silent partners in some venture . . . a Burger King franchise, or UPS store, a restaurant."

"No shit."

"It can be a good investment. I'll say this: Kenny knows the restaurant business cold. Frankly, I was impressed. I went to McLaughlin's and looked the place over."

"No kidding."

"Roddy, I'm going back next week with a guy who brokers restaurants. I examined their books and tax records and did a cash-flow analysis."

"You did all that?"

"Kenny's proposal could be a solid decision."

"Okay . . ."

"For one . . . McLaughlin's has been there for fifty years. It has a steady client base."

"Danny, I know *shit* about the restaurant business."

"We'll get to the business end . . ."

"Hey, Danny . . . you're not gonna get into balance sheets and all the lingo, are you? I can't handle that crap."

Danny laughs. "I know, Roddy, but let's just talk common sense. Here's the deal: you have a motivated seller, the son. McLaughlin Junior's not suffering from seller's pride. The father died and it's an estate situation. The son just wants out."

Roddy nods.

"Next, there are ten years left on the lease. So a huge cost factor is stable, predictable. There's no rent hike coming anytime soon."

"Understood . . ."

"It's in a top-notch location. Lots of midtown traffic: businesses, shoppers, and theaters."

Danny goes on and explains that the combined cost of food, labor, and rent shouldn't be more than a certain percent of total revenue. "And the place has done well, even during the recession. The tax returns tell it all."

Danny talks about how to set a price on the operation. He goes on about multiples, return on investment, depreciation, and amortization of debt. Roddy's head spins. "C'mon, kemosabe, you're killing me with this esoteric shit."

"Listen, Roddy, McLaughlin's willing to finance half the thing."

"Meaning . . . ?"

"He only wants half the money up front. We can pay the rest over five years, with interest. In other words, McLaughlin lends the other 50 percent. It's like a mortgage."

"How much interest?"

"Three percent. Roddy, by taking only *half* the bucks up front, McLaughlin's betting the restaurant'll do well enough that the new owners will pay off the balance."

"Understood."

"And there's no prepayment penalty," says Danny.

"So, it's like my mortgage. It can be paid in a lump sum at any time."

"Even better," Danny says, "McLaughlin's willing to sign an agreement that we won't have to collateralize the loan."

"Meaning . . . ?"

"Meaning McLaughlin's lien would only be against the restaurant. Not personal assets. If we can't make the payments he can raid the restaurant, nothing more."

Roddy nods; he understands.

"Now I had to negotiate McLaughlin down on his price."

"You got that far?"

"Yup. McLaughlin claims lots of income's been in cash—mostly at the bar. His father never reported it to the IRS. He claims the place earns more than the books show. He wanted a higher price for those unseen profits."

"Sounds like bullshit to me . . ."

"I said if his father cheated the Uncle, that was his business. But the buyer shouldn't pay for it. We went back and forth, and he caved."

"So what's the bottom line?"

"One million dollars. Five hundred thou up front, with the rest paid out over five years at 3 percent annual interest rate."

"Dan, I don't wanna make a commitment to . . ."

"Roddy, it's a good investment."

"For *me?*"

"For *you* and for *me* . . . along with Kenny."

"The three of us?"

"Haven't you noticed I've been saying *we,* not *you?* Like it's always been, Roddy, you and me . . . together."

It's like a spotlight suddenly turns on in a dark theater. Roddy's aware that Danny knows finances, cold. He plans trusts, taxes, estates, and loopholes. He has corporate clients—even some blue-chip honchos—and he's as familiar with business as Roddy is with the innards of the human body.

"You and me in business together?"

"Why not, Roddy? It'd be great. It could really pay off."

"How much money?"

"A hundred thou each," Danny says. "Here's how it breaks down. There's a half million due up front. Kenny says he can put up $300,000."

"Three hundred? Kenny McGuirk . . . I mean *Egan?* Fucking *Kenny?* Are you shitting me?"

"Kenny checks out. He's saved plenty. Made a ton of dough in Vegas. Shit, the guy even showed me his bank accounts—a CD, savings account, and checking account. And I contacted two of the major credit agencies—Experian and Equifax. Kenny's credit is fine. I called the federal bankruptcy district court in Las Vegas. He's never filed for Chapter 7—personal bankruptcy. There's *nada.*"

"He actually has *that* kind of money?"

"He's ready to write a certified check. So what's left to investigate? That leaves $200,000 split between you and me—a hundred each."

Roddy realizes his head is bobbing up and down.

"Kenny'd be the managing partner. He'd own three-fifths of the business—you and I each have one-fifth," Danny says. "Each year we owe McLaughlin $103,000, including interest. Based on the breakdown, Kenny pays McLaughlin $61,800; you and I pay $20,600 a year. In five years, we own the place.

"I've calculated it down to the penny. Right now, with gross revenues, there's a yearly profit of about $470,000, after costs. It isn't really very complicated, Roddy."

"It is for *me.*"

"Kenny draws a salary, which is part of the cost before profits, which are distributed according to the proportion we each own. We take out $60,000 a year—each—from which we make payments to McLaughlin. Roddy, when the arithmetic's done and taxes paid, it's nearly a 20 percent return each year. For each of us."

"You sound high on this thing . . ."

"Look, Roddy, Kenny puts up the most money; he takes the biggest risk and reaps the biggest reward. That's capitalism," Danny adds with a laugh. "The restaurant runs like it has for fifty years. We're silent partners."

"And you'd be the accountant . . . ?"

"I'd charge my usual hourly fee. It's part of the cost of doing business."

"You think Kenny can manage a place like this?"

"Roddy, I made some phone calls. Kenny was the assistant manager of Neros. And he comanaged the Prime Steakhouse at Bellagio. His comanager said Kenny's a pro at massaging the patrons."

"I'm just trying to get my head around this, Dan. I mean . . . you made the financial crap very clear. But why'd Kenny come to *us?*"

"A good question. And I grilled him about it. He wanted to come back to New York, and he went back to the old neighborhood. He heard about us and wanted to reconnect. He didn't give me any hearts and flowers bullshit about being old friends.

"He felt he could trust us . . . especially *you.* He's never owned a place of his own. For him, McLaughlin's is the chance of a lifetime. You don't often run into an estate situation like this. It's almost like a postdivorce distress sale."

"Danny, my last business venture with Kenny almost landed me in Attica."

"Roddy, that was thirty years ago. But, if the truth be told, I'm impressed. Kenny's changed."

"He asked me if *I'd* changed . . ."

"Roddy, you're proof that a guy can change. I think the church calls it an epiphany."

"You know Dan, we really don't need the money."

"Yeah, but it *is* interesting. And it gives us a little diversification aside from the usual—you know, stocks and bonds."

"You feel comfortable with Kenny as a partner?"

"Roddy, I'm not saying Kenny's a saint. But his gambling ended twenty-five years ago."

"According to *him*."

"The credit reports don't lie. And he has a track record," Dan adds. "But still . . . I'm bringing in the restaurant guy. And don't forget, Kenny's putting up three hundred—a certified check."

Roddy nods, sees the chips falling into place. And with Danny in on it, it's on the up-and-up.

"And Roddy, we're not *marrying* Kenny. It's an investment."

They sit silently.

"Besides," Danny says, "A hundred thou isn't a huge deal at this stage of the game. Talk to some of your surgeon friends and see how much they've sunk into silent partnerships."

"You know me, Danny, I don't like long shots."

"Look, kemosabe, the restaurant's a vanity investment for us. Just for kicks. Why don't you talk it over with Tracy?"

"That's exactly what I'll do."

Chapter 9

Danny sips Barolo. Glancing around the dining room, he feels a sense of deep satisfaction. Angela has decorated their house exquisitely. The English-style walnut breakfront holds a set of Coalport Arcadia English bone china—service for twelve. The Kashmeri Persian rug offsets the gleaming hardwood floors, and the room has a comfortable lived-in feel, as does their entire house. And it's not by accident; he and Angela have put plenty of work—sweat equity—into the place and Danny knows he's a bit house-proud.

"Angela, your lasagna's still the best," Roddy says.

"Sure beats my Irish stew," Tracy adds with a laugh.

"It's always a pleasure having you guys for dinner," Angela says. "Especially you, Roddy. Your appetite can make any cook feel appreciated."

"Oh, I'm quite discerning," Roddy says.

The wine makes Danny feel he's floating, but his head's crystal clear. He gazes across the table at Angela's dark hair, her olive complexion, and brown eyes. Danny knows he's lucky to have Angela, a woman whose common sense and no-punches-pulled advice is always right on target. She never hesitates to tell him when she thinks he's being overly circumspect.

"Well, guys," Dan says, "we've been kicking this thing around like a soccer ball, so let's make a decision."

Caution is good but don't let it turn into paralysis, Dan thinks.

"Danny, do you feel confident about Kenny?" Tracy asks. "From what Roddy says, he was a schemer."

"I'd put a different spin on it," Danny says. "Kenny was resourceful—a streetwise guy with an inside track on things; he always came up with an angle."

"Yes, but why does he come to you and Roddy all these years later?"

"It's a chance to reconnect. But different from years ago."

"We can't redo the past," Roddy says.

"Not *redo* the past, but *reconnect*—in a better way. It really shows how far we've come."

"And you're sure Kenny's for real?" Tracy asks.

"He's not a guy with a big hat and no cattle. His bank statement doesn't lie."

"What do you think, Angela?" Tracy asks.

"Danny can be *too* conservative. Sometimes, you have to go for it."

"Danny, you see any risks?" Roddy asks.

"There're risks in every business. Some you can contain, some you can't," he says with a shrug. "There are always variations in the business cycle, or trends that make a place sizzle one year and go ice-cold the next. That's life."

"Don't you try to control risk?"

"Sure, but there are risks you can't foresee. Take 9/11, for instance. Aside from the horror of it, it was a near-death experience for plenty of Manhattan eateries. They nearly starved after the attack. Those that hung on took time to get out of the red. Should that kind of risk be a deal breaker? And besides, Roddy, this isn't a lifestyle change for us. Like I said, it's a vanity project."

"We know surgeons who've sunk fortunes into some iffy things," says Tracy.

"Actually, I find this sideline very attractive," says Danny. "But lemme be clear, I stand to gain more than anyone. I could meet my clients at McLaughlin's and we'll talk taxes over dinner. The restaurant writes it off as advertising and it's good for my accounting business and the restaurant. It's cross-pollination."

"*Cross-pollination*," says Roddy. "A good business term."

"It's my business to think business," Dan says. "After all, I don't do surgery."

They all laugh.

"There's something else," Danny says, reaching for the wine bottle. "Owning a piece of McLaughlin's puts some Broadway in our dull suburban lives. I don't have to tell you, there ain't much glamour in accounting."

"Just don't get *too* glamorous on me," Angela says, narrowing her eyes.

"Think about it," Dan says. "We can go out for an evening—to our own place."

"So the bottom line is what?" Angela asks.

"It comes out on the plus side," says Dan. "For once I wanna drop the balance sheets and numbers. The sweet spot's being in business with all of us. *That's* the real return on the investment."

Danny looks across the table, fixes his gaze on Roddy, and says, "Just look at the irony. That botched burglary landed you in the army. In a way, it led you to medicine and then to Tracy. It turned out good as gold."

Roddy closes his eyes and nods. Tracy sets her hand on his.

"You know what I think, Roddy?" Angela says. "You have to own your past. Make it work *for* you."

Roddy glances at Tracy; she smiles expectantly, squeezing his arm.

"And Roddy," says Dan, "I'm in there counting beans. If the place sinks, we're out in a heartbeat."

"Just like that?"

"Sure. You can dissolve the partnership. Force the other guy to buy you out. It's not like we'd be hostages."

"Okay."

"Roddy, here's the worst-case scenario," Danny says. "The restaurant goes south. McLaughlin enforces his lien—seizes the restaurant's assets and sells 'em off. We're shielded personally. We've spent a hundred thousand apiece, but we've made money during the life of the business. Whistle blows; game's over. Any loss is tax deductible. That's it."

■

Roddy knows he's had a hard time letting the past go, forgiving and forgetting. He thinks about the brawls he had as a kid—in and out of the boxing ring—and all the wrongs done to him. Not just his mother and father. Not just that bastard Horst. There were fights in barrooms, in school, on the streets, in alleys—everywhere. His rage would superheat on itself—like an underground volcano—and then explode. He'd turn into that mad dog—the beast he fights off in his dreams.

If things had gone badly—if a guy fell and hit his head on the pavement and never got up—it could've led to a manslaughter charge. He'd been told he had lethal hands; he'd nearly killed a thug who tried to mug him when he was sixteen. Then there'd have been no army, no medicine, no Tracy—no life as he now knows it.

So here he is in Danny and Angela's Tuckahoe home and it occurs to Roddy that Danny's right: the botched burglary was a turning point in his life. Bad led to good. He turns to Tracy and says, "What do you think, honey?"

"I say as long as Danny and Angela are in, I'm fine with it."

Roddy says, "Danny, I know you longer than anyone in my whole life."

"Same here, Roddy, except for my mother."

"God rest her beautiful soul," Roddy says. "Dan, I know this isn't the Hallmark channel, but . . . ," and Roddy's voice cracks, "you're godfather to our children, and you're the executor of our estate. And if you're in, Tracy and I are good to go."

Lightness fills Roddy's chest. Then he says, "You know, sitting here in your beautiful house, sharing this great meal, and talking about being in business together—all four of us—and Kenny, too, it's a measure of the distance we've traveled."

"Yes, it is," Dan says.

"Maybe it's a chance to reconnect with the past, Dan, but in a successful way, the way Kenny put it. It's a reminder of the lives we live now."

Roddy feels tears welling up in his eyes.

"You know, Roddy, people reconnect all the time," Danny says. "That's why they go to high school and college reunions . . . even fifty years later."

Roddy nods and squeezes Tracy's hand.

"So maybe it's a map of our own personal journeys," Danny says.

Roddy looks around the table, wants to say more, but knows he doesn't have to; the words that count have been spoken.

So he simply says, "The distance we've traveled . . ."

Roddy shifts his gaze from Tracy to Danny and Angela, knowing he loves these people deeply.

"If the restaurant guy okays it, should I have a lawyer draw up the papers?"

"It's in your hands," Roddy says, looking into Tracy's eyes.

"It'll get done, Cochise."

"Yeah, kemosabe."

Chapter 10

"We've been in business three months," Danny says as he and Roddy enter McLaughlin's on a Thursday night. The noise level is oceanic.

The place is so mobbed, so boffo-busy, the walls seem to pulsate. According to Danny, the place peaks to feverish action on Friday and Saturday nights. And business isn't bad on Sundays either; they get the Broadway matinee crowd, and then a Sunday evening throng of heavy drinking beef eaters shows up before the workweek begins.

Roddy's reminded of Wal-Mart or Macy's on Black Friday, or a fire sale at one of those electronic stores near 42nd Street. Roddy recalls those National Geographic programs about the African plains—the wildebeest migration across the Serengeti—an immense herd, looking for greener feeding grounds during the dry season. And it looks like they've found one: McLaughlin's. Danny's analysis was right on the money. And for sure, Kenny's doing something right.

"Kenny's placed ads in the right places," says Danny. "*New York* magazine, *The New Yorker,* and some others. Remember *Field of Dreams?* 'If you build it they will come.'"

The reservation desk is mobbed by would-be diners waiting anxiously for tables. The cacophony is Yankee Stadium–loud. "This place is Fat City," Danny shouts above the din.

The telephone trills incessantly. Roddy's certain if this was a cartoon, the receiver would be bouncing off the cradle. It's a high-voltage mix of Miami, L.A., the Hamptons, and the old Borscht Belt in its heyday. Roddy sees a huge tourist and pretheater crowd. Everyone's there: the dowdy, Peoria types, the *New York Review of Books*–reading Upper West Siders, the youngish East Siders using anyone's plastic but their own.

Roddy's certain he spots some oil-rich Middle East guys—Kuwaitis or Saudis, dripping lucre and dropping cash—and a few Eurotrash players, too. Apron-wearing waiters scurry frenetically trying to keep up with the crowd's appetite. It reminds Roddy of midweek rush hour traffic at the George Washington Bridge. Is there really a recession going on? Yes, McLaughlin's has *chops*—the ones you eat and the place has stature with the steakhouse set.

"It was like this a few weeks ago when Angela and I were here," says Danny. "And it was a weekday night, too. Roddy, you and Tracy should come once in a while."

"I haven't had time, but maybe Angela and Tracy can arrange it."

Omar, the assistant maitre d' Kenny hired, is desperately trying to keep up with the pressing crowd. People clamor for a table; some shout, others plead. Either way, they order cocktails before they're seated.

Walk-ins amble into the place, swarm the reservations desk—plead with Omar—and glad-hand the guy with twenty-dollar bills, just to sit among the steakarati.

"And tonight's typical," Danny says. "Kenny really doped this place out."

Roddy admires the décor. It's old fashioned: dark, wood walls with wainscoting, definitely steakhouse style—masculine, high-end, and clubby-looking, but not overdone. *And it's not overly Irish,* Roddy thinks. *Not seedy, like the Brooklyn Irish chophouses back in the day. But it's not overly posh either. Nothing to turn off the bridge-and-tunnel crowd from Brooklyn, Queens, and North Jersey. The* lighting is perfect: makes the women look beautiful while the men look well-heeled and handsome.

When you first walk in there's a linen-topped credenza with a bountiful display of top-notch California and French wines. A few haute Italian vintages, too. But no Chilean or other low-end stuff to save some penny-pinching diner a few bucks on lesser fermentations.

The bar is rich-looking, glossed mahogany, reminiscent of the early twentieth century—maybe even the days of the speakeasies in brownstone basements, places with small peepholes and huge bouncers. Bottles are stacked behind the bar in impressive battalions, all backlit in a colorful wash of well-placed lighting. It makes a definitive statement—the emphasis is on *the booze.*

"It's the Willy Sutton concept," Danny says. "You go where the money is. And it's at the bar."

Heavy white linens drape the tables. The room radiates elegance but in a rugged way, nothing that would denude its sturdiness or potency. There's an open flaming grill at one end with two grill chefs wearing white jackets and tall toques working the grill pit. A beef eater's delight.

With the crowd, the clatter of dishes and clinking glasses, and the booming laughter, the place exudes a muscular animation.

It's typical steakhouse fare: highly marbled porterhouse steaks, other cuts of prime beef, some seafood dishes, and the usual assortment of starters, from crab cakes to Caesar salads. As in all the beef joints, everything's à la carte. You pay to play and the price-point is just right—a Goldilocks approach—not too high, but not too low. The place is jammed with suited-up power brokers: thick-necked steak devotees—real carnivores—who devour gargantuan portions of meat. It's expense account heaven.

Roddy glances toward the bar area; two bartenders serve a clot of clamorous drinkers bellied up to the bar—three deep—washing down high-end whiskies and wines. Roddy sees bottles of Stoly, Bombay Sapphire gin, and pricey single-malt scotch whiskey whipped out by the barkeeps who keep pouring. And the cash register rings repeatedly. It's ka-ching heaven. Just as Kenny said, the bar is the profit center—it's a Niagara of cash.

■

Roddy, Dan, and Kenny sit at the table in the back office. Dining room din seeps through the door.

Kenny's at the wet bar; he pours Roddy and Danny glasses of Dewar's on the rocks. A tumbler of club soda sits in front of him. "Gotta stay sharp for the dinner crowd," he says.

Kenny's hair is stylishly coiffed. His fingernails are impeccably manicured, buffed to a pinkish glow. And that subtle cologne fragrance: probably Bulgari or Versace—just a hint of it—adds a touch of elegance. With his thin frame and height, in the tapered tux with its pleated, ivory-tinged tuxedo shirt and cummerbund, Kenny looks Fred Astaire–debonair. He exudes a toned-down buoyancy; and yes, Kenny looks exactly like the owner-manager of a Manhattan steakhouse should: urbane, brimming with bonhomie, and ready to do his meet-and-greet thing. After all, it's Kenny's house and he's hosting the party.

"Kenny virtually lives in the place," Danny said as he and Roddy drove into the city. "He's in by midmorning, supervises everything: sets up, preps for the lunch and dinner crowd, orders inventory, deals with the health inspectors, the whole works. He takes one evening off a week, that's it. I swear, Roddy, he operates like a surgeon."

"Now that's impressive," Roddy said.

"He knows how to maximize profit," Dan says. "Some items bog down the kitchen. Like Lobster Newburg—time consuming to prepare and expensive. So he replaced it with a surf-and-turf special— grilled steak and lobster tails. Very popular. Less inventory, more sales. The guy's a guru at this game."

"Kenny, the numbers look great," Danny says across the office conference table. "Like I always say, the books tell the story."

"I knew we'd make this place work," Ken says.

"To McLaughlin's and to us," Dan says, raising his glass.

"Here's to you, Ken," Roddy chimes in, clinking his glass to Kenny's.

"To being with old friends," Ken says.

Buoyancy fills Roddy's chest. "Here's to being partners."

Danny drains his glass and bangs it down on the table. Roddy knows Danny's amped.

"Kenny," Roddy says, "you're a master . . . like a skilled surgeon."

Kenny sets his club soda on the table and looks like he'll choke up. He peers at Roddy, then Danny, and his eyes grow wet. "I owe you guys big time," he says. "You've given me a gift . . ."

"Hey Kenny," Roddy says, feeling his throat close. "Remember back in the old days how you wanted to run your own card game?"

"I sure do."

"Well you can't do better than this."

"*This* is my game, now," Kenny says, nodding toward the door. The roar of the dining room is punctuated by the high-pitched laughter of a woman.

"I know I was skeptical," Roddy says, "but you've done something good here . . . and it shows how we've changed our lives."

"Amen," Kenny says, sipping his club soda.

So now, sitting in the back office, Roddy thinks it's true: the restaurant embodies the changes they've all made.

"Hey, Ken," says Danny, "before you went to Roddy, you visited the old neighborhood, right? Hear about any of the old crowd?"

"Truthfully, I wanted to find you guys, because this is where we're at now . . ."

"Still, it's good to hear about the old days."

Yes, Kenny ran into some of the old crowd. Frankie Messina served time and then became a truck driver; and Kenny had heard a little bit about Joey Sansone, Richie Hart, and Jackie Kurtz. They're all slogging along with their lives.

"I *did* hear about Cootie Weiss," Kenny says with a grin. "I'll never forget that fight, Roddy. How you ripped off that son of a bitch's ear. I still think about it . . . you standing with his ear in your hand, holding it up like a trophy."

"He's a dead issue," Roddy says.

"Dead is right. Got clipped by the Russians. Horned in on the Ecstasy trade."

Just the mention of the old names—especially Cootie Weiss—telescopes time for Roddy. He expects to be flooded by a wave of feelings—menace and wariness—the dark threat of the streets. But they've faded away in the haze of years. *Just like that song, "Dust in the Wind,"* Roddy thinks.

"Roddy, I heard your mother died," Kenny says. "I'm sorry about that."

"Drank herself to death," Roddy says with a sigh. "Wasted her life."

He recalls last seeing her. He was twenty-five years old, living near the medical school. Neighbors called the cops. The stench from her apartment wafted through the hallway. She was found half-dead, delirious from booze and body breakdown.

Seeing her in the bed at Coney Island Hospital, Roddy knew she wouldn't live beyond a few days. As a medical student he understood the metabolic catastrophe brought on by years of drugs, drinking, and dissipation.

She was forty-five—looked sixty-five—and floating in a confused delirium. Her hair was a dry nest of thinning frizz. Her color was the hue of a pumpkin. Jaundice. Liver failure. Her belly was bloated. Her skin was dry, cracking, wrinkled, and withered.

Roddy inhaled an ammonia-like smell—her breath—reeking of toxic waste and decay. Incoherent, babbling, she gazed at the ceiling. The not-so-faint odor of feces lingered in the air. She was shutting down.

"Mom . . . ?"

She mumbled something.

"Mom. It's me."

Gibberish came through her cracked lips—an incoherent stream of word salad.

"Mom . . . it's Roddy."

"Horst?" she mumbled. "Horst. Why'd you leave me?"

Her eyelids fluttered.

"It's me, Mom. Roddy."

"Horst. Why'd you leave me with that lousy kid?"

"Mom . . . ?"

"He was my biggest mistake, that kid . . ."

Nearly reeling, Roddy wanted to shake her, have her acknowledge him—her own flesh and blood.

"Horst?" she called.

Death was creeping through her. It was terminal toxicity.

A short while later, she was a wasted corpse.

And what did he feel?

Loss? Sadness? Regret? Relief? Anger?

He felt them all—raw, ripping—like a swarm of gnats settling in his brain.

Now, sitting in the back office of McLaughlin's, Kenny says, "They still talk about you back in the Bay, Roddy. A Golden Gloves champ who could've been a pro boxer, a Green Beret, and then became a doctor . . . you're a legend."

"Roddy doesn't wanna remember shit about those days," says Danny.

Sitting at the conference room table in McLaughlin's back office, a glass of scotch in front of him, the din of the crowd bleeding through the door, with Danny and Kenny at the table—two guys from a past best forgotten, a past now transformed for them all—with Tracy and the kids waiting at their lovely Bronxville home, Roddy thinks of the stream of time in his life and the changes the years brought. He looks across the table and says, "Hey guys . . . we're *here* now. The past is over and gone."

"Agreed," says Danny. "The past is dead."

"Here's to the future," Kenny says, lifting his glass.

"Long live the future," Dan says.

Chapter 11

Roddy sits with Tracy, Danny, and Angela at a banquette. It's their third time at McLaughlin's in the last few months.

The room is so filled it seems ready to burst. Drinkers are stacked at the bar. Kenny and Omar are seating patrons at NASCAR speed. Kenny's moving so fast Roddy's reminded he was a high school track star back in the day—was a jackrabbit who ran the 100-meter dash in record time at citywide meets. The moment a table is cleared, the busboys swarm over it, have a new setup in place, and Kenny or Omar appears with another cluster of diners.

Kenny's hired a hostess, a tall blonde with a trout-pout look on her plump, Juvederm-enhanced lips. Her hair is up in an elaborate chignon. She wears a supersized push-up bra—shows Grand Canyon cleavage—and has lust-inducing legs. She's wearing a black, stretch-satin sheath, open at the back, cut midthigh. She slinks about in stiletto heels. Pheromones waft from her body, mixing with the aroma of sizzling steak. Sex and beef swirl in the air. Every man in the place stares at Crystal. It's instinctual.

"Kenny still thinks he's in Vegas," says Roddy.

"Crystal's good for business," Dan says.

"*Crystal* . . . ?" asks Tracy.

"A *hostess* . . . ?" Angela says, chortling.

"Looks like a hooker," adds Tracy.

"Adds to the ambience," Dan says.

"It's nine and people are still waiting to be seated," Tracy says. "So why some empty tables?"

"Kenny told me a couple reserves a table for four," Dan says. "After they're seated, they tell the maitre d' the other couple won't show. Now, Kenny sits them at the bar until at least three people show. *Then* . . . they get the four-top."

Tracy and Angela laugh.

"If you don't do that, you end up using only a percentage of your table space."

"Even if your wine glass is half-full, the waiters keep pouring."

"Kenny calls it *flooding*," says Danny.

"Flooding . . . ?"

"Wine has a 400 percent markup. By flooding, you sell much more. Pure profit."

Kenny's like a bumblebee on steroids. He glad-hands everyone, kisses the women, and hands the men off to Crystal. She leads them to their tables while they stare at her ass. Ken's pocketing huge gratuities. Hugs and air-kisses abound.

"So, what do you think?" Kenny says, suddenly at the table. His eyes dart quickly toward the room's expanse, then back again.

"Looks great," says Danny.

"The food's excellent," says Angela.

Kenny beams. His hair is brushed back, glossed with gel.

Roddy's sure Kenny's changed over the last three months. Gone is that Fred Astaire look; it's been replaced by a buttery slickness. He reminds Roddy of a wet eel. In fact, Kenny's sweating so much, he looks like he's just surfaced from the greenish, oil-slicked waters of Sheepshead Bay. Suddenly Kenny's overseeing a new setup.

"What's up with Kenny?" Roddy whispers to Dan.

"He's on top of everything."

"I mean the sweat, the running around . . . ?"

"Roddy, he's working like three guys."

"He looks wired."

"The guy's running on ten cylinders," Danny says.

Kenny's back at the table and says, "Can I offer you an after-dinner drink, on me?"

"What do you mean *on me?*" Roddy says. "It's on *all* of us. Don't forget, Kenny, we own 40 percent of this operation."

Kenny bows. "Can I offer you a cognac—*three-fifths* on me?"

There's laughter. Kenny whirls; then he's gone. He glides, dips, and flits kinetically from table to table. He's definitely not the Kenny Egan who walked into Roddy's office six months earlier.

Now, Kenny's back at the table, sets down four cognacs, and plants a sloppy kiss on Angela's cheek. Then he lopes to the bar and gestures frenetically to a waiter.

Roddy watches Kenny meet and greet a party of four; then he's back to the bar rummaging through bottles. He serves drinks and then steers toward a table of six men, carrying a bottle of Veuve Clicquot.

Kenny's at another table, whispering to a couple of tough-looking types—two pinstripe-suited guys with their jewelry-draped girlfriends. *Total goons*, Roddy thinks, *real wise-guy types*, and a sense of discomfort threads through him. Crystal's there, too, her hand on one guy's shoulder. Two high-end wine bottles sit on the table. Looks like French stuff—a Bordeaux and a Burgundy. And an empty champagne bottle—Dom Perignon—is plopped upside-down in a silver ice bucket. It's a table of big spenders luxuriating in Kenny's ass-kissing courtesies.

Roddy nudges Dan and says, "Look at that."

"Kenny's massaging the clientele. That's the business he's in."

"He looks pretty cozy with them."

"It's business, Roddy."

"What about those guys?"

Danny squints and leans toward Roddy.

"Brooklyn . . . born and bred," he whispers. "Maybe north Jersey."

"Either way."

"Russian or Italian, can't really tell from here."

"Connected fucking guys."

"Roddy, it's a *steakhouse*."

"Maybe Al Capone's ghost'll walk in. Or Tony Soprano."

"I don't care if fucking Paulie Walnuts waltzes in. It's business."

"I'll bet those guys pay cash."

"Cash is king, especially with that type."

"What type?"

"*That* type."

"I don't like it."

"It's splashy. I love it," says Dan.

Roddy hears a nasal cackle. It's that insane Kenny laugh from the old days in that shit-pit known as Brooklyn—Sheepshead Bay to be precise. Roddy recalls that hyena howl that would erupt whenever Kenny won a hand at poker—when he'd plop down a full house or royal flush on the table and then rake in the cash. Or drag some slob over the coals in a game of eightball after ramping up the betting odds. He hasn't heard that insane laugh for decades, until tonight. And it's back, like a recurrent dream—in the middle of this vanity operation known as McLaughlin's.

Roddy eyeballs Kenny greeting another bunch of wise guys. All suited up in dark threads, chalk-stripes, hundred-dollar haircuts, and heavy-duty jewelry. It's a fucking costume, a dress code for these guys. Winding their way to a table, Kenny yammers away to the oldest one—maybe a mob underboss and his ass-kissing cronies. Definitely not doctors and lawyers. Not Garment District types, either, though they'd be at home on 8th Avenue or in the Diamond District—pulling a protection shakedown on some small-business owner.

Fucking racketeers, right down to their hard-looking faces and pricey threads. It's the whole testosterone-bloated swagger, jutting jaws, the streetwise look of guys who intimidate, goons who ooze threat, guys who're little more than fear profiteers.

It's been six months and McLaughlin's looks like a mobster hangout on Mulberry Street. Or maybe on Brooklyn's Brighton Beach Avenue—Little Odessa by the Sea. Roddy recalls that De Niro film, *Goodfellas*. The mob congregated at some Queens restaurant—turned it into a wise-guy clubhouse—wormed their way in, trashed the place, sold off everything, and put the owner out of business.

Roddy wonders if it could happen to McLaughlin's.

He scans the room and sees Kenny with another group. He's yakking, laughing, backslapping, and glad-handing. Roddy can only imagine his act with the Vegas junketeers—and wonders if this is Kenny's real self. He hasn't seen him drinking, but he's so high octane it's off-the-charts bizarre.

Roddy spots a squad of tough guys at another table. One of them—looks like a silver-haired Don—gets up. He wears a few thousand bucks of cloth on his back, with a $200 silk tie. No doubt the clothes fortuitously fell off a truck or were bought with cash at Emporio Armani on 5th Avenue.

The Don—made his bones years ago—saunters over to the other table of goons. And Roddy's certain they're Casa Nostra or the Russian Bratva, some syndicate, a conglomerate, a combination. Call them what you want: criminals, crooks, gangsters.

The head honcho stands—gotta be a Don, too—and there are hugs and backslaps, laughter, a few whispered words back and forth; some strange voltage streams between them. The older of the two points to another table—one Roddy hasn't noticed—and now he sees these gorillas. Huge guys, mob muscle, sitting with their overly made-up molls. *Jesus*, Roddy thinks, *what a carnival.*

Queasiness invades him, like it used to before a boxing match from a thousand years ago. It's that feeling of gut-sick weakness in the bowels, the churning stomach, the adrenaline-saturated priming of every nerve in his body: dry mouth, tingling lips, closed throat, damp skin, sharpened vision, twitching muscles—the whole fight-or-flight response—readiness to do battle.

With his thoughts swirling, Roddy excuses himself and meanders through the restaurant. He feels he's being pulled by a dark un-
dertow, something unseen but powerful. He passes dozens of tables
peopled by beef-chomping diners. He looks for mobster-types and
makes a mental checklist of guys who look like graduates of the New
York College of Criminal Activity.

He floats through a crescendo of voices and clatter, through
the near-deafening din of diners, and hears salvos of laughter and
snatches of conversation—intonations from Brooklyn, Queens,
Scarsdale, Jersey, Nashville, and beyond—and Roddy gets an eye-
ful of porterhouse cuts, strip steaks, shrimp cocktails, and quarter-
heads of iceberg lettuce doused in ranch dressing and bacon bits;
he sees creamed spinach, baked potatoes, bottles of Veuve Clicquot,
and goblets of Cabernet, Sauvignon, Malbec, and Pinot Noir.

He finds himself in the corridor leading to the men's room; he
pushes the door, walks inside, and nearly collides with a huge, steep-
jawed guy. He's NBA-tall and wide as the Volga River. The giant bris-
tles with barely disguised belligerence. In a heavily accented Slavic-
sounding voice, he mumbles a half-assed apology and shoulders his
way past Roddy, who's nearly pressed to the wall.

Roddy collects himself, inhales, and strides into the men's room.
Two guys are inside: one stands facing a *pissoir;* the other runs sink
water, washing his hands. At a urinal, Roddy sees the pissing guy
out of the corner of his eye: he has a telephone pole–thick neck. Just
above the collar are tattooed letters of the Cyrillic alphabet. Roddy's
sure the guy's torso is covered with a riotous swarm of azbuka—a
hallmark of the Russian underworld—the gulag of Soviet jails.

Roddy faces the wall, stares at the gleaming white tiles, and focuses on the gray grouting between them. The place smells antiseptic and reminds him of an OR. His piss hisses out of him and
splashes onto the mint-scented deodorant disc at the bottom of
the porcelain-white American Standard urinal. The guy at the sink
splashes water on his face, grunts loudly, pats his cheeks, turns off

the water, and shakes his hands.

With the faucet off, the bathroom goes quiet. Roddy hears the bull-necked guy's thick piss stream swish onto the deodorant disc of his urinal. The one at the sink rips paper towels from the metal dispenser and the sound clangs through the tiled restroom. The guy mutters a few words in a basso voice. Roddy feels his heartbeat in his neck as he shakes, tucks, and zips. He turns from the urinal toward the sink, and the automatic flush kicks in. Water swishes and swirls in the urinal and Roddy heads for a sink.

The tattooed guy—still at his urinal—answers the other one. They share a laugh and then talk as though Roddy's not there or they don't give a shit that he is. The guys' voices echo in the tile-encased room.

Roddy's no linguist, but he recognizes Russian when he hears it.

■

Danny sits at the banquette, waiting for Roddy to return from wherever he's gone. Dan thinks it's absolutely incredible to gaze out across the room; he can *feel* the buzz, the supercharged energy of the place. It's simply amazing. And to think he, Roddy, and Kenny are owners of this prime time steakhouse. It's fanfuckingtastic.

He casts a glance at Angela and Tracy. They're huddled together at the corner of the banquette, heads together, talking girl talk or whatever women discuss; it's always been a near-divine mystery to Danny. It's part of what he loves about women: their inscrutability.

Angela and Tracy look absolutely radiant tonight. He knows the blush Angela gets when she's filled with pride and the hot flush of accomplishment. Like here, at McLaughlin's, because they've made this investment and it's working like a charm. That same look spreads over her face when the kids do well at sports or pull down As at school. But this isn't school: it's McLaughlin's. Danny realizes again he's *house proud,* and he knows he tends to be overly prideful, which could be considered a sin. But who cares? He's busted ass, along with Kenny, to make this place work.

And it is working. It's the goose laying golden eggs. Angela was dead-on right: he's sometimes too conservative with his investment strategy. This place is a hands-down winner. He recalls last week having dinner here with John Harris, a Donald Trump–type mega-bucks magnate with tons of glitz and media savvy.

"Dan, this steak has the beefiest flavor I've tasted in a long time," Harris said. "It's grilled to perfection. And this Merlot; it's like nectar."

"It's Swansons, Napa Valley . . . a great American Merlot," Dan said.

"We Americans can do anything we want once we set our minds to it," Harris said.

Just then Kenny appeared at the table. "How is everything, gentlemen?" he asked.

"Just great," Harris said. "I'll have to bring my people here. This room would be perfect for our Christmas party. You could accommodate us—a hundred people—right, Kenny?"

"Mr. Harris. It'll be an exclusive. Your guests'll have a fantastic experience."

Harris beamed like a baby bloated on a bottle of warm milk. "Great, Kenny. I'll have my secretary call you."

When Kenny was gone, Harris leaned forward and said, "Dan, I'd like to shift some Westchester-based work over to you. But I'd like your expertise for more than just bean counting. I hope you don't think I'm denigrating accountants' work . . ."

"Not at all, John."

"Because, Dan, I've had my people look into your track record," Harris said with a knowing smile. "You're a certified financial planner with an emphasis on corporate work and I could use your expertise. I'm buying a Westchester golf course and planning to convert it into an assisted living facility. That's the big new thing: residential properties for baby boomers about to dodder into the sunset."

"John, I'd love to get involved."

"Maybe you and your partners can get in on the ground floor . . . make a savvy investment. I understand you have a third partner . . ."

"Yes, a surgeon. I've known him all my life. Dr. Rodney Dolan."

"I'll bet he's a very smart man."

Dan nodded, thinking of Roddy's considerable intellect.

"Well, Dan, if you, Kenny, and the good doctor get in on this, it'll change your financial equations. We can get into more details, let's say next week, at my office."

Later, after Harris left, Kenny said, "The guy could be a whale . . ."

"A *whale?*"

"Yeah. A guy who brings in loads of patrons. That's a whale."

Sitting here now, Dan knows part of what impressed Harris was Kenny's hands-on service. Danny knows Kenny's just perfect for this place. Sets the right tone—goes for broke trying to please the patrons and keep the cash register humming. Okay, he can be a little over the top, and there's no question he's getting his rocks off with his maitre d' act.

But it's a steak joint, not The Four Seasons or Daniel. You gotta know who and what you are. Sure, Dan noticed that for the first time since they opened, the numbers were a little off last month, and he'll discuss it with Kenny. But Angela was right when she said, "Danny, you focus too much on details. Don't lose the forest through the trees. Look at the larger picture. McLaughlin's is booming. As they say, if it ain't broke, don't fix it."

But Dan's certain that Kenny's doing too much. One man can't stay on top of everything. Kenny's putting in sixteen-hour days. Yes, he takes off one evening a week, but he's here seven days a week and six nights—until midnight, sometimes later.

Between being maitre d' and dealing with the employees, sundries, and a million other things, Dan knows Kenny's overworked. It occurs to Dan that there's no way Kenny can keep accurate figures; after all, there are just so many hours in a day.

Dan thinks maybe they should hire a part-time bookkeeper to

track inventory and keep tabs on cash flow—receipts and expenses. If it costs $40,000 a year, it's well worth it since it would spring Kenny for managerial things. After all, bookkeeping is detailed and tedious—not Kenny's style.

Dan wonders what's taking Roddy so long. It seems he's been gone for a good ten minutes. Danny can tell his kemosabe's not comfortable with some of the crowd. After all these years, if Danny couldn't read Roddy, he'd be a world-class dunce. Roddy keeps glancing at those wise guys—that table across the way—right out of *The Godfather.*

So what if some of these guys have a sit-down at McLaughlin's? After all, McLaughlin's is a meat house. You're not gonna draw the Metropolitan Opera crowd.

In a watering hole like this, you get the bridge-and-tunnel set (like the four of us), some well-heeled yuppies—if they're even still called that—your ad execs, a few banker and investment types, the pretheater crowd, out-of-towners, and for good measure, some of the Big Apple's sniff-worthy underbelly. That's life in Manhattan.

But when Roddy left the table, he looked ashen. Danny knows his blood brother like the back of his own freckled hand. Danny's certain Roddy's worried some mob bullshit will go down at McLaughlin's. Like the rubout years ago at Sparks Steakhouse on East 46th—where a couple of John Gotti's button men clipped Paul Castellano.

Sparks became famous. You name it: the *Post,* the *Times,* the TV stations, magazines; everyone hyped it. People came from everywhere to gape at the sidewalk where the mobster died in a pool of blood. And the bottom line? Sparks became a tourist attraction. Business skyrocketed.

Because deep down, people thirst for blood, guts, and gore. Like the dunderheads who rubberneck at a wreck at the side of a highway. They're like piranhas. People are turned on by violence.

But Roddy? He just can't get his head around it all—can't see that once in a while, if you're really lucky, something good can come out of the bad shit in your life. Something like McLaughlin's.

And sitting at the banquette amidst the noise and super-animated energy, thinking about John Harris and what may come, Danny knows this could put him, Angela, Roddy, and Tracy over the top. It's a far cry from those dog days back in Brooklyn.

Jesus, just thinking about it makes Danny's blood rush; he realizes what a good move this was. Even if they go out of business tomorrow, the Harris contact alone makes the deal worthwhile. *John Fucking Harris.* It's a high stakes venture with a known winner at the helm.

What was it Roddy said the night they made the decision about McLaughlin's? *The distance we've traveled.*

■

"Kenny's doing a tremendous job," Dan whispers as Roddy sits down.

Roddy thinks to himself that it *is* amazing. They're doing land-office business—on an ordinary weekday night.

"Just keep one thing in mind, Roddy," Dan whispers. "This isn't The Four Seasons. And it's not Burger King, either."

Roddy laughs softly and nods.

"It's a fucking steakhouse."

"You're right, Danny. It's McLaughlin's, and it's ours."

"Goddamned right. It's not one of those New Age places serving up tiny portions of fusion food—some Asian-American bullshit—where you pay a fortune *not* to eat. Where you leave the fucking place and wanna scarf down a burger 'cause your stomach's as empty as your wallet."

Roddy punches Dan's shoulder, gently. "You're right, kemosabe."

"And lemme tell you something, Roddy. I was here last week with John Harris."

"*The* John Harris?"

"Yes. *The* John Harris. He wants to meet you and talk about an investment in Westchester, a new property he's acquiring. We can get in on the ground floor. It could open some very big doors."

Roddy nods and then looks out across the expanse of diners.

"Imagine that, Roddy. John fucking Harris."

"When do you look at the numbers again?" Roddy asks.

"I've been reading about the guy . . . he's gonna out-trump Trump."

"The numbers, Dan. When do you look at them again?"

"Next Monday."

"They're good?"

"Yup," Dan says, after what seems to Roddy a long pause. "Just look at this crowd," Danny says. "I swear Roddy, I feel born again." Dan laughs and sips his cognac.

"You sure?"

"About what?"

"The numbers. They're okay?"

"I'm sure, Roddy. As a matter of fact, I'm thinking of hiring a bookkeeper."

"How come?"

"I think we could use some help."

"But everything looks good?"

"Oh, sure . . . sure . . ."

"Kenny sure loves working the crowd," Roddy says.

"You know, steakhouses aren't known for their gentility," Tracy says. "I think Kenny's perfect for this place."

"I agree," Angela adds. "He fits right in. And the place is a gold mine."

"So, Angela, I wasn't too *conservative*, was I?"

"Not at all," Angela says with a smile.

Roddy shoots a glance at the wise-guy table. They're big-bellied beef eaters—Bensonhurst or Brighton Beach types, for sure. Polyester-slick, rat-tail-file rough, not your corporate alpha males, not tweedy types either. One guy's gut's so ponderous, Roddy's certain he could gobble down a trencherman-cut beef slab in a heartbeat.

Kenny's palms rest on the shoulders of a bada-bing bad boy. He whispers into the guy's ear. The hood leans back and bursts out with an open-mouthed hoot of laughter. His maw looks like a wet, yawning hole. Thick threads of saliva hang down from his upper lip—real slobberchops.

And Crystal's bending over the other guy, whispering so closely, her breasts nearly burst out her top. The guy's ape-like arm curls around Crystal's waist; he's fondling her ass.

Slobberchops laughs as Kenny's cackle—nearly a shriek—pierces the air.

It's Kenny's circus and he's the ringmaster.

And Roddy's bought a ticket to the show.

Chapter 12

Traffic is light as they turn off the Henry Hudson Parkway.

"The food was excellent," Tracy says.

"Uh huh . . ."

"And Kenny sure took good care of us . . ."

"Yup . . ."

"Danny's really high on the place."

"Yeah . . ."

Tracy hears Roddy sigh and knows she's seen this before: Roddy's answering her, but with one-word responses, and he's remote. It's *Star Wars* time; he's in a galaxy far, far away. While driving, he's aware of the road, but the Sequoia might as well be on automatic pilot. It's like he's in a haze—isn't it called a *fugue?*

Tracy always knows when Roddy dwells on something, when it festers like an abscess. And she's certain Roddy's cogitating about McLaughlin's. She could tell when he went to the men's room because Roddy has a bladder like a camel, never has to go when they're out for dinner. Ever. And when he left the table, he looked chalky white; the blood had drained from his face. After all their years together, Tracy knows he'll break out of it and say something. She only has to give him an opening. But right now, she thinks it's best to change the subject.

"I got a call from Ann Johnson today . . ."

"Really . . . ?"

It's that absent voice of his: *Really?* It's conversation filler—mere padding signaling he's light years away.

"She wants to know if we'll rent the cottage at Lake Rhoda this summer."

"But it's only March," he says.

"She wants to lock us in now."

"You want to go?"

"I'm not sure, Roddy. Thomas'll be thirteen and won't want to spend time with us." Tracy can already envision Thomas's sullen pout, his dismissive look when she says something he finds contemptibly inane, which is virtually any utterance.

"I can ask him," Roddy says, checking the side-view mirror and then changing lanes.

"He'll just want to hang out with his friends," Tracy says visualizing a pack of bored preteens, wearing baggy jeans and constantly texting each other—overindulged kids who'll be getting Volvos or BMWs as high school graduation presents.

"Honey, he's nearly thirteen. That's when it starts."

"What starts?"

"Sex, drugs, and rock 'n roll . . ."

Roddy looks like he's ready to break out in a grin.

"Speaking of sex . . . ," she says.

"Yes?" he says, smiling now, his eyes on the road.

"The kids are on sleepovers . . ."

"You trying to seduce me . . . ?"

"Of course." She slips her hand onto his thigh. Tracy's certain he's back in the moment.

"I can pull onto the shoulder . . ."

They laugh and then fall quiet. He drives for a while, saying nothing. So Tracy decides to use the direct approach. "What's bothering you, Roddy?"

"Nothing . . . really . . ."

"C'mon, I know that look . . ."

"What look?" he asks.

"*What* look?" she says, shaking her head.

"Yeah, *what* look?" he repeats; it's the Abbot & Costello routine.

"That far-off gaze."

"I'm not familiar with that one . . ."

"That *I'm-worried-but-I-don't-want-to-worry-her* look . . ."

That crooked smile of his melts her like drawn butter. God, she's always been such a sucker for him. And she loves it.

"No secrets?" he asks.

"Not from me, lover-boy."

"I'm not comfortable with this McLaughlin's thing . . ."

"Why?"

"You see that crowd in there tonight?"

"Yes, it was packed."

"I mean . . . the mobster types."

"Like Danny says, honey, it's a steak joint. And Roddy, it's a free country."

"Kenny seems to know them all."

"Have you talked with Danny about it?"

"He's not concerned. In fact, he had John Harris there for dinner . . ."

"The real estate guy?"

"Yup, that's the one. And Harris would like to talk with us about a new property."

"So what's the problem?"

"Not Harris, those other guys . . ."

"The mob guys?"

"Uh huh."

"Look, Roddy, if you're not comfortable with it, then get out."

"You see that hostess?" he asks.

Tracy realizes he's deflecting her comment—about getting out.

"She turn you on?"

"Honey . . . I'm a man."

"So, *my* man. Did your blood flow to all the right places?"

"That's what *you* do."

"Only me?"

"Mostly you."

"So you're turned on by other women?"

"Trace, do I look like I'm dead?"

"How alive are you? Down there . . ."

He laughs. Keeps his eyes on the road.

"But some of the clientele . . . it looked like something right out of *The Sopranos.* And these Russian gangsters . . ."

There's silence as they move through the Westchester suburbs.

"Okay, Roddy. You're not comfortable with it. Some Tony Sopranos. And Russians, too," she says. "Look, honey, Danny was very clear. You can get out any time you want."

"I don't know, Trace . . ."

"Roddy, what do you mean *'I don't know'?*"

"It's just that . . ." and he shakes his head.

"Just *what?*"

"I feel trapped . . ."

"*Trapped?* How?"

He sighs. "Danny's so high on the place. It means so much to him."

Tracy waits a beat. "Okay, so Danny's excited about it. What does that mean?"

"It's just . . . well you know how I feel about Danny . . ."

"What're you saying, Roddy?"

"I don't wanna let him down."

"Did you go into this for *Danny?*"

"No . . . but . . ." He lapses into silence.

"But *what?*"

"Oh, Trace, we don't need the money. And . . . I don't like it."

"Then get out. Roddy, nobody's forcing you. Danny would understand."

"I *love* being in business with Danny, and it if weren't for him, I wouldn't have gotten involved."

"Roddy, you're a forty-five-year-old surgeon. If you don't like it, then get out. Call Danny tomorrow."

"I'll think about it."

"Roddy, you should do what *you* want."

"I hear you."

"And Roddy, you've made big decisions for years, and they've been good ones. You do what you feel comfortable doing."

"You're right, honey."

"Roddy . . . since this McLaughlin's thing, you've been talking about the past. About *growing up in the Bay,* as you put it. The crimes, the fights and gang wars. That botched burglary, and the army."

"I've never kept it a secret . . ."

"But you're harping on it, now. I know this McLaughlin's thing's been on your mind."

"You're right, honey. I'll take care of it,"

They turn onto the Bronx River Parkway and then drive in silence.

"I'll tell you what's bothering *me,*" Tracy says.

"What, honey?"

"Thomas. Because I have no idea what he'll do this summer. And we can't leave him home alone."

"What's going on now?"

Tracy hears tension thread through his voice. Whenever Thomas comes up, it's like a shadow passes over Roddy.

"He's still zoning out in school. I got another call today. The teacher says Thomas is *throwing away* his potential."

"Oh, honey, you spoke to Brookings. I've spoken with Tom. We've heard all this before. And I hope you're not calling him *Thomas* anymore."

"No, I'm calling him by his preferred name . . . Tom. Like a turkey . . . Tom, Tom," she says, with a brittle laugh. "This whole thing with his name is a diversion; it's just another pimple in his sullen little life. He's still surly . . . with me *and* with the teachers." Tracy's thoughts turn to Thomas's beneath-the-breath mutterings—his string of snide comments about everything—school, the house, his sister, his parents.

"Is he getting into trouble?"

"He's just snotty."

"It's that adolescent angst thing."

"Maybe. But these shorthand labels are too easy . . ."

"Maybe a private school's the answer. The teachers might be right, he's not challenged enough."

"If he'll even *go* to one." She pauses. "But what about his attitude at home? Is *that* because he's not challenged enough?"

"Honey, he's a work in progress . . ."

"Like you were at that age?"

He laughs. But she can tell: her comment punctured him.

"I'm sorry, honey," she says, touching his thigh.

"There's nothing to be sorry about."

"No offense."

"None taken. I'll talk to him again, okay?"

"I wish you would, Roddy. Just talk to him. He really needs you."

■

He pulls up the driveway and presses the remote on the sun visor. The garage door rises; he guides the Sequoia inside and throws it into "park." The thing rumbles until he kills the engine. They unbuckle their seatbelts. The garage door lowers.

They sit beneath the slowly dimming dome light. Tracy peers at the well-ordered garage: the Peg-Board with its dangling tools: Stihl, Black & Decker, Snapper—saws, drills, nail gun, sander. Shelves stacked with an assortment of tools and a cornucopia of garden supplies—the implements of domesticity. God, how she loves this house and everything they've built together.

Roddy sits, hands on the steering wheel. The engine ticks as the vehicle cools.

"What?" Tracy asks.

"What, what?"

"What's on your mind?"

That smile of his spreads over his face. Uh, oh, she could melt again.

"Roddy . . . ?" she says softly, nearly laughing.

"You know *what*, honey," he says in that far-off voice.

"I'm waiting . . ."

"When we talk about the restaurant, and then about Tommy . . ."

"Yes . . . ?"

"It makes me think . . . ," he says, drawing closer.

"About what?"

"About what really counts," he whispers. "The restaurant's nothing, Trace. You and the kids are *everything* to me."

"Oh sweetheart," she whispers, leaning toward him. Her heart feels like bursting.

"I love you so much. I swear Trace . . . you, Tommy, and Sandy are my life."

A lump forms in her throat, and for some strange reason she feels she'll burst into tears. She clasps his neck as his arms enfold her. She buries her face in his chest and breathes in his manliness. She feels so loved in his arms. Tracy adores the feel of his stubble as he nuzzles her. She loves smelling his breath with its residue of wine mixed with the hazelnut aroma of cognac. An erotic rush fills her, as though he emits an electric field that makes her tingle. Her hand moves to his bulge. She feels him grow hard.

"I love you, Roddy. More than anything," she whispers.

And it's true, there's never been anyone she's loved this way, so deeply and completely. More than she could ever say.

Their lips meet and they kiss tenderly. Her mouth opens slightly, and so does his. Her tongue slides lightly over his. He tastes delicious to her, always has. And there was never a man who could fill her with desire the way he does. "Make love to me," she whispers as her voice trembles

"Here . . . ?"

"Yes, here . . . like we're kids . . ."

His hands move to her shoulders as her lips press against his neck. He reaches behind her, unzips the back of her dress and undoes her bra. She feels his hands on her breasts, tender, light, and loving. That electric charge spreads through her and makes her insides quiver with pleasure.

They pull at each other's clothing. His mouth presses against hers, and his hands move over her body, everywhere. Then, they're kissing so hard she thinks her lips may bleed, and she pulls him down onto her as the feelings heighten to an exquisite intensity.

Soon, they're naked, and they start slowly, right there, in the Sequoia, parked in the garage of their lovely Tudor home in Bronxville, where they live such good lives, and she wishes that this would never end, that they could go on like this, forever.

Chapter 13

Squinting at the spreadsheets, Danny feels his pores opening. A prickling sensation begins at his hairline. He feels his lungs closing off and knows the constriction's starting in his airway. And mucous is building up, thick and sticky, and soon it'll begin bubbling deep in his chest. Fucking asthma; it always kicks in when he gets upset. The print seems out of focus, he squints and his vision sharpens. The numbers don't lie—they never do.

They've been in business six months now, and for the second month in a row, the numbers don't match up. Last month, the numbers were off slightly, but this month, even though business is in the stratosphere, receipts have plummeted into the deep debit zone. A few more like this and they'll all be swimming in red ink.

Picking up the telephone receiver, Danny realizes his hand is shaking. He dials Roddy and gets Brenda, the receptionist. After some friendly banter, he asks for Roddy.

"He's tied up with patients. Shall I have him call you back?"

"Sure, Brenda. As soon as he's free. I'm at the office."

Danny feels antsy—pins-and-needles jittery—waiting for Roddy to get back. He knows he won't be able to concentrate on anything until this gets settled. And his lungs feel like collapsing bellows; soon he'll be sucking air. Just to be on the safe side, he opens his desk drawer, pulls out the Advair, and primes it by shaking the canister. He slides the mouthpiece against his tongue, presses the top, and inhales slowly. He can feel the airway opening.

A half hour later, the telephone rings.

After a moment of banter, Danny explains. "You know Omar gives me McLaughlin's computer data every month. I'm going over the numbers and there's a problem . . ." Danny's toes curl. And he hears high-pitched squeaks coming from deep in his chest—he's avoided an asthmatic attack but knows the wheezes will stay for a while.

"What kind of problem?"

Danny senses his own hesitancy; he wonders if he's blinded himself to the obvious, but now there's no denying it: the numbers never lie, not even when liars concoct the numbers. The figures are the flesh and blood, the DNA of a business. *Any* business.

"Roddy, tomorrow's Saturday; can you come to the office?"

■

Morning light floods through the office windows. Roddy and Danny sit at the conference table.

"It's obvious there's a problem," Danny says, after explaining the numbers to Roddy.

"Did you notice anything before this?"

"Last month I did, but not as bad. I suggested that we get a book-keeper, but Kenny nixed it."

"Can he do that?"

"He has controlling interest, Roddy. He said he'd take care of it. I've been tied up with John Harris. We're getting close to the April 15th tax deadline and I've been swamped." Danny inhales deeply and coughs. "But it's clear: we're buying the same amount of food, alcohol, and supplies. Labor costs are the same, but income's dropping like a rock off a cliff."

Something cold eddies through Roddy. "So, Dan, someone's stealing."

Dan gets up from the table. "My restaurant guy said internal theft's part of the cost of doing business."

"Then we're in some fucked-up kinda business," Roddy says.

Dan walks over to the window and peers out.

"So whaddaya think's going on, Dan?"

"Don't know . . ."

"That's right! *You* don't know and *I* don't know. Dan, let's face it. As absentee owners we don't have a *clue*."

Danny returns to the table and sits down.

"Dan, McLaughlin's is ripe for pilfering."

"I agree. Kenny can't possibly keep up with everything."

Danny stares off into space.

"Like Kenny once said, he knows all the tricks," Roddy says.

"Ken's doing a good job as far as . . ."

"You know, Dan, with a botched surgery, I can stop the bleeding, but I know shit about a restaurant operation. Looks like we're hemorrhaging money."

Dan nods and frowns.

"Danny . . . the last time we were there, business was booming, and Kenny looked like a madman."

Danny's lips twist into a grimace.

"So, Dan, here we are—an accountant and a surgeon—in the *restaurant* business."

Danny nods.

"And we're down 14 percent this month. When business is going through the roof."

Dan shakes his head. He looks milky white.

"Lemme ask you something, Danny . . ."

"Yeah?"

"Are you looking at this thing clearly?"

Dan's eyes widen.

"I'm gonna quote you, Dan . . . *The numbers don't lie.* I know you're hot for this John Harris thing, but frankly, Dan, are you seeing the red flag in this little vanity project?"

"So whaddaya wanna do?" Danny asks.

"Let's sit down with Kenny."

Chapter 14

It's been four weeks since he last saw Ken. It strikes Roddy that over the last six months, Kenny's changed—drastically. The guy's pale, Dracula-white with grayish-looking pouches beneath his eyes. His cheeks look hollowed out. He's shed a good fifteen pounds and looks gaunt. His tuxedo looks a couple of sizes too big. Sweat glistens on his forehead and his foot beats a nervous tattoo on the floor as Danny rummages through the spreadsheets.

Danny shoves the papers aside and then says, "What's changed, Ken?"

Kenny shrugs. He lights up a Lucky Strike, inhales, and blows thin trails of smoke through his nostrils.

It's Tuesday night, 9:00. They're in McLaughlin's back office, near the supply room leading out to West 46th Street. A computer screen sits on a table off to the side. The wet bar is in the corner.

Omar is running the front of the house, along with Crystal the man-eater, still showcasing every bodily crevice. Restaurant clamor bleeds through the door.

"Kenny, the place is packed, but the numbers are going south," Dan says. "What's going on?"

"A lotta shit, that's what," Ken mutters, shifting in the chair. He sucks on his butt and blows more smoke.

"What kinda shit?"

"You don't wanna know . . ."

"Yes, I do, Kenny."

Roddy sees the sheen on Ken's forehead and hears his voice warble like a songbird's. Roddy's heard that vocal quaking before: when paratroopers hooked up to the static lines at 1,500 feet; in patients waiting for a dreaded diagnosis; and years ago, before a fight.

Roddy's listened as Danny winnowed the numbers like a patient teacher, pointing out discrepancies in costs and profits—some as glaring as the sun in a white sky.

"We're going down the crapper," Danny says.

Ken coughs up a wad of phlegm, gets up, and spits it into the wet-bar sink. Sitting down again, he clears his throat, blinks rapidly, and sweats like a boxer in the twelfth round. He's jumpy, revved; he reminds Roddy of a car driven in low gear—ready to lurch. Ken lifts the cigarette in his nicotine-stained fingers, puffs, and exhales another cloud of smoke.

Jesus, Kenny," says Dan. "You're *killing* me with the cigarettes. My asthma."

Kenny sighs and crushes the butt out in an ashtray.

Kenny's left shin crosses over his right thigh; his foot shakes so fast, it could whip heavy cream.

Roddy feels taut, primed, but says nothing.

"So, Kenny," Dan asks. "Why are waiters leaving?"

"Restaurant people come and go," Ken says. "The old ones retire, who knows? I been replacing 'em with Ecuadorians and Mexicans. The kitchen help's a bunch of illegals looking for somethin' to tide 'em over the winter till they get back to the burbs to mow lawns."

"What's with the bar?" Dan asks. "It used to be the profit center. Now it's a money pit."

"I had to fire some barkeeps . . ."

"Why?"

"I caught one guy under-ringin' sales and pocketing the difference. I didn't know the money was gone till I saw the booze outlay didn't match the receipts."

"So that's one guy. What else?"

"I caught another one runnin' a scam."

"How do you mean?" asks Roddy.

"Ya mean I gotta explain this shit?"

"*Yeah,* Ken . . . you gotta explain it," Roddy says, feeling heat in his face.

"Shit! Howdaya like that? Fuck me."

"We gotta know why the numbers are dropping," Danny says.

"Okay, okay. I caught one guy sneakin' in his own bottles. Settin' 'em up at the bar—a bottle of gin and one of vodka. One label says Bombay Sapphire, but it was rotgut. Another said Stolichnaya, but it coulda been kerosene. He'd take an order for Sapphire or Stoly, serve up the piss-water, and pocket the money. Never rang it up. Was using his own inventory, so the register matched up."

"How'd you catch him?" Roddy asks.

"I made a drink. The gin tasted like weasel piss."

"But Kenny, food receipts are down big time," Dan says.

"I caught a prep man stealin' steaks . . ."

"Stealing *steaks?*"

"Yeah. They come twelve to a case. Fuckin' guy'd unload a couple of twelve-packs and toss 'em in a trash bag out back. They're in vacuum-packed plastic, so when it's cold, nothin' rots. End of the day, the fucker fishes out the packs and makes tracks. I canned his ass. And he wasn't the only one."

Dan casts a glance at Roddy.

"Now I'm usin' clear plastic trash bags instead of black ones. Can you believe it? There I am, manager and owner and I'm lookin' through *garbage bags* every night."

"It's a den of thieves," Roddy says. "This happen in Vegas?"

"It happens in *every* restaurant, Roddy." The sweat sheen on Kenny's forehead is now a dense field of droplets.

"I don't know how any restaurant stays afloat," Roddy says.

"Stayin' afloat? I'm doin' all the rowing in this fuckin' boat. I'm doin' *every* fuckin' thing." Kenny's eyes bulge.

"Hold on, Kenny . . ."

"What're you sayin', Roddy? You accusin' *me* of stealing? You guys think I'm *stealin'* shit? What're you, outta your fuckin' *minds?*" Kenny's face goes beet-red; veins pop out on his neck. "I own three-fifths of this operation . . . so I'm stealin' from *myself?* That what you're sayin'?"

Roddy's chest tightens. Acid bubbles up his gullet. *Holy shit*, he thinks. They could be bickering in front of The Johnny Fell Inn—a thousand years ago in Brooklyn or standing on the corner near the Greek's. It's all coming back in a swill of polluted tide—from the waters of Sheepshead Bay. Kenny even sounds the way he did back then: the clipped cadence, the rough-edged street talk, the aggrieved tone and dropped consonants. Brooklyn—thirty years back—harsh and tough.

"Nobody's accusing you of anything," Dan says. "But it's all going downhill."

Ken whips out another Lucky, lights up, sucks inward, and then exhales contrails of smoke. He shoots an incensed look at them both.

"Kenny, we gotta understand what's . . ."

"No!" Kenny shouts. "I'm *stealin'?* How the fuck ya like that? Accused by guys I know forty years."

He bolts up from the chair, stands, hands on his hips, and looks like an angry version of that actor, Roddy thinks—Adrian Brody. His face is so pallid it borders on sea-green. "Jesus! I put up my own fuckin' money—*300 large*—so I'm stealing from myself?"

"Kenny, we just wanna know what's going on."

"I don't know, Danny. I don't fuckin' *know.*"

"How many drinks are you comping?" Roddy asks, trying not to sound accusatory.

"A few. Just to the regulars."

"Because I saw high-end champagne at lots of tables when I was here."

"So . . . ?"

"Are they being comped?"

"Some."

"How many, Kenny?" Roddy asks.

"Who the fuck counts?"

"So, Kenny . . . how 'bout the clientele . . . ?"

"Whaddaya mean?"

"A lot of them look mobbed up to me."

"What the *fuck're* you talkin' about, Roddy?" Kenny squints, looking offended.

"Plenty of Mafiosi. And Russian goons, too."

"It's a fuckin' steakhouse," Kenny shouts.

"Kenny's right," Dan says. "Every steakhouse feeds wise guys."

"You seemed pretty cozy with 'em, Kenny."

"Fuck you, Roddy, I don't control who walks in the door."

"I'm talking about comping these guys, because . . ."

"You *gotta* massage the regulars, Roddy. This isn't medicine; it's a restaurant. We don't have patients; we have clients. Ya gotta understand, it's *entertainment.* That's the business we're in, Roddy."

"Are you comping us right *out* of business, Ken?"

"Not a chance."

"What about the steaks?" Roddy asks. "Who's stealing now? Because Dan says we're ordering way more than we're selling."

"If anyone's stealin' now, I'm not seein' it, Roddy. I'll spend more time in the kitchen . . . in the garbage, too." Kenny draws hungrily on the cigarette and looks like he's sucking wind. He blinks like a parakeet, and his leg shakes like a metronome.

Roddy leans against the wall and feels himself seething. "Ken, you know every restaurant scam, right?"

"Hey, Roddy, this place is runnin' on my energy."

"And it's going down the tubes, Kenny."

"You're a tough guy to work with, Roddy. And who died and made *you* fuckin' king? Huh?"

"You have a short fuse, Kenny."

Roddy pushes away from the wall, leans his palms on the table, and peers into Ken's eyes. They're narrowed, shifting back and forth between Danny and himself.

"What the fuck you lookin' at, Roddy?"

"You. You're on edge, Kenny. Hopped up."

"Yeah? How the fuck would *you* feel if your partners accused you of stealin'?"

"Nobody's accusing you, Kenny," Danny says.

Roddy moves closer to Kenny, nearly chin to chin. Kenny blinks repeatedly, but Roddy gets a good look.

"What the fuck you lookin' at?" Kenny asks, scowling. He leans back in the chair, sweat dribbles down his forehead.

"I'm looking into your eyes."

"Fuck you, Roddy. What? You think you're my fuckin' doctor?"

"I *am* a doctor, Kenny, and I don't like what I see."

"What the fuck you talkin' about?"

"Your pupils are pin-point. And you're sweating like a pig even though it's cool in this room. And you're paranoid . . ."

"Fuck you, Roddy. If I want an opinion about my mental health, I'll see a shrink."

"It doesn't take a shrink, Kenny."

"Fuck off!"

"Using drugs?"

"Huh . . . ?" Kenny sinks lower in the chair. His mouth opens.

"YOU USING DRUGS?"

Kenny's eyes bulge like globes. Makes his pupils seem even smaller—black dots in a sea of bleary-eyed emptiness.

Roddy moves closer, face-to-face. Yes, Kenny's eyes are wet, unfocused, crisscrossed with fine red squiggles, and his pupils are pinpoint specks. There's a strange vacuum there. Like he sees nothing. Roddy's sure the guy's junked.

"What about it, Kenny? Using drugs?"

"C'mon Roddy, gimme a fuckin' break. Just some booze."

"How much?"

"A drink every now and then."

"Don't *fuck* with me, Kenny. I'm a doctor."

"Okay . . . okay . . . I snort a little coke. Just here and there. It's rare."

"*How* rare?"

"Once a week, I'll do a line. Maybe less."

"*Maybe* less?"

"Fuck you, Roddy."

"Before coming to work?"

"*Never*. Later, at night—if I go to a club."

"Don't b*ullshit* me, Ken. Is every other buck getting sucked up your nose?"

"No fuckin' way. And you *are* accusin' me of stealin'. Jesus Christ. My own partner accusin' me of—"

"Because, Kenny, you look *wired*. And you know what? You *are* paranoid. You're stoned."

"Not true, Roddy. I'm *never* stoned. And like I said, I'm doin' the work of—"

"You snort, or skin pop, too?"

"Snort. A line here and there."

"What do you mix it with?"

"Some alcohol . . ."

"What kind?"

"A little scotch, maybe some gin . . ."

"Anything else?"

"Like what? What the fuck you talkin' about?"

"Like amphetamines."

"Speed? *Na.*"

"You sure?"

"What is this? The fuckin' Spanish Inquisition?"

Ken's foot shakes like a Mixmaster.

"We're partners, Kenny. We have a right to know," Roddy says.

"It's recreational, and like I said . . . it's *rare.*"

"Hey, Dan," Roddy says, "you buying the shit-sandwich Kenny's serving up?"

Danny sits at the table; his eyes lock onto Kenny.

"I don't know, Roddy. You're the doctor."

"Because this stinks like an army latrine."

"What the fuck are you sayin', Roddy. I put up 300 large. I cover the spread. I'm walkin' the walk, and you're sayin' I'm fulla shit?"

Roddy feels his hand curl into a white-knuckled fist.

It's unbelievable. We might as well be back in Brooklyn with the threats, the cursing, the whole street thing.

"You know what this is, Danny?" Roddy says. "It's Irish hari-kari. We're going down the tubes with this fucking guy. I don't know if it's booze, drugs, women, or some other shit, but I don't see any reason to stay in this game."

Roddy turns to Kenny. "Look, Kenny, at the rate you're going we'll be out of business soon. Danny and I'll be fine. This isn't our main play."

Ken looks stunned; he stares with glazed eyes.

"But Ken," says Roddy, "your 300's getting flushed down the toilet. We'll go bust and it's over. Your $120,000 salary and tips'll be down the crapper. Fucking gone."

Kenny's soaked and trembling like he's got a thermometer-bursting fever.

"You saving any money, Kenny?"

"That's none of your fuckin' business, Roddy."

"So long as we're partners, it's my goddamned business."

"Bullshit. It's personal."

"Well, Kenny, is your personal life fucking up the business?"

"No. And who the fuck you think you are? I don't take orders from you."

Roddy's guts clench and his body goes taut. He thinks back to the last few minutes in this cramped office at the back of the restaurant—he's cursing, bellowing, threatening, and feeling like he could explode, detonate like a time bomb. Just like the old days back in the Bay. It all rushes back in a corrosive moment of gut-wrenching recollection. That night: Mom and that bastard Horst.

Who the fuck you think you are? I don't take orders from you. The same words Horst used that night.

He was fifteen years old that winter evening, just home from a night out with Danny and the guys. He suddenly recalls Kenny ran the table at Sammy's pool hall and conned a hundred bucks off some dupe, just like Fast Eddie Felson in *The Hustler*. It all comes back now in a heated mind-rush.

Roddy got home and saw Mom on the couch, passed out. Her face was pulpy looking, raw and bruised, and her eyes were swollen shut. She'd been beaten and one arm was angled obscenely, looking broken. The stew she'd been cooking had burned to cinders. The place stank like an incinerator.

Roddy knew instantly what happened: Horst had come home, found her drunk, smelled the burned stew, and beat the shit out of her.

Horst emerged from the bedroom and reeked of booze.

"Get out," Roddy said.

"You little Irish shit," Horst sneered. "Who the fuck you think you are? I don't take orders from you."

He loomed over Roddy. "I'm gonna cut your mick heart out."

Horst rushed into the kitchen and came back with a huge steak knife and a wild look in his eyes. Roddy dodged the thrust and kicked Horst in the crotch. Horst doubled over, howling in pain. Vomit shot from his mouth. The knife fell.

Horst bent at the waist, retching. A string of mucous hung from his lips. Roddy closed in, clamped his hands behind Horst's neck, and then yanked downward. He thrust his knee up into Horst's nose. Bone and cartilage crunched and blood sprayed. Roddy lost it—went insane. He began pounding Horst—furiously. Horst spewed more vomit, and blood spattered the floor.

Fury poured through Roddy's fists and feet. He kicked and punched Horst, again and again with power shots until Horst went down. Roddy straddled him, locked his arms around Horst's neck, and wrenched upward. There was a cracking sound.

The EMS guys carted Mom and Horst away. Horst had a broken nose, a smashed eye socket, a fractured skull, cracked ribs, contusions everywhere, bleeding kidneys, and a partly crushed windpipe.

That was the last he ever saw of Horst.

And now, here in McLaughlin's smoke-filled back office, Roddy realizes he's drifted off in the middle of this verbal smackdown with Kenny—he's downshifted to thirty years ago, and every muscle in his body quivers while Kenny curses and sweats like an icy bottle of Bud on a hot day. The restaurant's crammed with drinkers and steak-eaters, yet he and Dan are chin-deep in shit after being sucked into this proposition that's flushing down the toilet, swirling counter-clockwise in a maelstrom of overwrought bullshit. And amidst Kenny's drug-fueled paranoia and the mounting tension, Roddy's floated back to the tar pits of his past.

"You all right, Roddy?" Dan asks.

"Huh?"

"You okay?"

"Yeah . . ."

Now, Kenny looks like a sullen kid. Reminds Roddy of Tom when he's trying to get to first base with the kid—get him to see the larger picture. But this isn't adolescent kid-shit; it's not growing pains angst. It's big bucks and bad business.

"What about gambling?" Roddy asks.

"I haven't gambled in forever, Roddy."

"How long?"

"Nearly a quarter century. What the fuck —"

"Don't *lie* to me, Ken. Bullshit hour's over."

"No way, Roddy. I'm *over* that shit."

"Not even a friendly game of poker?"

"Not a fuckin' thing. What're you tryin' to—"

"You still go to meetings—Gamblers Anonymous?"

"Nah . . . don't need to anymore."

Roddy glances at Danny.

Dan's arms are folded across his chest. His face is a blank, a total nonread.

"Lemme tell you something, Kenny," Roddy says, circling the table. He tells himself to stay calm: no ranting or shouting, no threats or cursing. But Roddy knows it's truth time. Bullshit done, last round, the bell's gonna ring, fight's over.

"So fuckin' tell me already," Kenny shouts. "What the fuck you wanna tell me?"

Restaurant hum penetrates the door, a back roar, low level and steady. The fluorescent light drones like an insect. Roddy's blood hums and his neck pulses.

"I see no reason to stay in business with you, Kenny."

"That's not fuckin' fair."

"I'm pulling out."

"You can't do that to me."

"I can get out whenever I want. You'll have to buy me out."

"You know I can't do that," Kenny cries in a burbling voice. He looks ghostly and sweats rivulets. "I spent every fuckin' nickel I had on this place. And now you wanna kick me to the curb? You're fuckin' me where I breathe for Chrissake."

"Means shit to me, Kenny. We're going down the tubes and I want out."

"Look, Ken," Danny jumps in, "I know where Roddy's coming from. It's not worth the trouble. If push comes to shove, we're outta here. Got it?"

At the wet bar, Dan pours himself a shot of Johnny Walker, tosses it back, and stares long and hard at Kenny, who looks mortified.

"Kenny," says Dan, "we know each other a long time. So, I'm willing to give it a chance, but I . . ."

"You're kidding, Dan," Roddy cuts in. "Don't you see where this is going?"

"I see it, Roddy. I do. But for old times' sake I'm willing to hang on, but not for long." Danny turns to Ken. "Kenny, if you don't turn this around soon, Roddy and I are outta here."

Kenny nods, looking porcelain white.

"You'll hafta buy us out and there's not a bank on earth that'll give you a loan with your books lookin' like they do. You'll hafta put the place up for auction. Tables, chairs, equipment . . . everything. You'll pay McLaughlin off and it's over. We all move on." Dan sets his tumbler on the table and stares at Ken. "I hate to sound so bottom line, Kenny, but if that's what it comes to, we'll do it. We take our losses, write 'em off, and move on."

Kenny blinks, looks up at Dan, and then peers at Roddy.

"In the long run, Kenny, we're not doing you a favor by helping you limp along."

Kenny nods, a quick bobbing of his head. He swallows hard. Looks like he's been stunned by a Taser.

"Now look, Ken, I asked if you needed a bookkeeper, and you deep-sixed it. But I don't wanna hear 'No' for an answer. I'm gonna get someone in here to oversee the money end of things. That clear?"

Kenny nods like a bobble-head doll.

"Ken, you have forty employees, and you're still doing everything."

"Yeah . . . forty employees," Ken mutters. "Forty paid enemies."

"Kenny, lemme ask you something else," Dan says.

Kenny peers up at him.

"You need any other kind of help?"

"Whaddaya mean?"

"For alcohol. Coke. For anything. After all, Roddy knows people . . ."

"C'mon, Danny. I use once in a blue moon."

"Kenny, when's the last time you had a physical?" Roddy asks.

"Who the fuck knows?"

"Because you look like shit."

"What're you . . . the designated driver of my life?"

"Kenny, we *gotta* know."

"I'm fine, Roddy. I'm just stressed out. You have no idea of the pressure runnin' a New York steak joint. Between the help and the stealin' and . . . shit, I already told ya."

"You wanna tell us anything else?"

"Na, Roddy. There's nothin' . . ."

"You sure?"

"I said there's *nothin'*."

Kenny peers at Roddy, then at Danny. "There's one thing I do wanna say . . ."

"Shoot . . . ," says Roddy.

"I'm gonna make this place work. I swear. You guys oughta know that most restaurants lose money during the first six months—even turnkey operations like this. It takes time to get the kinks out. But I'll turn it around."

■

"So what do you think?" asks Danny.

They're on the Henry Hudson Parkway, heading toward the Tuckahoe train station, where Danny left his car before taking Metro North into Manhattan.

"Dan, I'm getting out. Six months to sort things out? And we began like gangbusters."

"Roddy, don't make a hasty decision. This is too—"

"I've been thinking about it for weeks. I want out."

"But Roddy, it's only this last month there's really been a downturn. I'll get a bookkeeper and—"

"Kenny's using drugs."

"Only here and there."

"Bullshit."

"You sure?"

"Of course. The sweating, the jitteriness, his whole look. He's skinny as a pole. And he's paranoid; he jumped down our throats the second we asked some questions."

"Well, he's under stress . . ."

"He looks wasted," says Roddy.

"*Wasted?* As in using drugs?"

"Yup."

"Why'd you ask him about gambling?"

"It used to be his thing."

"Hey, Roddy, it's decades since guys tossed dice in the school bathroom."

"Danny, I want out."

"Look, I've met with John Harris twice and he wants—"

"Fuck John Harris. I don't need a real estate venture, Danny. I'm financially solid, thanks to you, and I'm happy with my piece of the pie."

"Roddy, you don't wanna pass up this chance."

"I don't need it. And lemme tell you the truth, Danny, because I gotta be up front with you. It's about you."

"C'mon, Roddy, you can't offend me."

"Danny, you're too caught up in this McLaughlin's thing. And you're too willing to give Kenny a pass. You're not letting yourself see the truth."

Danny stares out the window; Roddy's not sure he's listening.

"Lemme ask you something, Dan. What the fuck are we doing? You're an accountant and I'm a surgeon. We deal with death and taxes and we make great money doing it. So why're we going into—"

"Roddy, this is a chance to—"

"Fuck John Harris and fuck McLaughlin's, Danny. We don't need 'em." Roddy shoots a look at Danny. "Look, kemosabe, I didn't like the fucking goons I saw in the restaurant. I don't like how Kenny cozied up to those John Gotti wannabes, and I don't like that business is booming, but receipts are going south.

"I've got a bad feeling about this—bad fucking vibes. And Danny, the last time I didn't listen to my gut and went into a little venture with Kenny McGuirk-Egan and Frankie Fuck-up Messina, I ended up facing felony charges."

"Roddy, that was forever ago."

"Doesn't matter, Dan. I'm out. I don't want Kenny or McLaughlin's or John Harris or anyone else. It smells bad to me."

"Roddy, do me a favor?"

"What?"

"Wait a week. *One* week before you get out."

"Why, Dan? What's that gonna do?"

"You'll have time to think about it. Especially this Harris thing."

"I've already thought about it."

"Just a week. And if you still want out, I'll buy your interest. But it won't be any good without you."

Roddy drives, saying nothing.

"How 'bout it? A week."

"Okay . . . one week."

Danny sighs, shakes his head, and then says, "You know what beats the shit outta me? The guy blows into town, and he wants to go into the restaurant business—with *us.*"

"Yeah . . . ?"

"He puts up $300,000, cold cash. We make the down payment and we're on our way. The place takes off. But now we're goin' into the red. It makes no sense."

"Hey, Danny, can you make sense of anything in this world?"

Chapter 15

Danny thinks about the meeting with Kenny two nights earlier. He replays it in his mind and wonders if he really wants to stay with McLaughlin's. The pleasure—the whole brothers-in-arms, the Cochise and Jeffords thing—will go missing without Roddy. By now, the John Harris venture has legs of its own. If he really lets himself think it through, the glitz of owning a restaurant may not be worth the damage to his reputation if McLaughlin's goes Titanic. Roddy's no dope. It might be wise to pull out now.

The telephone rings.

Danny picks up the receiver and hears Kenny on the line. "Dan, we got a problem, a very big problem."

"What's going on?" Danny's heart starts to jackhammer.

"I need to see you. Roddy, too."

"What's up, Kenny?"

"I can't talk about it now. But it's important." Ken's voice sounds shaky.

"What do you mean, *important?*"

"Can you and Roddy come in tomorrow evening, let's say seven?"

"Kenny, I don't have time. It's April and tax time's right around the corner. What's going on?"

"Please, Danny. Talk to Roddy. I need you to come tomorrow night."

"Kenny, let's get something straight . . ."

"Dan! *Please*. I wouldn't kid about something like this."

"You wouldn't kid about *what*, Kenny?"

"Jesus, Danny. I can't talk right now," Kenny says, his voice trembling. "Please, just be here. Both of you. Tomorrow at seven."

"Look, Kenny . . ."

"Please . . . promise you'll be here."

"Kenny, this better be important."

"It is."

"Okay, Kenny. I'll talk to Roddy."

"Thanks."

Danny hears a click. The line goes dead.

■

"So, Mr. Grange, what can we do for you?" Roddy asks, as low-voltage current sizzles through him. They're in the back office at McLaughlin's.

John Grange is a very big man, Roddy thinks. *No, he's bigger than big. He's sumo-sized huge—the size of a military Hummer—a good 350 pounds, maybe even close to four bills.*

"Kenny didn't tell you?" Grange asks, a smile threatening to erupt on his jowly face.

"He said he couldn't talk on the phone . . ."

"That right, Kenny?" Grange says, casting a look at Kenny who sits to Roddy's left. "That what you told these guys, your *partners?*"

Kenny nods and peers down at the table.

"So you weren't honest with these guys."

Kenny says nothing; he has that sweat sheen on his face and still looks cadaverous.

Roddy looks across the table at Grange. The man is sloppy-looking, on top of being huge. His dark hair has thinned out in front. Flakes of scalp decorate his shoulders like granules of sugar. His jowls give him a tough hangdog look. Brooding eyes peer out beneath hooded lids.

"A guy who can't be honest with his partners ain't a guy you can trust," Grange says.

Roddy can't get his eyes off Grange. The fat man's lips are thick and wet; his lower lip hangs like a glistening slab of liver. Multiple chins form accordion folds above an open shirt collar. His sausage-like fingers sprout thick, black hairs. One outsized digit sports a ring with an immense star sapphire.

"You guys're takin' a big fuckin' risk dealing with this Kenny Egan character," Grange says. "A guy who keeps secrets from you . . ."

The restaurant is as loud as Shea Stadium. Omar and Crystal are running the front of the house. The office seems tomblike. Roddy's blood pulses in his ears. Heat flushes through his face and seeps to his neck. He can see Kenny peripherally; the guy's virtually cringing. Danny is on Grange's side of the table, to the fat man's left.

"You wanna tell your partners why we're here, Kenny?"

Kenny shakes his head.

Standing in the corner, leaning against the wall, is a fifth man.

If Grange is a Hummer, this guy's an 18-wheel Mack truck, thinks Roddy. *Parked, with its engine idling.* He reminds Roddy of Ivan Drago from that *Rocky* movie. The guy must stand six five and tip the scales at 270. Pure, rock-hard muscle. His crew-cut blond hair is slickly gelled; his face—especially those cheekbones and that lantern jaw—could be carved from granite. He, no doubt, spends countless hours at some muscle emporium. Pure muscle, but probably clumsy; he would go down fast if Roddy drove a flurry of punches into his gut and face. A gold earring pierces the guy's left earlobe. The drape of the jacket on his Schwarzenegger shoulders shows a bulge on the left side. The guy's packing some serious hardware. Mack Truck stares blankly and stands rock-still, hands clasped in front of his gargantuan body.

Roddy can virtually smell testosterone in the air.

Grange's thick lips curl into a smirk as he eyes Kenny, then Roddy, then Dan.

The heat in Roddy's face feels combustible.

"What can we do for you, Mr. Grange?" Roddy asks. He feels strangely calm.

"So you're the spokesman for this group of losers," Grange says. His deep voice rumbles through the floor and buzzes up the chair, into Roddy's legs.

"Why'd you want to meet with us?" Roddy asks.

Stay calm, don't go Irish on this fat bastard.

"You have no fuckin' idea . . . ?"

Roddy senses his kemosabe is scared shitless, and Dan's terrible at hiding his feelings. That pale Irish face and his dilated blood vessels—those rosy cheek blotches—are his Gaelic giveaway.

Roddy thinks: even if Grange's real name doesn't end in a vowel or rhyme with beef stroganoff, the guy's connected. This is industrial-strength mob shit: hard-core gangster crap—with muscle on the side. There's one certainty as Roddy looks at Grange and Mack Truck: this isn't some amateur-penny-ante-Brooklyn-Irish-boys-on-the-street bravado. Those days are history—gone forever. The man sitting across the table could be cast in *The Sopranos* or maybe as Clemenza in *The Godfather*—some mob captain or underboss—Italian, Russian, Ukrainian, Albanian, it doesn't matter.

The edges of the room darken and the air in the room feels so close Roddy can barely suck it into his lungs.

"Now lemme see . . . ," Grange says in that basso voice. "We got a doctor here . . . an MD, that's *you*, right?" Grange asks, pointing a fat finger at Roddy.

"And we got an accountant, too," Grange says, glancing over at Danny.

Dan nods and then swallows hard.

"And we got a restaurateur." Grange nods at Kenny. "That right, Mr. MD?"

Roddy's head bobs up and down.

Mack Truck looms silently. Like Gibraltar.

"Why're we here, Mr. Grange?" Roddy asks, as a sickened feeling floats up from his gut.

Grange glances to his left and spies the wet bar. "Whaddaya got there?" He points to the bar.

"Whatever you want," Roddy says.

"Gimme your best single malt scotch."

At the wet bar Roddy says, "We have Glenfiddich Ancient Reserve . . ."

"How old?"

Roddy reads the label. "Aged eighteen years."

"Oh, yeah," grunts Grange. "Gotta be at least a hundred a bottle."

"On the rocks or straight up?"

"Straight up." There's a pause. "By the way, I got a nickname . . . it's 'Ghost.'"

Mack Truck bends his neck to the side and cracks his neck bones.

"Because I come and go like a ghost."

The storeroom freezer's compressor kicks in, rattles, and then hisses. Dishes clatter in the kitchen amidst muffled Spanish shouts. Restaurant din seeps through the door.

Roddy pours the Glenfiddich, carries the glass to the table, and slips it in front of Grange. Roddy feels Mack Truck's eyes bore into his back.

"To your health, motherfuckers," Grange says, sipping the scotch. "Divine. Just fuckin' divine." He guzzles the rest.

"Another . . . ?" asks Roddy, still holding the bottle.

"I never have more than one. But this fuckin' stuff's great," Grange says, holding up the empty glass.

Roddy's eyes meet Dan's—briefly. Then he sits down, across from Grange.

"So, Mister Fuckin' Doctor and Mister Fuckin' Accountant . . . I guess you're wonderin' why I'm here . . ."

Dan looks greenish now, like he belongs on an autopsy table.

Ken's pouring sweat and looks shriveled.

"Let's just cut to the chase, Mr. Grange," says Roddy.

"You're the tough guy in this bunch, aren't you?" Grange's unblinking eyes—deeply set, gray, lifeless—crawl over Roddy.

Roddy feels prickly sweat all over; it reminds him of entering the boxing ring.

"Yeah, I can tell you're a tough guy—starin' at me like some streetwise punk, like some tough-motherfuckin' hood, some fuckin' ex-con right outta Sing Sing. Yeah, you don't take shit from nobody, right?" Grange's eyes lock on Roddy.

Now Roddy recalls the prefight stare downs, eyeball-to-eyeball, two boxers, midring—a light sweat-sheen on each—staring murderously at each other.

"But lemme tell you somethin', Mr. Fuckin' MD. Lemme tell you this . . . tough-guy . . . that's no way to look at your partner."

More silence as the fluorescent light buzzes.

Roddy's thoughts reel back to the paratroopers at Fort Bragg. He hears the jumpmaster's words: *once you've jumped from an airplane, there's nothing can scare you. Nothing at all, young troop.*

The storage room freezer hums louder; the restaurant sounds like a muted roar. Iciness seeps through Roddy, yet sweat leaks from his pores.

"Okay, lemme spell it out." Grange sets his lunch-box sized paws on the tabletop and clasps his fingers. "This fuckin' loser over here . . . ," he says, shooting a bulbous thumb at Kenny, "this piece-of-shit-in-a-suit borrowed *250K* from me. Ain't that right, Kenny?"

Kenny's head jiggles up and down.

Roddy's heart feels like a mallet in his chest. The room goes bleached white, washed-out. Roddy's innards coil as though a snake coils around his guts. On the Richter scale of intimidation, Grange hits a full-blown 10.

"You *did* that, Kenny?" Roddy hears himself ask. Craning his neck, he looks over at Ken.

Roddy knows he shouldn't be shocked. After all, this is

Kenny-I'd-bet-my-mother's-life-on-a-whim-McGuirk, or Kenny-Fucking-Egan-McGuirk-from-Brooklyn, also known as Kenny "Snake Eyes" from Sheepshead Bay. Numbers runner, dice-thrower, poker player, pool shark, a scrounger, pilferer, and wannabe Jimmy the Greek or Nathan Detroit out of *Guys and Dolls*. Jesus Christ. *How could they've not seen this coming?* Roddy wonders.

"That right, Kenny?" Danny asks. "When you showed me your bank statement, it was *his* money?"

Kenny nods. A sweat droplet hangs from his nose and falls to the table.

Roddy's nerve endings tingle. His right lower eyelid twitches and goes into spasm.

"You borrowed a quarter of a million?" Danny asks. "And never told us?"

"And the juice is runnin'," says Grange.

"And just how much juice is running?" Dan asks.

"Your partner borrowed 250K at 12 percent a month."

"Twelve percent a *month?*"

"That's right, Mr. Fuckin' Accountant."

"That's *144 percent* a year." Danny's half-standing, but glances at Mack Truck, sinks into his seat.

"However you wanna figure it . . ."

"That's *usury*," Danny cries, crimson-faced.

"Usury?" chortles Grange with a thick-lipped smile. "That's juice." His dewlaps jiggle as he laughs. Mouth open, his wet tongue shines in the fluorescent light; he shows a phalanx of yellow teeth.

Suddenly, Grange's huge fist crashes onto the tabletop. The thump thrashes into Roddy's legs. His body pulses.

"Like I said, it's 12 percent a month, Mr. Fuckin' Accountant. Normally, I collect on the 12 percent every month . . . that's the vig."

"*Vig* . . . ? asks Roddy.

"Yeah. Vig . . . juice . . . interest. But with this fuckin' loser," he says, pointing at Kenny, "because of the loan's size, I forgave the monthly vig so I could collect 20 percent after four months. And so far, I got *nada*. Ain't that right, Kenny?"

Ken nods, still looking down.

"This skinny turd hasn't paid back one fuckin' nickel. Not in four months . . . not in five months . . . and not now . . . six months later. He's in over his Mickey Finn eyeballs. Me and my associates ain't waitin' any longer."

Grange turns to Dan. "Hey, Mr. Accountant, I'll bet you can figure how much this skinny bastard owes."

"This is *insane*. First of all, it's—"

"Insane? It's *life*. And *you* and your *doctor*-partner here owe big time."

"We didn't take a loan from *you*."

Roddy's insides quiver.

"Oh yes you did. I got a lien on your restaurant."

"You can't enforce that kind of lien," Dan says.

"I got plenty of enforcement power."

"You can't hold us responsible for that."

Grange's laugh sends a vibration into Roddy's feet, like a drill press buzzing through his bones.

"Lemme tell you something, Mr. Fuckin' Accountant. I'd never've loaned the money if this restaurant wasn't backup. Or as *you* would say . . . *collateral*."

"Mr. Grange," says Roddy, keeping his voice steady, "if Kenny borrowed the money six months ago, how much does he owe?"

"Lemme correct you, Mr. Fuckin' MD. *You* borrowed the money. You *all* borrowed it. The Three Musketeers." He casts a choleric glance at Roddy. "But to answer your question, Mr. MD and partner of this full-time fuck-up sittin' to your left, the three of you—as of tonight—owe . . . ," he pauses and removes a slip of paper from his breast pocket.

Roddy's brain is ready to explode through his skull.

"You three fuckers owe $493,454 and zero cents. That's what you owe *tonight*. By tomorrow, it'll be higher, because the juice is run-nin'. And *this* skinny, fast-talking Irish son of a bitch hasn't paid one fuckin' cent. So . . . now it's *your* fuckin' problem."

Dan looks like he'll faint. Kenny looks catatonic.

The storage room compressor kicks in again.

"Look, Mr. Grange," Danny says.

"Yeah . . . ?"

"We don't have that kind of money." Dan's shivering, as though they're in an arctic whiteout.

"Do I look as stupid as this motherfucker?" Grange pokes a thumb at Kenny.

"No, but . . ."

"But *what*, Mr. Fuckin' Accountant from Tuckahoe with a nice house on Maple Street and an office on McLean Avenue in Yonkers? Whaddaya wanna tell me? With two kids goin' to private school. Just what the fuck you tryin' to tell me?"

Roddy hears Dan's breath leave him.

"But that kind of money is . . ."

"Is *what*? You tellin' me you don't have money Mr. Fuckin' Accountant whose wife's a nice-lookin' Italian girl, drives an A-6 Audi. A fifty-thousand-dollar car? You tellin' me you can't get money?"

"No . . ."

"You earn good money helpin' your goddamned clients cheat the government. And that's what you'll pay with."

Grange shifts his gaze to Roddy, his face scorched with malevolence.

"And you, Mr. Fuckin' MD. How much you get for a hernia, huh? Two, three thousand . . . four?"

A coppery taste forms on Roddy's tongue.

"Whaddaya do, three, four, maybe five operations a day? How much you rake in a year . . . five, six hundred? How 'bout a mil-lion, motherfucker? You didn't bust ass all those years to make shit-on-a-stick for money, did you? You cut those slobs up for good bucks. From insurance companies. And Medicare pays plenty, doesn't it? And don't try to tell me you never scam the Uncle like all the other fuckin' crooks out there. Everyone pays the doctor . . . and the undertaker. You ain't cryin' poverty, are you?"

Roddy shakes his head, tells himself to stay calm, just roll with the punches from this fat bastard. Then, somehow—deal with it.

"You got securities, don't you—after cuttin' up all those losers at Lawrence Hospital? Right?"

Roddy nods his head.

"Yeah . . . keep noddin', Mr. Fuckin' *Tough* Guy. 'Cause you got plenty of dough. Even your wife works, like you need the money. That's what I love about you doctors, lawyers, and accountants. You got securities, assets. Ain't that the way to put it, Mr. Accountant? *Assets.* Right?

"Don't cry poverty to me, Mr. Fuckin' MD, with your house in Bronxville, right on a golf course, whose pretty little wife with the blonde pony tail works at Sarah Lawrence. Shit, if all librarians looked like her I'da spent more time with the books. Don't tell me you can't rustle up the money."

That taste on Roddy's tongue now feels like a mixture of copper and zinc. Acid froths in his gullet. He feels the hairs on his arms stand.

Grange says, "You sell some securities and you got money to pay up."

Grange's gaze shifts back to Danny. "And you . . . you got securities, too, right?"

Danny looks paralytic.

"*Answer* me. You got securities, right?"

Danny nods quickly.

"You pay up. Because the juice is runnin'."

Voices and clatter come from the kitchen. The dining crowd sounds like roaring from afar—muffled, as though Roddy's ears are clogged.

Kenny's cigarette smolders in an ashtray.

Mack Truck stands in the corner, looking bored.

Grange's manhole cover–sized hands thump on the tabletop. "The shit hits the fan for this pussy posse. It's do or die."

"Okay, Mr. Grange," Roddy says. "We'll get in touch. You have a card?"

"You'll get it soon."

"We'll need some time," Roddy says, knowing his voice can be his Great Betrayer because it gets hard, steely when he's about to explode. He's known it all his life. But not now, not in this cramped little room at the back of McLaughlin's across the table from this fat fuck backed up by Ivan Drago or Kimbo Slice or the Terminator; no, not with this blubbery slob who's made barely veiled threats against them and Tracy and Angela, who's jeopardizing everything in their lives. This mobster makes Roddy feel like chewing on galvanized nails, and yet, there's not a trace of hostility in his tone; no bravado bullshit, no macho I'll-kill-you crap. His voice sounds soothing in his own ears. Yet his veins feel icy and his face is on fire.

"How much time you need?" Grange asks, drumming his fingers on the tabletop.

"We can't get our hands on money like that overnight," Roddy says.

Grange stares coldly with those hooded eyes.

Roddy looks straight into Grange's eyes and holds the fat man's stare. *Steady . . . steady*, he tells himself, *keep your eyes locked on his. Don't even blink because this is a man-on-man-no-holds-barred-stare-down. Like before a fight.*

"The juice'll be runnin'," Grange says.

"We understand. The juice always runs . . . ," says Roddy.

"*You* understand?" Grange asks, turning to Danny.

Danny nods and looks down.

Grange pushes away from the table and stands. His bulk is

Texas-size ponderous.

Mack Truck moves his mass from the wall and fills the room.

Grange turns to Roddy and asks, "What's the name of that scotch?"

"Glenfiddich, Ancient Reserve . . ."

"That's some good shit," Grange says and purses his liver-lips. Heading for the door, he stops, looks at Roddy, and says, "Like I said . . . you'll get my business card, real soon."

Then he and Mack Truck are gone.

Chapter 16

The office seems like a crypt.

Roddy's heart feels like a battering ram pulsing through his chest and his fingers cramp.

Danny erupts from his seat, red-faced, fists clenched. "You piece of *shit*," he barks at Kenny. He barrels around the table with fury in his eyes. "You no-good son of a bitch. I'll kill you," he cries, and lunges for Kenny.

Roddy leaps in front of Dan, grabs his shoulders, and pushes him back.

Danny's arms flail wildly, but Roddy shoves him against the wall.

"Lemme at him," shouts Danny. "You son of a bitch. I'll tear your fuckin' heart out."

"No, Dan," Roddy says, "it's not the way to go."

"Lemme *go,* Roddy." Froth forms at the corners of Dan's mouth. "You sneaky bastard. I'll . . ."

"Dan, we gotta stay calm."

Dan grunts and writhes, but Roddy holds him and hears wheezing coming from Danny's chest.

"Dan, *stop* it."

Dan goes limp against the wall. The wheezing grows louder; then come gasps for air. Still holding Dan, Roddy turns to Kenny.

Ken sits in the chair, ghostly pale and trembling, looking like he'll shatter into pieces.

"Roddy, this fuck-up's just ruined our lives," Dan grunts. Mucous bubbles in his chest; then comes a high-pitched wheezing.

"Danny, stay cool."

"Roddy, that fat fuck knows all about Angela and Tracy. And the *kids*. He knows *everything*."

Roddy turns, still blocking Dan. "Kenny, how'd he learn about us, our families, where we live?"

Kenny's eyes bulge like small balloons; he shakes his head. He dribbles sweat. "I . . . I don't know . . ."

Dan coughs up phlegm, swallows, and staggers back to the table. He glares at Kenny. "We're all mobbed up," he rasps, red-faced, hands on the table. "I swear to God, if I had a gun right now, Roddy, I'd shove it down this bastard's throat and pull the trigger. I don't *give* a shit. Throw me in fucking jail."

"Take it easy, Danny."

"What the fuck'd we get into?" Dan shouts. He coughs, goes to the wet bar, leans over it, brings up phlegm, and spits into the sink. He pulls out his Advair, sucks it in, and then breathes heavily and closes his eyes.

"Dan, pull it together," Roddy says. "We gotta figure out something. Going after each other's no way to . . ."

"There's *no* way, Roddy," Dan shouts. Another jag of coughing begins. Dan's fist covers his mouth; he gurgles and then looks up again. "This skinny prick let a shylock—a fucking loan shark—into our lives."

Mucous rattles in Danny's chest; the sound bubbles through the room.

"*Dan*. Your asthma."

"*Fuck* my asthma."

"You all right?"

"Yeah . . . yeah." Dan coughs, brings up more phlegm, and spits into the sink. He stands at the bar; a string of mucous hangs from his lips. He swipes it away. His hands go up and clutch the sides of his head.

They wait. Finally, Dan lets out a deep breath, shudders, and leans against the bar.

"Dan, can you stay calm?"

Danny nods and closes his eyes. "I can't believe it," he mutters. "In all the years I've known you, Roddy, you never took shit like that."

"Dan, it's not the schoolyard anymore. And the big dude was packing."

Danny sinks into a chair, sets his elbows on the table, and rests his head in his palms.

"Let's be practical . . ."

"*Practical?*" Dan shouts. "The juice is running . . . even as we *speak.*" Danny groans and then looks up. "Figure it out, Roddy. At 12 percent a month, the half-million grows by *two grand a day.* By next month it'll be three Gs. Ninety thousand a *month.*"

"But let's . . ."

"What the fuck does *practical* mean?"

"It means we learn what we're dealing with."

Kenny sits quietly, looking ghoul-green, sweaty.

Dan's wheezing subsides. The Advair is working.

"Hey, I'm sorry, guys," says Ken. "I didn't think it'd come to this . . ."

"What the fuck'd ya think it'd come to?" Danny shouts. "How'd you expect to pay that bastard?"

"We got a fuckin' gold mine here. The business we're doin' is—"

"Tell me something, asshole," Danny shouts. "What made you go to this guy?"

"This was a once-in-a-lifetime shot. I wanted somethin' of my own."

"So you went to a fucking *shylock?*"

"No bank would give me that kinda dough."

"Tell me, Kenny," Danny says, "you ever go to a shark before?"

"Never."

"You have no experience with a shy . . . a guy like you?"

"No personal experience. No."

"Tell me something else, asshole, how'd that fat bastard know all about our families, where we work? How'd he know all that?"

"Danny . . . I swear to *God* I didn't tell him a fuckin' thing."

"Dan . . . these days we're just a click away," Roddy says. "We're on Facebook or anyone can Google us. It's easy."

"Did you think of the consequences of your shit?" Danny asks. "For even for a second?"

"Hey guys . . . I thought we'd score big. And you can see—"

"Score *big?* Yeah, like you did with the appliance store?" Danny shouts. "Like you let Roddy and Frankie take the rap, you bastard. Grange was right. You're a piece a shit in a suit. Jesus, I forgot the simple fact that people never change."

"Danny, forget the past," Roddy says. "We gotta handle this now."

"What the fuck's *that* mean?" Danny's face reddens again. He's nearly frothing at the mouth. "We owe that shy big bucks," he shouts. "And more every day. The juice is runnin'. The goddamned *juice.*"

"We gotta dope out Grange," Roddy says, trying to stay calm.

"Yeah? How?"

"I don't know."

"Roddy, you can't deal with the mob," Danny says.

It occurs to Roddy that his life's been so *clean;* there's been a kind of self-anointed innocence to his existence for twenty-five years. And now, this: a heart-freezing development comes out of nowhere, like a snarling grizzly leaping out of the brush.

"Roddy," says Dan, "we're dealing with the fuckin' *mob.*"

Roddy turns to Ken. "Look, Kenny, we gotta know the full deal. You hear me?"

Ken nods; his chin trembles.

"Did you contact anyone else about a loan?"

"No."

"No associates of Grange's?"

"Not a soul."

"You tell anyone else about Grange?"

"No. Who the fuck's there to tell?"

"Why'd you go to him?"

"Like I said, I had a shot at making this place work. And it's booming."

"Yeah, asshole?" shouts Dan. "And now we're losing money."

"Dan, I didn't—"

"Forget it," Roddy says. "Kenny, how'd you get hold of this guy, Grange?"

"Through a gambler I knew in Vegas."

"A *gambler*? Who?"

"Guy used to lose at blackjack. Name's Collins."

"How well did you know him?"

"Enough to know he was a loser. Always cryin' in his beer . . ."

"Was he connected?"

"Nah. Just a sad-assed joker. From L.A. In the entertainment business. Hollywood type. Fucker was feedin' a huge cocaine habit. His nose was half-eaten away."

"What's the connection between Collins and Grange?"

"Collins got money from him. Lost big time at the tables . . . at Caesars and Bellagio. Had a thing for showgirls, too. Was hittin' the clubs, snortin' his brains out, payin' for high-end pussy."

"How'd he know Grange?"

"I have no idea. You never know with these guys—who they know or how . . ."

"But why'd you go to Collins? You said he was a *loser?*"

"He was tapping a money source . . . always got more, that's why."

"So what'd you do?"

"I asked Collins for Grange's number."

"So what do *you* know about Grange?"

"Just that he's a shy here, in New York . . ."

"Does he have an office?"

"I have no idea."

"Well, *who* is he? Where's he from? Brooklyn, Queens, Jersey . . . where?"

"I'm tellin' ya, Roddy, I *dunno* . . ."

"*I dunno* . . . ," pules Dan. "*I dunno* . . . you dumb motherfucker." He leans across the table. "You know *anything*, you stupid bastard?"

Roddy sits next to Ken. He leans in, real close.

"How'd you contact him?"

"Telephone."

"You got his number from Collins?"

"Yeah . . ."

"Still have it?"

"Nah . . ."

"Is Grange connected?"

"I don't know."

Danny gets up and paces. "You don't even know if he's with some mob?" Danny shouts.

"He's not Italian and he's not Russian," Kenny says. "I dunno what he is . . ."

"Is Grange his real name?" Roddy asks.

"I have no fuckin' idea." Kenny shakes his head. "Could be a guinea . . . or a kike. Or something else. He ain't Irish, that much I know. The only thing I know for sure, he's not a nigger."

"Very fucking funny, asshole," Dan mutters.

"Do you know a *thing* about this guy? *One* thing?"

"Just that he came up with money."

"Ever hear him talk about anyone with an Italian or Russian name? Any foreign-sounding name? Middle East . . . Eastern Europe, anything . . . ?"

"Nah."

"So, maybe he's a lone operator?"

"I dunno."

"So you don't know who you're dealing with?"

"What can I tell ya, Roddy? I make a fuckin' call; the guy shows up. All he talks about is money . . . the loan, the terms, and he looks at the operation. He doesn't talk about his friends. He just talks the talk."

"What about the muscle?" Roddy asks.

"Looks like a bouncer to me," Danny says.

"A bouncer? What makes you say that?" Roddy asks.

"He doesn't look mobbed up. Blond, a body builder, right out of Central Casting," Dan says with a sneer.

"He could be Russian, from Eastern Europe, any fuckin' thing," Kenny says.

"What're you saying, Kenny?"

"Guy didn't say a word. It's hard to place him."

"He looks like a bouncer," says Dan. "One of those big dudes the clubs hire to tame the drunks. They get a couple hundred a night, maybe pick up a spare job here and there . . . like maybe tonight, with Grange," he says.

"How do you know this shit, Danny?" asks Roddy.

"Had a client who owned a club. He used to hire NFL dropouts and other sleaze-bags as bouncers, the bigger the better."

"Can you contact this guy? Maybe we can learn more."

"He died last year."

"That dude was carrying," Kenny says.

"So what?" Dan says. "Anyone can get a piece in this town."

"Jesus," says Roddy. "We're half a million down; we got a shark with threats and a guy packing; we have juice, or vig, Vegas, and a whole lotta shady shit."

"You can thank this skinny bastard," Danny mutters. Though calmer, Dan's voice warbles. And he's still beet red.

"Man, am I sorry I bought into this vanity project," says Roddy.

"I hear you . . . ," Dan says. "Me, too."

"So," Roddy says, "let's assume Grange is a solo operator. He's not mob connected. He hires a bouncer as muscle."

"I don't know if we can just assume that," Ken says.

"You don't know jack shit about *anything*, do you?" Danny snarls.

"I know what I know . . ."

"Roddy, you betting the guy's not connected?" Danny asks.

"Connected or not, we gotta do something."

Dan sighs and shakes his head. His hands shake.

"Kenny," says Roddy, "when you met Grange, was he alone?"

"Yeah."

"Where'd you meet him?"

"At the restaurant. He looked the place over and spoke to McLaughlin, too. Made sure the deal was legit."

"You have a contract?"

"These guys don't work like that."

"So there's no record of any deal?"

"No way. These guys operate on a handshake."

"And the fucking collateral is *this restaurant?*" Danny shouts.

Roddy ignores Dan and looks straight at Kenny.

"So he checks the place out, and then what . . . ?"

"Then the money . . ."

"A check? For a quarter of a million?"

"No . . ."

"Roddy," Dan says, "the money was *wired*. No doubt from a foreign account . . . the Cayman Islands, maybe Costa Rica, some offshore tax haven where nothing's real anyway. It's in cyberspace. It's dummy corporation shit. You can't track him that way."

"But, Dan, you checked Kenny's accounts, right?"

"Yeah. And the statement showed the balance in a ninety-day CD. It didn't say where the money came from."

"Danny's right," Ken says. "The dough was wired."

Roddy nods. "And how'd Grange get to the restaurant?"

"By taxi."

"And he was alone?"

"Yeah."

"And the only time you ever saw the blond guy—or anyone else—was tonight?"

"You got it," Kenny says. "Jesus, I'm scared shitless," he says, and pulls out a Lucky Strike. "Believe me, guys, I never thought it'd come to this. I thought I'd pay this Grange bastard off in maybe seven, eight months."

"You *prick*," roars Danny. "Seven or eight months? With the juice running, you'd pay out over *half a million.* With these loan sharks you're in for the rest of your no-good *life,* you dumb bastard. And believe me, soon we'll owe that scumbag a million bucks. A *million fucking bucks.*" Dan's eyeballs bulge; the veins on his neck look like they're ready to pop as he stares long and hard at Kenny. "And you involved me and Roddy? How fucking *dare* you?"

"Dan, I never thought—"

"You didn't realize the restaurant's the only reason he gave you the goddamned money. And now, *we're* up to our ears in *your* shit."

Kenny looks like he's shivering. His hand shakes so violently, he can't light the cigarette. He stubs it out in the ashtray.

"Kenny, you okay?" Roddy asks. He's certain Kenny will lose it soon, fold like a beach chair. Is it cocaine, speed, alcohol, or just plain Kenny?

"Yeah, Roddy, I'm okay."

"All right. Get outta here. Danny and I gotta talk."

"About what?" Kenny's eyes flit from Roddy to Danny.

"About how to come up with the money."

"Hey guys," Kenny says, standing. "I'm sorry. I fucked up . . ."

"It's not the first time, Kenny," mutters Danny, grabbing the Glenfiddich. He pours a shot into a tumbler.

"Believe me, I'll do anything to get us out of this."

"How about giving us a quarter million?" Danny asks with a sneer. He guzzles the scotch, slams the empty glass onto the bar top, and wipes his lips with his hand.

"All right, Kenny. Just take care of the diners," Roddy says, leading him to the door. And now, in this cramped, suffocating back office of McLaughlin's Steakhouse filled with flesh-chomping Sybarites, Roddy recalls the evening Kenny came to him and how he didn't recognize the guy. It's clear to Roddy that not only had Kenny changed his looks, but he—Roddy Dolan—never *wanted to see* the truth; he didn't want to look beyond the veneer of who sat in his office: Kenny Snake Eyes McGuirk.

What the hell made him so blind? It occurs to Roddy that maybe he was sidestepping what it meant to have Kenny McGuirk back in his life. Kenny and Frankie Messina and Sheepshead Bay, Coyle Street and East 19th Street, Horst and his mother and that fucked-up burglary, the cops, the judge, and all the seediness of his life as a kid. Maybe he wanted to nurture an illusion, maintain the belief that his past had faded, simply ghosted away in the brilliance of his new life as a husband, father, and surgeon living the good life with Tracy in the Westchester suburbs.

As the door opens, the restaurant's roar rushes into the office, assaulting Roddy's ears. God, how he hates all the beef-eating, wine-guzzling, bullshitting, backslapping steakhouse camaraderie.

"Hey, Kenny," Danny calls out.

"Yeah," Kenny says and turns back.

"Go fuck yourself."

The door closes with a click.

Now, it's just Roddy and Danny.

Chapter 17

Angela heads west on Heathcote Road in Scarsdale. It's a dark, humid night, and the Audi hugs the turns on this narrow road, slinking like a panther. Soon, she'll get on Route 22, heading south toward Tuckahoe. It sometimes feels to Angela that the car could drive this route itself since she makes this trip twice a week to visit Mom.

She glances at the dashboard clock: 8:30 P.M. Danny and the kids are home; they've probably polished off the tray of lasagna she left in the refrigerator. The kids have finished their homework and by now, are watching TV. Dan's no doubt studying his spreadsheets, preparing to file clients' returns electronically. The April 15th deadline is near and he's in his annual frenzy.

Angela thinks about these visits to Mom. She's seventy-five years old, a widow, living alone in a house that's way too big, especially with her emphysema and crippling arthritis. But Mom's so attached to the place, she won't consider downsizing, moving to an apartment. Too many memories float through the house—like shimmering ghosts. And Mom will never move in with her, Danny, and the kids. She insists on having her freedom, even though she's becoming more reliant on Angela by the day. She won't accept a housekeeper or part-time home health aide—it's the whole *independence* routine. Angela's sister, Lorraine, lives in Houston, so it's all fallen onto Angela's shoulders. Back in the old days, she'd be living in a mother-daughter house in Bensonhurst, Brooklyn, with Mom comfortably ensconced upstairs. But not now, with everyone in the suburbs.

There's a thick layer of dust on Mom's furniture and the pipe below the kitchen sink sprang a leak. Angela discovered it when she smelled a moldy odor. Opening the cabinet door, she saw a layer of green, cottony stuff mixed with mouse droppings. Angela will call a plumber and an exterminator first thing tomorrow. And Mom's becoming more absentminded. Angela noticed an overdue MasterCard bill on the dining room table. Mom's been making partial payments, so interest is mounting. *My God*, Angela thinks, *if Danny sees the statement, he'll throw a fit; he absolutely abhors usury. He always says it's what the credit card companies truck in.* Angela's sure she and Dan will be forced to take over Mom's finances. They'll have to talk about it.

Angela's thoughts turn to Dan, and even as they do, she feels her grip on the steering wheel tighten. She knows he's been *really* stressed these last few days.

"Dan, I've never seen you so uptight as this," she said last night.

"Oh, honey, you know this happens every year."

"Not this bad. You're not sleeping . . ."

"I'm getting my six hours."

"Danny, you're up at two and you go downstairs . . ."

"I'm working on clients' returns."

"You look . . . I don't know, you look worried. Is everything all right?"

"Angie, it's just . . . there's a lotta crap on my mind."

"There's plenty on your plate, between the clients, this John Harris thing, and the restaurant."

When she mentioned McLaughlin's, Dan blanched. And Angela was sure she heard a wheeze bubble deep in his chest.

"Danny, your asthma's been acting up."

"Well, it's April. The trees're pollinating."

"You're not allergic to tree pollen."

"Sweetie, these things happen as you get older . . . ," he said, sounding irritated at her persistent questioning. It's unlike Danny, who always asks her advice, especially when he's uptight.

"Honey, I think it's stress," she said. "Is it the restaurant?"

Again, when she mentioned McLaughlin's, Dan's face contorted, as though she'd yanked a raw nerve in his jaw.

"Oh, Angie," he said, "the place is a pain in the ass."

"What do you mean?"

"I'm not sure it's worth the aggravation."

"Aggravation? I thought Kenny was running a gold mine. Only a week ago you were high on the place."

"Well, it's complicated . . ."

"How?"

He hesitated, swallowed hard, and then said, "It's more than I want to take on . . ."

"Maybe you're overextended."

"The truth is, Angie . . . I might get out. Roddy too."

Angela thought it was odd. For months Dan's been high on McLaughlin's, how the restaurant and accounting practice were feeding off each other. *Cross-pollinating.* It'd become his favorite expression. And this John Harris thing . . . it's been a huge deal. Lately, it's all he's talked about, and how he had McLaughlin's to thank for it. And now? Suddenly wanting out? It seems strange.

Heathcote Road snakes westward toward Route 22. You don't see any houses. Most are recessed from the road. Each side of Heathcote is heavily wooded. And there are no streetlights.

Angela reaches for the radio dial—she'll hit the preset button for 100.7 WHUD, an FM station out of Peekskill. It plays good contemporary music.

As her thumb nears the button, an explosive whiteness fills the car. Brilliant light bounces off the mirrors and sears her retinas. Angela squints, peering into the rearview mirror. Huge headlights—halogen bright and blinding—approach fast; then comes the roar of a huge engine. The lights fracture into kaleidoscopic beams, streaks of white heat so bright she closes her eyes for a moment and the thing is so close it seems ready to pour through her rear window.

She speeds up, but the lights loom closer. If she brakes, she'll be rear-ended, so she stomps on the gas pedal. The Audi lurches ahead.

The monster behind her—a truck of some kind—is on her tail; its horn blows, sounding like a boat's air horn. Angela veers right amidst the squealing of tires. She's almost on the shoulder, but the thing stays on her tail, blasting its horn again—deafening—and she flinches, realizes she's doing fifty, and suddenly, the monster swings out. There's a shadow to her left: immense, dark; it veers closer; it seems ready to swallow the Audi. She jerks the steering wheel to the right; it rattles in her hands; gravel crunches and smacks up into the wheel wells; the car bounces; trees and bushes rush by; rubber shrieks on asphalt; then comes a leap and a hard rebound and Angela feels she's losing control. She's off the road; her headlights dip, then rise; her teeth rattle, and the car plunges down and the shoulder harness snaps against her chest. As the Audi dips into a swale, the seat belt grabs her hips and yanks so tightly she feels her ribs compress. The car plows ahead—there's a boom with a jarring impact, and she's thrust forward as the airbag deploys. There's a strange odor: oil, some weird chemical smell, and there's powder, or is it smoke?

Angela hopes the car hasn't caught fire, and she suddenly feels faint. God, no! Don't pass out, not if there's a fire, but she's alert now and realizes the Audi's tilted; the car's hit a huge rock; it's partly suspended in midair, a wheel spins, and the Audi's tangled in a nest of roadside euonymus. Sitting half-dazed amidst clanking and knocking, Angela can barely believe she's alive.

Breathless, she reaches for her cell phone.

Chapter 18

Roddy pulls the Sequoia into the garage, kills the engine, and listens to the ticking from beneath the vehicle's chassis. He's suddenly aware that his hands clutch the steering wheel tightly. He loosens his grip, opens and closes his hands, and tries relaxing his fingers, but they spasm. He waits for the contraction to ease up.

Roddy's flooded by thoughts of the telephone conversation with Dan this morning.

"Roddy, Angela was run off the road last night."

"What? Is she okay?"

"She's fine. She called 911 and they took her to White Plains Hospital. Just a few bumps and bruises and some burns from the air bag."

"Thank God. She was *run off the road?*"

"Bastard came up behind her and forced her into a drainage ditch. The car's totaled."

"Dan, are you thinking what I'm thinking?"

"Roddy, I *know* what happened."

"How would that bastard know where she'd be?"

"She's being followed."

"Have you heard from him?" Roddy asked.

"Nothing directly."

"You mean the hang-ups?"

"Roddy, there've been a dozen hang-ups the last three days. We have caller ID and the screen just says, 'Private.' And you?"

"Same thing. Tracy wants to change our number. She thinks it's some crank. And Brenda said there've been hang-ups at the office."

"It's Grange."

"Dan, let's go to the police."

"You gotta be crazy."

"They could pick him up and—"

"And what? We can't prove a thing. We don't even know if Grange is his real name. Look, Roddy, this bastard's upping the stakes. And we know squat about this guy."

"We could set him up and have the cops waiting."

"Yeah? Lemme paint the picture for you, Roddy. He gets arrested and he's out in a few hours. And then what? You're at a red light and a car comes up behind you. You're gonna wonder who it is. Or you're walking to your car in the hospital garage and there's some guy standing there. Whaddaya do?"

"How 'bout Tracy's delayed coming home from the library? Or she's going to Nordstrom in White Plains? You'll worry yourself sick. You gonna shit a brick every time the kids leave the house? And, Roddy, how long does it go on? A month? A year?"

Roddy hears Danny breathing raggedly into the phone.

"You got the picture?" Danny asked.

"I got it."

"So, we don't call the cops."

"But how does he know about Angela being in Scarsdale last night? About Tracy at Sarah Lawrence?"

"Fuck if I know, Roddy. But forget the cops. We don't know who's out there."

"That's the way he wants it."

"I say we pay up. The longer we wait, the more we pay."

"Dan, what if he's *not* connected?"

"Meaning . . . ?"

"Maybe we can negotiate. Get him to lower the payoff."

"Roddy, I never dealt with this kinda thing. I know jack-shit about it."

"So we just cave?"

"Roddy, we either pay or someone could get hurt."

"How about if we hurt *him?*"

"C'mon, Roddy. What're we, back in Brooklyn?"

"I'm just wondering," Roddy said as his thoughts tumbled. "You think we can negotiate with this guy?"

"He's a shylock, not a murderer. He just wants his money."

"One question, Dan . . ."

"Yeah?"

"Will he stop at half a million?"

"Who knows, Roddy. Let's give the bastard the money and hope he goes. And we get out of McLaughlin's and lose Kenny."

"Another thing, Dan. Will he stop the clock till the debt gets paid?"

"I have no fucking idea."

Then Roddy said, "Hey, Cochise . . . this really sucks."

■

Sitting in the Sequoia, Roddy reminds himself that Tracy's oblivious to all this. She's so sensible, so practical—always comes up with a reasonable suggestion for any situation. Roddy knows it's one of Tracy's many life skills—her ability to see through the static-filled flack of daily life and then make rational decisions, stay balanced and lucid. Tracy doesn't go Irish. There's no *mad dog* in her. She has what Roddy thinks of as social intelligence—a way of doping people and things out. She thinks things through. She knows the price you can pay for acting too quickly, for giving in to your feelings.

Injudicious . . . that's how she'd describe going ballistic, losing control, going mad dog.

There was the time he'd been passed over for a promotion to associate professor at Cornell back in the days at New York Hospital.

They were dining at La Panetiere, in Rye, and Roddy'd consumed nearly a bottle of Chateau Figeac. In a swell of self-pity, he'd guzzled the wine and then asked the sommelier for a glass of Remy Martin VSOP.

"I've busted ass," he said, feeling a wine-buzz. "I've shown the residents the latest techniques in abdominal surgery. And for what? To get kicked in the ass? Passed over?"

"It's only for this year, Roddy . . ."

"I swear, Trace . . . I could go to Columbia, get a top appointment in a heartbeat."

"Roddy, you're only thirty-four years old. You'll get it next year. Don't be rash and don't be in a rush."

"But I feel . . . I feel so . . ." He was at a loss for words.

"You feel rejected. *That's* what you feel."

"Okay, rejected."

"And angry. Angry at being, how shall I put it . . . cast off? *Unwanted?*"

"Okay."

"A familiar feeling, Roddy? Floating? Motherless?"

Jesus. She knows him so well.

"It's all in your head," Tracy said. "It's not reality. You're way past your childhood and you're on the way up."

He recalls staring into her soft eyes through a booze-induced haze, thinking, *God, how beautiful she looks. And so unbelievably intelligent, sensible, and loving. How did I ever land her?*

"Don't let anger take over, Roddy."

"But everyone knows I was passed over. I feel so exposed."

"These feelings are temporary, Roddy. Never make permanent decisions in a temporary state of mind."

Never make permanent decisions in a temporary state of mind.

Roddy thinks of it as Tracy Wisdom.

Are his feelings *now* temporary? About Grange and the money and Angela getting run off the road? And his worry about Tracy and the kids? Will they pass? Roddy wonders if it would be best to tell Tracy what's going down.

Keeping secrets from her, being duplicitous: not a way to go.

But one thing's certain: it would frighten her to death. He knows she'll want to call the police.

Tell her or not?

We make our choices . . . and we live with them.

He consoles himself thinking he's sparing Tracy worry and fear.

But secrets have a way of unraveling, of ruining everything.

Sitting in the Sequoia, he looks around the garage: drills, hammers, wrenches—all the power tools—Skil, Bosch, Black & Decker, you name it. They're emblematic of their lives: the cozy Tudor house, Tracy's perennial gardens, her colorful splashes of annuals, the screened-in porch, a birdbath, a backyard facing the golf course, the manicured front lawn with its yews, boxwoods, and magnolia tree.

Domesticity. A home life.

While the house is only a physical structure—wood, stone, cement—it signifies their lives together—so carefully constructed, so meticulously planned. Now and into the future.

But now, everything's unknown.

■

Tracy's at the stove, stirring an All-Clad stockpot. The kitchen is redolent of chicken broth and vegetables. *God, it's good to be home*, he thinks, enveloping Tracy from behind. He kisses the back of her neck. She smells as delicious as ever, especially her hair. And the taste of her skin: indescribable. He even begins feeling momentarily aroused. It never fails.

"You're home early today," she says, turning to kiss him lightly.

"No evening hours," he says.

"How was your day?"

Roddy's stomach flutters.

"Straightforward surgeries. No problems. Now . . . I relax."

She's making vegetable soup, her mother's recipe from the McDonald side of the family. It's strange: soup is comfort food—best served in wintertime, but she's making it on a gorgeous spring afternoon, as though she intuitively knows he needs nurturing.

"Ann Johnson called again," she says. "She wants to know if we're renting the cottage. I told her I'd let her know tomorrow."

"Well . . . should we?" Roddy knows he sounds calm, but his insides are humming. His blood feels electrified.

"Tom hasn't said yes or no."

"We can't let him decide our summer," he says, wondering if there's a future beyond the summer, if he and Danny will get beyond this Grange situation.

Parallel trains of thought shuttle through his brain: the here-and-now with Tracy at home—and tunneling beside it, images of Grange, Kenny, Danny, and McLaughlin's. His insides feels jumpy as though something lurks inside him, and Roddy remembers that scene from *Alien* when that reptilian *thing* bursts through the poor bastard's chest.

"We can't force Tom to go," Tracy says, breaking his reverie.

"Let's take the place," he says.

"Okay. I'll call tomorrow."

He kisses her neck and whispers, "I love you."

They hold each other. Roddy wonders if she can feel his heart slamming through his chest. He thinks, *I've never kept secrets from her, but if I tell her this, what'll happen?*

Dumb question, Roddy decides, because he knows Tracy would call the police, and a special unit from the Westchester DA's office would show up. Maybe FBI agents, crew-cut guys with dark suits and skinny ties. The whole cliché.

Then what?

"We'd like you to wear a wire, Dr. Dolan," the agent would say.

And then? Grand Jury testimony.

About what? Shylocking? Extortion?

And then? Danny's words crawl through his head.

How about when Tracy's at the mall? Or a guy's standing in the hospital garage?

It's unchartered territory. Is it the Witness Protection Program? Can't be. Their lives as they know them would be over, gone for good. He turns, about to head upstairs to change clothes, when Tracy says, "Roddy, we got two more hang-ups this afternoon. I'm calling the telephone company to change our number."

Roddy's heart thumps like a bass drum.

■

Upstairs, Roddy changes into jeans, a work shirt, sweat socks, and his New Balance cross trainers—his usual homecoming ritual. Then he'll do a little garden work before dinner—turn some soil and prepare the beds for spring planting. Keep busy and don't think about McLaughlin's or Grange or Kenny.

Tracy loves when he preps the flower beds. And it's great exercise; it will dissipate the nervous energy jangling through him like a hot current. He'll move his muscles, letting his thoughts flow to a million things as he slips into a work rhythm. It's like jogging; it gets his blood flowing, thoughts roaming. Maybe something'll come to him. A solution, if there is one. There've always been answers, ways to handle situations.

He recalls Sergeant Taylor from army basic training at Fort Jackson—a million years ago. "A good soldier finds an answer to any problem," Taylor said when he couldn't find his bayonet. And then in Ranger training, Sergeant Dawson, an Alabama hard-ass, a real redneck but a guy with a good soul who said, "You young troopers gotta learn there're two kinds of soldiers . . . the quick and the dead."

Soldiering. Airborne. Rangers.

A lifetime ago. Another life, one long gone and over.

Sandy comes out of her bedroom. Her eyes are red-rimmed. Her pretty face is pale and looks drawn. She has dark circles beneath her eyes and the corners of her mouth are turned down.

He knows that look. "What's wrong, honey . . . ?"

"Nothing, really, Daddy . . ."

Nothing, really.

It's that unprompted denial of what's really on her mind, Roddy thinks. *Nothing, really . . . means really something.* Because Roddy's bullshit filter is fine-tuned—always has been, but even more so now, after all the years of hospital work and now, this McLaughlin's thing. And Sandy's voice is also a giveaway—that barely detectable warble signals she's troubled, ambushed by some inner turmoil. She's asking for some gentle paternal persuasion.

"Oh, c'mon, sweetie. You can tell me."

Her blue-green eyes look haunted. "Someone came to see you today . . ."

"What?"

A fist thumps through Roddy's chest. His hands go weak. His lips tingle.

"Who, sweetie?" he whispers as every pore in his body opens. The hairs on the back of his neck bristle.

Standing there, Sandy twists her fingers. Another of her kid cues: the finger twist—waiting to be nudged into talking. It's a ten-year-old's paucity of social subtlety; she lacks the skill of artifice we develop with life experience.

"Tell me," he says, feeling his insides quiver.

Sandy looks down. Roddy gets the feeling she wishes he wouldn't push her, and suddenly he has that coppery taste on his tongue. He wonders if he's bitten the inside of his cheek; maybe it's blood? Or stomach acid. Could be bile. Something poisonous rising from inside, devouring him.

"Please, sweetie, tell me," he says, forcing a weak smile.

"You won't tell Mommy?" she asks, moving to her bedroom. She's very circumspect, tentative. He follows her—now certain she'll talk, but where they won't be overheard. He sits on a chair. Sandy stands in front of him.

"I won't tell Mommy," he says as his head spins.

"Promise?" Her eyes are wide, imploring.

"Oh, honey, you know I can't keep secrets from Mommy," he says, thinking now how he's bullshitting Sandy—and Tracy, too.

God, how we lie to our kids.

Her fingers twist into a knot of flesh.

"Okay. I won't tell."

"Promise?"

"I promise . . ."

Now he's made the commitment.

"I didn't do anything bad," she whispers, looking down.

The afternoon sun floods the room, highlighting her blonde hair with its tinge of McDonald red. God, she's such a beautiful child.

"I know," he says, as he marvels at her Irish conscience. Christ, being a kid's tough. "You said someone came to see me today . . . ?"

"I was in front of the house with my bike . . . and he walked up to me."

Roddy thinks, *What the fuck is this?*

"And what?"

"He asked me . . . he asked . . . is your daddy Dr. Dolan?"

"And?"

A glacial sweat covers him. His thighs begin quivering.

"He said he's a patient and he wanted you to call him."

"A patient?"

She nods.

What patient? he asks himself. Which fucking patient would know where he lives? Someone came to the house? The thrashing in his chest accelerates.

"Did he say anything else?"

"Just that you would know why he was here . . ."

"Well I can't know that unless I know who the patient is."

"He gave me something for you."

He's soaked. Every nerve ending in his body fires and jangles, and his skin prickles.

"What is it?"

At her desk, Sandy picks something up.

His brain teems with images—tumbling wildly. Something dark penetrates his flesh and chills his bones—to the marrow.

She hands him a business card.

With shaking hands, he reads it:

"John M. Grange & Associates."

His heart drops into his stomach.

Beneath the name is a telephone number. The area code is a give-away: it's a Manhattan-based number, probably a cell phone.

"Did he say anything else?"

Sandy's quiet. More finger-twisting; she looks down.

"He said I'm pretty . . ."

"Well he's right. You're very, very pretty," a small, distant voice says. Roddy no longer feels his fingers. His stomach eddies; nausea rises. He's her father, her protector. And now, this?

"Honey? You said you didn't do anything bad . . ."

She nods, nearly squirming.

"Why did you say that?"

"I don't know . . ."

"Were you scared?"

"Yes."

"Why?"

"He was very big, and fat. And he had a very deep voice. I didn't like him."

"Why not?" asks that quivering voice.

Roddy waits, but she says nothing else.

"Sandy, did he do anything else?"

"No. He just touched my hair. And . . ." She looks up at him.

"And what, honey?"

"His breath stinks."

"How do you know?"

"He kissed me . . . and he smelled terrible."

"He *kissed* you?"

Roddy's chest thumps and his heart races and feels like it's dribbling its blood into his body cavity, as though it's leaking, or maybe bursting. That fat, wet-lipped, slobbering fuck came to his home? Approached his child? Touched his daughter? Kissed her?

"On the cheek . . . ," Sandy says.

"Is that all he did?"

"Yes . . ." She looks into Roddy's eyes.

"Honey, did he say anything else?"

She nods and looks away. Roddy detects her trembling.

"Please tell me, Sandy."

"He said he'd come back and we'd go for ice cream . . ."

Poison seeps through his veins, hot and toxic.

Sandy's eyes get wet.

"What's wrong, Sandy?"

"I don't want him to come back, Daddy," she says and then sinks into his arms.

He hugs her and feels her trembling.

"He won't come back, sweetie," he whispers. He kisses her head and holds her tightly.

"How do you know?"

"I just know," he whispers, closing his eyes. She feels so small and fragile in his arms. Roddy's on the verge of tears.

Oh my precious child . . . my little girl.

"Honey . . . ?"

"Yes?"

"What happened then?"

"He left."

"Where'd he go?"

"To his taxi."

"A taxi?"

"Like the ones at the train station." A brief pause.

A sob threatens to burst from his throat.

"Daddy . . . ?"

"Yes . . . ?"

"Please don't let him came back."

"He won't, honey. He won't."

"I love you, Daddy," she says with a sudden laugh.

"And I love you so much," he whispers hugging her again.

Roddy stands on wobbly legs. They're turning to liquid. He feels faint. He waits for the feeling to pass.

He goes to the door, turns, and looks at Sandy. "I promise. He won't come back."

Sitting at her desk, she smiles.

Outside Sandy's room, he stands in a haze, as though he's in the English moors on a foggy night. In a horror movie. He's floating down the stairs, though he can't be sure. It's the strangest feeling, something he'd expect in a dream, but it's real. This is actually happening in his life, to his family, and in Danny's life, too. Pangs of rage and fear stab at him. A lethal fuming leeches through him—a toxic bubbling of repugnance. This is unimaginably grotesque, the ugliest thing that's ever happened in his life. Sandy's his *daughter*. Ten years old. *Innocent*. Naïve. Unsullied by the ugly shit and corruption in this fucked up world.

Something molten stirs inside him. Incendiary. It threatens to erupt.

Roddy thinks: *This bastard*. This slobbering wet-lipped fuck comes to his home, walks up to his *child* whom he would do anything to protect—absolutely *anything!*—and asks for her father, and tells her she's pretty.

And he fucking *touches* her . . . *kisses* her with those wet, sloppy liver-lips and his rancid saliva lingers on her skin. He moves his ponderously obese body close to her so his putrid breath's in her face. And says he'll come back. *For ice cream*. A fucking threat—abduction, kidnapping—like Elizabeth Smart out in Utah.

Grange, you scum-of-the-earth motherfucker. Scares the shit out of Sandy, his daughter. Makes her feel dirty, like any child abuser would, makes her feel sullied and worthless because he's a pervert, a predator, that's what he is, a wormlike mind-fucker, working his filthy shit on her, getting his rocks off—laughing to himself, knowing she'll tell her father—because he knows she fears him without even knowing why, but in her ten-year-old kid's mind she knows he's loathsome, dangerous, and dirty; and Grange is certain Roddy'll get the message.

He's mind-fucked Roddy's little girl, because he planted some ugly shit in Sandy's brain; he might as well have used a scalpel and suturing needle because he embedded a bucket of filth inside her she'll never forget as long as she lives.

And now, Roddy's in some fucked-up fuming state, seething, standing in the den—yes, he's in the downstairs den now, though he doesn't remember how he got here—but he's pacing like an animal as adrenaline pumps through his body, and he's feeling heat, seething with rage, a scalding fury—right here in the den of the lovely home where he and Tracy have made their lives, the home this loan shark violated . . . and it's not just telephone hang-ups here and at Danny's house and at the office; there was Angela being run off the road, and then, *this.*

Roddy now understands the expression *making my blood boil,* because he can *feel* his blood vessels throbbing, feels blood bubbling through him, feels his arteries spasm—feels his brain pulsing in his skull. And Roddy feels more venomous than a cobra, he feels like an incendiary device—a roadside bomb in Iraq or Afghanistan, ready to detonate.

Sandy, Sandy, Sandy . . . my little girl.

Roddy waits for it to ebb, but it's an insane flood of love and fear and rage and worry and overwhelming uncertainty. He shudders as he tries to calm himself, and he thinks that maybe his thoughts will stop their frenzied tumbling. Maybe his heart will slow and this poisonous brew will somehow drain away and leave him feeling steady, rational—so he thinks of Tracy at the stove and imagines Sandy studying and Tom probably sulking in his bedroom. He knows—at least for the moment—they're safe; Roddy knows too that he must think clearly and realizes he's got to choke off the fury and stifle the adrenaline flooding every cell in his body.

He asks himself if it's truly happening, if Tracy and the kids could *really* be in danger. Isn't that what Grange wants him to think? Isn't *that* the game? The threat?

Maybe he *should* tell Tracy. It might be best for her and the kids to spend a few weeks at her sister's house in Nutley. Just pack up, pick up, and leave.

And do what? Pay Grange?

Would that put an end to this? Make him go away?

Or, is that what a patsy would do? Pay up and shut up?

And then what? Get bulldozed into paying more? Like a weak-willed chump who can be steamrolled into paying and paying and then ponying up even more. A candy-assed loser, a piss-poor pantywaist terrified for his family's well-being. Isn't that what extortion's all about? You pay, and then you cough up more because Grange defines the worst in human nature—predatory greed and the need for *more*. And more after that. He preys on fear, like a vulture needs carrion, like a parasite needs a host.

It's a highjacking. Guys like Grange truck in fear. And Grange knows that he and Danny—Kenny, too—are rank amateurs, just a threesome of schmucks, ripe for picking.

Jesus. It would feel comforting to tell Tracy. But he can't do that. And moving the kids? Ripping them out of school, having them live with their cousins in Nutley? For how long? Absurd.

Okay, maybe Grange is connected, Roddy thinks. *Why does his card say* Associates? *Is it real, or just some cheap masquerade designed to intimidate nobodies like the three Irish know-nothings who've fallen into this shit pit. Won't this slimy bastard just want more?*

An avalanche of thoughts pours over Roddy: Grange, Kenny, Danny, McLaughlin's, Tracy, the kids; and there's Angela, Danny's kids, money, threats. It streams through his brain and fills Roddy with rawness that makes him feel like he's swallowed shards of glass.

Grange is a threat—to their future—to their whole way in the world. The danger is real, and it's out there. Waiting. It has to be handled.

Chapter 19

R oddy tells Tracy he forgot something at the office.
"I'll be back in forty-five minutes at most."

His insides churn; it's that queasy, sick sensation he had as a kid, just before a fight went down. But it's more than physical: it's a gnawing dread, a profound sense of his own smallness in the face of a dark and vast unknown.

Roddy thinks there must be a way to take control—to make the unknown less daunting, more knowable. And then he wonders, *How do you downsize fear?*

"No rush, honey," Tracy says. "We won't eat till 6:30, maybe later."

He mentions papers for a committee meeting as he rushes out the kitchen door.

Lies, deceit, secrets . . . but there's no choice, not now.

He jumps into the Sequoia, raises the garage door, and backs out. He stomps on the gas pedal; the tires squeal and he heads toward the town center. He suddenly realizes he's doing fifty. Jesus! Gotta be careful not to drive like a maniac, which can happen when he gets zoned out and goes into another world.

He lets up on the gas pedal, The Sequoia rumbles, slows, cruises down Midland Avenue, turns onto Pondfield. Roddy passes a botanical garden, a music school, glances at the speedometer, and realizes he's hitting fifty-five.

Slow down . . . slow down . . . take it easy. You'll be pulled over and get a ticket.

But his innards are bursting; they feel like a rat's scrambling around in his guts. His hands are weak—like string—on the steering wheel. His thoughts swirl furiously; he hears a car horn blare, swerves, almost passes a red light, and realizes he can't recall driving to this intersection. He's in some kind of altered state.

Further down Pondfield, he pulls over to the shoulder, throws the Sequoia in "park," and steps on the emergency brake. He sits there, kills time, and knows if he waits long enough, calm will come.

Right now, he can't think rationally—it's all a mind rush, a charged feeling like his nerves are in a synaptic frenzy. He's so primed he's sure he has a fever. Jesus, he can't be a fucking cave man. He remembers "Doc" Schechter, the trainer at Herbie's gym saying, "You can't be an animal in the ring, Roddy. You go in there and execute a *strategy.*" And he learned to do that—fight according to a plan, not just swing wildly.

Same thing in the Rangers. Sergeant Dawson always said, "You don't just wait for the enemy. You formulate a plan and then execute it, soldier. You make it happen and do it *your* way."

So Roddy closes his eyes and breathes slowly, steadily. He ignores the ramped-up slamming of his heart. His chin drops to his chest; he drops his arms so they hang limp. He feels his legs loosen, he can feel the muscles easing, like a stretched rubber band losing its tension.

Just relax . . . try to decompress, he tells himself. *Can't go numb, but can't keep feeling so jangled. Gotta move on from this point—just flow forward, like a river—not get caught in a backwash of swirling eddies. Move downstream, with the current, toward some conclusion.*

In Ranger school you always made a plan. Then you went on offense. You never played defense. And now, you're a grown man with a man's ability to know the world—and you *deal* with it.

Just fucking deal with it.

Isn't that what you did as a Ranger? Isn't that what Sergeant Dawson would say?

Soldier, you take away the enemy's advantage; you take the ini-tiative and make your move. And the enemy? You deal with that sumbitch.

He was an Airborne Ranger. Jumped out of planes and hit the ground running. Handled every kind of life-threatening shit: swamps, deserts, mountains, snow. There was Survival School, Jump School, Sniper School, infiltration, demolitions, field surgery, counterinsur-gency—everything. There was danger every day, and being a Ranger meant that threat, even menace, was part of the job description.

And remember, now you're a surgeon. You deal with life and death every working day of your life. You're no stranger to death. It sits in waiting every day of your life. That's what surgery's about.

And this Grange affair is like surgery.

As Dr. Henry Dennis, his mentor during his residency would say, "Before you operate, you weigh everything: the risk of surgery against the danger of doing nothing. You consider the pros and the cons. It's a balancing act."

Or as Danny would say when it comes to investing, "You've got to know your own risk-tolerance and your investment goals. It's a risk-reward ratio."

Do the risks outweigh the possible rewards, the benefits?

What risks? What benefits? What, what, what . . . ?

This Grange thing boils down to one thing: do you take a chance on doing nothing weighed against the chance of doing what you know must be done?

Because this sumbitch will come back; he definitely will. Grange's words to Sandy are telegraphic, predictive—he'll come back for more. It won't be a one-shot payoff.

Roddy suddenly realizes he's at the side of a major town road late on a weekday afternoon. People are getting off from work; they stop off at the mall or go to the supermarket to buy fixings for dinner. The town is after-work busy, just tumbling with people. They're going about their usual routines in a state of benighted normalcy—like a

Norman Rockwell painting. People are cruising by in their high-end SUVs—Escalades and Mercedes crossovers—maybe they'll think he's got car trouble. Or possibly, he's sick and can't drive. Needs help. It's a town of good neighbors.

They'll hit the Bluetooth button or pop out a hand-held cell phone and call 911.

Within minutes, a Bronxville cop will pull up, get out of the car, and approach slowly, maybe even warily, because these days, a routine traffic stop can be deadly. The cop'll turn on the recording device strapped to his belt.

Are you in trouble, sir?

And, he *is*.

He's in deep-shit trouble.

And, exactly what does he do?

People have told him he funnels things down to basics. The residents, interns, and medical students he teaches say he's a master at making complexities simple and digestible. Other surgeons and OR nurses have told him that under stress—of surgery, or anything for that matter—he's a *clear thinker*.

So think clearly, Roddy Dolan. Use what you learned in the Rangers. And what you've learned as a surgeon. But more important, use what you know about life, and people. Use what you learned as a kid on those hard Brooklyn streets. The learning curve had to be worth something. What do you know about Grange? And what do you know about Danny—and Kenny? These are the players.

What makes them tick?

What does each gain in this situation? What does each lose? How does this play out? He recalls telling Tom there are consequences to every decision in life.

And this thing impacts the rest of their lives, and their families. Once you act, there's no going back.

Sitting behind the wheel, he weighs everything. A throbbing headache begins deep in his skull, moves forward, and stabs into his eyes. Looking at the dashboard clock, Roddy realizes he's been sitting behind the wheel for a half hour. Has it been that long? Seems like a minute—maybe two. Roddy realizes he's thrashed through a dozen scenarios; he's gone through all the alternatives and permutations. He's funneled things down to basics, and it *is* basic. It's elemental, maybe even instinctual.

■

He's decided what to do. It's chancy, even dangerous, but there's no risk-free choice. They're in a swamp of danger, worse than anything he encountered at Fort Jackson or Fort Bragg in the Carolinas. But he knows something must be done. Because one thing's certain: *we're all creatures of habit*, he thinks. In a sense, we're all the same, yet a bit different, too. And that goes for Grange. Once we find a melody we like, we keep dancing to it, again and again. Habits and patterns tell the story. Therein lies the solution to Grange. Character defines us. It's a way of being.

He fishes out his cell phone and presses a speed-dial number.

Dan picks up on the first ring.

"Danny, it's Roddy. You alone?"

"Yeah. What's up?"

Expectation seeps through Dan's voice. It's nervous energy, tense and edgy. It's been three days now. And the juice is running.

"Grange came to my house today."

"You're *kidding.*"

Roddy hears Dan's wheeze through the phone.

"He spoke to Sandy and gave her his card."

"That fat bastard."

"He came to my house—where I *live.*" Even as he says it, a high-pitched ringing begins in his ears. "And he kissed her."

"There's no doubt it's a threat, Roddy."

"Oh, it gets better. He said he'll come back and take her for ice cream."

"My God."

Roddy pictures the spittle on Grange's lips. His mouth suddenly feels dry.

"Look, Danny, I know you've got cash in your safe deposit box."

"Yeah . . . so?"

"Can you come up with fifteen grand in hundred-dollar bills?"

"Sure . . ."

"I'll do the same . . ."

A momentary pause. Dan's wheezing big time now.

"Roddy, that's thirty grand. A month's interest. It's barely a dent."

"I have a plan."

Dan's breathing sounds like a steam engine. He could launch into a full-blown asthma attack. "A plan? What kinda plan?"

"It's a first step. I'll handle it," Roddy says.

"Whaddaya mean, *handle* it? Thirty thousand's nothing."

"I know." Roddy's guts clench.

"What're we gonna do?"

"Dan, I'll take care of it . . ."

"Roddy, you can't buy time with this guy. For him, time *is* money."

"I'm not buying time."

"Then what's up?"

"You'll see."

"C'mon Roddy, don't jerk me off."

"*Dan!*" he shouts.

Dan's wheezing like an accordion. Roddy waits. Dan's breathing more evenly.

"Danny, you trust me?"

"With my life, but . . ."

"If you trust me the way I trust you, you'll do exactly what I say." Roddy's tongue feels like a strip of leather in his mouth.

Dan goes silent; the wheezing lessens. They say nothing. But somehow, his kemosabe seems to understand.

"Roddy . . . ," Dan says, his voice trailing off.

"Dan . . . trust me . . ."

"Roddy, this guy isn't Cootie Weiss, and we're not back in Brooklyn.

"Dan, if we don't want to be hung out to dry, you gotta trust me."

Except for some low-level static, there's silence on the line.

"Dan, tomorrow morning, first thing—go to your safe deposit box and take out $15,000. I'll do the same."

"Yeah . . . ?"

"I'm calling Grange. I'll ask him to meet us at McLaughlin's tomorrow evening, 6:30. Get into the city by train. Leave your car at the Tuckahoe train station."

"Why?"

"Because I *said* so. Just get to McLaughlin's. We'll meet there at six."

"What then?"

"Dan, just have the cash. At six."

"Roddy . . . I need to know what . . ."

"Just *do* it. And one other thing."

"Yeah?"

"Don't say a word to Kenny."

"I wouldn't give that asshole the time of day."

"I'll call Grange and get back to you soon."

"Roddy, you sure about this?"

"I'm sure, Cochise."

■

The Stop & Shop's a madhouse.

The place teems like a roiling ocean. The noise is stentorian. Little kids are screaming, running in full glucose withdrawal, and grabbing at Kit Kats and Starbursts and Twizzlers. Mothers are on cell phones—harried, steering shopping carts like bumper cars. There are women in sweats, black Spandex running tights, Fila shirts, athletic shoes; kids are in jeans and baggy pants, jabbering, texting, and laughing; confused older men are trying to decipher shopping lists, wandering around the store's mysteries. Everyone's scurrying and shopping; there are people walking, chattering into cell phones, and wearing headsets and iPods—it's bedlam.

There's an endless maze of produce, piled packages, canned goods, jars, stock boys, butchers, fishmongers; there's the deli counter; dizzying aisles stocked with sodas, bottled waters, juices, and countless dairy products all beneath a cavernous florescent hue. Roddy finds it upending. Maddening.

How on earth does Tracy deal with this every day?

He's been here hundreds of time, yet he feels lost.

At the service counter he asks where the disposable cell phones are kept. The woman points to an aisle at the far end and resumes working the Powerball machine for a line of customers.

He passes the produce section—it's piled high with out-of-season fruits from Chile and Mexico. *Eat that shit and you're lucky you don't get salmonella or E. coli,* Roddy thinks, *or some other gut-twisting, parasitic infection.* Roddy moves to where the woman pointed. After passing ceiling-high stacks of cereal boxes—Apple Jacks, Kix, Froot Loops, and Rice Chex—Roddy realizes he's in the wrong aisle.

He knows he's totally primed, and with the bright lights, Yankee Stadium noise level, and shrieking kids, he's not thinking clearly. *Empty your head,* Roddy tells himself. *Everything's on the line and this is no time to let feelings—anger, fear, or uncertainty—take over. Man up, jackass. Time to take charge.*

He sees an array of cell phones, sifts through them, and picks a Motorola TracFone. He reads the package instructions. It's a prepay thing, costs $9.99. A cash deal, no bill. No contract. Just use it and toss it.

Disposable.

Untraceable.

Prepay cards hang from the display. He grabs one with thirty minutes on it.

Roddy sees a line at the service desk, at least ten people. He glances toward the cashier lines—they're backed up like traffic on I-95; not an option. So he stands at the service desk line. The wait seems interminable. Tracy's expecting him and wondering what's keeping him. His feet feel like moving; he wants to jump up and down, like when he had to piss real bad as a kid.

Roddy feels immobilized, rooted into forced passivity. Just standing there, waiting, reminds him of his time in the Rangers when they were on a forced march in the Carolina swamps. Ticks were sucking his blood, but the platoon couldn't stop. They had to get out of the bog first, and he endured a slow bleed while every cell in his body screamed for him to rip off his fatigues, strip down, and burn the ticks off with a cigarette. But they had to get to the target—and meanwhile, get drained.

And now he's being sapped, not by ticks, but by a loan shark because the juice is running, each minute of each day, and he's standing in line amidst the clamor of this loony bin. A thought comes to him: he could bolt from the store, phone in hand. Like when they were kids stealing comic books and candy from Leo's. Just cop the merchandise and take off.

But it's not an option.

What the fuck's taking so long? Roddy wonders. He cranes his neck and sees a woman at the counter arguing with the clerk, something about a price discrepancy. Her voice rises above the din, it's ear-drum-piercing, shrill. The clerk tries to placate not agitate the woman. At least two more minutes pass; Roddy could explode. Finally, the dispute is resolved.

The line moves quickly. Only three more people before him.

It's his turn. He pays cash.

The clerk scans the prepaid airtime card to activate it.

At the end of the counter, Roddy sets the TracFone down, peels away the metallic-gray strip on the prepay card, and sees a fifteen-digit number. He enters the PIN number into the "Add Airtime" screen beneath the phone's "Prepaid" menu. It'll take a few minutes for the phone to register; once it's activated and Roddy's plugged into the network, he'll have thirty minutes of talk time.

■

Parked in the Sequoia, he sees the cell is registered. Some invisible wave has floated through the ether, slithered into this plastic device—and not into any other—and done its thing. Electronics. Fucking amazing.

Roddy fishes in his wallet and slips out Grange's business card. Just looking at his name brings on queasiness; his hands go weak.

Pressing the numbers, he almost drops the phone. He misdials and tries again.

"Yeah . . ."

"Mr. Grange. It's Roddy Dolan."

The fat man breathes heavily into the phone. *It's gotta be tough getting enough air to oxygenate all that pendulous flesh*, thinks Roddy.

Hearing Grange suck air in and out, Roddy wonders if Sandy heard the same sound.

The static-filled silence is excruciating.

"I see you got my message," Grange rumbles.

"Message received."

Roddy's throat feels like a porcupine is sitting inside. The late afternoon sun pours in through the Sequoia's windshield, and Roddy feels like he's baking in an oven.

"Whatcha gonna do, Mr. MD?"

"We have money."

"Yeah?"

More puffing as air rushes past Grange's hair-filled nostrils.

"Can you come to the restaurant tomorrow evening at 6:30?"

"What's your rush?"

Is this bloodsucking leech kidding?

Roddy's legs tighten. If he squeezes any harder on the cell phone, it'll shatter.

"Let's get this over with," he says in an even voice.

"That's pretty quick, Doc."

Roddy's heart stampedes and then stutters. For a moment, he doubts he can go through with it. But he hates wavering; he loathes indecision.

"I said we have money." Acid roils in his stomach and crawls up his gullet. That strange taste coats his tongue, metal mixed with sulfur. Hot steel and rotten eggs.

A burst of static fills the earpiece.

Roddy is thinking: this is agony. How do I get through the next minute?

"I might just show up, motherfucker," Grange rumbles. "Gotta make a phone call, though . . ."

More static, crackling.

Grange speaks, but Roddy can't make it out.

"What?" he says.

Another snag of static; Grange's voice fades and then breaks up.

"You there . . . ?" he hears Grange ask.

"I lost you. What'd you say?" asks Roddy.

"Nothin', Doc."

The static clears. Grange comes through clearly.

"One thing, Mr. Grange . . ."

"Yeah?"

"Let's keep this civil. We just want to get this done. So come alone."

Don't blow it. Stay calm.

"Whatsa matter . . . you don't like my guy?"

"We're running a respectable place and we don't want thugs."

"I *always* have protection."

A volt of panic thrums through Roddy.

"Protection? From *us?*"

Roddy sounds appalled, aggrieved. Protection? From a doctor, an accountant, and Kenny Egan, a skinny Irish wannabe?

"I'm respectable looking, is that it?"

"That's it," Roddy says.

"What if I bring someone?"

"Look, Mr. Grange, we're four businessmen," he says, sounding beseeching, like some namby-pamby-I'm-scared-shitless kind of guy.

More silence.

Roddy wonders, *What was this thing about his making a phone call?*

"So I'm hearing you correctly, Mr. MD? You got the money for me?"

"We've got money for you."

Another pause, interminable. The reception begins fading. The call could be dropped. Fucking cheap cell phone. Roddy twists around—leans left, then right—angling for a better transmission wave.

"Six-thirty?" Grange asks.

"Six-thirty."

"You have the money. I'll be there."

Grange hangs up.

Roddy presses the off button.

The phone slips from his hand and drops to the seat.

Thunder crashes through Roddy's head. The parking lot spins. He closes his eyes and waits for the dizziness to pass.

Suddenly, Roddy slams his open palms against the steering wheel. Then again, violently, with a deep thump. His fingers wrap tightly around it, pushing, bending it back. Then pulling, hands locked on the leather-covered wheel, his feet press to the floor, thighs and legs extended. The steering wheel quivers in his grasp. He imagines it's Grange's throat and he's crushing his windpipe. He opens his eyes and squints at the sun glare bouncing off car bumpers and windows. A torrent of pressure builds in his skull and blood surges behind his eyeballs.

Roddy goes limp and feels weak, near collapse. He waits for the feeling to pass.

Calmer now, he opens his eyes, looks down, and then flips his own cell from its holster. Dialing Danny, his fingers still shake. He feels damp, drained.

Can I go numb? Drift into that zone where I feel weightless . . . like jumping from an airplane . . . the wind-rush, just floating . . .

"What's up?" Danny says.

"We're on. Tomorrow evening, six thirty. Be there by six with the cash."

"Listen, Roddy . . ."

"Oh, and Dan . . . ?"

"Yeah?"

"It'll be a late night, so tell Angela."

"How late?"

"Midnight. Maybe later. We gotta talk taxes."

"Jesus, Roddy. Can't we . . . ?"

"We can't talk now, Dan. Tomorrow at six."

He hangs up.

He feels clammy, cold. His insides ripple like the surface of a windblown lake.

Calm down . . . just stay cool . . .

He dials Ivan Snyder's home number. Ivan's wife, Sylvia, answers. They pass a few pleasantries. Tension threads through him as moments tick by.

"Sylvia, is Ivan home?"

"No Roddy, he's at the club. You have his cell phone number, don't you?"

"Sure, Sylvia. I'll call him. And thanks."

He gets Ivan on the phone. Roddy hears conversation and glasses clinking. Music is playing. Then comes a burst of laughter.

"Hey, Roddy, what's up?" Ivan says.

"Ivan, I need a favor . . ."

"Sure, partner. What is it?"

"Ivan," a woman's voice says. It's creamy, *sotto voce*. "Is it your wife?"

"Hold on, Roddy," Ivan says.

Ivan's hand goes over the mouthpiece. Roddy hears muffled voices.

"What's up, Roddy?" Ivan asks, back on the line.

"I have a light day. My last surgery's at one. An umbilical hernia repair—Mrs. Morelli. Can you do it for me? Something's come up and I have to leave early. I'll make it up to you."

"Sure thing, Roddy. No problem."

"Thanks Ivan. I owe you."

■

Roddy drives to a nearby Shell service station. Suddenly he's thankful for the Sequoia—this gigantic vehicle with its 26.4-gallon gas tank. Only the other day he was thinking seriously of dumping the guzzler. But for now, it's a keeper.

He gets out of the Sequoia, slips his credit card into the slot, punches in his zip code, hits enter, and waits for authorization. Moments pass; the read-out tells him to pick up the nozzle and start pumping. He clunks the nozzle into the gas tank aperture and begins filling up with premium, not the midgrade stuff he usually uses. He'll need high performance from the Sequoia.

The lever on the pump head snaps; the tank is full. He tops it off with a few extra pumps. Not supposed to do that. Something about leaking hydrocarbons increasing atmospheric carbon dioxide. Climate change, global warming, shit, the world's coming to an end.

Fuck the environment. His personal space—his sanctuary—needs saving.

Squeegee washing the car's windows, he thinks about the plan. Plenty could go wrong. After all, there's no such thing as perfection. Not in medicine, not in surgery, not in life. But there's no choice. Leaning against the Sequoia, he goes over it again. It'll require careful preparation, just like surgery. But it's more complicated than surgery because others are involved and they're not necessarily on the same team. There's no common goal.

Roddy gets back in the Sequoia and heads home. Driving by a mini-mall he pulls into a parking lot in front of a Burger King. An odd thought comes to him: *I'll bet that fat bastard Grange can down five Double Whoppers in five minutes.*

Using his own cell phone, he dials the restaurant.

Kenny picks up.

"Look, Kenny, I spoke with Grange. He'll be at the restaurant tomorrow night at six thirty, so be there. We have money."

"You got it all?"

"Just be there."

"Sure thing, Roddy. I knew we could count on you."

Roddy ends the call and slips the cell into his holster.

He thinks about the conversations he's just had with Grange, Dan, and Kenny. And about other talks he, Dan, and Kenny have had.

Now he must execute the plan.

Just like surgery.

Like in the Rangers. He'll have to make it work.

And there's no going back, not now.

He drives home and pulls the Sequoia into the garage.

There's work to do. He's gotta think it out—every detail—because he has to control whatever he can. The rest is up to fate . . . and luck.

Roddy knows he'll keep it simple. Simple things are best.

It *has* to get done. The right way.

Because now, there's no choice.

Chapter 20

It's nearly noon when Roddy leaves the hospital. He barely slept last night; an endless stream of thoughts reeled through his head like a movie track. He revisited the plan, again and again, trying to think about every variation and possibility. Lots could go wrong, but for the hundredth time he tells himself there's no choice.

Bone-tired, he got out of bed and trudged through his morning rituals. When Tracy asked if anything was wrong—she can read him like a wall clock—he said, "Just a headache."

"That's a first," she said. "Are you uptight about tonight's meeting?"

"Not really. You do what you have to do. We're getting out."

He dragged himself to the hospital and did his surgeries. While in the OR, he was needle sharp; everything else evaporated. He was in by 7:00, out by noon; he now feels energized. *Surgery always does that*, he thinks. It's restorative. Roddy heads down the hospital corridor, takes the elevator to the subbasement, and exits through a door leading to the garage.

It's a quick trip home, and when he gets there, he realizes he can't recall making the drive. There it is again: he was in that strange trance-like state, almost a fugue. Upstairs, he puts on a pair of slacks, a blue oxford shirt, and a tweed sport jacket. Downstairs, he grabs his North Face insulated nylon jacket from the hallway closet and tosses it into the storage area of the Sequoia. He goes to the mud room, snatches his Alpine Woods hiking boots, and stuffs them into the hatch area, too.

At the dinette table, he grabs a pad and writes a note for Tracy. His hand trembles, so he writes slowly, trying to keep it neat, and hopes it won't reveal how wired he feels. The cursive writing looks like a child's script. Ridiculous. A total giveaway something's wrong. Tracy'll pick up on it in a second. So he crumples the paper, tosses it in the kitchen trash bin, and begins over, printing in block letters.

TRACE:
HAVE LEFT FOR THE CITY. MEETING WITH DANNY AND KENNY. THEN GOING TO DANNY'S OFFICE TO DISCUSS RESTAURANT AND TAXES. I'LL BE HOME LATE. DON'T WAIT UP.

LOVE YOU,
RODDY

He leaves the note on the table, goes to the dining room breakfront, opens a drawer, and grabs the key to the safe deposit box.

In the garage, he eyes the gardening tools. He shoves the rakes, hoe, weed-whacker, and brooms aside and grabs two long-handled spade-shaped shovels and a heavy-duty pickax. He sets them in the Sequoia's hatch area. He cuts thick plastic from a roll, wraps the tools, and ties them with twine. He jams the bundle into the space.

He takes four Rayovac Workhorse twin-tube lanterns from a shelf, sets them in a corrugated box, and shoves the container into the hatch area. He sets a beam searchlight into the box.

At the workbench, he snaps open his three-tiered toolbox. It brims with hammers, screwdrivers, a wire-cutter, pliers, an assortment of tools. Must weigh forty pounds. He snaps the latches shut, hauls the box to the Sequoia's rear, and nestles it against the box of lanterns. It's all secure; it won't jiggle around.

On the workbench are boxes of Hefty garbage bags. He extracts a few—two different sizes—and stuffs them into the front passenger's door pocket.

He decides to get new work gloves, gets into the Sequoia, and drives into town. At Keeler's Hardware, he buys three pairs of canvas work gloves, for a total of forty-five dollars. He pays with his MasterCard and asks the clerk to cut off the plastic tags.

He tosses the work gloves into the hatch area and then heads to the Chase Bank on Palmer Avenue. He approaches the assistant vice president, Ginny, a tall, white-haired woman who's been branch manager for years. "How are you, Doctor Dolan?" she asks with a broad smile.

"Fine, Ginny. I'd like to get into my safe deposit box," he says, realizing any attempt at small talk will fail miserably. He's too primed.

"How's Mrs. Dolan?" Ginny asks, as they walk to the safe deposit file.

"Just fine," Roddy says, trying to sound upbeat, but he knows his act is lame.

Ginny hands him the sign-in card. He signs it; she slips it into the electronic time-stamp machine, and he's admitted to the safe deposit area. The teller, a young man with gelled hair and tortoise-shell glasses, uses two keys, opens the door, extracts Roddy's box, hands it to him, and escorts him to a booth.

Inside the enclosure, Roddy counts out fifteen bundles of hundred-dollar bills, all banded—a thousand to a bundle. He slips the bills into an oversized brown envelope and stuffs it into his breast pocket. He returns the box to the teller and leaves the bank.

Roddy slips the envelope into the glove compartment and locks it. He drives home, returns the safe deposit key to the breakfront, and then drives to the office. Parking behind the building, he enters through the rear entrance. He passes a white-coated technician from the dentist's office on the first floor, nods, and keeps walking. He hustles up the stairway to the second floor and enters the office. It's empty. Brenda won't be in until 3:00 when Ivan's office hours begin.

In examining room 1, Roddy opens a cabinet and peers at the

array of pharmaceuticals. Over the years, drug company representatives have flooded him and Ivan with samples. They pitch the latest in their ever-expanding pharmacopoeia of miracle medicines, even Viagra and Cialis—to surgeons. And they've changed tactics: they used to send male representatives—"detail men"—but now, it's another story: stylish young women oozing estrogen materialize in the waiting room. Pharmaceutical reps—gorgeous and smart. It's a whole new ballgame.

He rummages through the cabinets: lidocaine, prednisone, Klonopin, Xanax, Lyrica, Prozac, Zoloft, Kadian, Vicodin, Oxycontin, and a host of salves, creams, lotions, along with samples of pills and capsules for every conceivable ill.

Roddy narrows the choice down to two: clonazepam or lorazepam—generic preparations he's used hundreds of times over the years. He thinks about their pharmacologic actions and the duration of each drug's effects. Roddy chooses clonazepam, otherwise known by its trade name Klonopin, a standard benzodiazepine—a benzo or trank, as it's called on the streets—used by most physicians in their daily practices. With his desk calculator, he does some fifth-grade arithmetic—converts kilograms to pounds and calculates the dosage he wants.

Back in the examining room, at the countertop near a sink, Roddy empties the tablets onto a paper towel. For good measure, he adds two more. He goes to his consultation room, takes a white porcelain mortar and pestle he bought on eBay a few years back for $14.99 as an office decoration, and brings it to the examining room.

He tosses the tablets in the hollow of the mortar, and, using the pestle, grinds them to a fine powder. He pours the powder into a plastic vial, caps it, and slips the vial into the side pocket of his sports jacket. He rinses the mortar and pestle with tap water, dries them, and returns them to the consultation room.

Back to the countertop: he removes two gloves from the box of CareMates disposable, powder-free latex gloves, slips them on his hands, and then pulls two paper towels from the metal dispenser on the wall.

In the consultation room, Roddy inserts a key into the bottom drawer of his desk. He slides the drawer out and sees what he wants. It's been sitting in the locked drawer for years. Just looking at the thing makes him shudder and brings him back to another time in his life. Does he really want to do this? But Roddy decides this is no time for doubt.

Wearing the latex gloves, he picks it up. He's very careful, making sure to leave no fingerprints as he handles it, and does what he has to do. He slips it into his jacket pocket, goes back to the examining room, rips off the gloves, and tosses them in the bin labeled "Medical Waste." He decides to take the box of surgical gloves with him.

Sitting at his desk, he goes over his plan. Roddy knows the note he left Tracy is nothing but a pallid construction of lies—all bullshit. But that's life—at least that's his life at this moment. You do what you gotta do and go where you gotta go; that was the rule in Brooklyn and in the Rangers, too. Just get it done.

Roddy realizes it's 2:30. Time to go. He makes certain he has everything; he turns the lights off, locks the office, and heads down the rear stairs to the car. He rummages through the Sequoia's rear hatch, rearranges the toolbox, and sets it inside the spare tire well. He empties his pockets and makes sure he has everything. He sets the box of surgical gloves into the box with the lanterns.

He has some time to kill, so he stops off at a Nick's luncheonette. It's midafternoon and the place is nearly empty; just a few people sip coffee in two booths. The counterman approaches and wipes his hands on his apron. Roddy has no appetite, but it's gonna be a long day, so he'll force himself to eat something. "I'll have a tuna sandwich on toasted rye, no mayo," he says. "And a cup of coffee."

When the sandwich arrives, he feels queasy, realizes he must fight nausea, but manages to nibble half the sandwich and washes it down with black coffee. The brew tastes like sulfuric acid.

At 3:30, he gets into the Sequoia, drives through local streets, and gets onto the Cross County Parkway, heading west. He drives to the Saw Mill River Parkway and heads south.

Traffic is light in the Manhattan-bound direction, but the outbound highway is already choked with early rush-hour traffic. It seems that rush hour begins earlier with each passing year. The Saw Mill cuts through Yonkers and becomes the Henry Hudson Parkway, where Roddy drives through Riverdale, crossing the Henry Hudson Bridge into the Inwood section of Manhattan. Living in Manhattan, as he did during his internship and residency, seems a lifetime away. And it was—a different life from the one he's living now. A life that could screech to a complete halt if something goes wrong tonight. But there's no time to think about that.

He heads south with the Hudson River on his right and Riverside Drive above him on the left. He passes the Cloisters and the span of the George Washington Bridge arching over the water into New Jersey.

The parkway becomes the West Side Highway. He exits at West 56th Street and drives south on 12th Avenue, weaving through commercial truck traffic. The midafternoon sun is dazzling on this mild day, and he lowers his sun visor. On 12th Avenue, he passes parking garages, truck depots, industrial warehouses, a FedEx complex, some seedy-looking diners, a huge H&H Bagels outlet, and a sprawl of factory buildings and service stations.

Another ten blocks and he'll be within walking distance of McLaughlin's. Glancing at the dashboard clock, he realizes he'll get to the restaurant far too soon. So he'll park the car in the garage where McLaughlin's has a monthly arrangement for valet service. Then he'll meander around the theater district and gawk at the stores, restaurants, and theaters—watch the matinee crowds—just another anonymous soul wandering the city's streets.

Roddy does his best not to think of what he's planned, but he finds himself wondering about the chain of events that led Danny and him to where they are right now. He contemplates the quirks and infinite accidents of fate, quotidian happenings in the stream of time—unforeseen, strangely sequential—funneling down to any given moment in this thing called life.

If I hadn't been in the library that day, I'd never've met Tracy . . .

If I hadn't been in the Acropolis Diner that night, I'd never've been in on that burglary . . . if Danny's mother hadn't asked teachers to write those notes, I'd never've gone into the army . . . then no field surgery training . . . and then what? If . . . if . . . if . . .

You can go crazy thinking like this.

And though he tries not to, Roddy thinks about the nightmare ahead of him.

The next ten hours could decide the rest of his life.

Chapter 21

Roddy and Danny sit at the table in McLaughlin's rear office. Danny looks haggard, depleted. Purplish circles crouch beneath his eyes like puffy sacks of dough. His face sags.

"We were prey the moment Grange walked into this room," Danny says.

Roddy wonders if Dan's conceding something, because he hasn't asked about the plan. Roddy thinks maybe Dan doesn't want to hear it.

"Correction, kemosabe," Roddy says. "It began when Kenny borrowed money."

Nodding, Dan looks like a jackrabbit ready to sprint.

"I thought of moving Angela and the kids," Dan says.

"Where?"

"Her sister's place, in Queens."

"For how long?"

"I don't know."

"Just rip the kids out of school?"

Danny shakes his head and presses his lips together.

"You think they can't be found?"

Danny shrugs his shoulders, looking beleaguered.

"There're always choices, Roddy."

"Yeah? What choices?"

"We pay up . . ."

"And then what? Grange just goes away?" Roddy asks.

"I have no idea."

"You tell Angela?"

"Of course not. You tell Tracy?"

"Not a word."

"You got the money?" Roddy asks.

Dan taps his breast pocket. "So what do we do?" Dan's voice is shaky.

"What we have to . . ."

"What does that mean?"

"You don't wanna know. Not right now."

Dan nods, a barely discernible movement. Dan's foot shakes—violently. He says, "If I had a gun I'd shoot that fuckin' Grange in the heart."

"And you'd shoot Kenny in the mouth."

Whorls of dilated blood vessels cover Danny's cheeks.

After a long silence, Roddy asks, "Danny, how long've we known each other?"

"Jesus . . . I can't remember . . ."

Dan's legs jump like jackhammers. Roddy feels the table shaking. He knows Dan wants out of this situation—desperately—but this is where they are, with no way out. The only certainty is the mutual trust of blood brothers.

"Dan, when you stole from the poor box at St. Andrew's, did I rat you out?"

"You *knew* I did that?"

Roddy nods.

"Shit. You never told me you knew."

"Danny, have I ever let you down?"

"Never."

"And I could always count on you and your mother. She saved my life," Roddy says, recalling Peggy Burns taking him in after Horst beat him. She fed Roddy and Danny cooked cabbage and bacon, lamb stew, potato and leek soup—dishes Roddy never got at home. And she nurtured him with a gentle touch and nursed his injuries for weeks. She wanted to call the police, but Roddy feared Horst would kill his mother if she did.

And it was Peggy Burns who asked his teachers to write letters to the judge before Roddy's sentencing. Peggy Burns helped him avoid prison and a life of crime. She was his savior. And Roddy knows Dan's thinking they are godfather to each other's kids; they'll care for each other's family if either one dies.

Dan's eyes gleam; liquid forms at the corners, the prelude to tears.

Roddy's throat tightens. He can barely swallow.

"Roddy, it's all ancient history . . ."

"Danny, it's *our* history."

Sitting there, Roddy aches, thinking of those days.

Finally, Dan says, "So what happens next?"

"We take care of it, Dan."

Silence. Roddy hears the restaurant roar through the office door.

"Have you thought this out?"

"It's all thought out."

Dan closes his eyes.

"This bastard won't go away, Dan . . . ever."

Danny nods.

"Just trust me," Roddy says.

This is the sickest thing I've ever done . . . but you go where you gotta go.

"Where's Kenny?" asks Roddy.

"Front of the house, waiting for Grange."

"Good. I told him we had money."

"You tell him how much?"

"No. And I didn't tell Grange either."

By the knowing look in Dan's eyes, Roddy's certain he understands.

They wait. The overhead light buzzes. It's hard for Roddy to keep his legs still. It feels like an electric motor churns in his chest.

■

A knock on the door.

It opens. Restaurant noise pours into the office.

In comes Kenny wearing his maitre d' tux. He looks pale and gaunt, with a hollowed-out look in his dark eyes. He's a goddamned junkie, for sure, a dyed-in-the-wool doper.

Behind him, Grange fills the doorway.

Roddy's heart throbs with a deep thudding rhythm. He tries to look casual, but his eyes are fixed on the doorway. The fat man glances around the office and shuts the door. No Mack Truck. No protection. Roddy's pulse rate climbs.

Roddy knew it would happen this way. He just knew it. Greed, Grange's logo—it might as well be stamped on his forehead—is a great predictor. Each man in the room has a mental road map, a hierarchy of needs and wishes, an immutable personal trajectory that defines him.

Yes, you have to know the players and their patterns.

Grange trundles into the room. Kenny walks behind Roddy; he takes the same seat as last time, to Roddy's left. Kenny's breath reeks—gin or vodka, Roddy's certain.

Grange takes the same chair—across from Roddy, to Dan's right.

Habits . . . patterns . . . never change.

Grange has that hangdog look: dewlaps, blubbery lips, and pendulous earlobes that remind Roddy of melting wax dripping down to his fat-padded, round shoulders.

"I'm glad to be back," Grange says.

Roddy's heart gallops wildly. He feels his tongue dry out and stick to the roof of his mouth.

Grange clasps his meaty hands on the table. Roddy stares at that obscene ring partly covered by black knuckle hairs. And there are still flecks of dandruff on Grange's shoulders. Roddy is thinking, *You kissed my daughter, you fat fuck . . .*

Kenny shrinks into his chair; he reminds Roddy of a worm burrowing into soil.

"So . . . you got something for me," Grange says.

Roddy nods. For half a second, he feels an impulse to smash the fat man's face.

Roddy and Danny reach into their breast pockets, extract the envelopes, plop them on the table, and push them toward Grange.

Roddy feels his toes curl inward and feels his teeth clench. He knows Grange can't possibly think the two envelopes hold nearly a half-million dollars. Will the fat man go for it? Roddy stares into Grange's eyes. Neither man blinks. Roddy hears the ticking of Grange's wristwatch. The wait seems endless.

Grange's eyes shift to the table; he grabs the white envelope first—Danny's.

He runs a thick finger through the sealed flap and dumps cash onto the table. Neat bundles of hundred-dollar bills wrapped with rubber bands sit beneath the glow.

Roddy watches the fat man's nostrils—they quiver as though he's inhaling the smell of the bills. Grange lifts a packet, bends it, fans it, and then whips off the rubber band and counts the bills. His fingers are bank-teller quick. His thick lips move in a sibilant whisper as the bills fan in a blur.

"Three thousand . . . ," he murmurs; he then rewraps the bundle.

He moves the other packs closer, fans swiftly through them, and checks the denominations. All hundreds. He doesn't bother unwrapping and counting them. Instead, he reaches into the middle of one and extracts a bill.

He holds it up to the light and his eyeballs roll over it; he flips it and examines the other side. He nods and slips the bill back into the pack. The corners of his lips curl in a budding smile. He corrals the bills and stuffs them back in the envelope.

"Five packs. Fifteen thousand . . . ," he says, and he slides the package aside.

He grasps the brown envelope—Roddy's—and repeats the procedure; then he lets out a soft grunt.

He pockets both envelopes. His jacket bulges.

"Okay . . . so whaddaya got here? Thirty thou . . ."

Roddy nods. His legs feel like coiled steel. He knows he could clutch Grange's windpipe, squeeze and pull, and rip it out instantly. An Airborne Ranger move—gouge the throat and watch the enemy collapse, gasping for air. Hear the death rattle deep in his chest. Smell shit slide from his bowels in the throes of death.

Stay calm, stay in charge . . . let it happen the way you think it will . . .

"So where's the rest?" Grange asks.

"It's the first month's interest, plus some . . ."

Roddy's breath churns in his ears. He feels blood pool in his cheeks. He hears the buzz of the overhead light, a hornet drone.

"Where's the rest?"

"We'll have it in two days."

Grange's face is a fleshy mass. His lips purse; his eyes narrow. He leans his bulk forward, as though he'll slither across the table.

"You said you *had* the money."

"I said we have *money*. I didn't say we had *the* money."

Roddy's certain his voice is calm—firm but not belligerent, and not overly placating.

The storage room compressor kicks in. Kitchen clatter seeps through the door.

"You sure you're a surgeon?" Grange says. "Because you sound like a fuckin' *word* doctor. You didn't say *the* money, you said we have *money*. I love guys who tease apart their fuckin' words. A regular Bill Clinton is what we got here." His blubbery lips go agape in feigned awe. "Depends on what the meaning of *is*, is . . . huh, motherfucker?"

"It's a good-faith down payment," Roddy says.

Roddy wonders what calculus meanders through Grange's reptilian brain. He asks himself if this covetous bastard can resist the lure of cold, hard cash.

A woman's high-pitched laugh penetrates the door. The restaurant noise pulses. It's a good-time throng out for an evening's pleasure.

Roddy wraps his feet around the chair legs—just to keep them from jumping.

Dan stares straight ahead, tension on his face, waiting.

Kenny stays silent.

Voltage streams through Roddy.

"Where's the rest?"

"It's a lot of money, Mr. Grange," Roddy says, his voice measured, calm. "We sold some mutual funds and bonds. I'm sure you know the settlement date for the sale of securities is three business days."

Grange stares at him with those lifeless shark eyes.

Dan's eyes are locked on Roddy.

Kenny's sweating out every tortuous second of this parrying; Roddy knows it.

"Tomorrow's the settlement date," Roddy says. "We can have our brokerages transfer the money by wire, or have bank checks made out, not personal ones."

Grange's unblinking eyes stay fixed on Roddy.

"After all, any cash withdrawal greater than $10,000 gets reported to the IRS."

There's a long pause. Roddy's pulse amps up. The room feels cold.

"You'll wire the money to my account," says Grange.

"We'll need your account information."

"You'll get it tomorrow. I'll call your office."

"I'll be there," Roddy says. "And tonight, you leave with $30,000."

Silence swells in the room.

"And this loser pays nothing?" asks Grange, nodding toward Kenny.

"We're *partners,* Mr. Grange. It's from all of us."

Grange's lower lip hangs nearly to his chin. "One other thing . . ."

"Yes?"

"The juice. She's still runnin'."

"We gotta talk about that," Roddy says.

"Talk."

Grange's stare is intense. But the jumpmaster was right all those years ago: not even a low-life like Grange scares Roddy.

"The settlement date's tomorrow, which is when we transfer the money. So, the juice stopped when we sold the securities two days ago."

"I can't do that, Mr. MD."

"Yes you can."

Keep calm; remember the greed factor . . .

"That's not the way I do business."

"Then the deal's off."

Dead silence. The fluorescence hums. The compressor in the back room chugs and then whirrs. Roddy's heart hammers; blood rushes in his ears. His mouth is so dry he feels he'll gag.

Grange stares at him.

Roddy stands and pushes the chair back. His legs quiver, feel weak.

Danny's face goes bloodless. His eyes shift back and forth.

Roddy hears Kenny's exhalation, a desperate huff. Roddy's sure Kenny's dribbling sweat like a leaky faucet.

Grange's breath whistles through hairy nostrils. "You gonna kill the deal?"

Roddy moves toward the door. He stops, turns back, and faces Grange.

"Look, Mr. Grange," he says, "tonight you walk out of here with thirty grand. Cash. Tomorrow the rest is wired to your account. You'll have half a million dollars on an investment of two-hundred-and-fifty-thousand dollars. Double your money in six months."

Grange stares, unblinking.

"So, you'll forego two day's interest."

Everything slows and turns to sludge. Roddy hears the restaurant buzz, more laughter. He waits, trying to quell the ramping beat of his heart.

"You got some fuckin' pair of balls, Doc," Grange says.

Roddy stands there, saying nothing. He hears Grange's wristwatch ticking away.

"Okay, it's a deal," Grange says, extending a thick hand across the table.

Roddy moves to the table, leans over, and grabs Grange's hand. It's a plump slab, yielding, doughy. Roddy could give him a finger-crippling squeeze, but he shakes it gently.

"Deal," says Roddy.

Their hands separate.

Grange stays seated.

Roddy feels the wire-like tension fade. Kenny sighs; relief, deliverance.

Danny sits, rigid, unmoving, and granite-faced.

Roddy wonders what happens next. He reminds himself that the less said, the better. The silence seems excruciating, and he wonders if he can hold Grange's baleful stare a few moments longer.

Then Grange says, "Don't you think this calls for a little toast, Doc?"

Grange leans his bulk back in the chair and looks contented, triumphant.

"Yeah," Kenny warbles. "How 'bout a drink?"

Grange peers toward the bar. "Hey, Doc," you got more of that great shit . . . that Glenfiddich?"

Roddy nods and moves to the wet bar.

"Straight up. And be generous," Grange calls.

"How 'bout you Danny?" asks Roddy.

"A Coke . . ."

"Kenny?"

"Gin and tonic . . ."

"Coming up," Roddy says, busying himself. His hands tremble. He keeps them behind the bar and hopes they can't be seen.

"Hey, Doc, you got a pretty daughter," Grange says with a sniggering laugh.

Roddy's stomach churns and knots on itself. He feels he'll heave any second. He glances at Danny, whose features darken. Roddy's sure he's thinking about Angela.

Roddy sets a glass of Coca-Cola in front of Danny. Dan gazes ahead, as though looking at an imaginary horizon.

Returning to the bar, Roddy lifts the bottle of Glenfiddich from beneath the counter and pours a tumbler full—no ice—for Grange.

He sets the drink on the bar top.

Using the hose, he sprays club soda into a glass of ice for himself. Then he grabs a bottle of gin and pours a shot into an ice-filled glass. He fills the rest up with tonic.

He sets Grange's drink in front of him and carries Kenny's in his other hand. After setting down Kenny's drink, he returns to the bar and grabs his own glass.

"Here's to tomorrow," Roddy says.

Tension threads through him like a piano wire. Roddy wonders if his voice sounds as high pitched to the others as it does in his own ears. It can be a giveaway.

Can he lift his drink without his hand shaking? Will the ice rattle, the soda spill?

Grange lifts his glass; so do Kenny and Danny. Grange sips his Glenfiddich. "Ah . . . smooth as a baby's ass," he says, and then grunts contentedly.

Kenny guzzles his drink. Then he's at the wet bar, pouring himself a shot—straight gin, a good two ounces. With shaking hands, he sips, closes his eyes, and then slurps the booze. He returns to the table and sits down.

Roddy sips his tonic; the effervescence burns his throat. He's ready to gag.

Danny stares straight ahead, still fixed on some distant point.

"Careful, Kenny. You don't want to get drunk on a work night," Roddy says.

"An Irishman never gets drunk."

Roddy peers at Danny. No eye contact.

Roddy is thinking: *Yes, we're here: three schmucks and a shylock.*

Grange's rotund body drapes over his chair like a hillock of wrapped flesh.

Grange lifts his Glenfiddich. Roddy can smell the scotch's smokiness across the table. "This fuckin' stuff's so good, I could break my rule about havin' only one," Grange mutters, and then smacks his lips.

"Rules are made to be broken," pipes up Kenny, oozing relief.

"Man, this shit's good," Grange says, and then paws the glass, lifts it, and takes a huge slug.

He sets the glass down with an emphatic thud.

Dan says nothing and looks calm.

Roddy is thinking: *Dan's a good soldier.*

Another minute passes. There's hissing in Roddy's ears. It grows louder.

He gets up, goes to the wet bar, fiddles with some bottles, and returns to the table.

Grange swills down the last of his scotch. He belches.

He sets the empty tumbler down. It spins like a top on the table.

Grange's face is ruby red and looks porcine, sweaty. He peers across the table and says, "Yeah . . . I'll have another . . ."

"You sure?" Roddy asks.

Grange's eyelids droop languorously.

Silence. A few minutes pass; but for the restaurant hum and fluorescent buzz, everything's quiet.

Grange's eyelids slide shut. His mouth opens; he speaks, but the words are slurred.

"What's that, Mr. Grange?" asks Roddy.

Grange's shoulders sag; his arms hang at his sides. He leans back in his chair and opens his eyes; suddenly his eyeballs roll up into his head. A snore erupts from his throat.

Roddy looks at Dan and Kenny. His index finger goes to his lips. Danny nods.

Kenny turns pale. Sweat dribbles from his hairline; droplets sit above his upper lip.

The restaurant throng sounds like a choral whine.

Roddy tries to gauge his feelings.

Fear? Yes.

Exhilaration? Maybe.

Expectation? Who knows?

Grange snores steadily. It's a sloppy, noisy sleep, just what Roddy expected.

Kenny looks frightened, perplexed—he knows jack-shit about what's happening—his face asking, *What's going on?*

"Mr. Grange is tired," Roddy says.

Kenny's eyes dart back and forth; he looks confused, almost disoriented. Above all, he looks frightened.

"Don't worry, Kenny. Our friend here is taking a little nap," Roddy says as he gets up, goes to the telephone, and dials the in-house extension. Someone at the reservations desk answers.

"It's the back office. Put Omar on," he says.

Roddy grips the telephone tightly. He controls the trembling.

Roddy glances at Kenny, who sits there; his eyes widen. His lips and chin tremble. His hands go up, questioningly. Roddy winks at him, but Ken still looks confused. Roddy can almost hear Kenny's thoughts churning, cogitating. Kenny stands, peers at Grange, then at Dan. He shakes his head and then looks questioningly at Roddy.

Roddy winks again.

Kenny seems to gather his composure. His hand goes to his

mouth. Then, a half-smile forms on his lips. Yes, he's getting it.

"Omar here . . ."

"Omar . . . it's Roddy Dolan. How're you doing?"

"Fine, Doc . . . and you?"

"Great. How's business tonight?"

"Full house."

"Good. Listen, Omar . . . Kenny's here in the office. He's not feeling well; he has to go home." Roddy sees Kenny nod his head. Yes, he understands.

"That's too bad, Doc."

"You're in charge. You'll close up, too."

"Sure thing . . ."

Grange's bulk slips downward; his head hangs over the back of the chair. The snoring continues.

"Omar, ask a valet to go to the garage and bring my car around to the side entrance. We're taking Kenny home. Have someone come back to the office for the garage ticket."

Roddy hangs up.

"What'd ya do?" asks Kenny, his teeth nearly chattering.

"It's the Glenfiddich," Roddy says.

"That's some strong shit," Kenny squeaks.

Roddy puts his index finger to his lips. Kenny nods.

There's a knock on the door.

Roddy opens it slightly; a cauldron of noise rushes into the office as he fishes out a garage stub and hands it to a busboy.

He closes the door and locks it. "We'll take Mr. Grange home," Roddy says.

"Where's he live?" Kenny asks.

"Upstate."

"You're shittin' me," Kenny says.

"My car'll be here soon. Let's get ready."

Roddy tosses Grange's glass into the half-sink filled with soapy water. He swishes it around and then rinses it under the faucet.

Grabbing a towel, he dries it. He sets it back on a shelf. Grabs the Glenfiddich bottle, turns it upside down in the other half-sink, and pours the scotch down the drain. He holds the bottle under the faucet, fills it halfway, caps it, shakes it, and empties it. He tosses the empty bottle into the bin beneath the bar.

Dan and Kenny get up and toss their glasses into the sudsy water.

Roddy can almost hear a rush of thoughts in Kenny's head. *His gears must be really turning*, thinks Roddy.

"A nice April evening," Danny says. "Perfect for a drive."

Grange's mouth is open; his tongue protrudes like a slab of ham.

Roddy walks down the corridor and ambles out the side door onto West 46th Street.

The valet sits in the Sequoia. The engine's running. Roddy hands him a five-spot.

The valet thanks Roddy, gets out of the vehicle, and heads back to 46th and Broadway where he's stationed at McLaughlin's front door.

Roddy turns the ignition off, extracts the key, puts the blinkers on, locks the vehicle, and heads back.

■

"Okay, let's move him out."

They haul Grange out of the chair. The man is a behemoth, a mountain of flesh. They nearly topple under his weight. But once they get him to his feet, Grange responds sluggishly.

As Roddy expected, he's in a twilight state, only able to follow simple commands. His arms are draped over Roddy's and Danny's shoulders while Kenny clasps him around the waist. Grange's legs move indolently, one lurching thrust after another.

They guide him down the corridor. Grange totters from side to side.

Roddy's glad he's stayed in shape all these years: the weights, the treadmill, the long walks with Tracy. It's paid off. Still, Grange feels

like a load of bloat, lead weight wrapped in a size 60-plus suit. For
sure, he's a 350 pounder, maybe close to four bills.

Out on 46th Street, it looks like they're hauling an intoxicated
man to a forest-green Toyota Sequoia. Roddy looks left and right.
The street is gloomy. A sodium vapor lamp lights the area. The
street's deserted.

Roddy presses the remote, unlocks the doors, and then opens
the right rear door. They shove Grange onto the bench seat. He tumbles in, spreads across the leather, and snores like a hibernating bear.

Barging into the SUV, Kenny and Danny maneuver Grange into
a semi-sitting position behind the driver's seat.

"Kenny, sit back there with him," says Roddy. "Dan, get in the
front."

"Why do I hafta sit with this fat fuck?" Kenny whines.

"Because you're strong, Ken. We may have to move him."

Roddy locks the doors, starts the engine, and pulls away from
the curb.

"Where the fuck're we going?" Kenny asks.

"To a place I know," replies Roddy, heading east on 46th Street.

"What's the plan?" Kenny asks.

"We're taking him someplace . . ."

"This is fuckin' unbelievable," Kenny says; then oddly, he cackles.

Roddy turns onto 8th Avenue, heads north and then hangs a left
onto West 57th Street. The streets teem with nighttime pedestrians.
Roddy waits impatiently at a red light. People cross the street in
throngs, squadrons of theatergoers looking eerie beneath the street
lights, like apparitions.

The traffic light takes forever; Roddy's left foot taps a tattoo on
the floor.

"What'd you do, slip him a Mickey Finn?" Kenny asks.

"Something like that," Roddy replies.

The light changes. Roddy drives west on 57th Street.

"Imagine that. Roddy became a fuckin' MD so he could learn

how to make a date-rape drug," Kenny says, and then laughs. It strikes Roddy that Kenny's fear and confusion have quickly turned into willingness to take extreme steps.

A hollow pop sounds in the rear.

Roddy knows that sound: it's a plastic lid snapping off a pill bottle. Glancing in the rearview mirror, he sees Kenny downing a pill. On top of at least a glass and a half of gin—no, more than that since he reeked of booze when he came into the office. The guy's getting stoked; he needs help getting through what's going down. Yes, Kenny's figured it out.

The ramp leading to the West Side Highway looms ahead.

Another red light.

Roddy stops and waits. Moments pass; this light takes forever. Roddy feels edgy, like his skin is curdling. This is excruciating—the beginning of a nightmare.

"How long's that shit work?" asks Kenny.

"Hard to know. Maybe six, seven hours . . .," says Roddy, clutching the steering wheel.

"He's sleeping like a fuckin' baby," Kenny says. He laughs again, that nasal cackle. He sounds pumped, high.

The light changes—finally.

Roddy steps on the accelerator and drives to the entrance ramp.

"Ya gotta gimme the formula for that shit, Roddy. I'd make a fuckin' fortune."

Soon, Kenny's jabbering about the hassles of McLaughlin's, how tough it is to stay afloat. "I'm not sure Omar can be trusted. Can't trust those A-rabs," Kenny says with a snort. "Not those Indians or the Pakis, either . . . lyin' thieves." Another laugh. "And the wetbacks . . . *fuggedaboudit.*"

Roddy peers at the fuel gauge. It's nearly full, and he's again thankful he pumped a megaload of gas in Bronxville. The only mileage he's put on was the hitch into Manhattan.

Roddy rethinks the preparations he's made. If they take it one step at a time, it should go as planned.

"How long's this gonna take?" asks Kenny.

"From here, maybe an hour, hour and a quarter, depends on traffic . . ."

Another popping sound comes from the rear.

"What're you taking, Kenny?" Roddy asks.

"Just some shit to stay awake."

Roddy knows Kenny's on drugs, probably crap he's been taking all night long. One thing's certain: Kenny's a junkie.

It occurs to Roddy that Kenny was using that night he first saw Crystal and those mobsters at the restaurant. He was wired. Totally amped. And the night he and Danny confronted him about the nosedive in receipts. He was paranoid. Probably speed or coke. And who knows how long he's been using?

"You're not gonna fall asleep on us, are you, Kenny?" Roddy asks, wanting to hear if Kenny slurs his words.

"Not a fuckin' chance. I'm in for the duration."

Roddy hears another pop in the back, but traffic sounds smother it.

"So how far's this place?" Kenny asks.

"It's a way off," Roddy says, thinking how their lives will be changed.

Completely.

Forever.

But there's no *forever* for anyone.

Chapter 22

They're on the West Side Highway.

Heading north along the west side of Manhattan, traffic is moderate, less than Roddy expected on a weekday evening when the rush to the burbs peaks. The Sequoia takes the bumps and potholes with barely a shake or jiggle. The thing is like an Abrams tank.

On their right, above the highway, the lights on Riverside Drive form a glittering man-made palisade. On the left, beyond the traffic stream heading south, are the dark waters of the Hudson River. Roddy drives beneath the arch of the George Washington Bridge and then heads over the Henry Hudson Bridge. They leave Manhattan and enter the Riverdale section of the Bronx, heading north. Roddy thinks how odd it is: only a few hours ago he'd crossed this same bridge and driven the same highway, but Grange wasn't asleep in the back seat, and Kenny and Danny weren't with him. Now, it's all changed.

The Sequoia's huge radial tires hum smoothly on the road. They hammer and drub on the occasional rough patch of highway and then resume their rubberized drone when the roadway smoothes.

The Henry Hudson Parkway courses its serpentine route through the Bronx; it then becomes the Saw Mill River Parkway in West Yonkers. Traffic thins. Roddy's thoughts spin wildly as they move north. It's 7:15. By now, people are home, eating dinner, thinking about tomorrow's work, or they're watching *Jeopardy*, before they

tune into some sitcom or their usual TV pabulum. Roddy's own routine would ordinarily be similar.

But not tonight.

This morning, after he told her about the meeting, Tracy said,
"Roddy, you've been so tense these last few days. If McLaughlin's is
bothering you, you're doing the right thing. We have so much right
here. We don't need anything more."

Lies, lies, and more lies—to Tracy, of all people in the world.

But everyone lies and keeps secrets, too. Some people's secrets—
if revealed—could send them to prison. Is all the good he's done
about to wash away? And Danny too? He wonders if the distance
they've traveled could be undone in one night.

But why ponder this bullshit now? Roddy asks himself. He's thought
it through—and he's exhausted all ideas. Now he's got to focus on what
must be done. And he doesn't want to think of Tracy or Tom or Sandy.
Or his patients, the hospital, or how his life's gone all these years. This
isn't the time to think of the normal cadence of things.

You do what you gotta do . . .

He drives at a moderate speed, rarely exceeding fifty-five. The
headlights going south are sparse. A thin necklace of taillights lies
ahead of him. The Sequoia's dashboard seems eerie with its orange
lights, numbers, letters, and gauges. It's ghostly.

They pass through Ardsley, then Elmsford. Soon, the highway
snakes through Hawthorne, where they come to an intricate maze
of cloverleaf entrance and exit ramps.

■

Roddy follows the on-ramp to the Taconic State Parkway, heads
north, and picks up speed.

Within minutes, the road looks different—rustic, eerily deserted. Stands of tall pine and spruce line the highway. They fill the
median, too, a massive, black tree line in the night. Two lanes head
north. There're no overhead lights and darkness envelops them. The

Sequoia's high beams shoot long shafts of white light ahead. The vehicle cruises like an ocean liner; it swallows its own light beams as they glide through an arcade of crouching trees.

Another hollow pop comes from the back.

Roddy glances in the rearview mirror.

Yes, Kenny's getting stoked. He needs courage in a capsule.

Grange's snoring in the back seat sounds like a chainsaw.

Dan stares straight ahead, hands clasped, knuckles white.

The road slips by; the Taconic's white line streams through the night. Gleaming reflectors sit on the guardrail along the roadside—like eyes in the night. It's all foreign-looking and strange.

Roddy breaks the silence. "Kenny . . . give Dan the money."

"We're really gonna get rid of this bastard, aren't we?" Kenny says, his voice an octave higher than usual.

Definitely drugs, thinks Roddy.

"Just give Dan the money."

Kenny reaches into Grange's breast pocket and hands Danny the envelopes.

Danny slips them into the glove compartment.

"It's a lot of good dough," Kenny says.

"Yeah, sure . . . ," mutters Danny.

There's something in Dan's voice. Is it resignation? Not really. Anger? Yes. At Kenny? Yes. At Grange? Definitely. At himself? For sure.

"Take off Grange's jacket," Roddy calls.

Kenny tries to maneuver the fat man. He grunts, tugging at the jacket. "This fucker's too goddamned heavy. I need help."

"Never mind. We'll do it later," Roddy calls back.

Roddy glances in the mirror again. In flickering shadow, he sees Kenny's hand go to his mouth. Roddy hears a gulp.

"What're you taking?" Roddy asks.

"Some shit my doctor prescribed."

"What shit, Ken?"

"None of your fuckin' business, Roddy."

"Speed? Vicodin? Valium?"

"Fuck off."

"You asshole . . . ," Dan mutters.

"Fuck you." Kenny shouts.

"Hey, asshole," Danny shouts, "we're getting you out of this, so shut up."

"Getting *me* out?" Kenny yells. "Getting *me* out? You're getting *yourselves* out; you're not doing *me* any favors."

"Yeah?" Danny shouts. "And who got us into this shit?"

"Both of you shut up," Roddy calls. "Let's just get this done."

Roddy's certain the guy in the back seat isn't the same Kenny Egan he was a few months ago.

"He's stoned," Roddy mutters.

Danny nods.

"Whaddaya sayin'?" comes from the back seat.

"Nothing, Kenny."

"I fuckin' heard ya."

Roddy knows Kenny's snagging a brain jolt. It's coke, speed, or some other mind-blowing shit. But there are more important things in the mix, shit that matters.

"Dan," says Roddy, "in the door pocket next to you there's some plastic bags. Grab one and open it."

Danny struggles with the bag and snaps it open.

"Kenny, take Grange's wallet and drop it in the bag."

Dan undoes his seat belt, turns around on his knees, leans over the front seat, and holds the plastic bag open.

"There's lotsa good money in here," Kenny says.

"Just drop it in," Dan says, nearly snarling.

"Why don't we grab his credit cards?"

"You asshole," Dan sneers. "Put it in."

Kenny drops the wallet into the bag.

"Look through his pockets for keys, coins, papers, anything . . . toss them in there," Roddy calls.

Kenny pats Grange down. Out come keys, a cell phone, and a small pillbox.

It all goes into the bag.

"Search his jacket . . ."

Kenny goes through Grange's jacket. "Nothin' here . . ."

"We'll get the jacket when we're there."

"Where?" Kenny shouts.

"*There*," Danny yells.

"Grab his watch and toss it in the bag," Roddy says.

"It's a Rolex."

"In the *bag*," shouts Dan.

It drops in.

"What a waste," Kenny moans. "I could get a thousand for that thing."

"And that ring of his," Roddy calls. "In the bag."

Kenny pulls, grunts, and curses. "I can't get it off this fat fucker."

"Spit on it . . ."

Kenny coughs up a wad of phlegm and spits. Roddy hears grunts. "It's stuck. You fat *fucker*," Kenny shouts.

There's a sharp, clapping sound as Kenny slaps Grange. And another. Then the thump of a fist hitting flesh and bone. A stream of curses flows from the back seat. The sound of another punch comes from the back.

"Stop it, Ken!"

"The fuckin' ring won't come off."

"We'll take care of it later."

"Okay, okay," Kenny says. And for good measure, he slaps Grange again.

"Cut it out, Kenny."

"He can't feel shit anyway, Roddy. I oughta smash his fuckin' brains in."

"Just leave him alone."

■

The Sequoia hums along the deserted highway and the tree line thickens. The terrain changes as the SUV glides to higher elevation. Dan's window slides down for a moment. The wind rush is powerful, smelling of pine and resin.

Roddy's glad for this oversized monster—the SR5 with four-wheel drive and a 4.7-liter V8 engine. With just a few options—not anything near the deluxe package—the damned thing ran him nearly forty thousand. A full year's salary for Tracy at the library.

It would be better not to think of Tracy or the kids. Not tonight.

Roddy wishes he could empty his mind, go numb, and know nothing. Sometimes, to distract himself, he imagines a surgical procedure. He can visualize a person's innards—the organs, blood vessels, fat, and fascia—it's like flipping a switch in his mind. It turns feelings into something simple, concrete, surgical, into an intellectual exercise. It's one of his failings, and tonight he's in touch with his flaws. There are so many of them—deep and telling fault lines in the foundation of his being.

He's tried so hard all these years, struggled to undo the shit from his past. He's done good things as a surgeon, husband, and father. But maybe it doesn't matter; maybe you just dribble downhill in your life, like a river. Maybe evil's just part of him, embedded in his DNA. Irreversible. It can't be changed.

Like father, like son.

Does it linger within, forever? And is tonight simply a small part of forever?

I wanna be an Airborne Ranger. I wanna live a life of danger . . .

That was the chant at Fort Benning, during Ranger training: 200 men—Bravo Company—sweat-drenched soldiers trotting along dirt roads, tramping through green forests and barberry thickets, wading through fetid swamps, scaling steep ridges shouting in a macho sing-song chorus, training to be a lethal fighting force.

There are only two kinds of Rangers . . . the quick and the dead.

Ain't no use in lookin' back, Johnny's got your Cadillac. Ain't no use in feelin' blue, Johnny's got your girlfriend too.

Character. A way of being in the world. It's who you are; it pre-
dicts what you'll do.

Yes, character is destiny.

Popeye was right . . . I am who I am . . .

And all that bullshit.

■

They head north at a steady sixty-five.

Kenny's on a nonstop, drug-fueled diatribe. Roddy's certain if
he'd spent more time with Kenny over the months, he'd have realized the guy's a junkie. Kenny's going totally mental, prattling on
about the restaurant, how to get back in the black. It's an avalanche
of pressurized verbiage; he's riffing about the kitchen—line chefs,
waiters and busboys, city inspectors—about Crystal and Omar,
about everything.

"I'm glad we're getting rid of Grange," Kenny says. "This fat fuck's
gotta go." A laugh. "And that Rolex, what a waste. Hey, Danny, fish
that fuckin' thing outta there."

"Fuck you, Kenny," Dan shouts. He shoots an exasperated look
at Roddy.

Roddy keeps driving steadily and feels zoned out.

Now Kenny's spewing crap about a woman he met. His words
are rapid-fire, pressure-cooker intense, superheated. Roddy's sure
he's wired on speed, maybe cocaine or crystal meth. Who the hell
knows?

"She's only eighteen," Kenny says. "I'm tellin' ya, there's nothin'
like a young woman—eighteen or nineteen. The younger the better."

Then comes another torrent of complaints about the restaurant.
"Believe me, I'm tellin' it like it really fuckin' *is* out there. People are
cuttin' back. It's personal plastic, now—no more corporate cash. No
splurging. And costs are going up—food, booze, every fuckin' thing.
Tell me . . . does *anything* cost less now?"

"Yeah . . . ?" Dan parries. "Every time I'm there the place is jam-packed."

"But the costs. I'm tellin' ya . . ."

"That's bullshit, Kenny," shouts Danny. "Because I see a restaurant that's filled every time I'm there."

"And the help. It's impossible," Kenny cries. "There're no more waiters. They're all *actors* and *writers;* it's part-time shit. Everybody wantsa get paid for doin' nothing. Ya gotta get Ecuadorians or Dominicans or some other Latino muthafuckas. And then ya know what? They'll rob your ass blind."

Dan sighs. Roddy knows Danny's having a tough time tolerating Kenny's clamor.

And it's all bullshit, thinks Roddy, keeping his eyes on the road. *Gotta tune out Kenny's drug-addled gibberish.* Roddy knows Kenny's off the charts when it comes to drug use: the guy's judgment is gone, wasted.

"You're fulla shit," Danny yells. "You've been running the place into the ground. And you know what, Kenny? You must think Roddy and I are stupid, because I can tell you're all fucked up on drugs. Isn't that right, Roddy?"

"That's what I'm seeing, Dan."

"Fuck you both," Kenny shouts. "I'm sick of hearing two holier-than-thou muthafuckas—I ain't listenin' to you."

Danny shakes his head, glances at Roddy, and mutters, "Goddamned junkie bastard."

Grange sleeps like a baby; though if shoved, he mumbles, moves an arm or leg, and grunts or belches. But he's in a twilight state, la la land.

Roddy thinks that as wasted as Kenny is, he's right about the Klonopin. It's potent shit and it's worked wonders on Grange. He feels absolutely nothing.

Roddy's used Klonopin for preanesthesia medication—to induce a twilight state in patients, who can't even recall being wheeled into the OR. It's simply a matter of the dosing—a bit more, and you've got a king-sized lump like Grange slumbering away in a brain-altered dream state.

Back in the office, Roddy estimated Grange at a good 350-plus pounds; he calculated the dose for a deep twilight state. He'd be out of it but could respond sluggishly to simple commands. In a few minutes, if downed quickly—especially with 80-proof booze—the ravenous bastard would be in another world.

This afternoon, when Roddy got to McLaughlin's, he went to the wet bar and poured the tasteless, odorless, Klonopin powder into the Glenfiddich. He swirled the bottle to dissolve the Klonopin. Then he slipped the bottle inside the wet bar so no one would inadvertently pick it up and pour a drink. Knowing Danny would ask for a soft drink and Kenny would opt for gin or vodka, there was no risk of anyone but Grange getting dosed.

Roddy was certain if the deal was made, Grange would make his power demand—a glass of Glenfiddich. Roddy'd counted on that. *If* the deal could be made. And deep in his bones, he'd known Grange would go for the up-front money with more to follow—a wired transaction to an offshore account. Like a shark smells blood in the water.

It was hairy for a while: would Grange show up without Mack Truck? Or some other Godzilla-sized bastard? Would he go for the thirty thousand with more to come?

He had to guess and hope for the best.

He'd doped it out correctly—down to the last detail. What does Danny always say about investing? Past return is no predictor of future performance; but with Grange, past behavior *was* predictive.

Roddy'd been sure, Grange's greed was voracious. The promise— the green elixir—would be too great for him to resist. Whether he'd show up alone was the only real question. And Roddy knew Grange would want that self-congratulatory drink—*that great shit.*

People always give themselves away, Roddy thinks. Greed's an insatiable human appetite, oozing to the surface like amber molasses. Roddy was sure the bastard would sing his song and dance his dance.

But if Roddy thinks too much about the step-by-step path leading up to this moment in the Sequoia drubbing on highway asphalt and nearing Dutchess County, it could drive him just plain nuts.

■

He picks up speed. The world is dark and seems endless in the night. They pass Fahnestock State Park and enter Dutchess County. Roddy takes this route every time the family goes to Lake Rhoda, but this isn't a time for family. *Just stay focused*, he tells himself.

"This fuckin' guy's breath stinks," Kenny calls.

Roddy's reminded of Sandy's comment about Grange's breath, but he concentrates on the road.

He's doing a solid seventy. During the last half hour, they've passed only two cars going north, three others traveling south. They're in Columbia County—cow and chicken country. The foothills of the Berkshires loom darkly above them. Lights from a few distant farmhouses are visible. Rustic, serene—a world far removed from McLaughlin's or Tuckahoe or Bronxville. Light years away from Brooklyn and Sheepshead Bay.

At the Ferris Lane exit, they're maybe five miles from where they'll exit the Taconic. Roddy slows down and calls back to Kenny, "Take off his shoes."

"What the fuck?" calls Kenny.

"I said take off his shoes."

"Whaddo I look like? A fuckin' valet?"

"Kenny, just *do* it." Dan says.

There's grunting in the back.

"They're off."

Roddy slows the Sequoia. He peers in the rearview mirror.

Nothing but blackness.

"Take *one* shoe and toss it," Roddy calls back to Kenny. "Just one."

Using the master control, he lowers the right rear window.

Kenny hurls a shoe into the night.

A couple of miles north, Roddy slows the vehicle again and tells Kenny to throw the second shoe.

Kenny does it.

"Take off his belt and toss it," Roddy says.

Kenny struggles, gets the belt off, and throws it out the open window.

Soon, Roddy sees Jackson Corners. It's the exit to get to Lake Rhoda.

On Jackson Corners Road he makes a left onto County Road 7. He's been on this road dozens of times, but it's always been in daylight. Everything looks different at night. They pass a few farmhouses. Some interior lights are visible, but it's quiet.

Roddy glances at the dashboard clock; they've been traveling over an hour. There's been zero traffic. And his thoughts have shuttled to countless things; it's like he's been driving in a dream.

"Where the fuck're we goin'?" calls Kenny.

"To a place I know," Roddy says.

"What place?"

"We're going wherever Roddy's going," shouts Dan. "Just shut the fuck up. I'm sick of your bullshit. And frankly, fuck-face, I'm sick of you."

"Listen asshole . . ."

"Cut it out, Kenny," Roddy calls. "You got us in this and now we're getting out."

Silence in the back seat. A reprieve.

No wind rush, no tire hum now. It's a quiet country road—desolate, black, noiseless.

Roddy hears the vial pop. Then there's a gulping sound.

"What're you taking, Kenny?"

"Gotta stay awake."

"It's not even eight o'clock, you jackass," Danny says.

"I'm tired."

"Taking speed, Kenny?" Roddy asks.

"Nah . . . NoDoz . . ."

"Lemme see the bottle."

"What're you, my mother? It's none of your fuckin' business," Kenny screams. "Who died and made *you* king? What're you . . . some goddamned guinea goombah Mafioso? Fuck you, you shanty-Irish, muthafucka."

"He's stoned out of his mind," Roddy mutters.

Dan nods. "What a fuckin' mistake . . . getting involved with this bastard." He turns back to Kenny and shouts, "You doped-up piece of shit. We should never've got involved with you."

"Do I look like I was born yesterday?" Kenny shouts back. "Like I don't know the fuckin' score? Whaddaya think I am? A nothin'? A nobody? Whaddaya think? Ya can shit all over me? Do I look like a fuckin' toilet bowl? Huh? Whaddaya think? I'm your goddamned Stepin Fetchit nigger?"

"You racist pig," Dan murmurs.

"Okay . . . Okay . . . you don't like *nigger* . . . so whaddaya think I'm your fuckin' valet? Your toe-sucking servant, your ass-kissing *negro? Yowsir massa Dan . . . yowsir, yowsir,*" he yells. *"Anything you say, massa."*

"God, I oughta kick myself in the ass," Danny says. "I'm sorry, Roddy . . . I'm so sorry. I apologize."

"Not your fault, Danny." Roddy sighs and keeps driving.

Roddy thinks Kenny's right in his way: Roddy's not his mother. And he's no kingpin, no boss or gang leader, either. But Kenny's drugs—bad news. Could blow the game wide open.

■

The deserted road winds through the town of Gallatin, then through Ancram, a collection of a few houses and a shuttered country store.

Route 7 meanders through the darkness. The Sequoia's high beams light the way. Huge trees arch over the roadway, forming a dense arcade.

"This fuckin' place is eerie . . . ," Kenny says.

Even though he tries to block them out, Roddy is flooded by memories of the summers at Lake Rhoda. There were times alone with Tracy—in the woods on a blanket, making love beneath the hemlocks—then time with the kids, teaching them to swim, roasting marshmallows at campfires, traveling to Great Barrington for ice cream at Friendly's, or driving to Bash Bish Falls to hike the trails.

They pass Upper Lake Rhoda, where he's gone fishing for perch and sunfish with Tom. Those were the summers before McLaughlin's and Kenny—or Grange. When things seemed easier, knowable, even predictable, if there's such a thing in this world.

A few minutes later Kenny begins yammering a cascade of curses, ramblings, and ruminations.

Then, Roddy sees it. In the darkness, amidst a stand of tall pines, a black space looms in front of them. Roddy hits the brakes.

"What're you doin'? Kenny calls.

"We're here," Roddy says.

"Where?"

"It's Snapper Pond."

Chapter 23

R oddy turns onto a rutted dirt road pocked by holes and swales deepened by the early spring rains. The Sequoia heaves and sways from side to side. Roddy clutches the steering wheel tightly; the SUV swings up and dips down, its springs squealing.

"This thing's a roller coaster," Kenny shouts. "And, it's fuckin' dark here."

A sliver of high crescent moon casts washed-out light on the still-bare and crooked treetops. The headlights throw piercing shafts into the blackness ahead.

"How do ya know this place?" asks Kenny.

"From summers here."

Roddy slows the SUV to a lurching crawl. To the right, maybe fifty yards, lies Snapper Pond, a marshy body of water thirty feet deep at the center. It teems with snapping turtles—huge creatures with diamond-shaped heads. They can crack your foot in half and shatter your bones with their powerful jaws. The bottom swarms with leeches, famished bloodsuckers that attach themselves with their cup-shaped mouths, boring into you in seconds. Roddy recalls reading their saliva has an enzyme that slows blood from clotting. So they drink your blood—no interruption—just suck until they're bloated.

One day Roddy and some hikers saw a swimmer stagger out of the water. Glistening bags of blood-filled leeches draped from his

legs, belly, and back. They were drinking him away. The guy looked
ghostly white and was being drained alive. Roddy and the others
burned the swollen creatures with cigarettes until they dropped off.
They stomped them, bursting their ballooned bodies into blood-
spattered remnants. The poor guy was transfused at a local hospital.

No one comes here. The pond is isolated, creepy. Corroded,
broken tree trunks poke out of the greenish, slime-covered water.
The air is still and the place smells like a putrid marsh. During the
summer, it's mosquito infested. The bastards whine incessantly and
fly into your ears, up your nose, swarming airborne bloodsuckers.
Either way—whether walking around, or in the water—your life's
blood can be sapped away.

"How's Grange?" Roddy asks.

"Out like a fuckin' light," Kenny says.

"Shake him. See if he moves."

Kenny shakes Grange violently; the man mumbles something,
grunts, and then snores.

"This bastard stinks like shit," says Kenny. "He has badass BO.
Don't you guys smell it?"

Roddy's sure Kenny's senses are heightened by drugs. He's a bundle of sensory overload, brain-jacked to some perversely heightened
level of awareness. He smells things no one else does, hears things
others don't, and maybe even hallucinates if he's had enough crank
or speed or booze. His liver must be suitcase-sized—from booze and
whatever other shit he's shot, slurped, or snorted. Jesus, why didn't
Roddy notice it before this?

The sound of a punch—a deep thump—comes from the back
seat.

"*Stop* it, Kenny," calls Roddy.

He pulls the Sequoia to an abrupt halt. They lurch forward.

Roddy thinks again that if he'd spent more time with Kenny over
these past months, he'd have seen how jacked the guy was. But he
was too busy living his real life—at home with Tracy and the kids,

going over Sandy's homework, doing surgery, reading journals—
not spending time at McLaughlin's where he'd have seen Kenny's
insanity.

It's too late for regrets . . . just do what you have to do.

Roddy throws the Sequoia in "park" and presses the emergency
brake pedal.

"Keep her running," he says. "And keep the headlights on. I'm
gonna look around."

He opens the door. The interior dome light goes on.

He walks around to the back and pops open the rear hatch. He
can see the back of Kenny's head over the seats. Grange is slouched
down, unseen. Blackness surrounds the vehicle except for the headlight beams shooting ahead into the woods.

Roddy takes off his sports jacket and tosses it in the hatch area.
He pulls out his nylon North Face jacket and slips it on. He extracts
a twin-tube lantern from the box in the hatch area. It's a bright area
light with a plastic handle. He grabs an Eveready lantern—it can cast
a light beam a hundred yards.

Leaning against the Sequoia's rear bumper, he removes his shoes
and puts on his Alpine Woods boots—ankle-high hiking shoes
made of Thinsulate material. Rubber coating covers the bottoms.
Totally waterproof and warm. He laces them up and tosses his street
shoes into the rear hatch.

Using both lights, he trudges toward the pond.

The grass is still brown and desiccated from the winter cold;
it hasn't yet begun its springtime growth. It crunches beneath his
boots. The twin-tube lantern casts a dull glow; the Eveready shoots
a sharp, white beam ahead.

Tall pines loom to Roddy's right and left. So do leafless maple
and linden trees. Their inky, twisted branches form an eerie trac-
ery backed by a sliver of crescent moon. The tree branches have
yet to sprout spring buds. The sky is star-filled and with the moon's
pale light, the place seems unearthly. It reminds Roddy of a horror

movie. Shadows sway as Roddy advances with the lantern.

It's all forbidding, alien.

Trudging ahead, Roddy realizes he doesn't recall so many pines. It seems to him there were more saplings and birch trees. But this is a pine and hemlock forest. Crickets are chirring in a strange cadence. And tree frogs peep in the night.

The road is farther from the pond than he's remembered. But then, everything seems different at night, distorted. The senses are misled by the darkness. Glancing back, Roddy sees the outline of the SUV with its headlight shafts piercing the night. He's walked a good fifty yards along the edge of the forest.

Nothing moves. It's a windless night; maybe a slight intermittent breeze brushes his face.

He comes to a small clearing. Dried remnants of fountain grass poke up from the ground—yellow, with tufted stalks, shriveled from a harsh winter. Roddy knows from his hiking experiences in Westchester County that this kind of greenery grows near water.

Yes, he's at the right place, not exactly where he thought, but close enough.

The pond is only about thirty feet away. Still water, it looks like a sheet of black ice in the night. He focuses the Eveready straight ahead. The light beam shimmers off the water's surface.

It's Snapper Pond, still water in all its barren ugliness.

The nearest house is miles away. There's no sign of human life, just a swarm of vegetation and countless trees. And the crickets and tree frogs. And whatever's in the pond—snapping turtles and leeches. The bulbous eyes of a bullfrog peer at him from the water's surface. The thing croaks and then sinks noiselessly into the water.

He moves back from the pond, shoots the light beam around, and then moves back another ten or fifteen feet. It's probably the best distance. The ground cover is stubby grass shoots and dried, tawny-colored weeds. Roddy slams the heel of his boot into the soil. It sinks in, no resistance. Soft earth, but not muddy.

Perfect.

The spring thaw began some weeks ago. Right now, the earth is soft and moist but hasn't yet turned wet and boggy. Wet soil can be tough to move—heavy and dense. There should be no rocks in this area. And he's in a clearing; no tree roots can get in the way.

Easy digging.

Am I really doing this? Is this what it comes down to? After every-thing . . . all these years later . . . is this where I am?

A chill runs through him, settling in his spine like an icicle. For a moment, an aura of unreality envelops him, as though it's some strange dreamscape, a nightmarish depiction of hell from one of Tracy's art history books.

He turns and plods back toward the SUV. The Sequoia's head-lights' shooting beams into the bare timbers are a focal point. As he moves through darkness, the thought hits him like a sledgeham-mer: this night, in this eerie place with its peeping frogs, chirring crickets, snapping turtles, and leeches—with Danny and Kenny and Grange—is like the night of the appliance store break-in so many years ago. It all comes together now, decades later, after so much that's been good and worthy and filled with love and commitment.

And now, because Roddy let Kenny Egan back into his life and then sent him to Danny and got his kemosabe involved, Roddy and Danny—who've gone so far in their lives—are sinking in a stench-filled quagmire—fast. They'll be criminals and act with deadly con-sequences, like Roddy's father did. And it could be the end of all good things.

It's another turning point in Roddy Dolan's life.

Chapter 24

Danny peers into the woods. *This is pure wilderness*, he thinks. There's nobody around for miles and there's total darkness, except for the headlights and Roddy's lanterns in the distance. And it's creepy with those weird peeping sounds mixing in with the nonstop sound of the crickets. It reminds him of *Invasion of the Body Snatchers*, otherworldly. Some horror movie . . . maybe *The Night of the Living Dead*. Jesus, this is the creepiest place on earth and this has gotta be the sickest thing he and Roddy have ever done.

Behind him, Kenny mutters. The crazed bastard just can't control himself.

I could kick myself in the ass for getting involved with this out-of-control psycho.

"I'd love to kill this scumbag," Kenny murmurs. A stream of curses and mutterings follow, nonstop gibberish—the rantings of an addled brain.

How'd all of this happen? Danny wonders. Why's he sitting in this car with Kenny Egan and a drugged loan shark in the back seat while Roddy scopes out some God-forsaken swamp?

But then Danny wonders how could he even ask such an asinine question? He knows *exactly* how and why it happened.

He, Danny Burns, *let* it happen.

He'd worked hard to get out of that shithole in Sheepshead Bay. He busted balls to become a CPA and a certified financial planner.

He'd gotten his CFP certification at NYU, learned all about investing, finance, and managing money. But when it came to this McLaughlin's thing, he'd been snowed by bullshit, lost his bearings, and failed miserably in his obligations to Roddy, himself, and their families.

Why'd he consider, even for a moment, the restaurant business—for himself or Roddy? So he could be a celebrity-host? Some watered-down version of Danny Meyer at Union Square Cafe? Feeding the stars and glad-handing the wannabes? Or suck up to the John Harris real estate rapists? Who'd he think he was trying to ingratiate himself with? The high-end tax dodgers, the corporate raiders, and venture vultures? What crap. If he's honest with himself, Danny knows it was the notion of celebrity, far more than money. And it didn't help that Angela always carps about his being too cautious when it comes to taking risks. So he took a chance—*God,* did he take a chance.

And Irish Danny Burns—know-it-all-CPA-hotshot-financial-planner and money-maven, a guy with a nose for fiscal prudence, a guy who can smell a rotten deal a mile away—did what? He let Roddy and himself fall into this septic field, this rancid deal leading to this unbelievable moment in the woods.

He got into the restaurant game, personally getting into bed with Kenny Egan and by extension, with this loan shark, Grange. And who knows what kind of criminal machine's backing Grange? A bunch of gun-toting goons and racketeers. He can't even begin to know.

And now, where is he? On a narrow, dirt road in the middle of nowhere, in the dead of night and he's waiting for Roddy to find a place to dump—let's face it, kill and then bury—this flab-assed bastard Grange.

And who's with him? Kenny "Snake Eyes" McGuirk—now known as Kenny Goddamned Egan—a guy who slithered out of some slime-ridden sewer from Danny and Roddy's past—and convinced them to get in on a good deal. A mere hundred thousand each and they were in. And he, Danny Burns, bought into it.

And now, there's no way out.

But one thing's certain. This bastard Grange made one huge mistake calling their homes. And running Angela off the road. And an even bigger one putting his fat lips to Sandy's face. Because he hit a raw nerve in Roddy's being. He reawakened something in Roddy, something that was buried and gone. Something lethal. Grange will never see that half million, nor will he see the light of day again.

So, try as he may to not think about it, Danny knows that tonight, they'll commit murder. They're gonna snuff out a life, and now, Danny's sweating rivulets as he waits for Roddy to return from scoping out where to plant this fat bastard.

Tonight'll be a nightmare. But he's gotta live through it. Somehow, he's just gotta grit his teeth and do what must be done. There's just no other way.

Grange coughs and sputters; phlegm rattles in his throat. He mumbles something. Danny can't make it out, but it's about "the deal" and then about "a ride." The bastard's half-awake, maybe even coming out of the half-dead zone Roddy put him in.

"What is it, muthafucka?" shouts Kenny. "Huh? What the fuck're you saying?"

A sharp crack comes from the back seat; Grange gurgles. Again, he says something about "the deal." Kenny punches him again; it sounds like a plank of wood slamming into Grange's face.

Kenny shouts, "What? What? What? Whaddaya say now Mister Fuckin' Shylock?"

Slap, thump. Again and again.

Danny rues the fact that after all these years, his life has come down to this.

He thinks back to his father. Poor guy, busted chops seven days a week. Poor Da, just upped and died in a pile of soot. And Danny thinks of his beautiful Irish mother, with her pale skin, red hair, and green eyes. After Da died, to make ends meet, she cleaned houses for the lace-curtain Irish in Ditmas Park; she spent the days on her knees, scrubbed shit out of their toilet bowls, made their beds, did their laundry, and came home with hands smelling of Clorox and borax—she slogged like a fucking slave just to keep food on the table and a roof over their heads.

Ma always said, *"Daniel . . . you're the best of boys. And even though he doesn't know it yet, Rodney Dolan's the best of boys, as well. You're both my Best Boys."*

She'd always ask, "How're my two Best Boys?" whenever Roddy stayed with them after Horst beat the shit out of him. Always called them by their formal names: Daniel and Rodney. Ma's two *Best Boys.*

And now this: an insane night in the woods and they're gonna do murder. Jesus, what has he done? What'll become of Peggy Burns' two Best Boys?

The lantern approaches. Roddy's coming back.

At that moment Danny knows he wants to drop to his knees, hit the ground, and pray. Just kneel down, put his hands together, gaze up at the moon and stars—those heavenly bodies—and utter some prayer, and like a true penitent, beg for forgiveness.

Danny's not sure he recalls it, but he begins whispering the act of contrition. *"Bless me O Lord, for I have sinned. I am heartily sorry for having offended Thee . . . ,"* but the words won't come to him; he's forgotten them, so he thinks it's the sentiment—the very real feeling from deep in your soul—that counts. Not words, because they're just bullshit.

Our father who art in heaven . . .

Forgive us our trespasses . . .

Danny feels like praying with all his soul.

Pray for what?

Forgiveness? Redemption? Salvation?

Who knows if they even exist?

The right rear window slides down.

Kenny calls to Roddy, "What's up?"

"I've found a spot."

"Let's bury the bastard alive," Kenny says, and then cackles.

■

What a fucked-up situation this is, thinks Kenny.

Now, Roddy and Danny know he's put up only 50K, not three hundred. But when this bastard Grange is gone, who's gonna own that 250K his money represents? Doesn't matter. Roddy and Danny are gonna want out.

The game's over.

Kenny was doing a helluva good job as manager—until a few months ago. That's when he *really* began the sticky fingers routine. Man . . . you can really do a lot of shit when you're an owner—not like when he was only a manager in Vegas. Owning the place is like walkin' through money fields. It's all there for the takin'.

The bar's a gold mine: all cash, all the time; and he can adjust the ticker and walk away with a thou a week in cash. Mother's milk.

And comping diners—the kahunas and kingpins—brings in monster-sized tips. Every fat-wallet honcho ponies up, if for no other reason than to impress the women. That's maybe another thou a week. All cold cash and tax-free.

And those steaks bring in top dollar—even when he sells 'em at half-price to that smart-ass purveyor, some guy who's cozy with the big-name chophouses.

But he's been kissing the money goodbye on the ponies and bettin' the spread on ballgames. The bullshit he fed Roddy and Danny about stayin' away from the tables could hold up for just so long. Especially when he got heavy into the coke and speed. He went loosey-goosey with that stuff and began bettin' his life away. The money's had wings.

But the party was over the second Grange popped up.

Because Kenny was supposed to have a full year to raid the pantry. But the fat fucker shows up after only six months. Greedy bastard. But his days are over.

And maybe with a little finagling, Kenny can reshuffle the deck with Roddy and Danny and work out a new card game. Kenny's certain Danny'll wanna toss him. And Roddy'll go along with him. Because those guys are thick as thieves—always *have* been, even as kids.

So, Kenny thinks, *the biggest problem is I been playin' the odds.*

Man, these days it's too easy.

You just pick up the phone and place a bet. Or boot up and go online. Kenny lost a bundle on college basketball—fuckin' March Madness—and then too, he got scalded betting on the Super Bowl.

So, he's an addict. Addicted to gambling, coke, speed, booze, money, and women. Hooked on good times.

The speed costs a fuckin' fortune. But the cocktail Roddy fed this fat bastard Grange, now that's some good shit, thinks Kenny. He's gotta get the formula. Those Russian guys got labs in Brooklyn; they could make that shit in bulk.

Danny was right: the deal with Grange was a disaster waiting to happen. The interest was too high. Jesus, if he'd only had the full year with the restaurant.

But by then, the interest would've climbed to a fortune. A million.

And you can't push a guy like Roddy too far. That's what Grange did—goin' to Bronxville, touchin' his daughter. Because Kenny remembers him as a kid; once he went over that edge, Roddy turned into a beast.

But Kenny's still got 10 percent of McLaughlin's. He could get another loan from the Fontana brothers, those greedy goombahs. He's comped them dozens of times at the restaurant. But he's already fifty Gs into them. Maybe he'll offer his share of McLaughlin's as backup. They'd *love* to have a greasy finger in the place. Then they'd spot him another fifty Gs.

But those guys charge weekly vig. And with those fuckers, you miss *one* payment, they break legs. They'd go after him *and* his partners. People could really get hurt.

It means I gotta win big at the tables.

He can get to Atlantic City and shoot craps—or hit it big at blackjack; that's always been his game. Gimme an ace . . . gimme a queen. Hit me, muthafucka.

Grange mumbles something about "the deal." Kenny snarls, "What deal muthafucka? What fuckin' deal? What the fuck you talkin' about you fat bastard?" He slaps Grange hard, right across his fat face.

Kenny shouts, "What? What? What? Whaddaya gotta say now, Mr. Fuckin' Shylock?"

Kenny rears back and slams his fist into fat-boy's face. Then another, and another after that. Grange lies across the seat like a clubbed baby seal.

Then, there're the Russians, thinks Kenny. He met a guy—Oleg Russakoff, comped him a few dinners—who can get him in on a massage parlor. For fifty grand. Russian and Ukrainian girls—with blonde hair and blue eyes—not the motley Koreans in the eighty-dollar shitholes. The whole sex-trade thing's the way to go.

If Kenny can wangle some more cash, Roddy might just let him stay on. Mad Dog's tough—has Mohammed Ali speed in his hands. But when push comes to shove, he's got a good heart. So maybe Roddy'll give him another chance to mark the deck and stack the cards.

He sees Roddy approach the car, so he lowers the window. Kenny feels so electric he hears his blood buzzing in a speed-rush. It's like a current coursing through him. Kenny thinks to himself there's no way he's gonna let this gig with McLaughlin's end.

Before he calls out to Roddy, he decides he needs a jolt.

So he pops another pill.

Chapter 25

"See the lantern?" Roddy says. "That's where we're taking him."

"This fucker weighs a ton," says Kenny.

Kenny's sweating. And his tuxedo shirt looks drenched. *His brain's wired like a utility substation*, thinks Roddy. And Dan looks washed out, really fucked up by what's going down.

"We won't have to carry him," Roddy says. "We'll just have to help him . . . like you would a drunk guy."

Roddy opens the Sequoia's hatch. He removes three more twin-tube lanterns, turns one on, and sets it behind the vehicle. He turns off the ignition and headlights. They get out of the SUV. Kenny's tuxedo jacket lies rumpled on the back seat. They haul Grange to the edge of the seat and swing his shoeless feet onto the ground.

Dan and Kenny get on either side of Grange and slip his arms over their shoulders. Grange's knees buckle and he lurches forward, nearly toppling. He lists from side to side, head drooped, but he trudges ahead.

Roddy carries the lanterns and walks toward the light on the ground. Kenny curses and grunts as he and Danny guide Grange toward the lantern. "You fat bastard," Kenny yells. "Roddy . . . lemme kill him, right here. Ya got a knife? Lemme slit him open."

"Just keep moving, Kenny."

They stagger and sway, making progress; finally, they near the lantern.

"Put him down over there," says Roddy. He turns the other lanterns on and sets them on the ground in a semi-circle.

"Let's get his jacket off," Danny says.

The loan shark lies on his back. They roll him over, pull the jacket, and strip it off.

"Go through it again," Roddy says.

Danny rummages through the pockets. "There's nothing."

"Stay here with him," Roddy says. "I'll be right back."

Moving toward the Sequoia, Roddy thinks this is the most insane thing he's ever done. Sheepshead Bay, the army—it all pales by comparison. He knows if a single thing goes wrong, all he's ever worked for comes to an end. His family, profession, everything.

Moving closer to the SUV, he can barely feel his legs. It's like walking underwater.

At the open hatch, he grabs the gloves, swings the shovels and pick over his shoulder, and heads back. The lights in the clearing look eerie in the darkness. The silhouettes of Dan and Kenny seem otherworldly. And the huge mound lying next to where they're standing—Grange—sends a bolt of tension through Roddy. Shadows are everywhere. The crickets keep up a racket; the tree frogs send out a constant peeping.

At the clearing, Roddy tosses the tools to the ground. He repositions the lanterns, forming a crude square. They stand in the lantern glow—huddled in the radiance of light—three men in a clearing amidst impenetrable woods. Outside the circle of light: darkness and the spooky sounds of the woods. Nearby, the blackness of the swamp. A frog emits a gulping sound; Roddy thinks he hears a hiss from somewhere over the water. A chill runs down his spine.

"Here's where we dig," Roddy says.

"What if somebody finds him?" asks Danny.

"Nobody comes here—ever. The nearest house is miles away."

"But if we dig a hole, somebody might find it."

"I know this area. Don't be fooled by how warm it is tonight.

There'll be another snowfall soon. The ground'll freeze again, and then thaw. It'll settle in. Then come the April rains. By June, there'll be weeds everywhere."

"Let's do it," Kenny says. He picks up a shovel. "Right here?"

"Right here," Roddy says. He swallows hard, thinking about what he must do before this night is over.

"I wish I knew," Kenny says. "I'd a dressed for this."

Dan takes off his jacket and tie. Roddy hands them gloves. "Better wear these if you don't want blisters."

Kenny puts on the gloves and picks up a shovel. With a quick movement, he plunges it into the ground. It sinks in with a slicing thwack.

Just as Roddy thought, the soil is soft, porous, no rocks or roots. Digging should go fast, very fast.

Kenny tosses a shovelful of dirt to the side and then pitches the blade into the earth again. It sinks in, to the hilt. Kenny bends at the waist and pulls up. A huge wad rises on the shovel. He tosses it over his shoulder.

Roddy raises the pick over his head and slams it down; it sinks in deeply. He tugs, feeling his back muscles tighten. The pick swivels on itself and yanks up a huge chunk of soil. He swings the pick upward and then down, then up and down again. After each thump of the iron into the soil, Danny's shovel scoops out a clump of dirt and tosses it. A few earthworms wriggle through the soil, their bodies glisten in the lantern light.

The hole deepens, widens, and gets longer—quickly. The air smells of damp earth.

Kenny moves like a human backhoe. But then, Roddy realizes he's on speed, or maybe he's all coked up—or on some weird combination of mind-blowing shit. He's pumped, crazed.

The hole expands. No water, rocks, or roots. They plunge the tools into the ground, gouge, scoop, and toss, again and again. It takes on a silent rhythm.

Pyramidal mounds collect nearby. They look strange, glowing in lantern light.

Grange moans, so Roddy climbs out of the pit and kneels down to check him out. He's in a stupor. Even by lantern light Roddy sees huge welts around Grange's eyes—obscene-looking swellings that make his face look mongoloid. His lips are swollen, split, and his jaw looks misaligned. Probably fractured from Kenny's battering.

Roddy pinches Grange's jowls; an aversive response follows, a twitching of Grange's blubbery lips, a slight moan: completely normal. *Responds to noxious stimuli* is how it's put, medically. He's in a twilight state, not quite sleeping but oblivious.

Peering at the loan shark, Roddy thinks, *So you'll come back for Sandy? Afraid that's not gonna happen.*

Back at the hole, Kenny's removed his shirt. His bare torso glistens with sweat; he shovels like the hopped-up addict he's become. Kenny grunts, mutters, tugs at the soil, and then lets out a high-pitched laugh. He's got a crazed work-rhythm going. Looks ridiculous in his black tuxedo pants with silk side-stripes reflecting the lantern light.

Roddy knows that for Dan this is grim work—the labor of malevolence. It's not his way of being. But Danny's been burned—Angela's near-death experience did something, it flipped some internal switch of anger, of desperation, even barely controlled rage. Dan digs like a good soldier.

They stop to rest. Roddy feels his back muscles tightening. Dan takes in greedy gusts of damp night air. He's not quite wheezing, but his lungs could start filling with mucous. "You gonna be all right?" Roddy asks.

"Yeah . . ."

"I mean the asthma."

"I'm good."

Kenny keeps up his rhythm; he mutters, heaves soil, and laughs like a lunatic.

"It's my fault we got involved with this guy," Danny says with a shake of his head.

"Forget it."

"You were right; I was snowed by the glitz, with Harris and all that shit."

"Let's just do what we gotta do."

Danny looks at his watch. "We've been digging for half an hour," he says.

Roddy can barely believe it's been that long. Time is gone, collapsed on itself. It seems like five minutes have passed. Time has lost meaning . . . past . . . present . . . it all comes together now. Nothing seems real. Everything's distorted, out of its own realm. It's crazy, a nightmare. Like that dog lunging for his throat in the dream. God, if only this was a dream.

Kenny's waist-deep in the hole. He's soaked; sweat dribbles down his torso, off his elbows. Soil particles cling to him on his shoulders and neck, too. Sweat forms jagged channels through his earth-covered chest and back. He doesn't give a shit.

Roddy watches Kenny squat down, his back against the side of the pit. He lights a cigarette and puffs away. He mutters some crazed crap, deranged nonsense about the restaurant and Grange, something about money—a madman's ranting. Shit, the guy's dribbling words like a leaky faucet. Kenny sucks on the cigarette and exhales, and smoke fills the pit, rises in spiral wisps, and then swirls in the lantern light.

"Hear that bastard?" Dan says, struggling to catch his breath.

Roddy nods. Breathing heavily now, his arms burn.

"Belongs in an insane asylum," Dan whispers.

Danny leans against the pit's wall, waves at the cigarette smoke, coughs, brings up a wad of phlegm, and spits it out. Roddy hopes Dan's asthma won't kick in. This isn't accountants' work. Nor is it a surgeon's.

But tonight's not about surgery; that's light years away—

gone —another life.

Kenny drops his cigarette and stomps it out. He evens the edges of the hole: slices off clumps of dirt, scoops them up, and tosses them to the top.

Despite his thin frame, Ken has sinewy arms, shoulders, and back; he still looks like the track athlete he was in high school. In those days he could run a hundred meters in no time flat. He was never beaten in a citywide track meet. Despite the years and the booze, and now, drugs, Kenny's still ripped. He heaves soil like a machine.

Kenny pulls a lantern down into the hole. He's in a strange fury; he shovels, scrapes, scoops, and hurls. He's lost in what he's doing: making a grave.

A cigarette jumps up and down between Kenny's lips. He looks up at Roddy, now standing at the top. "How much deeper?" Kenny asks.

"Another foot . . ."

"This fucker's gotta be four feet down . . ."

"We can't take chances."

"I shoulda joined the gravediggers union," calls Kenny.

Are they making another mistake—a huge one? Roddy wonders. *But there's no time for questions,* he tells himself. *You don't let doubt invade you after what Grange did to Angela. And touching Sandy? And the hang-ups, with Tracy getting worried. And the possibility of Grange coming back, wanting more . . . and then more. No,* Roddy thinks; *you just keep going. Like in the Rangers.*

Roddy jumps into the pit and grabs Danny's shovel. Dan, wheezing now, leans against the wall, trying to catch his breath.

The pit smells like rotting humus. The air is humid, hot, even wet. With Grange buried, bacteria will do their work—bring decay. *Flesh won't last,* Roddy thinks. *Turns to dust. Bone lasts longer but turns to powder, too. Though not always: don't they dig up dinosaur bones? A million years old. Something always stays. Can't worry about that.*

Nature will do what nature does.

Kenny still works like a maniac; he leaks sweat, laughs, and keeps digging.

He doesn't give a shit. About anything.

And Roddy? He knows what he must do.

■

Kenny moves like a jackhammer. It feels good, like he was back in the Bay—the good old days when he ran numbers and had sway with the Sheepshead Bay Boys, even had connections to Parisi's crew in Mill Basin.

And now, they're diggin' this fat fuck's grave. It's what this lousy shark deserves: bein' buried alive. What a way to go. Imagine bein' in this stinkin' pit, eatin' dirt, no coffin, nothin'. Drugged, dazed, awake, can't move. Dirt drops onto your face; it gets in your hair, your mouth, up your fuckin' nose. You gag and choke and can't breathe worth a shit. And it keeps comin', pressin', crushin' your chest. You suck it into your throat, your lungs—till you smother and black out. It's like drownin' but it ain't water.

Makes you wanna die fast—a bullet or something—quick and painless. It just goes black if you get it in the head. It'd be better if the fat fuck could be awake, feel the pain—the fear—and get the most out of the fuckin' experience.

But this Grange bastard's gotta go. Just disappear, *hasta la vista,* baby.

Now, he, Roddy, and Danny are stuck together—like triplets, joined at the hip.

Yup, together forever because now, each has somethin' on the other—*murder.* Big-time shit. Not some minor teenage bullshit like smugglin' cigarettes up from the Carolinas. Not your crooked back-room card game like he used to run for that greedy prick, Parisi. Not the penny ante Brooklyn Irish bullshit. This is a major league felony, the Big Show.

So now, it's like a marriage. They're together—in murder, and in life.

Till death do us part, muthafucka . . . till death do us part.

Chapter 26

They've been digging steadily. Dan's kept up the pace; not too much wheezing comes from his gunk-filled chest. At least not much that Roddy can hear amidst the raging of the crickets and frogs. Roddy's certain the grave's nearly six feet deep by now. It's a crude hole but can easily hold a body as large as Grange's.

He tosses the pick to the top. The others heave their tools up as well.

Roddy slaps his palms onto the top edge, digs his boot toe into the wall, and scrambles to the top. Soil sifts back down.

The smell of damp earth rising in the hole reminds Roddy of his Ranger days at Fort Bragg, then at Fort Benning. The infiltration course—nighttime. Live 30-caliber machine-gun slugs with phosphorous-tipped tracers—red and orange streaks, three feet off the ground—as they crawled beneath strung barbed wire. Flash bursts from deep holes momentarily lighting the course and then darkness and tracers. He was bellying through sand—beneath barbed wire—when he saw it. Just like Sergeant Dawson warned them: a rattlesnake in the night sand, cooling off.

"You come on a rattler, *don't* jump up," Dawson warned. "You'll be cut in half by tracers. Just freeze. The sumbitch'll slither away, or I'll kill it."

Snagged on barbed wire, eye-to-eye with a rattler, Roddy lay stone still.

He was the only man left in the sand when the guns went silent.

"Dolan. You caught on wire?" Dawson shouted.

He lay rigid, silent.

Overhead lights detonated; Roddy lay belly down, face flattened in the sand. The snake—thick and coiled, ready to strike—waited.

"Dolan, I can see you're snake-stuck. Stay still," Dawson yelled. "I'm comin' for you."

He stayed silent and heard his heart beating into the sand.

He heard Dawson trudging nearby.

A deafening boom. The snake was blown to bits—a blast from a .12-gauge shotgun with a choke to narrow the pellet pattern. Dawson clipped the wire. Roddy's ears rang for days.

On bivouac they were drained by ticks. The bastards crawled under your combat fatigues and latched on everywhere—your neck, in your ears, your groin, in every crevice—and sucked away. You'd all get naked—do a tick check on each other. Even in the other guy's ass. Then burn their blood-bloated bodies off with cigarettes.

Roddy recalls thinking it all *had* to have some meaning, a purpose.

And it did: Ranger training prepared him for anything.

But not this.

■

Roddy pats down his legs and slaps off caked soil. He kicks his boots together; dried clods drop off.

Danny and Kenny clamber out of the hole and stand at the top, panting. They beat at their trousers. Dusty clouds billow in the night air, backlit by lantern light. Dust gets into Roddy's nostrils and lines his mouth. Tastes gritty, makes him cough. Dan coughs, spits up phlegm, and wheezes heavily.

Roddy's arms feel rubbery and his legs feel like they've turned to liquid.

A cool breeze stirs. Shadows dance over them. The tree frogs and crickets keep up their nocturnal symphony. The cryptic sounds of woodland nightlife send chills through Roddy.

He wonders: *How did this come to pass?*

Stop thinking of the how and why . . . just do what's gotta be done.

"Okay, let's roll him in . . . ," says Roddy.

"Goodbye, you fat bastard," Kenny shrieks.

They start rolling Grange toward the hole.

"Wait!" shouts Danny.

"What for?"

"You wanted to get that ring off."

Roddy realizes he'd forgotten. He grabs Grange's finger and tugs at the ring. But a huge, swollen knuckle blocks it. No way is it coming off. Even axle grease won't do it.

"You'll never get it off this fat fucker," Kenny says. "Forget it."

"Can't forget it. Just stay here, I'll be right back," Roddy says.

"Where're ya goin'?" Kenny asks.

"Back to the car . . ."

Roddy picks up a lantern and heads back to the SUV.

■

Nearing the Sequoia, Roddy shivers.

He knows it's not the night air. It's something inside him: a sick, icy feeling taking over, because he knows everything will be forever changed.

For a moment, he can't feel his hands. It's as though they've dropped off his wrists. A hole forms in the pit of his stomach. Blood drains from his head and he feels faint, as though he'll sink to the ground. A prickling begins inside his body wall; he shudders and his heart feels too big for his chest.

Roddy closes his eyes and waits for the feeling to pass. He breathes in and out, steadies himself, and thinks, *Just do it and don't let it get to you.*

His heart slows; feeling returns to his fingers.

An image of Tracy flutters in his mind; he forces it away. *Gotta stay focused, like when you're doing surgery. Just think of what Grange did. Of what he'll do if he lives.*

Roddy reaches into the Sequoia's hatch, flips up the carpeting covering the spare tire well, and hoists out the toolbox. He opens it, peers inside, and spies the last two things he'll need tonight. He slips them into his pocket.

About halfway back toward the hole, Roddy realizes how strange it looks: two men are standing, another is on his back. Mounds of soil are piled nearby, backlit by lanterns.

All in the middle of nowhere.

■

"Whaddaya gonna do?" asks Kenny, rubbing his hands together. Sweat shines on his chest and shoulders. His eyes look glazed, absolutely mad.

"Take off the finger . . ."

"Lemme do it," Kenny squeals.

"No way."

" *Please* lemme do it."

"Fuckin' asshole," Danny growls.

"Fuck you!" Kenny shrieks. "Please, Roddy, lemme do it."

"You don't wanna do this, Ken."

Roddy holds the tool—a ratcheting cable cutter. It can slice through cable an inch-and-a-half thick.

"Please Roddy, I can do it."

Roddy shoves Kenny away and bends down over Grange. He slips the tool's aperture over Grange's ring finger and slides it below the knuckle, just above the ring. He squeezes. There's a sharp, snapping sound. Grange's body jumps.

Responds to noxious stimuli . . .

Blood spurts in a thin jetting stream from the stump.

Dan crumples onto his hands and knees, retching, then coughing.

"You okay, Danny?" Roddy asks.

"Yeah . . . ," Dan gurgles, and wipes his mouth. A thread of drool hangs from his lips.

"Ya fuckin' wimp," Kenny screams at Dan.

"Shut up you sick bastard," Dan sputters, still on his hands and knees.

A puddle of vomit shimmers on the ground. Dan spits, wipes his lips with his hand, and rubs the hand on the grass.

Roddy picks up the finger and slides the ring from the stump. His hands are covered with Grange's blood. The stump keeps squirting.

Kenny laughs insanely.

"You sadistic bastard," Danny yells.

Kenny looks skyward and laughs harder. "Fuck you, Danny Burns!" he shouts. "I *love* this shit. I just *love* it."

Dan gets to his feet, still coughing.

"Let's pull down his pants," says Kenny. "I wanna cut this fat fuck's dick off."

Kenny grabs the cable cutter from Roddy. The movement is so quick, it seems a blur. He rushes toward Grange's crotch and bends over the fat man, cable cutter in hand.

Roddy reaches for the tool.

Ken pulls away, thrusts an elbow at Roddy, and hits him in the thigh. Pain shoots through Roddy's leg and cuts to the bone.

Roddy slams a knee into Ken's back and sends him sprawling face down.

He straddles Ken from behind, keeps his knee in the small of his back, and bears down; Kenny howls in pain. Roddy rips the tool from his hand.

"Hey muthafucka. That *hurt*," Kenny whines, getting up. He gets to his feet and then wobbles.

"Try that again, Kenny, and I'll kill you."

Roddy turns, holding the tool, Grange's finger, and the ring. He grabs a lantern.

"Gimme that ring," Kenny says.

"Not a chance."

"That fuckin' thing's worth a fortune."

"Kenny . . . I'll end your life."

Roddy trudges toward the pond.

"What're you gonna do?" Kenny cries, following him.

"Toss it . . ."

"Get rid of it, Roddy," shouts Dan.

"Roddy. Wait!" Kenny calls.

Roddy nears the pond.

"I know a guy we can unload it on . . ."

At the pond's edge, Roddy hurls the finger and ring out into the blackness. Two splashing plops sound in the distance. Then, the croaking of a frog.

"What a waste," Kenny mutters.

Squatting, Roddy swirls his hands and the cable cutter in the water, shakes them, and dries them on the grass. He slips the cutter into his jacket pocket. He makes his way back to Grange; Ken follows, mumbling.

"Okay, let's roll him," Roddy says.

Grange's amputated finger pumps a thin stream of blood.

They roll Grange toward the hole, over and over, face down, then up. They avoid blood from the squirting stump.

Kenny's shoe thuds into Grange's side, then his back.

"Stop it, Kenny."

"You fat bastard; die and go to hell," Kenny shouts. He kicks again.

The fat man rolls toward the grave.

At the edge, Kenny shouts, "Good-bye, muthafucka," and with a final collective push, Grange tumbles into the pit.

He hits bottom with a heavy thump.

"Eat dirt, muthafucka," Kenny shouts.

They look down into the hole.

Grange is sprawled face down, partly on his side. One arm pokes upward at an unnatural angle. Roddy can tell the shoulder is torn; ligaments have snapped.

"Lemme check him out," Kenny says. He grabs a lantern and shovel and jumps into the pit.

The grave bottom is lit. Kenny moves Grange onto his back. He sets Grange's arms at his sides.

"Whaddaya say now, muthafucka?" Kenny shouts into Grange's face. He's so close he looks like he'll kiss the fat man's lips.

"Kenny, come on," Danny calls.

"What *now*, fat boy?" Kenny shrieks.

Roddy and Danny stare at each other.

"He's a fucking maniac," Dan says.

"He's jacked out of his mind," Roddy says.

"Kenny, *stop* it," Danny shouts.

But Kenny keeps bellowing at Grange's unconscious mass.

Suddenly, Kenny slams the shovel blade into Grange's face. A dull thud resounds from the hole's bottom and blood flies everywhere. Kenny bends over Grange, gripping the shovel handle near its iron blade. The lantern is next to Grange's face.

Kenny's arm moves to and fro and he keeps shouting into Grange's face.

Danny bends over at the hole's edge, retches, and then dry heaves.

"Kenny, stop it," Roddy yells.

Kenny stands up and drops the shovel. His hand goes to his ear.

"What's that you're sayin'?" He cups his ear. "What the fuckdya say?"

"Ken. Get up here."

Still cupping his ear, Ken looks up. "I can't hear ya, Roddy."

"I said . . ." Roddy's voice catches in his throat.

A smudge of blood blots Kenny's face, just below his ear.

"Whaddaya say, Roddy?" Kenny shouts.

"That fucking animal," Danny mutters.

Roddy realizes suddenly that Kenny's hand isn't cupping his ear; instead, he's holding Grange's ear over his own.

"Hey Mad Dog! Remember Cootie Weiss?" Kenny convulses with laughter; Grange's severed ear covers his own.

Roddy gapes at Kenny, at the ear and the bloodied shovel in the lantern's glow at the pit's bottom. Kenny cackles with his eyes closed. Spittle forms on Kenny's lips, and Roddy hears him shout, "It's Cootie Weiss, Roddy. It's Cootie Weiss and it's like yesterday."

Chapter 27

Roddy's not even at Snapper Pond; he's just floating somewhere, as though he's watching from afar. He's moving away from the hole, and it's such a weird feeling as he picks up Grange's jacket and drapes it over his arm—as if it simply rose from the ground. Then he's back at the pit where Kenny's sick laughter rises from the bottom. Danny curses and then coughs, and it's all dreamlike beneath the bone-white radiance of the moon and dull lantern glow rising from the hole.

Roddy's right hand slips into his pocket, and sure enough, it's sitting there—cold and heavy.

Out comes a .45 semi-automatic.

Grange's jacket wraps around the pistol—once, then again—and forms a bundle at the end of Roddy's arm. Wrapped and ready to fire.

Roddy feels the pistol's weight—so heavy he can barely hold it. His left hand slips beneath the jacket and goes to the steel ribbing on the slide, and he yanks it back—racks the weapon—and there's a muffled metallic slapping as a cartridge clacks up into the chamber.

Holding Grange's ear with his eyes closed, Kenny sees nothing. He's dribbling sweat, laughing, actually shrieking with his head back, mouth open, and in the lantern's glow he looks crazed and ghoulish.

Roddy's hand kicks upward as a stifled roar blows out from the jacket. The muzzle blast shears outward as a hot, fiery streak;

a percussive shock thrusts Roddy's hand upward. A violent jolt travels through his arm. As quickly as the pistol jumped, it lowers and Roddy squeezes the trigger again; another blast roars from the bundle.

Two holes burst through Grange's chest. His body jerks and splays against the dirt with the impact of the slugs.

Blood froths from Grange's chest—two lung shots. Two entrance wounds—bloody circles, crimson-black starbursts—spread out and soak through Grange's shirt and form wide circles in the fabric.

Kenny freezes midlaugh and goes statue-still. His mouth stays open and his eyes bulge as he peers up, bewildered and shocked.

Roddy knows there are grapefruit-sized exit wounds in the fat man's back as blood seeps into the soil; the fat man's life-blood spreads, and sinks into the dark earth where it mixes with the lead that tore through Grange. He's gone.

A wisp of smoke snakes from beneath the jacket and sifts into the air. Roddy smells burnt powder and feels heat as the smoke's acrid pungency singes the insides of his nostrils.

God almighty, am I in some kind of sick dream?

"What the fuck?" shrieks Kenny. He's now derailed from the insanity of his blood lust. "Whaddaya doin'?" Kenny cries as his hands drop to his sides. Grange's ear drops in the dirt.

Kenny glances at Grange and sees the bubbling holes in his chest, the last remnants of oxygen frothing through the lung blood like foam on a dog's mouth. Kenny's gaze shifts uncomprehendingly back and forth—Roddy to Grange and the widening circles of blood, back to Roddy. Kenny shakes his head in disbelief, sending sweat droplets flying.

Danny moves next to Roddy at the grave's edge. Short of breath, wheezing, he holds a lantern.

The biting odor of burned gunpowder fills the air.

Grange's jacket falls away and drops to the ground.

The pistol now feels light—weightless.

"Ya fuckin' wasted him," shouts Kenny.

Kenny's face goes crimson; his torso glistens. Covered with specks of soil, streaks of sweat, he rattles the shovel and shakes his head. More sweat droplets fly from his face.

"We don't torture people," Roddy says. The .45 floats in the air.

"You son of a bitch!" Kenny shrieks. His eyes bulge like golf balls and gleam wildly in the lantern light. "I wanted to work the fucker over for what he did."

The .45 slides sideways and Roddy thinks it's strange how it moves on its own—slowly, steadily—points at Kenny's chest, then rises, and hovers in front of his face.

"What the fuck ya doin', Roddy?"

Danny's breathing is heavy; mucous throttles through his chest. Sounds like a boiler factory.

Ken stares at the muzzle hole, eyes now wide with fear.

"Talk to us, Kenny . . . ," Roddy hears himself say.

"Don't point that fuckin' thing at me."

"Talk, Kenny . . ."

Roddy sidesteps at the grave's edge; the .45 hovers at Ken's head.

Kenny backs away, drops the shovel, and scrambles over Grange to the far side of the hole. His lower lip trembles. "Roddy, whaddaya doin'?"

"I'm pointing a .45 at your head."

"What the fuck for?"

"You gotta come clean, Kenny."

"You mean the business . . . ?"

"Yes, the business."

"I fucked up. So what?"

Roddy edges closer.

"It's truth time, Kenny."

Kenny cringes and turns his head away.

"Tell us . . . *now*."

"Fuck you!"

The .45 roars again and a slug thuds into Grange's corpse. The body jerks. Dirt sprays the air.

Ringing starts in Roddy's ears; his throat tightens.

"The next one's for you, Kenny . . ."

"You wouldn't."

"I'll blow your brains out . . ." Roddy says, pressing the trigger. *Jesus.* He's not even trying, but it's happening. The trigger begins to yield.

Sweating rivulets, Kenny sinks to his knees.

Blood no longer pumps from Grange's finger stump. The bubbling on his chest stops. He's gone.

"Whaddaya wanna know?"

"Everything."

"Okay. Okay." Kenny blurts, trembling. "I was taking cash from the register."

"How much?"

"Maybe four, five hundred a week."

"What else, Kenny?"

"I was comping people . . . desserts . . . extra wine . . . shit like that . . ."

Kenny's trembling spreads and ripples through him in a coarse shaking.

"Kenny, give it up."

It's so strange—Dan at his side, wheezing like a bellows, the light in the hole, the lanterns nearby, Grange's bloated corpse, the tree frogs, crickets, darkness, the .45 floating with such menace.

I'm really doing this . . . this is insane . . .

"I'm *tellin'* ya everythin', Roddy."

"You gambling?"

"Nothin', Roddy. Nothin'. I swear."

"We need the truth, Kenny. Grange can't tell us. But *you* can."

"What the *fuck* ya wanna know?"

"You *know* what, Kenny."

Kenny's putting out fear odor—like a dog. Roddy smells Kenny's innards; or maybe it's coming from Grange lying there in the dirt, bleeding out, leaking his life away, dribbling excrement. Roddy smells shit and blood and sweat and gunpowder and some strange mixture of fluids and solids, putrid waste, and God knows what else, but it hardly matters now.

"You couldn't pay Grange off—*ever*—not on those terms . . ."

"I know that *now*, Roddy. But the fucker's dead and we got his money. It's *our* business, Roddy. We got 250 of his dough. It's ours . . ."

Roddy shakes his head.

"Roddy . . . *please* don't do this."

"Don't beg, Kenny. Just talk."

Kenny's face contorts with fear as his jaw chatters. He kneels on Grange's corpse, gasping.

"Roddy, y'already know. The loan was too much . . ."

"Kenny, lie again and I'll kill you."

Gobs of spittle form on Kenny's lips. Snot dribbles out his nose, forming blistering bubbles at his nostrils.

"Promise you'll lemme me go."

"I promise you *this,* Kenny: you lie, you die."

"Okay. *Okay.*" Kenny looks up at Roddy. "So, here's the deal." He stumbles to his feet and stands shakily beside the body.

"I went to Grange . . ."

Roddy sidesteps along the grave's edge; the pistol shifts closer to Kenny's head.

Kenny swallows hard and then says, "I told Grange I had two friends from the neighborhood. I knew McLaughlin wanted the 500 up front . . ."

"Yeah . . ."

"I only had 50K. I needed 300 to be controlling partner . . ."

Roddy's chest constricts. He feels blood draining from his head; he's going lightheaded. Shit, in a second, he'll faint. So he squats beside the hole, the gun still at Kenny's head.

"I thought I could hit ya up for 100 each. So Grange would pop the 250 and I'd put in 50."

"And . . . ?"

"The catch was . . . ," Kenny coughs, gurgles, and spits phlegm into the dirt.

The woods are screaming.

"The *catch*, Kenny. What was the fucking *catch?*"

Kenny's eyes dart between Roddy and Danny.

Kenny says, "Grange and I were partners."

Danny gasps.

The woods shriek an insane choral whine. A band tightens around Roddy's skull: a crushing pressure so strong it feels like his brain will implode. His heart batters his ribs.

"Partners . . . ?" Danny rasps. "You were fucking *partners?*"

Kenny gulps and nods. He looks down. His arms cross his chest; he holds his elbows, still trembling.

"Then what . . . ?"

"Grange would show up in a year. With the vig, it'd be a million, give or take."

"And the 10 percent you'd pay Grange after four months?"

"Bullshit . . . just for your ears."

"Keep going, Kenny," Roddy says. The light-headed feeling's gone. A buzz hums through him.

"Grange would say I owed him the money. He'd threaten us. You guys would come up with the mill. Grange and I'd split it . . ."

"How . . . ?"

"He'd gimme 20 percent . . ."

"$200,000?"

"Yeah . . ."

"So it was a fucking *con*," Danny mutters.

Kenny nods and bows his head.

"But Grange showed up after only six months," Danny says. "Why?"

"The fat fuck was greedy. Couldn't wait."

"Surprised you, didn't he, Kenny?"

Kenny sinks to his knees.

"So we were just a couple of patsies, right?" Danny asks.

Kenny shoots Roddy a pleading look.

"The guy whose dick you were gonna cut off and whose ear you sliced off, he was your partner?" shouts Danny. "You fuckin' snake."

"Please, Dan. Please, Roddy . . ."

"You bastard . . . ," Dan shouts. He bends down and hurls a clump of soil at Kenny. It spatters in his face.

Kenny sputters and spits specks of dirt.

"And you passed yourself off as a *friend?*" Danny shouts.

Kenny's face is streaked with tears, sweat, soil, and snot.

"Roddy . . . you're gonna lemme go, right?"

"Why should I?"

"For old times sake."

Dan kicks dirt. It spatters on Kenny. Soil and saliva dribble from Kenny's lips and sweat pours off his chin.

The woods howl.

Roddy feels like his guts are being yanked.

"We can't trust you, Kenny," Danny growls.

Kenny knee-shuffles through the soil. His work gloves lie in the dirt. "Look guys, it's over," he cries. "You own the restaurant. It's yours—split two ways, and the 300K too."

"How much else you owe, Kenny?" asks Roddy.

"To who? For Chrissake, who?"

"To *anyone*," shouts Danny. "So you could use the restaurant and *us* as collateral?"

"Nobody. Grange is gone; I'm free and clear."

"I don't believe him, Roddy."

Kenny inches forward. "Gimme a break, Roddy."

Kenny's open mouth looks like a sucking hole.

"Like you gave us a break?" Roddy asks.

"So this is it? You're gonna shoot me like a dog in a hole?"

"Why shouldn't I?"

"I know why," Kenny says, his eyes widening, "Yeah, I know why ya wanna *do* me."

"Enlighten us, Kenny."

"I fuckin' know," Kenny shouts, frothing at the mouth, still kneeling with Grange's body beside him. "It's because . . ."

"Fuck you and whatever you think you know," Danny shouts. "Who else is in on this con?"

"No-fuckinbody, Danny . . ."

"Yeah? Tell me you son of a bitch, who ran Angela off the road?"

"I dunno."

"Shoot him, Roddy. Shoot the motherfucker."

"*Danny!*" Kenny shouts, "she didn't get hurt . . ."

"Who did it?"

"It was just to scare her . . . to get to *you.*"

"Was it *you?*"

Kenny nods, his head bobbing frantically; his body shakes and sweat dribbles. "We figured you'd get scared . . ."

"*Shoot* him, Roddy."

"Please . . . please . . . ," Kenny cries. He rises to his feet, backs away, trips over Grange's corpse, and lands on top of the dead man.

He sits on the corpse, amidst blood, soil, and sweat. Suddenly, a stain spreads over the front of his tuxedo pants.

"Look, Roddy, he pissed his pants," Dan yells.

"Dan! Roddy!"

"Gimme the gun," Danny cries. "Lemme shoot him."

Roddy's heart is throwing a tantrum inside his chest.

"You stalked our families . . . ," Roddy mutters.

Kenny shakes his head frantically.

"Grange came to my house, touched my daughter . . ."

"That wasn't me."

The stench of sweat, damp soil, and urine seeps up from the hole.

"And you nearly killed Angela," Danny shouts.

Kenny mutters something; his words are muffled; his hands come together, fingers clasped as though he's praying.

"Roddy, *shoot* him," Danny yells.

"Please, lemme go," Kenny squeals. "Danny, you wouldn't do this. You're not a violent guy like him." Kenny points a trembling finger at Roddy. "Don't let him do this. He's fuckin' *Mad Dog Dolan*. Remember back then? He was Mad Dog. Danny, you don't wanna *do* this."

"I can't help you, Kenny," Danny says.

Sobbing and shaking, Kenny grovels in the dirt and claws through the loose soil, panting. A string of mucous-filled saliva hangs in a glistening rope from his lips.

The .45 holds steady.

"Shoot him, Roddy," Dan whispers.

Roddy sees Kenny's hand move to his foot, nears his ankle; his pant leg slips upward. He swings around.

It's quick. Yet it's languid, happens in slow motion. Kenny's hand comes up from below and Roddy sees a metallic gleam in the lantern light. It swings toward him, and it's a gun, and in that instant Roddy realizes there's no time and his finger presses the trigger; his hand flies up with the pistol's kick, and there's a deafening roar as a slug slams into Ken's forehead, explodes out the back, spatters the dirt wall with a spray of brains, blood, and bits of skull.

Kenny's body thumps back to the grave wall, slides down amidst crumbling soil, and lands on top of Grange.

Chapter 28

Roddy's voice is gone. Just missing.

His hands shake violently while his legs feel rubbery. The lightheaded feeling returns and suddenly the woods look bleached. He feels faint and his knees wobble. His heart stampedes in his chest—a rampant thundering—and nausea rises from the pit of his stomach. He closes his eyes, knows he's still standing, waits, and hopes the feeling will pass.

It seems like forever as he and Dan wait beside the grave. He hears Dan's breathing—rapid, mucous-filled, heavy—and it sounds like Dan's dying. Dan says something, but Roddy's ears are clogged and ringing. Danny's voice is muffled, coming from far away.

Get it together, keep calm, do what you have to do.

Roddy's thoughts take on some semblance of coherence as his head clears. He bends down, picks up three shell casings, and slips them into his pocket. Though he's still a bit foggy, he's certain he fired four shots; but there's no fourth casing. He grabs a lantern, angles around the pit, and peers down. He circles the grave once, then again. No casing.

"It's probably down there," he hears Dan say in a warbling voice.

Even in the pale wash of night and lantern light, Dan looks ashen, bloodless.

Roddy hasn't uttered a single word since the shot.

He pockets the .45 and lowers himself into the grave. The pit is humid and hot and smells fetid in the lantern light. He sifts through the dirt and rummages around, damp soil slipping between his fingers; he feels grit beneath his nails. A tide of fear rises through him. Where is it? Where's the damned shell casing? He winnows through the dirt again, but there's nothing.

Ken lies on top of Grange. A small pistol lies next to his body. A holster is strapped to the inside of Kenny's left ankle. Roddy's careful not to touch it.

By lantern light, he sifts once again through the soil.

No casing. Just two dead bodies.

"Forget it," Dan calls down.

With weak hands, Roddy goes through Kenny's pants pockets, pulling them inside out. Nothing. No jewelry. He rips off Kenny's shoes, tosses them up to Danny, and throws Kenny's work gloves to the top. He slips the shovel over the edge, then wedges Kenny onto Grange, and jams the corpse in tightly.

He looks closely at Ken. A tide of revulsion threatens to overcome him.

Roddy's seen plenty of dead people—in the hospital, in the morgue. In the Rangers, too, when soldiers died in drunken car crashes or failed parachute jumps; he saw guys splattered with blood and guts everywhere and saw heads bashed in, mutilated beyond recognition.

But he's never seen anything like this. It's from Zombieland. Ken's face and head look like a smashed doll's. His open eyes stare at nothing. Totally blank, they're dull, clouded over by a gray film. From a seedy life to death in a split second. The flesh of Kenny's face sags lifelessly. It's a death mask. And behind the eyes, off to the side, there's a gaping hole in the skull. Red and white jelly, bits of bone, a mush of smashed brainpan.

The pit stinks of shit, piss, sweat, and blood. Dead flesh, too. Or is it his imagination running wild, Roddy wonders. And it's all mixed with gunpowder. Roddy thinks—or imagines—there's a burnt smell, maybe something from the depths of hell.

"What about his piece?" Dan calls.

"Leaving it down here . . ."

"Good idea."

He passes the lantern up to Danny. Dan extends his hand and yanks Roddy out of the grave.

They move away from the grave. Dan staggers sideways and then sinks onto the ground.

"You okay?" Roddy asks, feeling his breath go short.

Dan nods his head, but he's wheezing loudly. He sits with his knees beneath his chin, hugging his legs, rocking forward and back.

"Shit . . . what've we done . . . ?" Dan says; his voice, birdlike and warbling, sounds bubbly, riddled with mucous frothing up to his vocal cords.

Roddy's legs quiver; he drops to his knees, then leans back, and finally sits on the grass.

Dan's head droops; his chin is tucked to his chest. His breath comes in short, vicious spurts—mucous-ridden whistles rise in the night.

Roddy's heart still gallops like a stallion, feeling like it could pump through his breastbone.

The air feels wet, and Roddy realizes it's sweat, trickling every-where: on his face, inside his shirt and his pants; and, licking his up-per lips, he tastes his body's salt. It's mixed with something pungent, bitter: he's putting out fear odor—no, it's terror—mixed with regret, worry, remorse. Roddy feels like he's drowning in his own seepage. He can't stop shaking. It's a trembling from deep inside, from the core of him, a vibration, like a motor throttling within. Then comes emptiness, a dark void, as though his blood is washing away.

Time streams by—indifferently. Minutes, two, three, four, maybe more—he doesn't know. It seems unreal, as though time's flow has stopped. Like when he saw Kenny's pistol; everything moved through a sluggish film. And now, there's nothing but the woods, darkness, an endless expanse of vegetation and animal life, lanterns glowing, tools, mounds of earth, crickets and tree frogs . . . and Danny.

"So, we've done murder," Danny whispers.

"Yes . . . ," says a distant voice.

More silence. Roddy hears only woods in the night.

"I can't believe it," Danny says hoarsely.

"You all right?" Roddy asks.

"Yeah. It'll pass. Everything does."

Another few minutes drift by; nothing is said.

"Tell me something . . . were you gonna take him out . . . ?"

"The truth?"

"Yeah, the truth . . ."

A pause, with Roddy's thoughts tumbling in a sickening cascade.

"The truth, Dan? Yeah, I was gonna take him out."

More time passes. It seems like everything's gone dead.

Finally Dan asks, "You regret it?"

Roddy can't think of an answer. Coherence eludes him. He wonders if his mind is working, or maybe it's gone dead like the two men in the grave.

"He forced you," Dan whispers.

Roddy nods. His head feels heavy.

"He'd've killed you . . . me too . . ."

"I know."

How strange it is to be sitting here by lantern light, among mounds of dirt near the hole. Dead men down below. His best friend—all his life, Danny Burns—Danny, from the past, here with him now in the insanity of this moment. They're sitting in this clearing near a marsh, not far from the cottage where he's spent summers with Tracy and the kids in his life now, in the present. But it's all come together in an ugly nightscape, with blood and piss and snot and death, and Roddy finds it hard to believe what he's done. It's not a dream; it's real and it's part of his life, *this* life, the same one he's always lived, yet somehow, it all seems different.

Don't think of Tracy or Sandy or Tom, he tells himself, *not now . . . let it pass . . . it'll fade . . . wait . . .*

The crickets keep chirring in a mad symphony.

"Did you want me to shoot him?" Roddy asks.

"Yeah. I wanted you to take him out." Dan clasps his head in his hands. "For what he did to Angela, and for what happened to Sandy. Yeah . . . he had to go. They both had to go."

"Who knows what Kenny'd bring down on us?" says Roddy.

"Could still happen, kemosabe," Dan says. He coughs, brings phlegm up, and spits.

"We'll see . . ."

The air feels chilled and damp.

"The way Kenny wanted to mutilate that bastard . . . his own fucking partner. He turned on a dime. What a snake," Dan mutters.

Snake. Roddy has a brief flash of Fort Benning in Georgia: forced night marches, the Ranger platoon, deathly afraid of coral snakes in the Carolinas. Night stalkers. One bite—a milliliter of the reptile's neurotoxin—you're dead. You gag and smother and die of respiratory arrest. Jesus, that's the way he feels right now, like he's dying. It's tough to breathe. Maybe there's some vile poison seeping through him, flowing into every cell in his body—that's what anger and hatred can do, poison you, turn your soul to stone—and maybe the anger is eating away at him and killing him as they sit in this godforsaken place.

Snakes in the night.

Danny rubs his face. His elbows go to his knees.

Roddy closes his eyes. He wonders if his hands will ever stop shaking. He feels clammy, sick.

"Where'd you get the piece?"

"It's the one thing I stole from the army. An MP at Fort Bragg gave it to me . . . a thousand years ago. I kept it all these years."

"Where?"

"Locked up at the office."

They sit in silence.

"It's something . . . the past," says Roddy. "That bastard brought it back. Like it was yesterday."

"Yeah, but back then we never killed anyone."

"Well, now we have."

"*Mad Dog* . . . ," Danny mutters. "Haven't heard that in years."

"It's the one thing I never told Tracy."

"You never told her your moniker? Why not?"

"I didn't want her to think of me like that."

"It's nothing to be ashamed of, Roddy. That's who you were."

"But not now."

"Can't fight who you were, Roddy . . ."

Maybe that's what he *is*. Maybe he's the same animal he was back then—a mad dog. No matter how things seem to change, it's all an illusion.

Kenny the Snake . . . Roddy the Mad Dog. And Danny . . . ?

"Can't get past your beginnings," Roddy mutters.

They sit for a while, listening to the woods.

"So what now, kemosabe? We bury these two?" Dan asks.

"Can't bury the past," says Roddy.

"We can try," Dan says, standing, clutching a shovel.

Roddy nods. "Yeah . . . gotta try . . ."

They stand, shovels in hand, surrounded by the mounds of dirt.

They move closer and hug. Danny is shaking.

"Let's get to work . . ."

They begin heaving soil. The shovel blades hit mounds of earth, slicing, lifting, turning, dumping. Soil thumps onto the bodies. They shovel it in, arms heavy, grunting, straining, pushing. It feels good not to talk; just keep moving.

Work it off . . . dissipate the nervous energy, the anger, the hatred.

It's dark down there in the hole . . . the grave. Smells damp, earthen. Can't tell if the corpses are covered yet. Just keep at it. Don't stop, Roddy thinks.

Soil pours down, sifting, pounding, covering the bodies. Sounds solid, heavy, thick, a deep thudding, the thump changing as the level rises.

The pit fills quickly.

By 10:30 they stomp on the soil and tamp it down. It's solid, part of the earth.

They walk around the gravesite and check it out.

How obvious does it look?

Not very, Roddy decides. At least not at night by moon and lantern light. In daylight? Who knows? Time will tell.

Roddy's arms ache, but that sick, shaky feeling is gone.

"Roddy," says Dan, "in a few days the soil's gonna sink down and settle . . . so we better put a little extra on to make up for it."

"Let's do it. Then, like I said, after a while the place'll be covered with grass and weeds. Nobody'll notice."

"Yeah, but just for good measure, shouldn't we toss some branches around?" asks Danny.

They add more soil. Then, carrying lanterns, they rip off small branches from nearby pines. Then they sweep the grave with pine tufts, roughing out the soil, tossing a few branches about.

■

At the water's edge, Roddy pulls a rag from his jacket pocket. He wipes down the .45: the muzzle, handle, trigger housing, all of it. He holds it with the rag, careful not to touch it with his bare hands. Rearing back, he hurls the pistol into the darkness. It lands in the distance with a deep, gurgling plop. He wipes down the shell casings and throws them as far as he can. They splash lightly into the water. He wonders about the missing shell casing. But there's nothing he can do.

He dips the shovel blades and pick head into the water. He swirls them around and smells the pond muck as it stirs. Smells like shit, same as the grave.

He lifts the tools out, shakes them, and then wipes them down.

He dips his hands in the water and thinks of the snapping turtles. He pulls them out and shakes them. *Have to wash off any gunpowder residue*, he thinks, knowing it's on his clothing too. He'll take care of that later.

"Think we oughta toss their shit here?" asks Danny.

"No. Not in one place."

It takes two trips back to the SUV to bring the lanterns, rag, Grange's jacket, Kenny's wallet, jacket, shoes, shirt and undershirt, the shovels, pick, gloves, cable cutter—all of it—back to the vehicle.

At the rear hatch, Roddy pulls out the box of latex gloves. He and Danny snap them on and empty out Kenny's smoky tuxedo jacket. A few items, nothing much. Kenny's ruffled white dress shirt, undershirt, and shoes drop into the plastic bag with Grange's stuff. They toss the work gloves and wet rag in the bag.

Still wearing gloves, they go through the sack and take out both wallets. They empty out anything that could ID the dead men and toss these into a smaller plastic bag.

Roddy slips the dried tools into the plastic wrapping. He wedges them into the hatch. "I'll take care of these tomorrow," he says.

He sets the cable cutter into the toolbox and jams it back down into the spare-tire well. The lanterns get stowed in the box, wedged tightly into the hatch-area corner.

They pat themselves down, slapping away dried soil. Dust clouds form in the lantern light as they beat their clothing. They kick their shoes against the Sequoia's tires; caked soil drops to the ground.

Get it all off, Roddy thinks. Get clean.

They check each other's clothing. "Looks good," says Dan.

Roddy tosses the big plastic bag on the back seat.

Still wearing latex gloves, Roddy fishes around in the smaller bag and extracts Grange's wallet. A brown leather billfold. Roddy holds a lantern up, looks in it.

"What're you doing?" Danny asks.

"Let's see his driver's license. Or any ID. Find out who he is."

Hands trembling, he opens the wallet and peers into the compartments.

"There's nothing," Roddy says.

"Credit cards? Anything?"

"Just cash. Must be a couple of thousand here . . . large bills." Roddy tosses everything into the bag.

"How 'bout his business card? The phone number."

"Probably a disposable cell."

"But the card . . ."

"You can have it printed at any Kinko's. Means nothing," Roddy says.

"So we don't know who he is."

"He's a corpse. A ghost."

"You think Grange is his real name?"

"No idea, Dan."

"It'd help if we knew."

"How?"

"We might know what to expect . . ."

"You think so?"

"His associates," Dan says.

"Like he said, he's a ghost. For real, now."

"Let's hope he doesn't haunt us."

Roddy's head begins clearing. "Danny, tomorrow, first thing, take your clothes to the dry cleaners. And lose the shoes. Toss 'em somewhere, far from home."

God, how wobbly his legs feel. And there's a humming inside him, a blood rush of fear and worry.

"Roddy, we gotta get our story straight. What do we tell everyone at McLaughlin's?"

Think . . . think it out . . . logically.

Jesus. His head's spinning. He's gotta get it together. He'd thought about this before . . . actually, he came up with a story yesterday.

What was it?

"Okay, here it is," he says. "We dropped Kenny off near his apartment. He felt lousy and wanted to go to a pharmacy. After that . . . who knows?"

"Sounds good."

Roddy looks up at the sky, the sliver of moon, the stars, the shadowy outline of tall trees. He closes his eyes but through his eyelids, he sees the glow of lanterns and moonlight.

Just get through this . . . keep going . . . don't overthink it.

Everything's packed. Roddy carries the box of latex gloves and a scissors to the front seat and stows them in the storage compartment.

The crickets and tree frogs go silent.

They stand in the lunar silence. It seems to Roddy they're part of a moonscape. Nothing is real.

They climb into the Sequoia. Roddy turns the ignition key. The engine purrs to life. He makes a broken U-turn on the road and begins driving back toward County Road 7. Danny's slumped in the passenger's seat.

Suddenly the vehicle sinks down; the right rear wheel spins. It's in a deep rut.

Roddy revs the engine and rocks back and forth; no forward movement. He tries again. More spinning, whirring of wheels, and gravel and dirt spitting up into the wheel well.

Sinking deeper into the furrow. Shit. Stuck. *Here* . . . near the grave.

He shifts into superlow gear and steps lightly on the gas pedal. The Sequoia's 4-wheel drive kicks in; the vehicle lunges forward and leaps out of the hole.

They're moving.

The SUV bounces and sways over the cratered path leading from the clearing where he killed two men—one in cold blood, the other desperately. Self-defense. That's what it was—self-defense. Had Kenny not pulled the gun, would he have let him live?

Don't kid yourself. No way. He had to go.

Kenny was a madman, totally insane. Could he have killed him like a dog in a hole? Was he, Roddy Dolan, a mad dog?

Clutching the steering wheel, he feels weak, sick.

You did what you had to do.

Chapter 29

The Sequoia cruises along the Taconic, heading south.

The tree line hurtles past them in darkness. Roddy keeps steady pressure on the gas pedal. No speeding. He doesn't want to take the chance of being stopped by a state trooper. He tells himself to stay calm and just keep going because the night's work isn't finished.

"I know I said this before, but I owe you an apology," Dan says above the engine whine. He sounds more resolute, calmer, and the wheezing is gone.

"Forget it . . ."

"I gave you bad advice."

"I took it. It was my fault."

"No, Roddy, you were right when you said I was in love with the glitz, the glamour . . . and the John Harris thing. All I saw was the bullshit and the bucks, like I was trying to prove something to myself, and Angela, too. And I have to think the way you do, Roddy . . . I have enough. There's nothing wanting in my life."

"Forget it, Dan. We all make mistakes and we can't go back. No do-overs. It's done."

Dan nods and sighs. Roddy detects remorse, deep regret.

The Taconic is dark and deserted at this hour. The pine and spruce trees look eerie at the side of the road. Roddy's keeping at a steady sixty-five, again thankful for the Sequoia's twenty-six-gallon gas tank. Plenty of fuel. Nineteen highway miles to the gallon is how it was advertised. A good vehicle. It took them where they had to go.

Riding in silence, Roddy thinks there's no use in lamenting what happened, but he knows nothing will ever be the same. Ever. No matter how many lives he saves in the future, despite all the good he's done or will ever do, he's murdered—taken two lives, showed no mercy—and everything's changed.

"Can you believe what we did?" Danny blurts out. "I gotta try to forget it . . ."

"I know what I'm gonna do."

"What's that?"

"Keep busy. Do plenty of surgery. And I'll think of what might've happened if Grange was still around. Our wives, the kids, Dan. Just think about it."

"I don't *wanna* think about it."

The Taconic slips by in the night. No lights in either direction. There's silence as Dan seems to be thinking, he says nothing. It's the strangest thing to sit so quietly and just drive, but Roddy's thankful for the silence; it's hard to talk after what's happened.

"Roddy, lemme ask you something," Dan says as they pass through Dutchess County.

"Ask . . ."

"How'd you figure it out? The con . . ."

"I didn't."

"But when you had the gun on Kenny . . . and you pushed him?"

"I just had a hunch."

"What made you think of a con, that the bastard was playing us?"

"Remember, Dan, that night in the back office when Kenny thought we accused him of stealing?"

"Yeah, sure . . ."

"He said a restaurant loses money during the first six months. Even a turnkey operation like McLaughlin's?"

"Yeah. I remember."

"Well, after Grange showed up Kenny got into his bullshit about how he thought he'd pay him back in six months . . ."

"Yeah?" Dan nods his head.

"Well, lemme ask you, how do you take out a quarter-million-dollar loan at *those* terms if you think there's a good chance you'll *lose* money for six months?"

"So that tipped you off?"

"Not really, but when I heard the terms of the loan, I got suspicious."

"I never registered that," says Dan. "I'm a fucking CPA. I should've realized that."

"You didn't *wanna* realize it, Dan."

"You're right. I wasn't thinking straight . . . it was the glamour of it all. Let's face it, Roddy . . . I got seduced."

"Something else about Grange got me."

"What?"

"Tonight . . . when we gave Grange the thirty thousand . . ."

"Yeah?

"I handed him the bullshit about the three-day settlement period once we sold the securities . . ."

"Yeah?"

"He bought it. He forgave us the three days juice. Those bastards never forgive *anything*. The whole setup smelled bad; there was something going on, but I wasn't sure."

Evergreens on both sides of the Taconic form a solid wall as the Sequoia's headlights pierce the night air.

Finally Danny says, "You feel bad about Kenny?"

"I don't think so."

"I'm not sorry. Not at all."

More silence. Then Dan says, "Roddy, what if Kenny hadn't pulled a gun?"

Roddy doesn't really want to think about it, but he knows the answer. "I'd've still wasted him."

"You'd have just shot him?"

"We'll never know, will we?"

"We couldn't let him go, Roddy."

"Nope. He was a madman. Drugs . . . he was fucking crazy."

"Who knows what else he's into."

"We might still find out, Danny."

The Sequoia purrs south on the Taconic; the tires emit a low hum; the wind rushes as the night flies by.

"All things fade," says Roddy as they near the Saw Mill Parkway. "It'll seem like a dream . . . like it didn't happen."

"Don't kid yourself, Roddy."

"But think about Tracy, Angela, and the kids. That'll help get us through it."

Roddy thinks they're driving through some wild dreamscape—a surreal backdrop with wind and darkness—yet, it's not a dream; it's real and it all happened in their lives. It was the reality they lived through tonight.

"Roddy?"

"Yeah?"

"Lemme ask you something."

"Ask."

Roddy senses Danny's hesitancy.

"You believe in God?"

"You're killing me, here, Dan," he says, trying to force a laugh.

"I'm serious. Do you . . . ?"

"You mean a God who watches us . . . who gives a *shit* about what we do?"

"Yeah . . ."

"I don't know . . ."

A few minutes pass in silence. Roddy's thoughts flash seamlessly to a million things: Tracy and the kids, Danny and Sheepshead Bay—their past and what they did tonight—Lawrence Hospital and his surgeries, Kenny "Snake Eyes," Tom's troubles, his father's death,

Cootie Weiss, Horst, his mother, first meeting Tracy in the library, then back to his surgeries and the anatomy of the human body, and what he's done to two bodies on this night—murder—and a cascade of images swirls through his mind, and then—as though he's resurrecting himself from a dead zone—he's suddenly aware of Dan sitting to his right, staring ahead at the empty road and he says, "I'll tell you what, Dan . . ."

"What . . . ?"

"If you need that kind of thing, then there *is* a God."

"Think so?"

"Dan, for *you* there's a God."

■

"Time to go to work," Roddy says. "Grab the latex gloves and scissors. Put the gloves on and go through their shit. Cut it all up and keep it in the smaller bag."

Dan snaps the gloves on and cuts Kenny's ID cards, cash, license—all of it—over the open plastic bag. He shakes the bag and mixes the contents. Kenny's shoes are on the floor.

Roddy exits the highway at Briarcliff Manor. He drives along a darkened thoroughfare. At a red light he says, "Dump their cell phones into that sewer grating."

He opens the glove compartment and takes out the disposable cell he bought at Stop & Shop. Hands it to Danny. "Toss this one, too, but, first, open the backs and take out all the microchips and batteries."

Still wearing gloves, Danny extracts everything. He gets out of the car and tosses all the phones down the grating. A moment later, he's back in the passenger seat.

Roddy drives to a deserted KFC and pulls into the parking lot behind the place. Near a huge green Dumpster, he looks for a surveillance camera on a wall or nearby pole. He looks in every direction but sees nothing.

"Right here," Roddy says.

Danny nods. He gets out of the car and needs no further direction.

"Just a little bit," calls Roddy. "And watch out for rats."

Danny heads for the Dumpster, reaches into the bag, and tosses some paper pieces, one empty wallet, and the scissors into the side vent.

"Go to the back and take out one lantern. Then toss it in," Roddy says.

■

Farther down the road, at a Stop & Shop, Roddy drives to the back of the store. The place is poorly lit, deserted. "Look for cameras," says Roddy.

They look in every direction. There are no cameras to be seen.

Danny tosses Kenny's jacket and a shoe into one of two Dumpsters. And one more lantern. The air reeks of garbage.

Soon, they're back on the Saw Mill Parkway heading south.

A few minutes later, they exit the parkway at Hawthorne. Behind a closed Outback Steakhouse they pull up to a Dumpster.

Roddy sees a sign on a wall:

PREMISES UNDER SURVEILLANCE

He pulls away and drives to a nearby mini-mall. In the back, Danny gets out of the Sequoia and tosses more things into a Dumpster. Other items go into a second Dumpster.

At Ardsley and Hastings-on-Hudson, after they scope the place out for cameras, Danny tosses the remaining items into a Dumpster behind a Burger King.

It's all gone. History.

Back on the Saw Mill Parkway, they head south toward Tuckahoe where Dan's car is parked at the railroad station.

"Any regrets, Danny?"

"It had to be done."

"You know, Dan, sometimes I have bad dreams about the past."

"Listen Roddy, of all the guys I've ever known, you made the biggest change. You're not the same guy I knew back then. Your life's different now. *You're* different."

"Am I?"

"Yes."

"So I wasn't a mad dog back there?"

"You did what you had to. Kenny would've killed you. And me too. And Grange, that fat bastard, who knows what would've happened? We had no choice."

"We just gotta hope nobody comes for us," Roddy says.

"Let's hope."

"Let's not overthink this shit. Let's just get past it."

"That's it, Roddy. There's nothing left to figure out."

They drive toward the Tuckahoe train station.

"I can't help it, Dan . . . I just have this bad feeling."

Chapter 30

The Tuckahoe station is deserted.

In a few hours, the early morning commuters—"drones" are what Danny always calls them—will begin filing into the parking lot heading to Manhattan for a long day's work.

Danny's Audi is sitting at the far end of the parking lot, far from the red clapboard station house. It sits alone, the only vehicle in the parking area. Roddy pulls up beside Dan's car and turns off the lights and ignition.

They sit silently. Roddy knows he's reluctant to end the night. He feels a strange sense of comfort, sitting with Dan as though it somehow lessens the horror of the night.

So they sit. Roddy nearly drops off—but he's not falling asleep. It's different, as though he's losing track of time, just drifting in a rolling fog bank of memories. He recalls his childhood: the small apartment in Sheepshead Bay, sleeping on a pull-out bed in the living room, his father, drunk and enraged, beating his mother, the sounds of slaps and screams penetrating the bedroom door. She'd married a man who beat her, just as her own father abused her mother. And then Horst—violent bastard that he was—she couldn't get away from it, the beatings, the cruelty. It was a whole way of life.

His thoughts drift elsewhere and circle back on themselves like a carousel, and then comes a run of images, a quick-change rush of sights and sounds—the past, present, the future, what future?—and

Roddy knows these ramblings are fed by fatigue and the night's madness, and then Roddy looks at the dashboard clock. It's nearly midnight. He realizes he's been lost in reverie—for only a few minutes—and it seems he's replayed his entire life. It's all so crazy and it quickly rushes back to him.

"We hafta get our story straight," Dan says.

Okay, back to here-and-now, in this world.

"What're you gonna tell Angela?"

"That we had a meeting in the city."

"And we stick with the story about Kenny . . ."

"He didn't feel well so we dropped him off near his apartment," Dan says.

"You know where he lives?"

"Forty-Seventh and Ninth."

"Right. So we dropped him off where?"

"A block away . . . who remembers? It's not important, Roddy."

"Sometimes details are everything."

"Roddy, it's not surgery. We dropped the guy off and headed up 57th Street to the West Side Highway, the Henry Hudson. No big deal. He was going to a pharmacy . . ."

Dan lowers his window. Roddy thinks it's strange not hearing crickets or frogs, being away from the eeriness of Snapper Pond. There's only the stillness of a suburban train station late at night. And the humming of an overhead sodium vapor lamp casting a pinkish glow on the Sequoia and black asphalt of the parking area.

"And you'll tell Tracy what . . . ?"

"Same thing. But let's make sure we're on the same page, Dan. So, after we dropped Kenny off, I drove us to Yonkers, to your office."

"Right. Nobody's there at night. It was just you and me."

"No night watchman, no security or anything like that?"

"Nope."

"So nobody can contradict our story?"

"Right."

"No sign-in log?"

"Nothing."

"Any cameras in the lobby?"

"Nope. It's not Manhattan, Roddy. It's Yonkers . . . Nowheresville."

"Then what . . . ?"

"We talked about the restaurant. We don't like an operation we can't keep track of and that's dipped into the red. We decided to get out. And then we talked about your tax picture. Remember, it's tax season. And it got late, real late."

"So I drove you to the Tuckahoe station where you left your car before you took the train into the city for the meeting at the restaurant."

"And here we are."

"That's it."

"I have a thought," Dan says. "Let's call Kenny's apartment, ask how he's feeling, leave a message."

"Bad idea," Roddy says.

"Why? It jives with our story—that he didn't feel well."

"It's midnight," says Roddy. "Who calls at this hour to ask how a guy's feeling? And if anyone plays back his answering machine, it leads right to us. Let's leave it alone. We dropped him off near his place and drove to your office."

Dan nods. He's about to open the door. He stops and turns to Roddy. "How do you feel?" he asks.

"I don't know."

"Same here."

"You know, Roddy, we're gonna live with this . . . for the rest of our lives."

"Yeah. I know."

•

A deafening squawk.

Then a barrage of whoops behind them. A series of pops and

beeps penetrate Roddy's bones, his flesh. Roddy's heart freezes. His body jolts and every muscle coils in tensile readiness.

Red and blue lights pulse in a mad shuttling. The interior of the Sequoia is lit brilliantly. It's blinding. More lights flash from prowl cars at both ends of the station. Two squad cars pull up behind them and block their way.

Light and sound are everywhere; it's a carousel of confusion.

A hollow pit forms in Roddy's chest, rises to his head, and expands in his skull, and he wonders, *Is this real? Is this the end?*

A commanding voice booms through a loudspeaker. "Don't move! Stay where you are! Do not exit the vehicle! I repeat . . . do *not* exit the vehicle!"

Roddy feels like he's going dead.

He hears Dan wheezing, a sickening sound amidst the burst of lights and static. Roddy stares straight ahead and clutches the steering wheel, unmoving, quivering inside.

The lights gyrate in a multicolored frenzy.

"Oh, God," murmurs Danny.

"Do *not* move," blares the voice. "Keep your hands where we can see them."

Roddy stares ahead, knows his life is done. What'll happen to Tracy and the kids? Poor Tracy. How'll she ever live down what he did? And the kids . . . what'll this do to them?

Two more cruisers pull alongside them. One on each side. Tuckahoe cops. Four patrol cars. The Sequoia fills with white light— hot and blinding. Police radios crackle.

"Open the vehicle's doors—slowly—and exit with your hands up," commands the speaker voice.

They step out of the Sequoia with raised hands.

The lights are a brilliant explosion of prismatic flashes.

Silhouettes of six cops emerge from the lights. They advance slowly. Radio static is everywhere. Six men, in black, or is it blue? They come closer. Guns drawn.

Roddy's legs go rubbery. His arms feel heavy, like they'll drop to his sides and if they do, he knows he'll be shot. He'll take three or four slugs. It'll be over. Maybe it's better that way.

"Hands behind your heads . . . and clasp your fingers."

Roddy's hands move to his head, his fingers intertwine.

"Now turn around."

They turn, backs to the lights. Roddy closes his eyes.

Hands pat him down—beneath his arms, on his torso, his legs.

"They're clean," a voice says.

"Now turn around, slowly."

Roddy turns and sees men in dark blue uniforms, leather straps, badges, cop paraphernalia, and yes, pistols—lethal-looking Glocks—point right at them. There's a black O at the end of each one.

What if I drop my hands . . . make a sudden move . . . they'll blow me away . . . it'll all be over.

Yes, he could do it, let a bullet plow through his heart, maybe one through his skull, shatter his brains, the way Kenny died . . . real quick. And isn't that what he deserves? To be shot in the parking lot of a train station? A criminal on the run?

But there are Tracy and the kids.

This must be the end . . . somehow, we've been tracked. It's over . . .

"Sir, do you own this vehicle?" the officer asks, shining a flashlight in Roddy's eyes. He squints and sees concentric white circles in the dark—brilliant, dancing spots of light.

"Yes, Officer . . . ," he hears himself say.

"And who owns this other one?" the cop asks as his flashlight beam lands on Danny's Audi.

"I do, Officer," says Dan.

"May I see your licenses?"

The cop's face is flat, pugnacious-looking, jutting jaw, dead eyes.

They fish in their pockets and out come their licenses.

Holy shit. The guy's so close . . . he'll smell gunpowder on my clothes . . . he's inches away . . . I can smell it . . . it's gotta be crawling up his nostrils . . . this is it. It's over.

Flat-Face's name tag says "Caldwell."

Another cop's tag says "Smythe."

Both tags are visible in bursts of color and light.

Flat-Face turns back and goes to the patrol car, but Smythe is close . . . and he looks suspicious . . . he must smell powder residue.

Caldwell sits at a cruiser's dashboard computer. He begins talking into the handheld mike; Roddy sees the guy's lips moving.

Must be saying something to the dispatch clerk . . . about us being located . . . they've been tracking us . . . police technology is unbelievable . . . not like it was back in Brooklyn.

Whirling lights, radio static, crackling voices, transmission hissing from hand-held radios, exhaust from the prowl cars; Roddy feels like fainting.

What if they see my boots—the dirt? What if they open the hatchback? Do they have probable cause? Shit, they can manufacture anything they want.

He imagines questions, one after another, each one opening up new lines of inquiry. Where does it lead? What does he say?

The lights swivel and dance.

Caldwell returns. "You can lower your hands," he says. The other cops holster their pistols.

Roddy's chest deflates. Slowly.

"Sir," the cop says to Danny, "I'll need to see the Audi's registration."

"It's in the glove compartment, Officer," Dan says.

"Please open the vehicle and get it," he says, handing Dan and Roddy their licenses.

Danny extracts his keys. The Audi's lights flash; Dan opens the passenger door, then goes to the glove compartment, fishes around inside, and hands the cop the papers.

Using his flashlight, Caldwell checks the registration against the VIN on the Audi's dashboard. He returns to the waiting group.

A fine tremor threads through Roddy. His heart pumps madly, pulsing powerfully in his neck.

"Sorry to alarm you gentlemen," Caldwell says. "We've had big trouble here. Drug deals, muggings, car thefts. We've been staking it out."

Roddy waits and tries stifling the quivering in his guts.

"If you don't mind my asking, what're you doing here so late?"

"Dan's my accountant," Roddy says. "We met at his office in Yonkers and I drove him to the station so he could go home."

Roddy wonders if they'll notice his soil-caked boots. In the dark with the cruiser lights and flashlight beams, who knows? And the gunpowder, don't they smell it?

"It's not a good idea being here this late, gentlemen," Caldwell says. "This station's dangerous at night."

Roddy and Danny nod. Lights still flash in an insane spectral band.

The cops make a few friendly comments, apologize for the inconvenience, and then they're gone.

Exhaust fumes hang in the air.

Roddy's heart slows. He's drenched in sweat. His insides shudder like gelatin and he feels weak, exhausted. He and Dan stand behind the Sequoia.

"Did you notice their names?" asks Roddy.

"Are you kidding? I nearly shit my pants."

"Dan, it's the best thing that could've happened. We're on record as being in Tuckahoe after meeting in Yonkers. It's the alibi you were looking for. Just remember: one guy's named Caldwell, and the other guy's Smythe."

Danny snorts and shakes his head. "You're one smart guy, Roddy."

The parking lot is silent except for the hum of a sodium vapor lamp above them.

Danny goes to the Sequoia's glove compartment, extracts the envelopes and hands the brown one to Roddy.

"I thought for sure they'd find the cash."

"There's nothing illegal about having cash."

"It's just suspicious . . . drug money . . . you know?"

Roddy slips the envelope into his pocket.

"Think they suspected anything?" Dan asks.

"Like what?"

"I swear, Roddy, I'm gonna be paranoid from now on . . ."

"Yeah, me too."

They face each other in the rose-pink halo of light.

Roddy doesn't know what to say. But then, what can be said after a night like this? *I wish this never happened? I wish we never had any dealings with Kenny Egan? I wish we could do it all over?* But there aren't any do-overs, not once you're grown up.

"You know, we'll never talk about this again," Dan says.

"I know."

"Tonight never happened."

"Just the cops doing a check at the Tuckahoe station."

"Oh, yeah, *that* happened," Dan says. "Caldwell, Smythe, and four other guys, *that* happened. But the other thing, it never happened."

"What other thing?"

They look into each other's eyes. In that moment, Roddy can barely believe the tricks of time: they could be standing in front of the Shamrock Bar & Grill on a Saturday night thirty years ago, conniving how to get fake IDs, bribing some adult to buy them a six-pack of Budweiser at Carney's Wines & Spirits, or wondering if Tommy Hart will steal his father's Chevy Impala so they could take a nighttime joyride to Coney Island where, jacked on beer, they'll ride the Cyclone—scream in a half-drunken, utterly crazed state as the roller coaster rackets through the night air. Then they'll hop on the Steeplechase parachute jump, hit the top, float down to the glittering lights below, and then they'll pool their money, as blood brothers always do, and gobble fried clam bellies drowned in tartar sauce, then mustard-doused hotdogs at Nathan's Famous. Yes, Surf and

Turf at Nathan's, also known—in their private kemosabe lexicon—as Nathanial's by the Sea.

But no, it's thirty years later and they're *here,* at the Tuckahoe station, facing each other after an obscene night in the woods upstate— after they killed two men, buried them, and tossed their belongings in a meandering trail of upstate Dumpsters, and soon, decades away from Brooklyn and Coney Island, they'll drive back to their solid suburban homes where their wives and kids sleep safely, innocently, and where tomorrow they'll go back to their work-a-day little lives.

They embrace. Dan whimpers; it's a sound of wrenching inner pain, barely audible. Roddy's throat tightens.

He slaps Danny's back a few times; Danny does the same to Roddy.

They move back, their hands on each other's shoulders.

"It's over, Roddy."

Roddy nods.

"We won't see each other for a while," Dan says.

"Maybe, maybe not. Let's keep things normal."

"Yeah. Whatever that is . . ."

Dan moves around the Audi and opens the driver's-side door.

Roddy says, "We'll talk soon, Cochise."

"Soon . . . kemosabe . . ."

Roddy gets back in the Sequoia and heads home.

Chapter 31

Roddy pulls into the garage, the same one in which he loaded up the Sequoia this morning—and it seems a lifetime ago. No, two lifetimes ago, in another life. God, the insanity of this life is amazing, staggering.

He turns the ignition off, presses the remote device on the visor, and listens as the garage door lowers in its tracks. He sits in darkness, quietly, closes his eyes, and waits.

But for the engine ticking and the Sequoia's steel frame creaking, everything's silent. Behind the wheel, Roddy waits for his thoughts to slow because his mind has been going nonstop since he left the Tuckahoe station. He realizes suddenly he can't recall the drive home. He's been lost in some pensive haze. Very dangerous.

Driving while dreaming.

It's insane. Just like the night has been. And everything leading up to this moment has been totally deranged. Roddy toys with the notion that the night could have been a dream. After all, except for this very moment, everything in the past—each single moment and all the hours and days and months and years before this second—are nothing but a web of memory. An array of chemicals shuttling from one neuron to another. Nothing more than synaptic leaps, impulses, and electrical charges. That's all his memories are at any moment. It's almost as though each passing second is the death of time.

But it wasn't a dream. It was real, and it was horrific.

I've done murder. Like father, like son . . .

It hits him like a speeding locomotive: ending lives and burying the dead. He's a murderer, a killer.

And then, Danny's question.

You believe in God?

But Roddy knows there's no time for regrets. Nor for questions or doubts.

Or religion.

And there's no time to wonder if things could've been different, because it all happened and can't be undone.

There's only time to do what must be done now—for the future—so he rips himself from his thoughts.

He unlaces his boots, tears them from his feet, and sets them on the Sequoia's floor in front of the driver's seat. He slips into his street shoes and then shoves the brown envelope beneath the driver's seat. Fifteen thousand—had been in Grange's breast pocket, next to the warmth of his body. Does it smell of him? He cups his hands to his nose, inhales deeply—Jesus, sniffing for the dead. *The smell of death is a terrible thing,* he thinks. Corpses stink, they're putrid, and they turn to rot. Roddy knows; he's seen enough of them in his lifetime, but not decayed bodies, only those who'd just died. Rotting takes time, days, weeks, months, years . . . even longer.

Don't think about it. Gotta get beyond this. It'll pass. Everything passes. It all goes.

Roddy gets out of the car, opens the rear hatch, removes the wrapped tools, and leans them against the garage wall. He lifts the toolbox from the rear hatch, hauls it over to the workbench, and with weary arms sets it on top. He'll have plenty of work to do to-morrow—Thursday—his day off.

The garage smells of transmission fluid and brake lining, and there's the pungent stench of hot rubber. It's all mixed with soil and rot. And maybe gunpowder. Roddy can't believe the cops didn't smell it on him. He sniffs and inhales deeply. Seems to him he reeks of the stuff. The Sequoia radiates heat, still cooling, creaking, ticking.

Roddy waits in the dark and wonders whether he can magically undo what's happened tonight, but that would mean undoing his whole life. Because everything he is now is no more than a final pathway of everything that went before it.

Gotta forget all that shit. Just keep truckin' . . . like the character in the Zap Comix.

He enters the house through the door from the garage to the kitchen. It's dark, quiet.

He stands there, frozen, waiting.

He crosses the kitchen slowly, tiptoes across the tiles, and makes his way to the dining room.

He stands, waits, and listens.

Nothing stirs. The house is like a crypt.

Roddy hears his heart beating and feels it pulse through his neck into his head like a bass drum. His breath sounds ragged in his ears. It's so strange—standing in his own house, feeling like an intruder, feeling illegitimate.

Suddenly there's a flashing light—different colors—glimmering, coming from the living room. Flickering, changing color. Is it coming through the window? From the front of the house? No siren. A silent approach.

Tuckahoe cops? Or Bronxville? Maybe the state police.

His body jangles. His pores open; his skin dampens. Every nerve in his body fires.

He moves silently to the living room, his heart thundering.

He sees it: The television is on the Discovery Channel, some show about the Galapagos Islands. An image of Charles Darwin. It's on "mute." Aqueous, colored images fill the room with flickering luminescence.

Roddy sags onto the couch, closes his eyes, and waits for his heart to slow.

Tracy must've waited for him, hit the "mute" button, fell asleep, woke up, and went upstairs to bed.

He grabs the remote and clicks the TV off.

Roddy sits in darkness, slick with sweat. He feels as though his blood is simmering with voltage and knows he must calm his nerves. He pushes away from the sofa and moves stealthily to the dining room breakfront. He opens the lower cabinet door.

In the dark, he rummages among the bottles and pulls one out— he can see it in the pale light coming in from the street. It's a half-empty bottle of Stolichnaya—the shit Tom's been drinking; he hopes that's stopped. Roddy thinks, *Don't kid yourself, these things don't change; they don't just go away. What in this life ever changes? Have you changed, Roddy Dolan? No, you haven't. Change is an illusion.*

Roddy unscrews the cap, lifts the bottle of Stoly to his lips—and with his hands shaking—takes a swig. It feels hot on his tongue, burns his throat, sears its way down his gullet, and hits his stomach like lava. Heat mushrooms through his belly and moves to his chest. Another gulp. More heat, penetrating, incendiary. Roddy nearly retches. He screws the cap back on and shoves the bottle back in the cabinet.

He sits on the floor, his back against the cabinet, and waits for the vodka's dulling effect. Warmth spreads through his face. His scalp tingles. He closes his eyes. A few minutes pass, maybe more, he can't be certain. His hands still tremble; he wonders if they'll ever stop shaking.

The booze is quelling the fire in his brain and his thoughts slow, at least for now. Maybe they'll turn to sludge. He stands and takes off his jacket, pants, and shirt. He tiptoes to the mud room and stuffs it all into a laundry bag. Roddy tells himself to remember to get it cleaned, get rid of any gunpowder residue and Snapper Pond soil. Tomorrow.

He slips out of his shoes, pads to the stairway, stands, and listens. He hears sounds of a house at night, stuff you never hear in day-time—maybe the joists creaking, the furnace kicking in, or water churning in the basement heater; and it seems to Roddy that his every sense is primed, like an animal in the wilderness, wary of predators.

He climbs the stairs, slowly, carefully. His feet feel like lead ingots. The effort to lift each foot seems momentous and the climb takes forever. The wood beneath the stairway carpet creaks. Funny, he never noticed that before tonight. If only he could step more lightly, if he could weigh less, but things are what they are. He is *who* he is. He can't change a thing.

He slips quietly past Sandy's room, then Tom's, knowing they're asleep.

He eases himself into the bedroom, silently. He shuts the door, gently; the latch closes, barely a click.

Roddy hears Tracy's deep breathing and sees her form in bed, on her side, sleeping peacefully. It's the sleep of the innocent.

He puts his shoes on the carpet and makes his way toward the master bathroom; the floorboards groan. His body tenses; he holds his breath and stands rigidly, quivering.

Don't wake up, Trace. Don't wake up now.

Tracy stirs, mumbles, turns over, and stays asleep.

He feels like a burglar in his own home. Moving toward the bathroom, he winces with each tiptoeing footfall.

In the bathroom, he shuts the door and holds the doorknob so there's no clicking of the latch. He turns the handle slowly. Not even a soft tick.

He feels for the light switch, finds it, and flips it up.

He strips off his underwear and tosses it into the hamper.

He stands naked, dirty. He sniffs his pits. The odor—what is it? Gunpowder? Shit? Piss? Blood? Murder?

Roddy turns the shower spigot, adjusts the temperature, waits for the water to heat up and steps into the stall. He stands beneath a cascading stream of hot water. His legs can't stop quivering.

Just stay calm.

He turns the lever; the water gets hotter, as hot as he can stand it, nearly scalding. He soaps up amidst the downpour and steam and lets water flow over him. Closing his eyes, he tries to erase the night from his mind.

But Snapper Pond replays in endless loops, especially the grave, with Grange on his back, belly protruding, leaking blood. And Kenny. That metal flash, the pull of the trigger, the pistol's heavy jump in his hand, the fire streak as the bullet shatters Kenny's skull, the grave's smell, the blood, brains, bone fragments, the damp soil, even as the shower water pounds him, pulses hotly, sloshes over his skull, his neck, onto his back—everywhere. Heat and pressure and steam and lather—a cleansing, maybe a purging.

How do you get clean?

Out of the shower, Roddy towels himself; even a light touch feels ticklish, tender, like he has a fever. A glimpse of himself in the medicine cabinet mirror reveals a gaunt, wasted image. His eyes look hollow.

John M. Grange . . . and Associates.

At the sink, he turns on the cold water, cups his hands beneath the spigot, and brings them to his face—again and again. He grabs a bath towel, dries himself, stands, and waits for the jangling sensation in his body to subside.

■

Slipping into bed, he feels taut. It's that primed murder rush slamming through him, his blood coursing, nerves firing, brain pulsing.

Tracy stirs, mumbles something, and breathes heavily again. He nuzzles her neck, huddles against her, and inhales the scent of her warm skin.

Suddenly, he feels cold. It comes from deep inside him, a glacial feeling, as though he's dying. He rolls away from Tracy and shivers as iciness crawls through him. He draws his knees to his chest but can't get warm. His legs cramp; his toes curl in painful spasm. He waits, grimacing in the dark. The pain is exquisite.

Stretch . . . easy now . . . keep stretching . . .

The spasm passes.

Roddy lies there, suffocating on his own breath. Sweat-soaked, he'll need another shower. He knows what this is: night sweats, the shakes. Body-quaking, stomach-churning, gut-wrenching shakes.

He hears traffic on the street. His senses are primed: waiting, anticipating. Is there a car out there? Is it slowing down? Stopping? A light moves on the wall—a passing car? Has it stopped? Are they parking in front of the house? Should he crawl to the window? Look out? What'll he see?

Roddy folds the pillow over his ears to shut everything out. But through the pillow, he hears the deep thumping of his heart.

You believe in God?

Is Dan getting religion? Will his conscience rain down on him? Dan—his friend, his kemosabe all these years—will he cave? Talk to Angela? Can Danny keep it all under wraps? Can he be trusted?

No, he can't. Dan will give them away.

What's happening to me? Roddy thinks. *Can't trust Danny?*

Am I going insane?

He lies there, cold as the earth itself, waiting for that precious trellis of sleep.

Nervous jolts shoot through him. His feet suddenly kick out and Roddy realizes he can't control his legs. Sounds of the pond and woods come to him—frogs and crickets—and it's all in his head. Then, there's the stench in the grave, and the coppery smell of blood in his nostrils. He's drifting, falling away, but leeches bore into his flesh; snapping turtles tear at his toes, cracking the bones.

He bolts upright, seeping sweat.

Jesus! He was so calm, so unthinking when he killed Grange, and now? It's different; he's no longer in the moment. He has to keep going, stay alive—knowing he has killed. But there was no choice. It was do or die.

And then Roddy tells himself, *You'd have killed Kenny anyway— you had to. He was dangerous, crazed, was trouble waiting to happen.*

And then Roddy tells himself, *Don't whitewash it. You're a cold-blooded killer.*

And then Roddy tells himself, *You're a mad dog.*

Still shivering, Roddy feels dread, knows they'll come for him. Who will come? The police. Maybe other people . . . John M. Grange . . . and *Associates.* It's only a business card. But who knows what'll happen?

Roddy's drifting, slipping deeper into darkness, and then the dog comes with bristling fur, snarling with curved fangs and dripping saliva; it leaps at him, and Roddy shoots up, trembling, and he tries closing down his thoughts and finally—minutes or hours later—he drifts into a cold, shuddering sleep.

Chapter 32

In the morning, Roddy feels washed out, weak. Dread fills him, like a crab scrabbling around his insides. He heads downstairs on legs of cement. His head feels heavy, and a thick membrane squeezes his brain.

He sits at the breakfast table with Tracy. It's his day off, but today, he's aware of what he must do.

"What time did you get home?" Tracy asks.

"Oh, sometime after midnight, I think," he says, looking down at his coffee mug. "It ended late," he says.

Tracy nods; she's waiting to hear more. She squints; her forehead furrows. "Do you feel well, honey?" she asks.

He nods, unsure of what to say.

"You look pale . . . ," she says, reaching for him.

"I'm fine, Trace . . ."

But he feels that inner trembling and wonders if Tracy can detect it. She's got an exquisitely sensitive barometer, she can read his every nuance.

Roddy tries, but he can't eat a thing. Nausea washes through him, and the house feels cold. He finds his thoughts wandering to Danny; will he stick with the story? What if he blurts something to Angela? What if that Best Boy conscience grabs him by the short hairs? Can Danny deal with the nagging pull of the guilt he's bound to feel? *How're my two Best Boys? Lemme ask you something . . . do you believe in God?*

Roddy stares at the coffee steaming in his cup. He knows he'll vomit if he tries to drink it.

"How'd the meeting go?" Tracy asks.

"We've decided about the restaurant," he says in a voice sounding small and distant in his ears. "We're getting out. It's too much hassle; just isn't worth it."

"Danny agrees?"

"Completely."

"Then it's the best thing to do," Tracy says, placing her hand on his. "Roddy, I know it's been bothering you. You're doing the right thing," she says, and strokes his cheek with the backs of her fingers. "We don't need the money . . ."

The Toastmaster makes its metallic popping sound; Tracy's whole-wheat toast is ready, dark, crisp, the way she likes it. She gets up. "Oh, speaking of money, Roddy," she says, "I sent a check to Ann Johnson for the summer house. Tom says he'll come with us. Problem solved."

Roddy's skin prickles. Lake Rhoda. An image of Snapper Pond flashes in his head. Then the strangest thought comes to him, and before he filters it, the words slip out. "I was thinking about what John Biondo said to me a few weeks ago . . ."

Am I hearing my voice from another room?

"John? Your surgeon friend up in Vermont?"

"Yeah."

"What's that?"

"There's a high-level position open at the university hospital in Burlington. He thinks I should consider it . . ."

"Roddy. You want to move to *Vermont?*"

"It's beautiful up there. And Burlington's a very . . ."

"Oh, Roddy, you can't be *serious*. We love this house. And my job at the college. You and Ivan have a thriving practice, and you're so respected at the hospital. The kids have their friends, and school.

We're so—I don't quite know how to say it—we're so established here."

"It might be good for Tom. He could find new friends . . ."

"Oh, Roddy. Tom's who he is. He'll find the same kind of friends in Burlington. People don't change just because they move."

"I know," he says, weakly.

Such simple wisdom.

"This is where we belong. What's gotten into you, Roddy?"

He shrugs. "I was just thinking, that's all."

Thinking, but knowing it's not a real choice.

John M. Grange . . . and Associates.

Roddy shoves his coffee cup away. A hollow feeling gnaws at his stomach.

Tracy's running late, she says, and finishes her breakfast, gets her coat, and heads to the kitchen door.

He gets up, stands there, looks at her, and knows he feels like a kid. "You sure you have to work today?" he asks.

"Roddy . . . of course I do . . ."

"I wish you could stay home . . ."

"Honey? Are you okay?" She reaches her palm towards his forehead. "You look so washed out."

He nods and hopes she'll offer to stay home.

He knows he's clinging. He leans down and plants a kiss on her luscious lips. She tastes so sweet; he's tempted to kiss her longer, deeper. He smells coffee on her breath and kisses her again. Her lips are so moist. They linger for a moment, eye to eye.

"Tonight . . . ," she says with a seductive smile.

"Not now?"

"*One* of us has to work," she says, her eyes smiling.

He wants to tell her he loves her, more than anything in the world. He wishes he could tell her how frail and frightened he feels, how desperately he needs her, but that would be so childish. She'd know something's wrong.

How he wishes they could lie down together—on the bed or couch—just hold each other, so he could breathe in the scent of her skin, caress her hair, and brush his lips on her neck. How comforting that would be.

"Tracy . . ."

"Yes . . ."

"I love you. So much."

"And I love you." She smiles indulgently.

He's achingly aware of how much he needs her now. The feeling is so powerful, it's physical. God, he's such a kid.

For a moment, her eyes seem to question him. The corners of her lips turn up; she leans forward and plants a kiss on his cheek. "Later?" she asks.

"Later."

Yes, later, he thinks, because they both have things to do.

∎

With the house empty, Roddy listens to the hallway grandfather clock's Westminster chime: half past the hour. The world's going to work, yet he stays behind. Alone, he feels isolated, separated from everyone. Roddy wishes he could stay in the house for the rest of the day. No, beyond that. He'd like to stay here for a lifetime. At home—safe, secure, away from the unknown.

He finds himself wondering if he can do the simple things he does each day, questions how he ever got them done: getting to the hospital, greeting associates, his surgical team, doing surgery. Will he ever again feel comfortable with these simple, daily routines? But he knows he can't let himself slip into paralytic inertia. It's never been his style. And right now, he knows it's time to do what must be done.

Roddy retrieves the laundry bag from the mud room. Does it reek of Grange and Kenny? He opens it and sniffs. A vague odor—of Snapper Pond soil, of bodies and death, or is it his imagination working overtime? Roddy tells himself not to let his mind run rampant. Stay calm. Just keep going.

He backs the Sequoia out of the garage and heads toward the center of town.

At a mini-mall near the office, he maneuvers the SUV to the rear of the buildings. He locates a Dumpster, sits behind the wheel, and scans the parking lot. No activity. No cameras. Out of the vehicle, he looks around and then tosses one boot into the Dumpster.

Roddy drives to the other end of town. Passing a police cruiser, he feels like cringing but keeps going. He looks in the rearview mirror; the cop is behind him and Roddy's heart begins an internal rampage. A block later, the cop turns right and disappears. Roddy is nearly shaking but drives on. He locates a diner and pulls into the parking lot. At the rear of the place, he spots another Dumpster. He pulls into a parking space four cars away from the receptacle. He looks around, sees no one, and tosses the other boot into the vent at the Dumpster's side. He looks about casually. No one in sight.

His stomach feels hollow, aching for something to fill it.

Roddy drives to the part of town bordering Eastchester. He sees Dmitri's Diner, where he's stopped a few times over the years for coffee. He parks the Sequoia, walks to the entrance, and stops at a cluster of newspaper vending machines. He could pick up a copy of the *New York Times,* the *Post,* or the *Bronxville Bulletin.* He fishes in his pocket, but he has no change. He looks at the headlines, trying to appear casual, just killing time.

Entering the diner, Roddy smells home fries, bacon, and coffee. The aroma of food doesn't make him queasy. A good sign. Maybe he'll eat something.

He looks around, recognizes no one—not at the counter, the tables, or in a booth. Not a single soul. His own town—he's been living here for years. But he doesn't see one familiar face. Not even Dmitri himself. Roddy has that lost child's feeling of being alone in an indifferent world. All these people—maybe four dozen—and not a single person knows him, no one knows his name or a thing about him. And no one has an inkling he killed two men last night.

A raw charge stampedes through Roddy's chest. A Bronxville cop sits at the counter, a broad-backed guy—obviously a bodybuilder—who spends lots of time hoisting iron and gobbling supplements. A copycat Schwarzenegger. His uniform is custom made, tapered to showcase his pumped-up physique. A holstered Glock hangs from his hip. Roddy shudders, thinking of the Tuckahoe cops last night.

Smythe and Caldwell were their names. Don't forget them, ever . . . it's important. Will Danny recall their names? Doesn't matter.

Diner Cop sips coffee; his saucer-style cap sits atop the round stool next to him. Roddy thinks he's either waiting for his partner or he's an arrogant bastard, taking up two counter seats. For sure, no one's going to ask him to remove his hat. The bastard's engorged with his own sense of power, but Roddy wonders why he should give a shit. It's just that he now notices things he didn't before all this—especially cops.

Roddy waits for his heart to slow. He wonders if this is how he'll feel each time he sees a cop, anywhere.

He finds an empty seat at the end of the counter and sits amidst the morning chatter. He glances at the God Bless America sign on the wall above the polished aluminum Grindmaster coffee urn. He hopes Diner Cop doesn't notice him, but why should he care?

Roddy looks down at the paper place setting: a coffee cup and saucer are already waiting, as are a knife, fork, paper napkin, and a bottle of Heinz ketchup. Nearby sits a Plexiglas container with packets of sugar, Sweet 'n Low, Equal, and Splenda. A multipage, laminated menu sits to the side.

It feels weird to be among strangers, waiting for breakfast, a meal that should be taken with family, people you love. But he's alone in the morning crowd; he watches the overhead fans turn languidly; smells eggs, potatoes, bran muffins, and pancakes; and hears dishes clatter when the kitchen doors swing open. He sits amidst trilling cell phones and snatches of conversation—the Mets, Yankees, Afghanistan—and feels upended, lost and unknown, a complete stranger, even to himself.

The counter waitress—fifty-something, plump, dyed red-orange hair, ruby-red lipstick, with a world-weary look—fills his coffee cup without being asked to do it.

"What'll it be, hon?" she says, her eyes wandering restlessly over the crowd. Hesitating, he orders a toasted English muffin: well done, butter on the side.

"That's it, hon?" she asks offhandedly, removing the menu.

He nods and feels his shoulders hunch with tension.

When the muffin comes, Roddy opens a butter packet and smears some on the muffin's rough surface. The spread glistens and melts into the toasted crevices. Smelling the butter makes him feel queasy, as though a whirlpool swarms through his belly. He bites into the muffin. But there's no saliva. It feels pasty in his mouth— thick, like mucilage. He can't swallow and it feels stuck. He sips the coffee—it's greasy and bitter.

Roddy tries to gulp the wad down but feels himself gagging. It sticks in his gullet and he nearly spits it up; then he forces it down. He sips water to wash it down.

Catching the waitress's eye, he signals for the check.

"Is everything all right, hon?" she asks, glancing at his uneaten muffin.

He nods. He feels jumpy and can't wait to get out of the place.

"Can I get you something else?"

He shakes his head. He can't really talk. His throat feels raw.

The waitress rips the check from her pad, slips it onto the counter, and glides away.

The guy to his right lowers his *Post* and glances at him. Roddy fishes in his wallet, takes out two dollar bills, and leaves a tip. Just to make up for the small order, he rationalizes, like it really matters. Because he's not even an afterthought in her mind. Nor should he be anything more. He shakes his head and feels annoyed with himself. He spins on the stool top, stands on wobbly legs, and notices the guy at the adjacent stool staring at him.

Roddy can't really tell, yet he feels Diner Cop's eyes boring into his back. He tries to look casual, just another guy in a suburban diner on a weekday morning. He saunters to the cash register where he pays Dmitri's elderly mother. She takes the money, hands him change, and never even looks at him. Roddy stifles the urge to glance at the cop and leaves the diner in a hurry.

Back in the Sequoia, he sits, wondering if Diner Cop will come after him. If he does, what does he say to the guy? *This is ridiculous,* Roddy thinks, *what am I doing to myself?* He realizes today will be torture. Pure hell.

He heads to the dry cleaner Tracy always raves about. He drops off the nylon jacket, pants, sports jacket, trousers, and a few dress shirts for good measure. Feeling antsy, barely able to wait for the receipt, he makes a hasty exit.

He drives to the Chase Bank branch.

Entering the place, Roddy can barely believe he was here only yesterday. It seems a decade ago. He again greets Ginny; she looks surprised to see him. He realizes she must think it's odd seeing him here two days in a row. That's never happened before. Roddy feels naked, completely exposed.

At the safe deposit area, he's aware the sign-in card shows he's visited the box on two successive days. No big deal; it's done all the time. He tells himself to stop overthinking everything.

The same clerk as yesterday—the young man with gelled hair and tortoise shell glasses—punches the card and leads him into the safe deposit area. Roddy wonders what the kid thinks. The guy uses both keys and unlatches the little door. The box slides out.

In the privacy of a cubicle, Roddy slips the cash envelope into the box, closes it, and feeling furtive, leaves the booth and hands the box to the clerk.

He wonders if he looks overly secretive. Like he's doing something illegal. No, he decides it's all in his head. He makes a hasty retreat from the bank and gets back into the Sequoia.

.

On a weekday morning, the E-Z Car Wash in Eastchester is desolate. He's the only customer.

He orders a full wash with interior cleaning. Then, slipping the prep man a five-spot, he says, "Make sure they do a *really* good job, okay? I want the inside spotless."

After paying at the cashier's window, he waits for the car.

Roddy wonders how Dan's doing. Will he hold up? Should he call him? Not a good idea; the less contact the better for the time being. He can only hope Dan sticks with the story. It's basic. Believable. Confirmable. So far, so good.

Roddy sits on an outdoor bench watching the workers rag down the Sequoia. He waits until one guy vacuuming the interior glances his way; at that moment, he pulls a ten-spot from his wallet, holds it so dryer-guy sees it, then slips it into the plastic tip box.

Yes, the guy sees the bill, nods, and winks at him. Roddy nods in return. They're on the same page. Dryer-guy says something in Spanish to the other worker. They both smile. *Yes*, Roddy thinks, *money's a mover, the prime shaker of things*, and a flash of Kenny and Grange comes to him.

Roddy approaches the men wiping down the Sequoia and says he wants an extra thorough job done. "Especially the back seats and floor."

The men spend more time with the power vacuums. The gray, corrugated tubes sweep back and forth, whooshing through the car's interior. Roddy opens the rear hatch and asks them to vacuum it again. "I've been carrying garden tools; I need it really clean," he says, and then wonders why he's explaining things. The men go over the hatch area again, sucking up every particle. Nothing incriminating.

They wipe down the windows, the inside door handles, the dashboard, steering wheel, and rearview mirror—every inch of the interior.

The Sequoia's clean.

■

Back home.

Roddy wipes the shovels with a damp rag. He knows he must get rid of Dan's and Kenny's fingerprints. And any telltale dirt from Snapper Pond. He wipes, again and again. Just looking at the tools makes him feel squalid.

Then he carries the shovels and pick to Tracy's garden patch. Staring at the soil reminds him of last night. He slices into the ground with a shovel and turns over the soil. Smells humid, like at Snapper Pond. He does it again and then uses the other shovel to do the same thing. Then the pickax; he slams it into the earth, first the pick end, then the chisel blade.

Alternating tools, he turns the soil in the entire patch. Tracy'll be delighted when she discovers what he's done. Spring planting will be a lot easier for her this year.

Garden patch, soil, digging, spring planting. It's all so normal, so ordinary, the stuff of everyday life.

Soon the tools are covered with Bronxville backyard soil. He shakes them off and sets them back in the garage in their usual place. He makes certain everything in the garage is in order—all the gadgets, his toolbox, shovels, pickax—all the implements of crime.

He connects the garden hose to an outlet, washes the outside of the toolbox, lets it dry in the April sun, and then slips it back on the garage shelf.

Sitting on the living room sofa, he goes over a mental checklist. Has he overlooked some small detail, even the most miniscule thing? He rethinks each step he's taken, and reenvisions each moment of the last thirty-six hours. It's like doing surgery, going over everything before closing up. Roddy's certain he's left nothing undone.

Nothing but that shell casing, lying somewhere—buried deeply with Grange and Kenny for all he knows, or maybe on the ground nearby. Can't be certain. It was invisible at night. But Roddy knows four shots were fired, and he found only three casings. What if that fourth one's discovered? There's always the possibility of something going wrong. There are a thousand variables, a million unknowns. But why dwell on them? You can drive yourself crazy. Just let it ride. Besides, it's too late to worry about it now. What's done is done.

Roddy calls the office.

Yes, it's slow and, according to Brenda, Ivan will be finishing up early.

So far, so good.

But is it good? No, it's just a temporary reprieve.

John M. Grange and Associates.

It's the day after. The first of many to come.

It's another day in the life of Roddy Dolan, husband, father, surgeon . . . and murderer.

Chapter 33

Roddy loves the OR—the hydraulic table, circular lights, the argon beam coagulator—even soaping up before surgery, scrubbing every crevice of his fingernails, fingers, hands, wrists, and forearms. It's a cleansing.

The nurse holds the surgical gloves out, stretched at the wrists; he slips into them, feels them snap on and wrap snugly around his fingers, and he's ready to begin. The patient is draped, prepped, and covered with disinfectant solution and the team is ready. Pachelbel's *Canon* plays on the sound system.

The incision is straight and true and within minutes, the patient's exposed intestines glisten beneath the overhead light. Roddy dissects the diseased section of gut and begins the delicate removal. Blood seeps into the abdominal cavity; Dr. David Allen, Roddy's assistant, uses a cannula to suction it away.

"Keep going, David," says Roddy. "Keep the field clean."

More blood leaks into the field. "It's a severed artery," says Roddy.

"No Roddy," says Terri, the nurse assistant. "It's the usual seepage."

"You sure?"

"Yes. David's got it."

The cannula's sucking sound erupts in Roddy's ears; his scalp dampens and sweat forms on his brow. Terri wipes his brow and says, "You okay, Roddy?"

"Sure. Fine," he says, watching blood seep through the surgical drape and then drip to the floor. He hears a pistol shot and sees the patient's body jump; blood oozes everywhere.

"Keep the field clean, David," he says.

"It's clean."

The section of colon is out, hanging in the forceps. Roddy drops it into a metal tray, peers down, and sees quarts of blood in the gut cavity—it obscures the operating field as David sucks away with the cannula and Terri dabs with wads of gauze. Roddy's stomach lurches as he closes his eyes, opens them, and sees a clear surgical field. No blood.

"Can you sew it back together or do we go with a colostomy?" David asks.

"Let's spare the guy the misery of carrying a bag of shit at his side," Roddy says.

"It's a close call," says David.

"We can do it," Roddy says, as David begins sucking more blood. Roddy knows his senses are playing tricks, and he's working on nothing more than muscle memory because he sees nothing through the bloody debris. Roddy knows, too, that if he yields to the images, he'll see brain matter and shattered skull in the gut cavity.

His hands move quickly, steadily, and the two ends of the patient's shortened colon are reconnected.

"Good job, Roddy, but how do you feel?" asks the nurse-assistant.

"I'm fine, Terri."

"You look pale."

"I'm good," he says, recalling yesterday afternoon when he helped Tracy plant her first annuals. Digging soil brought an image of Kenny—bare-chested, sweating and cursing—and he could virtually hear Dan's wheezing. The smell of the garden brought back Kenny and Grange lying in the hole, and now, as he closes the patient up, Roddy wonders what's happening to the bodies at Snapper Pond.

Roddy knows nature's working on them—bacteria, worms, and

grubs—doing what they do: decomposing them, turning flesh and bone to dust and gas—bringing on rot. In time, they'll be gone. It all turns to nothing, or does it? Remember the dinosaurs. Millions and millions of years pass, and yet the bones stay. Yes, some essence of Grange and Kenny will keep—always. A person's being doesn't just disappear.

Tying the last few sutures, Roddy knows that each time he goes through the garage he ignores the shovels, pickax, toolbox, and plastic wrap; he won't even glance at the reminders of Snapper Pond.

And he hates driving the Sequoia and tries not looking into the back seat. Sometimes he even thinks he smells Grange's body in there. Or hears Kenny popping open the vial of pills. He hasn't driven the SUV for days; instead, he's borrowed Tracy's Honda Civic.

"I'm getting rid of this gas guzzler," he told Tracy.

"It's about time," she said. "You always talk about going green . . . so do it."

■

At the White Plains Nissan dealership on Tarrytown Road, the sales manager smiles and extends his hand. "I know you," says the manager, a portly guy with a receding hairline. "You took out my mother's gall bladder last year. You're at Lawrence Hospital, right?"

Roddy nods; he thinks it really can be a small world.

"She's crazy about you. She still talks about how kind you were."

So maybe I'm still a good person, Roddy thinks.

"Doc, I'll make you an offer on the Sequoia nobody'll match," he says. "That alone'll make the deal worthwhile And you'll get the $1,500 cash back, too."

Roddy drives out of the dealership with a graphite-gray Nissan Rogue. He loves the new car smell and how the crossover handles—has almost a sporty feel—and he admires its continuous variable transmission. It gets twenty-seven miles a gallon, has differential all-wheel drive, and handles like a sedan. It's a far cry from the truck-like feel of the Sequoia.

And neither Kenny nor Grange ever rode in the thing.

■

Danny's on the telephone. "Roddy, it's been nearly two weeks. I told the employees we have no idea where Kenny is. And McLaughlin's bitching about his nonpayment. He's gonna enforce his lien if we don't pick up the slack."

"So what'd you say?"

"I told him to do what he has to do. And I told Omar we're closing up shop."

"Sounds good."

"Roddy, we have to report Kenny to the police as missing."

"Absolutely."

■

Captain Jake Greene is commander of the NYPD's Missing Persons squad. He's a burly guy with steel-gray, crew-cut hair; he looks to be in his midfifties. His office at One Police Plaza, in lower Manhattan, is ultramodern, brightly lit. A large thermal-pane window looks out onto the neo-Gothic towers of the Brooklyn Bridge spanning the East River. Traffic proceeds soundlessly across the bridge's span and the Brooklyn waterfront is visible across the harbor.

"This isn't terribly unusual in the restaurant business, Greene says. "There are plenty of . . . how shall I put it . . . unsavory types in these setups. Present company excluded, of course," Greene says with a quick smile.

"Captain, it's been two weeks, and there's no sign of him," Danny says. "We had to close the restaurant."

"I understand," Greene says. "No one matching Egan's description has turned up at the city morgue. And there's no record of any Kenneth Egan, or Kenneth McGuirk, at a city hospital in any of the five boroughs.

"We spoke with his landlord. Nobody's seen Mr. Egan, who, by the way, was three months behind on his rent. We ran a full computer check on everything. His checking account at Chase wasn't closed out; he had $1,800 sitting there, and no checks were written for three weeks. We gained access to his apartment, and it was interesting."

Roddy's heart pulses in his throat. He restrains himself from glancing at Danny.

"There was lots of cash—I think it was about ten thousand in hundred-dollar bills—clothing, a toothbrush, toothpaste, personal hygiene things—everything was in place. It's not like he was getting ready to leave town. We found some street drugs, too. If Egan *did* leave town, it was unplanned. We logged into his computer. One thing's clear: he went to lots of gambling sites. Poker and blackjack seem to've been his favorites."

"You're speaking in the past tense," Roddy says.

Greene nods and presses his lips together. "Lemme put it this way, gentlemen," Greene says. His eyes flick back and forth between Roddy and Danny. "I don't wanna rattle you, but I'm sure some scary stuff was going on with your Kenneth Egan. The recordings on his answering machine give some clues about what might've happened."

Roddy's blood rushes in his ears.

"There were a few messages from your maitre d', Omar, and from you, Mr. Burns. We'd expect that when a guy doesn't show up at work, especially when he's managing a restaurant. But there were other messages. There were a few from two known midlevel associates of the Fontana brothers."

"The Fontana brothers? Who're they?" Danny asks.

"A North Jersey mob family. They're into narcotics, prostitution, loan sharking, you name it. They were hounding your Kenneth Egan for money, and the messages they left didn't sound friendly."

Roddy shoots a glance at Danny; his kemosabe looks directly into Greene's eyes, doesn't waver, and shows no emotion. No red, blotchy face.

"There were also messages from some guy with a heavy Russian accent," Greene says. "He didn't identify himself but he left a cell number, and we looked into it. It appears that Egan had some contact with the Russian mob in Brighton Beach. The Brooklyn Brotherhood. Very dangerous guys.

"My guess?" Greene says. "He left town. Probably for good. Guys like Egan come and go—just evaporate like a ghost, if you know what I mean. Probably owed money all over the place . . . to the wrong people."

A ghost . . . thinks Roddy. *Will we ever get past this?*

"Maybe he'll turn up somewhere," Greene adds, "like in the Jersey Meadowlands, deep in the marshes. Who knows? But I'll tell you this, he was messing around with the Mafia and the Bratva. Some very bad people."

Roddy does his best to appear confounded, even blown away. He exhales loudly and looks at Danny, who shakes his head.

"We did a background check on Kenneth Egan, once Kenneth McGuirk," Greene says. "Nothing at NCIC, and no criminal record in Nevada or New York."

Greene pauses, tilts his chair back, and laces his fingers behind his head. "The bottom line, gentlemen?" Greene says, looking up at the ceiling, "I don't think you'll be seeing Mr. Egan around for quite a while."

∎

"So, we're going out of business," Danny says as Roddy drives north on the East River Drive. "McLaughlin's gonna repossess everything. He's gonna look for another buyer. Said we're a pain in the ass . . ."

"Good riddance to it all," Roddy says.

"How you feeling?"

"A little better," Roddy says. "Tincture of time . . . it's the greatest healer, better than any medicine. That's what I tell my post-op patients. Time's your biggest asset for healing. Better than any physician."

Dan looks straight ahead as the Rogue clatters over the ridges of the Willis Avenue Bridge. "Yeah, but this isn't a physical thing. It's mental."

"Dan, eventually it'll be like a distant echo."

"You taking the place at Lake Rhoda this summer?"

"Yup."

"You're going up *there?*"

"Gotta keep things normal. Tracy loves the place."

"It's only a few miles from that pond . . ."

"Snapper Pond," Roddy says, wondering what it'll be like driving on County Route 7, near where it happened. Where crickets chirr, bullfrogs croak, with the smell of pine resin and country weeds in the air, the same smells as that night.

He decides he'll deal with it then, not now.

"How're you sleeping?" Dan asks.

"Could be better . . ."

"Me, too. Nights are the worst."

"You having any dreams?" Roddy asks.

"No. Just waking up three, four times a night, and thinking . . ."

"About that night?"

"Of course."

"Same here," Roddy says, knowing he bolts awake at night with his heart hammering. Then he lies in the dark, thinking, thinking, thinking—waiting for sleep to come, listening to Tracy's soft breathing.

"Think we're safe?" Dan asks.

"Probably."

"I don't mean the police . . ."

"It would've happened by now," Roddy says. "But who knows?"

"I gotta believe that; otherwise it'd be tough to keep going."

"Danny, we keep going. Like nothing happened."

"Yeah. Like nothing happened."

"It's our secret," Roddy says.

"Some fucking secret," Dan says.

"It's the secret of the Best Boys."

∎

Roddy's driving to the hospital two days after the meeting with Greene.

It's 6:45 and he has a full operating schedule. On Pondfield, he waits at a red light, reaches for the radio dial, but decides he doesn't want to hear the morning news. He glances into the rearview mirror and sees a black Cadillac Escalade in the early morning light.

The Escalade pulls up behind him. It moves closer; the front bumper is so close he can't see the vehicle's headlights. And the windows are darkened, pitch black. No way can he see inside the thing.

The light changes and he hits the gas. The Escalade follows, closely—he's being tailgated, even though he's doing forty-five in a thirty-mile-an-hour zone. His eyes dart to the mirror, back to the road, then the mirror—and the Escalade stays close.

Roddy's first impulse is to stop the car, get out, and confront the jackass—*What's wrong with you? Don't you know how dangerous that is?*—but he realizes at this stage of his life it's insane to go Brooklyn on whoever it is.

Suddenly the thought flashes in his head: *John Grange and Associates.*

A twinge of terror seizes him and explodes through his chest.

A black Escalade, darkened windows, this early in the morning, close behind me. Isn't the Escalade the preferred vehicle of gangsters?

Roddy's thoughts ramp into a frenzy as panic ambushes him.

A team of hit men could be in the thing, but he can't tell with the blackened windows. Barely able to grip the steering wheel, he stomps on the gas pedal and the Rogue darts quickly from the light. At the next corner, he turns left—no signal—and the Rogue careens around the corner and hugs the road. Roddy accelerates and the engine shrieks as Roddy speeds down the street. The Escalade turns left and the driver hits the gas; the behemoth pulls up and moves close behind him. A twist of panic seizes Roddy; it feels almost electric and his skin prickles.

He thinks the hospital might be a safe place. There're people and activity, even early in the morning. It's far safer than these deserted streets. If he stops at a light, some hit man could get out of the Escalade, run up to his car, and fill him full of lead. Roddy races to the next corner, barely slows at the stop sign, and hits the gas pedal so hard the tires burn rubber. A quick glance in the mirror: the Escalade follows, now farther behind.

Roddy swerves right at the next corner and hurtles down another street, his body taut and primed and his heart ramping as the Rogue hits sixty.

He glances in the mirror: the Escalade crosses the intersection—two blocks behind—keeps going straight, and doesn't follow. A surge of relief washes through him, but Roddy realizes they could be headed for the hospital. They'll wait for him there, in the garage where at this hour, it's nearly deserted. Roddy's pulse throttles through his neck and into his skull and pounds like an anvil. If the panic keeps up for long, he'll feel depleted. He realizes he can't let his imagination take him to the edge; he has to stop this insane thinking.

He heads for the hospital, his entire body damp and weak.

■

In the OR, Roddy's aware of a mournful adagio playing on the sound system.

"Who picks out this music?" he asks.

"I do," says Claire, a scrub nurse. "Don't you like it?"

"It's funeral music," he says.

"Mournful," says Terri Sanford.

"We have some other CDs," Claire says.

"Like what?"

"Italian opera . . ."

"Sounds good to me."

As Roddy begins the next surgery, a soaring aria from Puccini's *La Boheme* fills the OR. Roddy's scalp tingles as he makes the first cut in the patient's abdomen. The music is sublime, a thing of ineffable beauty, and he says, "Why don't we play opera from now on?"

"They're beautiful . . . but tragic," says the nurse.

"That's life," says Terri.

∎

That evening, after helping Sandy with her homework, Roddy sits on the living room sofa with Tracy.

"Things with Tom seem to be calming down," Tracy says. "I haven't had a call from a teacher and he's been better around the house."

"One thing's certain," Roddy says, "he likes being called Tom, not Thomas or Tommy."

"I've noticed that," she says with a quick laugh.

"He said Tommy's the *diminutive* form of his name."

Tracy laughs again.

"And I think he was right. It diminishes him."

"Maybe so. But it's affectionate . . . Tommy . . ."

It occurs to Roddy that he and Danny, and Kenny, too—when he was around—still use the diminutive forms of their names. *Roddy* instead of Rodney, or Rod; Danny instead of Daniel or Dan . . . and Kenny . . . Snake Eyes.

It strikes him that maybe it's a wish to remain boys, to keep things as they were when they were kids. But there's nothing he'd want to preserve from those days, except his ties with Danny. And Dan's mother, Peggy, the angel of his life. Until Tracy came along.

Then he recalls the Escalade this morning, how it was all in his mind—a car filled with goons, hit men, killers—how his imagination ran away with him, and he thinks of the Puccini arias in the OR, and Roddy hopes that maybe—just possibly—his dread about the police or a clutch of mobsters coming for him will fade the way blood soaks into gauze and the pad gets tossed and becomes no more than medical waste, and then it's incinerated and turns to ash—dust in the wind—never to be seen again.

Chapter 34

On this mid-May afternoon, he's finished early at the hospital. It's Friday. Roddy has no afternoon office hours. He can get home before Tracy and wait for her. It'll be a long evening together.

He stops off at Elmer's Wine Shop in the town center and picks up a bottle of Châteauneuf-du-Pape. Tracy loves the French burgundies and Rhone wines. They've been her favorites since they took a wine-tasting course last year at the Westchester Wine School in Rye Brook.

This evening, she'll be preparing coq au vin, and the wine will go wonderfully with the meal. He gets back in the car and heads home.

Driving down Crawford Street, right off Clubway near the golf course, Roddy sees their house. The Tudor style is unmistakable with the star magnolia tree out front. It's shed its blossoms, which lie on the grass in dried disarray. It's always seemed such a shame to Roddy that the blossoms are so short-lived; they fall within a day or two of their fullest blooms.

But it's May, and the air is fragrant with lilac and dicentra are everywhere. The sycamore trees form a gauzy lacelike canopy over the road; birds twitter and the Westchester sky is a deep blue.

Nearing the driveway, Roddy sees it.

His heart freezes and then drops to his stomach as a violent jolt shoots through him; then something inside him crumbles.

In their driveway, halfway up its length, sits an empty Bronxville police cruiser with its distinctive white color and blue side stripe. "Bronxville Police" is printed in slanted blue letters along the vehicle's side. The light bar and grill lights flash silently.

And parked out front is another empty patrol car with its lights blinking.

Behind that is parked another car. It's dark gray and has no markings; it looks like a detective's vehicle. A Crown Victoria? It looks like one. It could be a state trooper's car. And stranger yet: Tracy's Honda is parked in its usual place at the garage entrance.

Tracy's home early. Her hours at the library are set, inflexible. Police cars are in front of the house. Empty, with flashing lights. The cops are inside the house.

Roddy realizes it's unraveling. It's over.

He drives past the house while his insides are scrambling. He heads down the street—one block, then another.

In a glacial sweat, he pulls over to the curb. With shaking hands, he puts the Rogue in "park" and keeps the engine running. His heart pounds; tightness grips his throat, and he's desperate for air, choking on his own tongue. Adrenaline rampages to every nerve ending in his body. Sweat seeps everywhere and he's soaked. His shirt feels like shredded tissue paper.

It's been six weeks now. What went wrong?

Roddy begins asking himself questions and tries to dope it out. *Think it through*, he tells himself. How could he have been traced?

Had he or Danny left something at Snapper Pond, anything that could identify them? They were both so unnerved—so unglued—at the time; it's certainly possible. He rummages through his recollections.

Was that fourth casing lying there—in broad daylight? A shell from a .45—not an everyday find. If discovered, it could make the police search the area—carefully.

He'd been supremely careful when loading the pistol. He'd used surgical gloves handling the bullets. But there's always the chance he inadvertently fingered one shell. Maybe even years ago when he'd bought them. How long do fingerprints last? The casing could have been taken to a crime lab.

He'd been in the army, so his prints are on a database in Washington, DC and accessible by Internet transmission. Did someone find the casing—a tube of polished brass—and call the local sheriff, or the state police?

And from there, who knows what happened?

Roddy thinks back to all the movies he's seen, the crime novels he's read, the detective shows on TV. It's always some little thing that turns the tables, breaks a case—an inconsequential object or some minor glitch that leads to a crime being solved.

It could be any of a dozen other things.

Did someone see the Sequoia near a Dumpster? It would all look suspicious since he sold it soon after the night at Snapper Pond. Trying to get rid of incriminating evidence. A virtual admission of guilt.

Had he and Dan been recorded on a surveillance camera near any one of the Dumpsters? He'd checked for cameras, but it was dark; vision was limited. Cameras are used to discourage illegal dumping. These days it's a big deal because of medical waste, and then too, murder victims are sometimes discovered in Dumpsters. It might take a few weeks for the recordings to be reviewed, but that can be done.

Had some idiot gone through a Dumpster and found something? Hadn't he and Dan cut the driver's licenses, papers, and IDs into a million little pieces? Then dropped them in different Dumpsters in various towns? But how can he be sure there wasn't something in there that could start a trail of evidence?

Roddy wonders if someone stumbled onto the gravesite? Noticed the earth had been dug up and tamped down. Maybe some couple out for a woodsy stroll in mid-May discovered the gravesite. And what if they had a dog with them? Aren't dogs used to retrieve bodies buried beneath rubble in earthquakes?

Maybe some kids were tossing Frisbees or throwing a baseball near Snapper Pond. Or some moronic fisherman found something, a guy who knew nothing about Snapper Pond and thought it teemed with trout or perch.

Maybe someone saw them at Snapper Pond.

Saw the lantern lights.

Saw the SUV coming or going.

Heard their voices.

Heard Kenny or Danny shouting.

Heard those last two gunshots. Because when Roddy fired them he didn't have Grange's jacket over the pistol to muffle the reports. Sound travels at night, especially in the country. Even more over water.

But that was weeks ago. Why the delay?

Why are the police at his house today?

What about those work gloves? These items all have bar codes and serial numbers. They'd been scanned by the clerk at the hardware store, the bar code imprints saved on a microchip. He'd been stupid and used his credit card, not cash. Jesus! It's all on a True Value computer network. It could be traced to the point of purchase. What was he thinking? He should've used cash.

And the gloves could be coupled with other evidence.

What other evidence?

Back to cameras.

Aren't there cameras on tall poles along highways—used for live-feed traffic reports? Real-time security cameras are everywhere. In places like Burger King, KFC, and McDonald's. At virtually every mini-mall in existence. Like the ones they went to or passed that night looking for Dumpsters.

Don't they record every vehicle or person passing by? It might take weeks, but stored images could be reviewed, enlarged, clarified, and scrutinized.

The Sequoia's license plate could be easily read—a complete giveaway. Coupled with information about a lantern and work-glove purchases, a digital trail could start developing.

Leading where?

Maybe it was Grange. Could be he bragged about collecting from clients who owed him a half-million—the owners of McLaughlin's Steakhouse on Broadway and West 46th Street?

A fusillade of thoughts assaults Roddy and streaks through his mind. They flash so fast his brain feels like it's on fire. He considers one possibility, then another, then a variation of the first, leading to yet another, and with each variant, a new shadow of doubt infiltrates him and erodes his confidence.

When it comes to unforeseen twists—weird, unexpected developments—the possibilities are limitless.

Roddy wonders if he should get to the safe deposit box, grab cash and a few other valuables, and leave town.

Okay, so he snatches some money and takes off.

And goes where?

Does what?

Becomes who? Richard Kimble in *The Fugitive?* Ridiculous.

Just disappear? Evaporate? Leave Tracy and the kids?

Beyond the pale. Not a chance.

Besides, he knows nothing about fake passports or bogus social security cards, IDs, and driver's licenses.

I wouldn't even know where to begin.

And even if he did, could he ever leave Tracy and the kids?

Impossible.

He's just gotta face whatever awaits him.

Stay calm and composed, reason it out clearly, and take it step by step. Think, take your time, and use your brain.

He wonders if he should call Danny. No way. Dan's probably sitting in some interrogation room right now, sweating so much his skin is shredding. The cops will break him.

So think it out. There must be some way to handle this.

But nothing comes to him.

He might as well be floating in space. Upended amidst infinite nothingness.

It's got to play out to its conclusion. There's no other choice.

·

The police cars are still in front of the house. The cops are inside, waiting.

Roddy sits with the Rogue's engine idling. Finally, he kills the engine, gets out of the vehicle, and crosses the street.

This is it—the end of it all.

It's the last time he'll ever walk this stone path to their lovely Tudor house, the last time he'll see the slate roof, the dark timbering, and casement windows. It's the last of everything worthwhile in the meandering path of his life.

Roddy walks slowly—barely moving; he can't feel his legs. His hands feel heavy, as when he first held the loaded .45. His shoulders are hunched; every muscle in his body tightens as he nears the front door.

What awaits him?

It all streaks through his mind: the old neighborhood, its streets, alleys, and people. The days of his youth are a world away, yet it's only yesterday. The fact is that at nearly forty-six, he's been alive almost three times longer than when he was nabbed with Frankie Messina.

He remembers first seeing Tracy drop from the air; he recalls their dating days. He thinks back to first meeting her family. He re-calls barely believing a woman so beautiful and smart as Tracy—a Celtic queen who could've been a model if she'd chosen that path—could actually be interested in him, Roddy Dolan, a kid from the streets.

He thinks back to when Tom and Sandy were born. How excit-ing it was to be a father. And with their births, he would live—not just for Tracy and himself, or even his patients, but for another generation. And he would love and care for his kids in a way he never experienced as a child. He would be living his life to make it all better, to undo the past, a do-over as they said when they were kids.

And now?

Approaching the front door, he thinks of the days of his life, and it blitzes through his head in an assault of fear, fondness, love, and regret.

Fear and regret for what's happening now.

Fondness and love for his family and everything about Tracy.

Now there's the specter of an eight-by-ten cell; and he thinks of his father dying in a shower at Attica; and he knows he's no different—a man who killed two men . . . *like father like son.*

And what has he created for his wife and kids? Their husband and father: a cold-blooded murderer. Shot two men to death and buried them in a ditch in upstate New York. What kind of legacy is that for his family? How could he have ruined their lives, this way? And now? Roddy is mourning his own broken life.

Will there be two cops or three or four? Does he feign innocence? Does he clam up and talk only to his attorney? What attorney? He doesn't even have one.

Roddy wonders if they'll read him his rights, like on television? Will they snap handcuffs on him and lead him to a waiting patrol car? Will he be escorted away in front of the neighbors, people he's known for years? People whose mouths will drop in disbelief at what they're seeing—Dr. Roddy Dolan cuffed and being led away by the cops.

The ugliness, the shame. It would be unbearable for Tracy and the kids.

He'll be in lockdown with beasts. In a cage with the animals who prey on humanity, extruded from society.

Maybe Kenny was right. His moniker all those years ago was a fitting one: Mad Dog.

Things don't change. People never change. Not him . . . not anyone.

Here and now is the last time he'll ever walk as a free man.

It'll be hard time. Life with no possibility of parole.

The world he's known and the life he's lived are over—gone for good.

Chapter 35

On wooden feet, Roddy approaches the front door.

Opening it, he hears Tracy's pitiful sobbing. Her wailing makes him feel he's dying. Molten lead forms behind his eyes—heavy, hot, unbearable.

Roddy tries imagining the next steps: the arrest, arraignment, and the rest of it—a holding cell somewhere, possibly bail—no, not for first-degree double murder, then a trial or maybe just a straightforward admission. Why not? He's guilty, pure and simple—of intentional murder, thought out, planned exactly. Premeditated—down to the last ghoulish detail. Yes, that's what it was. First-degree murder—life without parole.

He thinks of Danny—whether they'll arrest him—maybe they have no idea he was involved. It's a possibility. But it's remote, after all, how could one man kill and bury two men, especially a guy the size of Grange?

No, Roddy's certain they've got it figured. The police are pros; they know what they're doing when it comes to a crime so simple, so obvious. And if Dan denies it, they'll sweat it out of him. He'll crack. He's got that Best Boy conscience. He's probably been picked up by the Tuckahoe police and is conferring with an attorney. Doesn't matter, the cops have the case locked up tight. It must've been that shell casing. And who knows what other evidence they've been collecting all these weeks?

Roddy tries imagining the outcome. Will he go to Attica, where his father died?

Like father, like son . . .

■

Tracy can barely breathe. Queasiness and disbelief wash through her. Pins and needles prickle her fingertips. And a strange tingling surrounds her lips. Coldness penetrates her bones. She shudders trying to comprehend what she's heard.

"Are you all right, Mrs. Dolan?" one officer asks.

She nods and tries to hold it together as tears well up in her eyes. She hugs herself, her arms clutched in front of her, sitting on the sofa. She rocks back and forth.

Tracy closes her eyes, trying to obliterate what the police said. *Oh, Roddy . . . Roddy,* she thinks. *How could this be?*

The officers are saying something but she can't follow a thing they say. Some internal trip-switch was flipped and she's moving parallel to them, on a different mental track.

Oh Roddy . . . Roddy . . . Roddy . . . how can this be? It's unbelievable.

The police are in her living room, and this is really happening in the sanctity of her home, of *their* home, the lovely house they'd worked so hard to build—together. It's horrible . . . beyond belief . . . and there's nothing she can do . . .

■

As Roddy opens the door, his heart aches. It's all come down to this . . . at last. He knows he'll be hauled away in a squad car. Right in front of Tracy.

Tracy's sitting on the living room couch, legs drawn up beneath her. Her eyes are swollen and tear-filled.

He could run to her, sink to his knees, beg for forgiveness, and tell her he was trying to protect her and the kids because he loves them more than anything in the world. More than life itself because really, they *are* his life. He'd go through anything for them—even as the cops are cuffing him.

The cops turn to him. Three uniforms and a guy in plainclothes—a detective.

Roddy's heart thumps madly; he feels faint. This must be a prelude to death—the way you feel with that sudden realization of finality, that you're about to face the darkness, that endless void.

Tracy leaps up, throws her arms around his neck, and sobs frantically. He holds her as tears well up in his eyes and he chokes. He feels her shudder as tears drip onto his chest. He closes his eyes and hears the words:

Rodney Dolan . . . you're under arrest for two murders. And they name the men he slaughtered: *John Grange and Kenneth Egan. You have the right to remain silent . . .* and the whole Miranda thing, said in a rushed monotone.

"Oh Roddy . . . ," Tracy cries. "This is so terrible . . ."

He looks over her shoulder at the officers.

A cop approaches. A big guy who looks serious and stares into his eyes.

Icy tingling covers Roddy's skin.

He closes his eyes and presses Tracy closer to him.

He feels he'll collapse in a moment—just sink down, fall away, then die.

Please, God . . . let this end . . . let it all be over . . .

"Roddy, how could this happen?"

So this is how it all ends.

The cop stands before him. Roddy feels a mixture of dread and relief.

■

"Tom? Is he all right?"

"He's in his bedroom," Tracy whimpers.

"It's kid stuff, Doc," the sergeant says.

"They'll take us to court," cries Tracy.

"Court? For two boys fighting?"

"We'll be leaving now, Doc," says the sergeant. "You'll probably get a civil summons. I'm sure you have a homeowner's policy . . ."

Roddy nods; then, on wobbly legs, he escorts the cops to the door. He's in a haze and feels leaden, but a sense of liberation seeps through him.

Tracy says, "We'll be sued . . ."

Roddy is astounded. Mute. Two kids fighting; the cops get involved?

"I'm so worried, Roddy . . ."

"Worried? About what—a fight?"

"Do you know what he *did?*" Tracy cries. She looks stricken.

"He beat the crap out of the other kid and . . ."

"He bit part of his nose off. Tore it off with his *teeth*. If the surgeons can't sew it back, that boy will be disfigured for life."

"I'll call the hospital . . ."

"Roddy? What kind of boy does that?" Tracy's chin trembles. Her eyes are swollen.

"Tracy, he's a kid. Let's give him a chance."

"For what? To kill someone? He's a beast . . . biting a nose off."

He shakes his head in disbelief.

"Roddy, I'm so scared. I'm worried we're living with a mad dog in this house."

Acknowledgments

No novel is a product of its author alone.

Many people contributed their time and effort to reading, making suggestions, and thereby improving the manuscript.

Deepest thanks to Kristen Weber for showing me the way of the novel.

Relatives and friends graciously devoted their time and talent to reading the manuscript at various stages and making valuable suggestions. They include Claire Copen, Rob Copen, Marty Isler and Natalie Isler, Helen Kaufman and Phil (The Man) Kaufman, Arthur (Arturo) Kotch and Jill (Chilly) Kotch, and Barry Nathanson and Susan Nathanson. Their suggestions, criticisms, and comments were marks of friendship and caring; they vastly improved what I'd written.

Other people, both living and dead, made their own (most, unknowingly) contributions to my knowledge base and authorial efforts. They include Dick Simons, Bill Console, Warren Tanenbaum, Sigmund Freud, Charles Darwin, Edgar Allen Poe, Jacob and Wilhelm Grimm, Edgar Rice Burroughs, Clarence Darrow, Jack London, Jim Kjelgaard, William MacLeod Raine, John R. Tunis, Rena Copperman, Melissa Danaczko, Bruce Glaser, Sharon Goldinger, Sam Kuo, Leonard Shengold, and a cadre of writers, artists, physicians, attorneys, and educators of every stripe.

My brilliant wife, Linda, was with me every step of the way. She's a source of courage, inspiration, and love. Thanks a billion, babe, and no matter what, let's keep on truckin.'

About the Author

Mark Rubinstein grew up in Brooklyn, New York, near Sheepshead Bay. After earning a degree in Business Administration at NYU, he served in the U.S. Army as a field medic tending to paratroopers of the Eighty-Second Airborne Division. After discharge from the Army, he went to medical school, became a physician, and then a psychiatrist. As a forensic psychiatrist, he was an expert witness in many trials.

As an attending psychiatrist at New York Presbyterian Hospital and a Clinical Assistant Professor of Psychiatry at Cornell, he taught psychiatric residents, psychologists, and social workers while practicing psychiatry.

Before turning to fiction, he coauthored five books: *The First Encounter: The Beginnings in Psychotherapy* (Jason Aronson); *The Complete Book of Cosmetic Surgery* (Simon and Schuster); *New Choices: the Latest Options in Treating Breast Cancer* (Dodd Mead); *Heartplan: A Complete Program for Total Fitness of Heart & Mind* (McGraw Hill); and *The Growing Years: The New York Hospital-Cornell Medical Center Guide to Your Child's Emotional Development* (Atheneum).

He lives in Connecticut with as many dogs as his wife will allow in the house. He still practices psychiatry and is busily working on other novels.

You can visit Mark Rubinstein at http://www.markrubinstein-author.com.

preview of

Crazy Love

A DRIAN DOUGLAS heads for the operating room doors. He glances back at the argon beam coagulator, the hydraulic operating table, and brilliant OR lights. As sterile as the filtered air and gleaming instruments may be, the place is a thing of ineffable beauty. It signifies a kind of artistry. Adrian realizes this after every successful surgery, and for the moment, the OR is the best thing in his life. He knows it's good to be alive and in the lifesaving business.

The patient had been dying—his heart barely able to pump blood. They had cracked open his chest, bypassed the clogged coronary arteries, and then closed up in near-record time.

A stitch in time...

"Great job, Adrian," Fred Bailey, the assistant surgeon, calls across the room.

"Thanks, Fred," Adrian says. "Thanks, everyone. Fabulous work, guys." He snaps off his surgical gloves.

"Hey, Adrian," Dottie, the chief OR nurse, calls.

"Yeah?"

"Chalk another one up for the good guys."

Though her face is masked, Adrian sees the shine in her eyes. And he hears the smile in her voice.

■

Still wearing surgical scrubs, Adrian dons his windbreaker and New Balance running shoes, takes the elevator to the hospital's main floor, and leaves through the emergency room. It's a balmy night in early September and a brisk breeze whips up the ambulance ramp. Though he's been on his feet since six this morning, he feels invigorated with the postsurgical high he loves and doesn't want to make the lonely drive back to his cottage in Simpson.

Looking up at the hospital facade, Adrian tells himself he's glad he left ground zero of the medical universe—Yale–New Haven Hospital—and took the job at Eastport General. He's in on the first floor of an exciting new heart surgery program. At Yale, he'd be just another guppy darting about an aquarium of sharks cannibalizing one another.

It's nearly midnight as Adrian crosses Fairfield Avenue. He passes a row of shuttered stores—a FedEx office, a Wendy's, and a Starbucks; Adrian knows there's no barista to serve up a latte, espresso, or foamed macchiato at this hour. It's time to go more downscale, so he heads for King's Corner, a watering hole two blocks away. He's grown absurdly fond of this dated pub with its beer-stained mahogany bar, neon Schlitz signs, potted snake plants, and 1950s-style, CD-filled Wurlitzer jukebox. It's so retro it reminds Adrian of the old Irish bars he frequented as a medical student in Manhattan.

Entering the place, Adrian hears the first lines of Led Zeppelin's "Stairway to Heaven." The acoustic guitar sends out a mournful melody; it's joined by the soulful recorder. Then comes the plaintive vocal by lead singer Robert Plant.

The place is dimly lit and smells of malt—actually, stale beer. And there's the faint odor of piss, or, Adrian wonders briefly, is it sweat? No matter. It's familiar, even comfortable. A muted cathode-ray television on a shelf casts an aqueous hue over the place as the Red Sox play the Yankees. Swivel-top, vinyl-covered stools line the length of the bar, like soldiers at attention before an iron-pipe foot rail. There's a vintage tin ceiling. The dim seediness seems welcoming after hours in an OR with its modular orbital lighting and antiseptic tile walls.

Vinnie, the thirty-something bartender, turns to him, his face creasing into a smile. "How ya doin', Adrian?"

"Good, Vinnie. You?"

"Can't complain."

"How're the wife and kids?"

"They keep me workin," Vinnie says and shakes his head.

Vinnie has a flattened nose and rough-hewn features and always sports a dark stubble of beard—looks like a guy who's seen his share of barroom brawls. He wears faded jeans and a tight-fitting, sleeveless T-shirt. His bloated biceps are covered with a riotous array of tattoos.

"Bottle of Bud, Adrian?"

"Right on, Vin," he says as the music in its minor key hits its ethereal stride.

Adrian and Vinnie usually talk about the Red Sox. As a former college baseball player, Adrian loves the game.

"The Sox are behind five-nothin," Vinnie says, setting the bottle on the bar.

A smoky vapor rises from the open top.

Adrian puts the bottle to his lips, takes a gulp, and feels the cold effervescence at the back of his throat. After a long day in the OR, the beer's warmth mushrooms through his belly and rises to his chest. Then comes a deliciously light buzz.

"That's damned good music, Vinnie," he says.

"Adrian—my *man*," Vinnie calls. "Nobody loves Led Zeppelin like we do." Vinnie moves down the bar.

He's had only one swig, but Adrian already feels a foamy web of warmth in his head. He seems to float in the bar's dimness.

Adrian hears a voice—but it's muffled by the music.

He takes another pull on the Bud. A haze settles in his brain.

"I said . . . *Adrian?*"

Startled, Adrian looks to his right.

A ruggedly built man in his midthirties stands at the bar. He stares, intensely, with cold, deep-set gray eyes. The guy's about six two, maybe taller—with sloped, powerful-looking shoulders and a broad, well-muscled chest. He has a bull neck with cordlike veins that look like blood-filled pipes. Even in a flannel jacket, his arms are thick, sinewy. His hands are huge, with thick, gnarled fingers.

"*Adrian?* Do I know you?"

Adrian suddenly feels a clenched dread. A knot forms in his stomach. A shudder floats through his chest. He draws back as if by instinct. The man is steely eyed and steep-jawed; he has a Vandyke beard and closely cropped blondish hair cut in a semimilitary style.

"I don't think so . . ."

"Oh, yes . . . I *know* you . . ."

The guy edges closer, looms larger.

Adrian thinks the man's nostrils quiver as though he's smelling something. Even in the bar's dimness, Adrian registers the grayness of the man's eyes with their pitted-olive black pupils reflecting a neon sign. Adrian sees a dark madness there, a smoldering rage, and something cold crawls through him.

"Adrian . . . That's a girl's name. You a faggot?"

Adrian's mouth goes dry. The guy reminds him of a beast—something lethal, soulless. Adrian's fingers tingle; his scalp dampens.

Holy shit. This is unbelievable. It's not from the life I've been living.

"Look, mister," Adrian says. "I don't know you and I'm—"

"Hey, *you,*" Vinnie growls from behind the bar.

The man's eyes shift to Vinnie. The guy has yet to blink.

Voltage charges through the air.

Except for the jukebox, the place goes quiet.

"Vinnie," Adrian says, "there's no need—"

"It's okay, Adrian," says Vinnie as his sumo-sized arm slips beneath the bar. "If you're looking for trouble, you son of a bitch, you've come to the right place." A blue-black baseball bat appears in his hand. "Get the fuck outta here. *Now.*"

Suddenly, the guy's arm lunges out in a mercury-quick movement; his beer bottle slams onto the bar. The bottle bounces, topples, and twirls wildly as foamy beer spurts out its neck. He glares at

Vinnie with those cold, unblinking eyes. "I'll be back," he says and then turns to Adrian. "And I'll see you too, faggot."

Adrian's skin feels like it's peeling. He goes cold, as though an ice floe encircles his heart.

The guy turns, casts another look at Vinnie, and saunters out the door.

Led Zeppelin's chorus fills the room.

Adrian's armpits are soaked. His heart batters his rib cage.

"You know that guy?" Adrian asks, surprised at the steadiness of his voice.

"Nah," Vinnie says, setting the bat behind the bar. "Been hanging around a couple weeks now. Looks like he's been waitin' for someone."

"Looks like he was waiting for me . . ."

"He's just killin' time—comes in around seven, stays an hour or two, leaves, then wanders in again around eleven, stays another hour. Nurses a bottle of beer. Strange guy." Vinnie swipes the beer bottle, tosses it into a bin, and wipes down the bar top. "In this business, you meet all types . . ."

Vinnie heads toward the grill area.

Adrian waits for the adrenaline rush to subside. He swigs his beer and it shoots right to his brain. His legs are unsteady. He plops down on a stool.

The last stanza of "Stairway to Heaven" resounds through the bar.

The front window shatters. A scorching air blast whooshes through the room as bottles detonate in a percussive blowout. Glass, liquor, and debris scatter as neon explodes and everything flies. Adrian drops to the floor.

Another blast sprays the place.

There's yelling as everyone hits the floor.

The lights flicker; one goes out.

Smoke, plaster, and dust float in the air.

"A shotgun!" shouts Vinnie; he leaps over the bar and rushes out the front door.

A dangling ceiling light sizzles.

A babble of voices rises; panic-level fear takes over as patrons stampede toward the back of the place. It's pure mayhem.

"Don't go out the door," someone shouts. "He could be there."

Vinnie bursts back in and looks around. "Anyone hurt?"

"What the hell was that?" someone calls.

Vinnie snaps open his cell phone.

A patron swipes shards of glass from his hair. Another guy curses. Someone whimpers. A few guys rush for the front door.

Adrian gets to his feet. "You see who it was?"

"Probably that bastard I kicked out," Vinnie says, dialing 911. "It was a black pickup, a big Ford or Chevy. With a steel toolbox behind the cab. He was goin' like a bat outta hell."

"You get his plate?"

"Nah . . . He was goin' too fast."

The place smells like malt and acrid smoke. A trace of whiskey, too. The walls are pocked with pellet holes. Ceiling wires dangle, spit, and sputter.

"It's King's Corner," Vinnie says into his cell. "There's been a drive-by shooting through my front window."

There's a pause as Vinnie listens.

"No . . . nobody's hurt . . ."

The music builds in a surge of guitars and vocals. The air is hazy, yellowish, caustic. It smells like a chemical factory. Booze drips from shattered bottles.

Vinnie's still on his cell, talking to the police dispatcher.

The music hits a crescendo and then goes serene.

A police siren burps, then whoops. Whirling lights carousel everywhere.

The Led Zeppelin vocalist ends the song in a voice that conjures up angels.

3/19
④
3/22
3 in SCA